THE GOVERNOR'S WIFE

THE GOVERNOR'S WIFE

Mark Gimenez

sphere

SPHERE

First published in Great Britain in 2012 by Sphere

A CIP catalogue record for this book
is available from the British Library.

ISBN 978 0 7515 4376 6

Typeset in Bembo by Hewer Text UK Ltd, Edinburgh
Printed and bound in Great Britain by Clays Ltd, St Ives plc

Sphere
An imprint of
Little, Brown Book Group
100 Victoria Embankment
London EC4Y 0DY

An Hachette UK Company
www.hachette.co.uk

www.littlebrown.co.uk

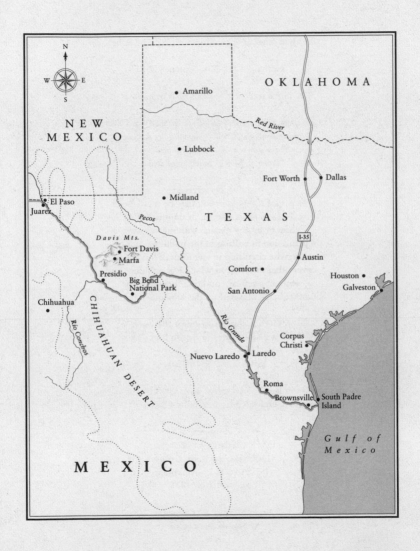

'If I owned Texas and Hell, I'd rent out Texas and live in Hell.'
— Union General Philip Sheridan

'Texas is a state of mind. Texas is an obsession. Above all, Texas is a nation in every sense of the word.'
— John Steinbeck

'We really stole Texas, didn't we? I mean. Away from Mexico.'
— Leslie Lynnton in *Giant* by Edna Ferber

'Poor Mexico, so far from God and so close to the United States.'
— Porfirio Díaz, president of Mexico, 1877–80, 1884–1911

Prologue

Dying is a way of life on the border.

And if her true identity ever became known, she'd be dead before the sun again rose over the Rio Grande. But here in the *colonias* on the outskirts of Laredo, she was just the Anglo nurse who made house calls. Not that the residences qualified as houses. They were just shanties constructed of scrap material—plywood, sheet metal, cardboard, even discarded garage doors—but they provided shelter from the hot sun if not the dry wind that blew in from the Chihuahuan Desert. It was early September, but it was still summer on the border. It was always summer on the border.

She ducked her face against the dirt that never ceased to blow and walked down the road to her next house call.

Barefooted children played in the gray dirt that was the road or in the foul water that was the river. Potbellied pigs lay in what shade they could find. Chickens pecked at the bare ground, and goats wandered aimlessly. Vultures circled overhead, waiting. Always waiting for death. Young women who looked old cooked beans and tortillas over open fires and wielded straw brooms in a losing battle against the dirt. They smiled and waved to the pretty nurse wearing a white lab coat over a bright yellow peasant dress and pink Crocs; a stethoscope hung around her neck. A scarf concealed her famously red hair from the world and a wide-brimmed hat her light complexion from the sun's harsh rays that had burned the land to a crisp brown. Everywhere in Texas, she was considered a glamorous forty-four-year-old woman.

Everywhere except the *colonias*.

Over her shoulder she carried a black satchel filled with medicine and supplies and hard candy. Small children ran to her and gathered around as if she were the Pied Piper, a dozen little voices pleading in Spanish and twice as many hands reaching up to her. She searched inside the satchel and dug out a handful of candy; she placed one piece in each open hand. Their brown faces beamed as if she had doled out diamonds, then they ran back to their *madres*. The sight of an Anglo in the *colonias* would normally send the women and children scurrying into the shanties and shadows. But she was welcome now.

Because while they lived with the fear of death, she was in the business of life.

She stopped at the next residence where a child's wailing could be heard from inside. A once colorful wool blanket made gray by the dirt that attacked it like a cancer covered the doorway. A clay flowerpot sat outside with a single yellow sunflower. She spit dirt then called out to the woman of the house.

'Maria!'

A hand yanked the blanket aside, and the distressed face of a young woman appeared in the doorway. Maria Teresa Castillo was only twenty-three years old, but she looked twice her age. Life in the *colonias* aged a woman. Maria was a Mexican national and a single mother of four children and pregnant with her fifth. The youngest had diarrhea. From the river water.

2

'*Señora*, thank God you have come,' Maria said in Spanish. 'Benita, she is very sick.'

She stepped inside and recoiled at the foul smell of the child's stool, suffocating in the small space. She blew out a breath against the odor then waited a moment for her eyes to adjust to the dim light. Electricity had not yet come to this *colonia*. She now saw the small child lying on a burlap pad on the dirt floor and crying against the pain of intestinal cramps.

'Maria, you cannot bathe her in the river,' she said in Spanish. 'The *parásitos* and toxins in the water make her sick.'

The Rio Grande was contaminated with industrial waste from the *maquiladoras* on the other side and human waste from both sides. She cleaned her hands with a gel sanitizer then dropped the satchel and knelt beside her two-year-old patient. She placed her palm on the child's forehead; her skin felt hot and clammy. She retrieved the tympanic thermometer from her coat pocket, placed a disposable cover over the probe, then inserted the probe into the child's ear canal and took her temperature.

'*Ciento dos.*'

She put on latex gloves and removed the child's dirty diaper. It was wet and pungent with urine, which was good; she was not suffering from dehydration. She cleaned the child's bottom with a sanitary wipe then applied petroleum jelly to ease her discomfort. She put a new diaper on the child then removed the gloves and searched her satchel for medicine to relieve the child's pain until the bacterial infection had run its course. In Spanish, she explained the proper dosage to Maria. Her instructions were interrupted by the sound of distant gunfire, which elicited no more reaction in the *colonias* than the sound of the wind. With Nuevo Laredo just across the river, gunfire was the car horns of the *colonias*. She continued her instructions until she heard a familiar voice outside.

'*¡Señora! ¡Señora!*'

'In here!'

The blanket parted, and Inez Quintanilla stood in the doorway.

'*Señora*, you must run away! You must hide!'

The doctor's young receptionist was breathing hard, her pretty brown face distorted with panic. That was not like Inez.

'Why?'

'They come for you!'

'Who?'

'El Diablo! And his *hombres*.'

Her respiration increased.

'He's here? In the *colonia?*'

'*Sí, Señora.*'

'*Why?* Why does he come for me?'

She heard the fear in her own voice.

'El Diablo, he knows who you are.'

'*How?*'

Inez's brown eyes dropped.

'I am sorry, *Señora*.'

Her eyes came back up.

'But you must run! He will take you away!'

'Where?'

Inez pointed south to the river and Mexico beyond.

'You must hide! They are coming!'

Inez stepped to the blanket that was the back door then turned to her.

'*Señora*, I pray to God for you.'

Inez disappeared through the blanket. Pray she might, but

4

there was no god on the border. There was only the devil. El Diablo. And there was no place for an Anglo to hide in the *colonias*. There was no place for anyone to hide. The river blocked escape to the south, the eighteen-foot-tall border wall to the north. The *colonias* occupied a no man's land, on the American side of the river but the Mexican side of the wall. The U.S. government had built the wall to keep the Mexicans out, but they had fenced the *colonias* in. Everyone in the *colonias* now lived at the mercy of the Mexican drug cartels.

Including her.

They would take her across the river into Nuevo Laredo, just as they had taken so many other Americans, who had never been seen again. But she was not just any American. She turned to Maria and gestured to the back door.

'¡*Ándale, ándale!*'

Maria lifted the child and carried her out back.

She was alone. She didn't need the stethoscope to know that her heart was racing; she could feel it pounding against her chest wall. She stepped across the dirt floor and peeked out the blanket door. She stared east. In the distance she saw women and children scattering from the dirt road and a cloud of dust kicked up by black trucks speeding toward her.

She did not have much time.

Everyone in the *colonias* knew of the Anglo nurse. But only the doctor knew who she really was. She had never revealed her true identity to anyone else, and no one here had recognized her. They had not seen her face on the news because there was no television in the *colonias*. They had not read about her or seen her photo in the newspapers because only the Mexican papers were sold here—the language of the *colonias* was Spanish. The *colonias*, like so much of the border-lands north of the river, were just suburbs of Mexico.

5

But Inez had learned the truth. And then she had betrayed her. How? And why? She did not understand, but it did not matter. All that mattered was that they were coming for her. And they would take her into Mexico. She fought not to panic—because what she did in the next few moments would determine whether she lived or died.

Think, Lindsay, think.

They would take her, but he would come for her. She was still his wife. Her husband had his faults—he was unfaithful, he was ambitious, he was a politician—but he was no coward. He would come for her. But how would he find her in Nuevo Laredo? Among five hundred thousand people living in five hundred square miles. A sprawling, lawless city controlled by drug cartels. And beyond the city lay the vast Chihuahuan Desert. She would be swallowed whole across the river. He would never find her.

Unless.

She grabbed the satchel and rummaged inside until she found her cell phone. She always turned it off when she arrived at the clinic each day because there was no phone service in the *colonias*, landline or cell. She now turned the phone on. The battery registered full. He had found her here on the border that first time when the Rangers had tracked her cell phone with GPS. He could find her again—if she had her phone.

But El Diablo's men would search her and take the phone. If they found it.

There was only one place they wouldn't find it.

She pushed the volume button to mute the compact cell phone then pulled up her dress and reached down inside her panties and between her legs and pushed the phone into her vagina. Then Lindsay Bonner waited for them to come for her.

And prayed her husband would.

SIX MONTHS BEFORE

Chapter 1

Bode Bonner woke next to a naked woman who was not his wife.

His wife was out of town, so Mandy had snuck upstairs the night before. She was twenty-seven; he was forty-seven. She made him feel young.

Alive.

Vital.

Relevant.

Sex with a younger woman allowed him to forget—at least for a few short moments—that he was a middle-aged man with his best years in the rearview mirror.

It wasn't a pretty sight.

But Mandy was. Her beautiful backside was to him. He slid his hand down her smooth side and over her round hips and firm bottom and down between her legs. She stirred and groaned.

'I'm sleeping.'

'Don't mind me, darlin'.'

He reached over to the condom box on the nightstand and shook it, but nothing came out. Damn. He turned back to his aide and inhaled her scent. Her bare bottom beckoned to him, and his body responded. At his age, he hated to waste an erection, especially since he often required a little help from the Viagra prescription. She had said he didn't need to wear a condom, that she was on the pill and unconditionally devoted to him, politically and sexually. Aw, hell, once wouldn't be a problem. He pushed into her from behind.

'Governor, you're an animal.'

He growled and bit the back of her neck.

Chapter 2

The sign on the closed door read: THE GOVERNOR'S OFFICE.

Inside, Bode Bonner sat behind his desk flanked by Texas and U.S. flags on tall standards while Lupe ran the boar bristle brush through his thick blond hair then shielded his eyes and sprayed shellac until his hair could stand tall against a Texas twister. Guadalupe Sendejo was a squat, middle-aged Mexican national who had been in the Bonner family service since she was five. She now served as Bode's personal valet, ensuring that his hair was sprayed, his shirts starched, his suits pressed, and his boots polished. He had brought her over to Austin from the ranch four years before when he had won reelection and the job had taken on a more permanent feel. She held the mirror so he could examine her work, but the mirror caught Jim Bob's amused expression from the other side of the desk. Bode nodded at Lupe.

'*Muy bueno. Gracias.*'

Lupe grabbed the brush and hair spray and shut the door behind her. Bode sipped coffee from a mug with an image of his smiling face and *Bode Bonner for Governor* stenciled on the side and stared out the second-story windows. The stark white, Greek Revival-style Governor's Mansion and grounds occupied an entire city block at the corner of Eleventh and Colorado in downtown Austin, as it had for one hundred and fifty-five years. Sam Houston himself had sat in this office and gazed out those windows, which now offered a prime view of the pink granite state capitol sitting catty-cornered across Eleventh Street. The capitol dome glowed in the morning sunlight just as Jim Bob's bald head glowed under the fluorescent office lights. Add in the pasty skin and pock-marked complexion—the man's got a face like a bowl of oatmeal—and James Robert Burnet looked more like a registered sex offender than the ace political strategist for the governor of the great state of Texas. Bode exhaled loudly enough to get his attention.

'What's wrong now?' Jim Bob said.

At first Bode wasn't sure Jim Bob was talking to him. His strategist had an earpiece that looked like a hearing aid on steroids wrapped around his ear, a newspaper in his lap, and an iPhone in his hands. His head was bent over, and his fingers fiddled with the phone like a squirrel with an acorn. Jim Bob texted on his cell phone more than Bode's eighteen-year-old daughter, and he carried on phone conversations while also conversing with Bode, which annoyed the hell out of him. Bode addressed the top of Jim Bob's bare head.

'You talking to me?'

'No one else in the room.'

'Then stop texting and talk to me.'

11

'I'm not texting. I'm tweeting.'

'Tweeting?'

'On Twitter.'

'Tweeting on Twitter—that's what I'm paying you to do, play on your goddamn phone?'

Still talking to the top of his head.

'You're paying me to win elections, and social networking is another way to connect with voters. Grass roots. So I tweet for you.'

'What am I . . . what are you tweeting?'

' "Nine A.M. and at my desk working hard for the people of Texas." '

'And they believe that?'

'Your three thousand followers do.'

'I've got three thousand followers? Hey, that ain't bad.'

'Obama's got ten million.'

Bode sighed. 'Figures.'

Jim Bob punched a button on his phone as if firing off a nuclear bomb then raised his head and eyed Bode over his reading glasses.

'Okay . . . so what's wrong now?'

Like a mother to her child who had come home from school with hurt feelings.

'What makes you think something's wrong?'

'Because you're frowning. Which I find hard to believe, given that you just had sex with a gorgeous twenty-seven-year-old girl. If I had been so lucky this morning, you wouldn't be able to slap the smile off my face for a month.'

Bode tried to block the image of Jim Bob and Mandy having sex from his mind.

'How'd you know we had sex?'

'Because that gal's just naturally horizontal.'

Bode's thoughts drifted back to that morning in bed. He had tried to satisfy his need for excitement with his young aide, but after a year the initial thrill of sex with Mandy Morgan had waned. Sex was much like big-game hunting in that regard. Bode's gaze turned up to the stuffed animal heads that adorned the four walls of his office: axis and mule deer, elk, Catalina goat, red stag, Aoudad sheep, impala, pronghorn, Corsican ram, sable, and his favorite, the wildebeest.

'Remember when I bagged the wildebeest?'

'I do indeed,' Jim Bob said.

Bode and Jim Bob had hunted together since middle school.

'A thousand feet out, one shot to the head.' Bode held an imaginary rifle, sighted in the wildebeest head through an imaginary scope, and squeezed an imaginary trigger. 'Boom.'

'That was a good shot,' Jim Bob said.

'That was a great shot.'

The memory of which almost brought a smile to Bode's face. Almost. But after killing so many creatures, the thrill of the hunt had also waned. The hunts had all started to seem the same. Like sex. There were only so many positions and places to have sex, just as there were only so many creatures to kill. Hunting. Sex. Football. Politics. He had always found fulfillment in those manly pursuits. But now he found himself searching for something more. There had to be something more. He sighed.

'Why am I in this office?'

'It's the Governor's Office. And you're the governor.'

'But why am I the governor?'

'You're a Republican in a red state.'

'No—what is my purpose in being governor?'

'To get reelected.'

Jim Bob choked back a laugh.

'Wait, I lost count—is this your third or fourth midlife crisis this term?'

Jim Bob shook his head then tossed the newspaper on the desk and gestured at the headline: 'Bet On Bode'.

'You're a hard man to please, Bode Bonner. You just won the Republican primary with one hundred percent of the vote, and you're not happy?'

'No one ran against me. Where's the thrill of victory in that?'

The state of Texas had held the Republican and Democratic primaries the day before. But Republicans didn't fight each other in March, and Democrats didn't win in November. The Democrats hadn't won a statewide election in Texas in twenty years. They were that incompetent. That irrelevant. And outside of Austin and a few border counties, statistically insignificant, as the pollsters say. Texas glowed bright red from Amarillo to Brownsville, Texarkana to El Paso; Republicans controlled all three branches of state government. Consequently, the general election was a mere formality, Republican voters rubber-stamping the Republican primary winners. Bode Bonner was as good as reelected for another four-year term. He had been declared the Republican primary winner by eight the night before (the polls had closed at seven), given his victory speech by nine (the party was over by ten), had sex with Mandy by eleven (his wife had left for the airport after his speech), and fallen sound asleep by eleven-thirty. No contest. No agony of defeat for his opponent. No thrill of victory for Bode Bonner.

'You want thrills, go ride a roller coaster. You won. That's all that matters. Like that guy said about football, "Winning isn't everything. It's the only thing." '

'Lombardi.'

'Same rule applies to politics. And yesterday goes in the books as a win. A win–win because we saved our campaign funds for the general election.'

'Like that'll be much of a fight.' Bode waved a hand at the newspaper. 'Even the Austin paper figures me for a landslide. And who are the Democrats running against me? A Jewish ex-country-western singer who dresses like Johnny Cash and sings like Dolly Parton. A goddamn serial candidate. He's run for damn near every state office except dogcatcher. He's a political punch line.' Bode threw his hands up. 'Where do they get these people? For Christ's sake, Jim Bob, I'm up fourteen points in the polls.'

'Eighteen.'

Bode sat up.

'You got the new poll numbers?'

'Yep.'

'Did I make the nationals?'

'Nope.'

Jim Bob pulled a thin black notebook from his briefcase— a notebook he guarded with the same paranoia as the army officer guarding the president's case containing the nuclear launch codes—and flipped open the cover.

'But you're kicking ass in Texas. Fifty-nine percent favorable rating across all registered voters—that's your all-time high.'

'What's the breakdown?'

Jim Bob turned the page. 'Anglo males, seventy-one percent favorable. Anglo females, sixty-two percent. African-Americans, seven percent. Mexican-Americans, four percent.' He looked up. 'NASCAR dads and soccer moms, they love you. Not so much the blacks and Latinos.' He chuckled. 'Hell, just be glad the Democrats are running a Jew instead of

15

a Latino. There's not but a dozen Jews in Texas, but there's ten million Latinos.'

'You don't figure they'll vote for him, do you?'

He could hear the hint of worry in his own voice.

'Not a chance.'

And that was the fear of every Republican politician in Texas: Would the Latinos vote? They never had before, but no Republican wanted to be the one who finally brought out the Latino vote—for his Democratic opponent.

'They're waiting for their savior . . . and they'll still be waiting come election day,' Jim Bob said. 'They won't vote.'

'Thank God.'

Every Texas politician understood a simple electoral fact: Anglos occupied the Governor's Mansion by the leave of Latinos.

'One day,' Jim Bob said, his voice taking on that familiar professorial tone—

James Robert Burnet held a Ph.D. and taught a class on politics at the LBJ School; consequently, he was known in Texas political circles as 'the Professor.'

'—there'll be a Latino sitting in your chair, that's a fact. But not on my watch.'

For the last decade, ever since Karl Rove had decamped to D.C. with George W., the Professor's opinion on all things political in the state of Texas had been considered gospel. So Bode Bonner breathed a sigh of relief: no need to fret about the Latino vote, at least not in this election. That settled in his mind, his thoughts quickly returned to his midlife crisis.

'My life peaked when I was twenty-two and playing strong safety for the Longhorns. Been downhill ever since.'

He fingered the massive UT college football ring that rode his big right hand like a hood ornament; the memories of

16

football flooded his mind. Sitting in the Governor's Office and recalling those glorious moments now, Bode couldn't believe how life had let him down. He leaned back and kicked his size 14-EE handmade elk skin cowboy boots up onto the desk. He had big feet because he stood six feet four inches tall and carried two hundred and ten pounds, his playing weight. He had blue eyes and good hair. He worked out at the YMCA and ran five miles around the lake every day. He had a working prostate and a valid Viagra prescription. Bode Bonner possessed the strength and stamina and sexual drive to keep up with men half his age. And women. He was still young enough and strong enough and willing enough to live life. He just needed something to do with his life.

'What am I gonna do the next four years?'

'Same thing you did the last four years . . . Nothing.'

'I don't want to do nothing the rest of my life, Jim Bob.'

'Bode, you're the governor of the second most populous state in America with twenty-five million people, a state that encompasses two hundred and sixty-eight thousand square miles, a state with a one-point-two-trillion-dollar gross domestic product that would rank it number fourteen in the world if Texas was still a republic, a state that's—'

'Bare-ass broke! I'm the governor of a goddamn bankrupt state, and I don't have any public money to spend or power to wield. I can't do a damn thing.' He pointed out the window at the capitol. 'Hell, I gotta go over there and beg those bastards to pass a bill before I can take a goddamn piss.'

The Professor nodded. 'Sam Houston thought power should reside in the legislature, so the state constitution provides for a weak executive.'

'Doesn't provide for much excitement.' Bode shook his head. 'I love the guy, but old Sam screwed the pooch on that one. I mean, what the hell is the governor supposed to do for four years? I can't play golf every day—some days it rains.'

That amused the Professor. He was fixing his coffee in a china cup—cream and five sugar cubes. Which explained his pudgy physique and why he had been the star of the chess club in high school instead of an athlete.

'What do you hear, Jim Bob?'

The Professor cocked his head. 'Nothing.'

'Exactly. This ain't the Governor's Office—it's the goddamn morgue. You know why?'

'I bet you're gonna tell me.'

Bode again pointed out the window at the capitol.

'Because all the action's over there. You want to play the game of politics in Texas, you don't come to the Governor's Office, you go to the capitol. Come January, that place is gonna sound like a cattle auction, lobbyists bidding for legislators' votes. Hell, they're already lining up outside the speaker's office, because he's got the power, not me. Because they don't need the governor. Because I'm irrelevant.'

'Irrelevant?'

'Like tits on a boar hog.'

Bode Bonner pulled his boots off the desk and stood then smoothed the coat to his dark suit. Armani suits and cowboy boots. And French cuffs. You could do that in Texas, if you were the governor. He was, so he did. He stepped over to the tall floor-length windows and stared out at Austin and Texas and the end of his life. He could see it all from the second story of the Governor's Mansion. He was the governor of Texas, but he was no different than every other forty-seven-year-old man in the state. The best years of his life were behind him. His glory days were gone. No one needed him anymore, not the state of Texas, not the UT football team, not his wife or his daughter or even the cattle on his ranch. He was just another unnecessary middle-aged white male waiting for a heart attack or a positive prostate exam to make the end of life official. And like most men when facing their own mortality or irrelevance, Bode Bonner longed for one more moment of glory, one final challenge in life, one more thrill of victory, one last great—

'Adventure.'

Jim Bob had returned to fiddling with his phone. He didn't look up.

'What?'

'I need an adventure.'

'An adventure?'

As if Bode had said 'enema.'

'I've gone as far as I can go in Texas, Jim Bob. Time to move up.'

'Senator?'

'President.'

He cut his eyes to the Professor, who was shaking his head.

'Don't even think about it.'

Bode fully faced the ranking political genius in the state of Texas—or at least his bald head. He wanted to snatch that goddamn phone and stomp the shit out of it.

'Why not?'

'The Bush legacy—no more Texans in the White House.'

'It could happen.'

'Not to you.'

'I'm a great campaigner.'

'Here in Texas.'

'What's that supposed to mean?'

Jim Bob exhaled as if his teenage son had just announced

19

at the dinner table that he had wrecked the family station wagon, then he turned his head up.

'That means, Bode, you're a good ol' boy cattle rancher from Comfort, Texas. Which means your bullshit sells here in Texas, but take it to the East Coast and West Coast, nobody's buying.' He leaned back. 'Look, Bode, you've got the perfect résumé for a Texas politician: Tall and handsome with good hair. Star football player at UT. Devout killer of animals and lifelong NRA member. Republican and rancher—hell, you're a real goddamn cowboy and you look the part, like John Wayne if he wore Armani. Which means you're immensely popular here in Texas. You see "Bode" was the second most popular baby name in the state last year?'

'What was the first?'

'Osvaldo.' Jim Bob chuckled. 'But you blew away Britney.' He thought that was even funnier. 'You're beloved here in Texas, Bode—at least by fifty-nine percent of registered voters—but north of the Red River, no one's ever heard of you. You're not even within the margin of error for potential Republican presidential candidates.'

'Doesn't matter. My message will resonate with the people.'

'Your *message*?'

'It's okay to be white and pissed off.'

'There's a bumper sticker.'

Jim Bob was smiling; Bode wasn't.

'I've got the Ph.D. in politics. Let me decide what your message is, okay?'

'Jim Bob, middle-class folks are desperate for a hero, someone who'll stand up and fight for them. For their America.'

'And you like being a hero.'

The Professor let out an exasperated sigh, as if a student had asked a stupid question.

20

'Bode, we've been best friends since fifth grade. You were a great football player. You're a great governor. And you're the best goddamn campaigner I've ever seen. But the White House? It's just not going to happen for you, buddy.'

'Who're we gonna run? Romney? A Mormon named Mitt? Sounds like the fucking family pet. Folks are sick of him—he's like a party guest who won't go home.'

'There's Bachmann.'

'She's half crazy.'

'Santorum?'

'Creepy.'

'Paul?'

'Kooky.'

'Cain?'

'Black.'

'Christie?'

'Fat.'

'Daniels? He's not crazy, creepy, kooky, black, or fat. And he's smart.'

'Sure, he's smart, but he's got the personality of a minivan, he's five-seven, and he's bald.'

'So?'

'So voters want a tall president with good hair.'

'Gingrich has good hair.'

'And two ex-wives.'

'What about Palin? She's happily married.'

'She's a goddamn *Saturday Night Live* joke to most Americans. She gets elected and takes that litter to the White House, it'll be the *Beverly Hillbillies Go to Washington*. Besides, Americans don't want a broad in the White House. They want a man, someone who'll take charge and make things better, and not for those greedy bastards on Wall Street'—he pointed out the window—'but for Main Street. For middle-class folks.'

'I hope you don't mean that.'

'I do.'

The Professor shook his head. 'Don't go populist on me again, Bode. Remember, politicians talk populism, but big business funds their campaigns.'

Bode paced the office; his adrenaline was pumping now.

'The tea party changed the game, Jim Bob. It tapped into the middle-class anger at government, same thing we've been doing. I'm the tea party's favorite son here in Texas—why couldn't I go national with them?'

'This ain't the Ice Capades, Bode. You want to go national, you do it with the Republican Party leadership, the Establishment boys in Washington, not the crazy cousins out in the country. Sure, they can energize the voters, but they're wild cards in the party—shit, they're not even sure they want to be Republicans. And they're sure as hell not interested in long-term careers in Congress, which is how the party keeps the members in line. You want to move up, you keep your head down, your mouth shut, and follow orders when a vote is called. You don't go on *Fox News* and buck the speaker. Tea partiers, they don't give a shit about moving up in Congress—they want to firebomb the fucking place.'

'I thought you believed in the tea party?'

'No more than a surfer believes in the wave.'

Bode stared at the Professor. He blinked hard.

'What the hell does that mean?'

'It means, just like that surfer respects the power of the wave, I respect the tea party's power to mobilize middle-class voters. We got two hundred tea party groups in Texas representing half of all registered voters. So we're going to ride

22

that tea party wave right through the election. You're going to tell those voters exactly what they want to hear. But that doesn't mean you're supposed to believe it.'

Bode pulled out his pocket-sized copy of the U.S. Constitution and held it in the air. The Professor groaned.

'Not with the Constitution again.'

'Like Reagan said—'

Another groan. 'Now it's Reagan quotes.'

'Jim Bob, I've been preaching the same Tenth Amendment, anti-Washington, anti-taxes sermon since—'

'Bode—you're *not* the wave. You're just *riding* the wave. You used to be a Democrat when Democrats controlled Texas. Then you switched to Republican when Republicans took over Texas. Now you're a tea partier because they're sweeping across Texas. That's what politicians do, at least the ones who win elections: they ride the wave.'

'I'm not the wave? I'm just riding the wave?'

'Bode, politics is like investing. Twenty years ago, I bought stock in Whole Foods. Not because I believed in organic— hell, I don't give a shit if my fried chicken was happy when it was alive—but because I saw the organic wave building and thought it might be a money-making opportunity. So I jumped on that wave, and I rode the stock price up and made a lot of money. Investing isn't about what I believe; it's about making money. Politics isn't about what you believe; it's about winning elections. The tea party is a political opportunity. It's the wave. Today. But that wave always dies out, and the tea party will, too. And all those middle-class folks will go back to work and church and the PTA and get on with their dull lives out in suburbia and leave politics to the professionals.'

'Which means?'

'Which means the tea party can't put you or anyone else

in the White House. Only the Establishment Republicans have the money for that. The Democrats are going to spend a billion dollars to keep Obama in the White House. Where's that money coming from? The unemployed middle class? No. It's coming from Wall Street. Same place Republicans get their campaign money.'

'Money's the only politics Wall Street knows.'

'Exactly—and they're sure as hell not going to bet a billion dollars on another Texas governor.' He blew out a breath. 'Look, Bode, you've got a good thing going here—governor-for-life. Don't fuck it up.'

'Why aren't the Republican bundlers in play yet? Why haven't the fundraisers committed to a candidate? Because they're all losers. We need a winner.'

'You?'

Bode stopped pacing and pointed a finger at the ceiling. Jim Bob looked up.

'What?'

'Not what,' Bode said. 'One. All I need is one big play.'

'One big play?'

'Every game I ever played in—won or lost—turned on one big play. A long run, a pass, a fumble, an interception . . . a game changer. One big play, Jim Bob, that's all I need to be president.'

'Bode, to put another Texan in the White House, it'd have to be the biggest Hail Mary in the history of politics.'

'It could happen. I could win. I've got the game to play in the big leagues, Jim Bob. I just need one big play to get in the game.'

Jim Bob shook his head and sighed.

'Higher office and younger women—the ambitions of a politician.'

Before Bode could defend himself, there was a loud knock on the door, and Jim Bob jumped.

'Might want to try decaf,' Bode said.

Jim Bob was always a little jumpy, as if worried someone might sneak up behind him and put him in a headlock like the cowboys in Comfort used to do to him in the middle-school restroom, until Bode took him under his wing. From that day, Jim Bob Burnet had pledged his undying loyalty to Bode Bonner. Another knock, and the door swung open on Jim Bob's new young assistant. He waved her in. She walked over and handed a stack of papers to Jim Bob. But she smiled at Bode.

'Mornin', Governor,' she said in a syrupy Southern drawl.

Her perfume drifted over and incited Bode's male hormones the same as waving a red flag at a bull. Bode's eyes involuntarily dropped from her face to her body and then slowly worked their way down to her feet and back up to her face. When their eyes again met, she winked. Damn, she was a frisky gal—whose name he couldn't recall.

'Morning, uh . . .'

'Jolene . . . Jo.'

'Jolene. Sounds like a country song.'

She gave him a coy smile.

''Cause I'm a country girl.'

'Are you now?'

Bode caught Jim Bob rolling his eyes.

'That'll be all, Jo,' he said.

Jolene sashayed out in her tight pants and high heels. Jim Bob shook his head.

'You're a goddamn rooster in a hen house.'

He put the stack of papers on the desk then slid the top document across to Bode. He sat behind the desk and grabbed his signing pen.

25

'What's this?'

'You're appointing Joe Jack Munger to the UT Board of Regents.'

'Munger?'

'Oilman out in Midland, went to UT.'

'He know anything about education?'

'He knows how to write a big check to your reelection campaign. Two hundred grand.'

Bode signed the appointment, one of the few powers of the office. The University of Texas had always been run by the governor's cronies and contributors, more like a real-estate venture than a university. Jim Bob pushed another document across the desk.

'Proclamation.'

'Proclaiming what?'

'A day of prayer for rain.'

'Damn drought. How are we doing on those wildfires out west?'

'Out of control.'

'Half of Texas is burning, and Obama won't declare those counties disaster areas so those folks can get federal funds to rebuild. Blue state fucking hiccups, he sends in billions. Red state, he lets us die in a drought.'

'It's called politics.'

He signed the proclamation.

'Next document.'

Bode read the title: 'Deed?'

'The land deal. With Hoot Pickens.'

'You run this by the lawyers?'

Jim Bob nodded. 'It's legal. And profitable. Half a million bucks. We put it in your blind trust, gives us deniability.'

Bode signed the deed. Jim Bob gathered the papers then checked his watch and stood.

'Come on, we're late.'

'For what?'

'Elementary school.'

Bode groaned. 'Aw, damn, Jim Bob—not reading to kindergartners again? I hate that shit.'

Jim Bob offered a lame shrug.

'You made education a major part of your platform—faith, family, and schools.'

'Just because Lindsay wanted something to do. Why can't she read to them?'

'She was supposed to, but I had to send her down to the border—Delgado's in from Washington. They're trying to get the Mexicans in the *colonias* counted for the census.'

'Why?'

'So Texas can get more seats in Congress. We've got thirty-two seats now. If we can get all those Mexicans counted, we can pick up three or four more seats. And once I'm through redistricting the state, every one of those seats will be Republican.'

'No—why'd you send Lindsay down to the border? Why couldn't I go?'

'Because you don't speak Spanish. She does.'

Chapter 3

'*No teman el censo.*'

'Yes, Mrs. Bonner,' Congressman Delgado said. ' "Do not fear the census." That is our message this day.'

Two hundred and thirty-five miles south of the Governor's Mansion and two blocks north of the Rio Grande, the governor's wife stared out the tinted window of the black Suburban as their five-car caravan rolled around the San Agustín Plaza in downtown Laredo. She had flown in the night before and stayed at the La Posada Hotel on the plaza. She would fly back to Austin that afternoon. Up front, a state trooper drove, and her Texas Ranger bodyguard rode shotgun. She sat in the back seat with the congressman. His aftershave reminded Lindsay of her father when she was a little girl riding in his lap and pretending to steer the old Buick. Congressman Delgado pointed out the window at a white church with a tall clock tower.

'The San Agustín Cathedral,' he said. 'I was baptized there. And that is the old convent for the Ursuline Sisters, but the nuns are gone. And the Plaza Theatre, it is shuttered now, but I watched many cowboy movies there as a child. That was, of course, many years ago.' He chuckled. 'I was born in Laredo, but I am afraid I will die in Washington.'

Ernesto Delgado had first been elected to Congress in 1966. He was seventy-eight now and had no thought of retiring.

'The plaza seems . . .'

'Dead?'

28

She nodded.

'Yes, it is March and our streets should be crowded with college students on spring break, staying in hotels on this side of the river and partying on the other side. Gin fizzes at the Cadillac Bar and pretty girls in Boys' Town—Nuevo Laredo once boasted the cheapest drinks and the best prostitutes on the border. It is legal in Mexico, prostitution.'

A wistful expression crossed the congressman's creased face, as if he had experienced all that Nuevo Laredo had to offer in his younger days.

'Now the Cadillac Bar is closed, and Nuevo Laredo has only the drugs and violence to offer, so the DPS issues travel warnings. "Avoid traveling to Mexico during spring break, and stay alive," the one this year said. So the students, they go to Padre Island instead. And the streets of Laredo are empty.'

The streets were empty. The few pedestrians on the plaza walked slowly, as if they had no place to go. Palm trees and old Spanish-style structures lined the brick-paved plaza, a few elderly tourists snapped photos, and some of the businesses still seemed alive—Casa de Empeño, Casa Raul, Pepe's Sporting Goods, Fantasía Linda—albeit protected by burglar bars. Other storefronts sat boarded-up, left to decay in the dry air. Faded murals, a fenced-off movie theatre, a forgotten convent—the streets of Laredo were paved but not with gold. The town seemed tired and weary, like an old person who recalled an earlier time, when her life had meaning. When she was useful. Lindsay Bonner was only forty-four, but she often felt like that old person. Or this old town. Old. Useless. Unnecessary. She still had the energy, the drive, and the desire to be useful and necessary, but she had no place. No purpose. Her husband was the governor and her daughter a college student; her jobs as mother and wife were finished now. She was the governor's wife, but that was not the same as being a wife. It was a role she played; it was not her. So she volunteered around Austin, but she was always the governor's wife. She could not escape that identity. That prison. Those cameras. That was her role now, a pretty face that brought out the cameras.

A photo op.

Local television and newspaper reporters and cameramen ready to record every moment of her visit to the border followed in vans with their stations' logos stenciled in bright colors on the sides. A Department of Public Safety cruiser manned by two well-armed state troopers led the way; a local police car with two well-armed cops brought up the rear. Security for the governor's wife and a U.S. congressman. Their DPS driver cocked his head their way.

'You know what they call an American in Nuevo Laredo?' He didn't wait for an answer. 'Victim.'

He laughed. He was Anglo. The congressman responded with a pained expression.

'Border humor. The cartels, they killed over one hundred Americans last year and kidnapped many more who have never been seen again. But the Nuevo Laredo mayor, he says we have only a public relations problem, that with better press, the tourists will return to the border. Of course, Nuevo Laredo is under martial law and the mayor, he sleeps on this side of the river. I think that is what they call denial.'

The caravan coursed through the maze of narrow one-way streets that was downtown Laredo and then past the bridge leading into Mexico. They turned north and accelerated onto Interstate 35. They drove through the city landscape at seventy miles per hour, only the palm trees distinguishing the journey from that through any other city in Texas, and the governor's wife had journeyed through most the last eight years. They exited the interstate and turned west on Mines Road. They soon reached the outskirts of Laredo, and beyond that, the city became the desert. The land lay vast and empty and flat, brown and parched from the drought, only scrub brush and dirt as far as the eye could see.

Lindsay Bonner had been born in Boston but had grown up in the Hill Country of Texas, a land of streams and rivers and lakes, so contrary to this land. She had been to the border the tourists see, but never to the borderlands. Her husband did not campaign here. He said it was simply a matter of getting the most bang for your campaign buck. There was little bang for a Republican on the border: the people who inhabited this harsh land were Democrats, poor Latinos who did not contribute to political campaigns and who did not vote. So to the politicians in Austin, they did not exist. Perhaps that was why she had jumped at the chance to come south.

She often felt as if she did not exist. And she was a Democrat.

She had never told her husband, of course, and she had never officially registered, but she had always voted straight-ticket Democrat—except she had always voted for her husband. The bonds of matrimony. Or the guilt of a Catholic: to love, honor, and obey, in sickness and in health, for better or for worse. Father O'Rourke had said nothing about a husband converting to Republican. It was worse. She was smiling at the thought of what her husband would say if he ever learned her secret—there would be profanity—when they abruptly veered off the highway and turned south onto a bumpy dirt road that cut through dense brush—

'Chaparral,' the congressman said.

—and bounced her about. The DPS cruiser in front

kicked up a cloud of dust that enveloped their Suburban. But visible in the distance through the dust was a low shadow that seemed to rise from the desert and extended east and west as far as she could see until it disappeared into the haze. The shadow grew taller and taller as they came closer until it loomed large overhead. But it wasn't a shadow.

'What is that?'

'That, Mrs. Bonner, is the border fence.'

'But it's not a fence. It's a wall.'

'Yes. Some portions along the border are fences, but here it is a wall. Eighteen feet high, constructed of steel with six feet of reinforced concrete below ground—apparently the Department of Homeland Security thinks the Mexicans will be arriving in Abrams tanks.'

'This is what Bush wanted in America? Our own Berlin Wall?'

'Obama voted for the border wall, too, Mrs. Bonner, when he was in the Senate. He was a politician before he became the president.'

They stopped in front of a massive gate guarded by two Border Patrol agents wearing green uniforms and wielding military-style rifles as if guarding the gates to a kingdom. Or a prison. Were they keeping them out or someone else in? Her Texas Ranger bodyguard threw open his door. Dirt blew in with the hot wind; Lindsay averted her face until the Ranger stepped out of the vehicle and slammed the door shut as if he were angry at the Suburban. He pushed his cowboy hat down hard on his head to prevent the wind from taking it north to San Antonio and marched over to the Border Patrol agents. After a brief discussion, the agents opened the gate, reluctantly it seemed. The Ranger returned, removed his hat, and got back in the vehicle, grumbling something about 'Feds.' They drove through the gates, and Lindsay sat up, anticipating what she would see on the other side, which was—

Nothing.

She saw nothing but more chaparral and dirt. She had expected something, perhaps a panoramic view of the majestic Rio Grande. But the river was nowhere in sight. The wall just cut through the land like a random mountain range.

'So the border wall isn't actually on the border?'

'Oh, no,' the congressman said. 'The border runs right down the middle of the Rio Grande, so the wall, it is off the border. Here, about a mile. Elsewhere, maybe two miles.' He chuckled. 'Over in Eagle Pass, the public golf course runs right along the river. The golfers, they would be hitting their balls and suddenly Mexicans would dart out of the *carrizos*, the thick reeds by the river, and race across the fairways and into town where they could mix in with the locals. So Homeland Security built the fence on the town side of the golf course, to block the Mexicans' path. But they also blocked the golfers' escape. So now the Mexicans jump out of the *carrizos* with guns and rob the golfers.'

He now gave out a hearty laugh.

'You cannot make that up,' he said.

'A border wall that's not on the border. That doesn't make any sense.'

'There is little on the border that makes sense, Mrs. Bonner. As you will see, this side of the wall is another world entirely—a world that is not *México*, but that is also not America.'

'Then what world is it?'

'This, Mrs. Bonner, is the *colonias*.' He turned to the window and pointed. 'Oh, look—a jackrabbit.' He turned back. 'Ah, we are here.'

The Suburban braked to a stop and stirred up dust that soon dissipated in the wind. The Ranger opened the back door for the governor's wife. Lindsay stepped out and immediately surrendered her hair to the wind. The ninety-degree heat felt like an oven after the air conditioning inside the vehicle. The press crew bailed out of their vans and began unloading their equipment. The troopers and police got out of their cruisers with their large guns strapped to their waists and stretched their large bodies; they must have recruited the biggest men on the force to guard the governor's wife. Congressman Delgado came around and stood next to her. They were both decidedly overdressed, she in a cream-colored linen suit and low heels, he in a tan suit and tie. He inhaled the dry air.

'Ah, spring on the border. It is the same as summer.' He extended a hand as if gesturing at a grand monument. 'Welcome to *Colonia Ángeles*, Mrs. Bonner. The border's version of a gated community.'

They stood at the entrance to this community of angels. But it was not heaven on earth. The dirt road continued on and seemed to disappear into the dust, just a rutted path winding through a vast shantytown of dilapidated structures that in the distance seemed to merge together to form a massive inhabited dump. Half-naked brown children played in the dirt road and down in the river, dull in the hazy sun. Women carried water from the river in buckets and cooked over open fires; smoke rose into the sky in thin spires. An enormous pile of smoldering refuse stood tall near the river; with each gust of wind, paper and plastic items broke free and danced across the dirt as if attempting an escape. Rats rummaged through the refuse. The congressman was right: this was another world. A third world.

'How many people live here?'

'Six thousand. Or perhaps seven.'

The women had stopped their work and the children their play, and they now stared at their visitors, as if frozen by the sight of the black Suburban and the police cars and the cameras. Or frightened. One barefooted little girl in a dirty white dress broke away and ran over to Lindsay. Her hair was stringy and gray with dirt. Her face was gaunt. She had pierced ears and dangling earrings. She carried a naked doll.

'*¡Qué lindo el cabello!*'

'She says your hair is pretty,' the congressman said. 'She has probably never before seen red hair.'

Lindsay leaned down to the girl and said, '*Gracias, mi amor. El tuyo también es bonito.*'

'Ah, you speak Spanish.'

'Enough to converse.'

'Juanita!'

A woman down the road called to the child then clapped her hands.

'*¡Venga! ¡Ándale!*'

The child twirled around and ran to the woman.

'She is afraid,' the congressman said.

'The girl?'

'The woman.'

'Why?'

'Anglos. Police. Cameras.'

The woman and child disappeared. All the residents seemed to fade into the shadows. The dirt road suddenly lay vacant except for a few stray dogs and chickens. Two pigs. A goat. The *colonia* was now a ghost town. The congressman leaned in close and lowered his voice.

'May I suggest, Mrs. Bonner, that the troopers and the police stay here with the vehicles. The Ranger also.'

'Why my Ranger?'

'Well, the Texas Rangers are not . . . how shall I say . . . well regarded here on the border.'

'Why not?'

'History, Mrs. Bonner. History.'

She turned to the police. 'Please stay here.'

They didn't argue.

She turned to her Ranger. 'You, too.'

He did argue.

'But, ma'am—'

'Ranger Roy—'

She felt utterly stupid calling her Texas Ranger bodyguard 'Ranger Roy,' but his surname was Rogers. Roy Rogers. Ranger Rogers was even worse than Ranger Roy.

'—if these people fear us, we won't accomplish what we came here for today.'

'Mrs. Bonner, your safety requires that I accompany you. The governor, he wouldn't be happy.'

Lindsay embedded her fists in her hips and craned her head up at Ranger Roy. He was a strapping young man of twenty-eight; he had played football at UT. He had been her bodyguard for her husband's entire second term; he had become something of a son to her. A very large son. She had no doubt he'd die before seeing her harmed.

'Who would you rather have unhappy with you—the governor or me?'

Ranger Roy had faced that same choice many times. He knew the wise answer.

'Uh, yes, ma'am, I'll wait here.'

'Thank you.' She gestured to the press crew. 'Let's talk to these people.'

They stood as if embedded in the dirt. A burly TV cameraman smoking a cigarette shook his head.

'No way. My producer didn't say nothing about going into the *colonias*. And we sure as heck ain't going in there without the cops.'

'Why not?'

'Because this *colonia* is controlled by the Los Muertos cartel.'

'*Controlled?* This is America.'

He snorted like a bull, and smoke shot out of his nostrils.

'No, Mrs. Bonner, everything on this side of the wall, it's just a suburb of Mexico.' He jabbed a fat finger at the vast *colonia* that confronted them. 'Ma'am, you go in there, you might never come out—you can't even call nine-one-one 'cause there ain't no phone service out here, landline or cell.'

Congressman Delgado must have noticed her face flushing with her spiking blood pressure; he took Lindsay's arm.

'Come, let me show you the river.'

They walked away, but she heard the cameraman grumbling behind her back.

'Don't see why I gotta risk my life just 'cause some diva from Austin—'

'Shut up,' Ranger Roy said.

Lindsay smiled. Roy was a good son. They continued a short distance to a low bluff overlooking a narrow strip of brown water. She had never before seen the Rio Grande. She had expected majestic. It was not.

'The Rio Grande disappoints you?' The congressman gave her a knowing nod. 'Yes, I understand. It is not what you had envisioned, this dirty little river. But you see only the tired old man, not the strong young *hombre* that was born in Colorado. I have stood where the river begins, twelve thousand feet up in the San Juan Mountains, where the headwaters are cool and clean and rapid, fed by the melting snow. The water you now see, it has traveled seventeen hundred miles through New Mexico and West Texas and it must journey two hundred miles more before it will empty into the Gulf of Mexico at Boca Chica. To the *Mexicanos*, it is not the Rio Grande, the big river. It is the Rio Bravo del Norte. The brave river of the north.'

But the river did not seem brave or big. It seemed ordinary, too ordinary to separate two nations. The congressman sniffed the air.

'Something has died.' His eyes searched the sky. 'Ah, yes. See the vultures?'

He watched the birds circling, then his gaze returned to the river.

'The dams and the drought take the water. Upriver, before the Rio Conchos joins the flow, you can walk across without getting your feet wet . . . or your back.'

He smiled at his own joke then gestured at the children playing in the shallow water on the other side below their own slums. They waved; she waved back. Less than two hundred feet separated them, America and Mexico.

'If not for the river, you would not know which side is Mexico and which side is America,' the congressman said. 'But it is a very different world, if you are standing here and looking south or standing there and looking north. It is hard to believe this sad river holds so much power over human life. The river decides if you are American or Mexican, if you deserve ten dollars an hour or ten dollars a day, if you live free or in fear. If your life will have a future. My parents had not a peso in their pockets when they crossed the river, but I am a member of Congress.' His eyes lingered on the Mexican children. 'If you were born on that side, would you not come to this side?'

'I would.'

'They do. *Mexicanos* have always been drawn north, for the pull of America acts like a magnet on their souls. They think the stars shine brighter on this side of the river. Perhaps they do.'

He stared at the river a long moment then held a hand out to Mexico, to the outskirts of Nuevo Laredo and the vast desert beyond.

'All this land was once *México*, and Laredo straddled the river. After the war, *Mexicanos* moved south across the river and began calling that side *Nuevo Laredo*. But families still straddled the river, and all through my childhood, we crossed this river daily as if it were a neighborhood street instead of an international border. There are still footbridges up and down the river, from the old days. It was nice on the border back then.'

'What changed?'

'Drugs. All that was nice was washed away in the blood from the drug war. This is now *un río de sangre* . . . a river of blood. Forty thousand Mexicans have died in the last four years. It is violence we fund, with our appetite for the drugs. One pound of heroin on that side of the river is worthless. On this side of the river it is worth one hundred thousand dollars. Our drug money has made Nuevo Laredo the bloodiest place on the planet. But we think, Oh, it is their problem. But it is just there, on the other side of this shallow little river. How long before the violence is here, on this side of the river?' He pondered his own words. 'Six nations have flown their flags over this land, but it is the cartels that now claim sovereignty over the borderlands.'

He squinted at the sky and seemed to contemplate the endless blue.

'We have put a Predator drone over the border, as if this is Afghanistan. Perhaps it is.'

'This is not what I expected.'

'No. The borderlands is not like the rest of Texas. The land and the people are brown, the language is Spanish, and the culture is Mexican. And we are burdened by history. In Dallas and Houston and Austin, people look to the future. Here, they look to the past. Wrongs beget by wrongs, so many wrongs over so many years, that there will never be a right. Not on the border.'

Lindsay turned and looked north toward the wall in the distance. Then she turned back to the river.

'The wall is there and the river here.'

'Yes, we are on the American side of the river but the Mexican side of the wall.'

'These people, they're trapped by the river and the wall.'

'They are trapped by much more than that.' He held a hand out to the *colonia*. 'They fled Mexico, hoping for a better life in America. But the wall blocks their path into America. And that is their dream, Mrs. Bonner, to live beyond the wall. But for now they must live here in this no man's land, neither here nor there—neither *México* nor America.'

The congressman took her arm and escorted her toward the *colonia* as if leading her into a fine restaurant. He was thirty-four years older than her with thick white hair that contrasted sharply with his wrinkled brown skin and thick in the middle and short, but she felt secure next to him, like a girl with her grandfather.

'Come, you are safe with me.'

He pulled his coat back to reveal a gun in a belt holster.

'You carry a gun?'

He shrugged. 'Of course. It is the border.'

The congressman led the governor's wife into *Colonia Ángeles*. Ranger Roy made a move toward them but retreated when she held up an open hand. They walked down the dirt road past shacks and shanties, small and odd-shaped and pieced together with corrugated tin sidings and cinder blocks and scrap wood with black plastic tarps for roofs and wood pallets stood upright for fences and seemingly held together with wire and gravity. They continued past lean-tos and huts with thatched roofs, lopsided travel trailers embedded in the dirt with sheet metal overhangs, and abandoned vehicles that lay as if they had been shot from the sky and left to die where they landed. A yellow school bus sat buried in the dirt up to its wheels; it was now a home. Clothes hung over droopy lines and flapped in the dry breeze. They heard babies wailing and Spanish voices. Small children splashed in dirty water that had pooled in low gullies, women and girls cooked and washed outside, and boys played soccer on a dirt field.

'Don't they go to school?'

'No. The buses do not come to this side of the wall. The bus drivers, they are afraid to come in here, and the mothers, they are afraid to take their children out there, afraid they will be detained and deported if they go into Laredo.'

'Don't the truant officers come looking for them?'

The congressman chuckled. 'No, they do not come into the *colonias*.'

'But there are so many children.'

'Yes, the *colonias* are like child-care centers, except no one cares about these children.'

The congressman pointed at large drums sitting outside some residences.

'Water tanks. Fifty-five gallons. The water truck comes each week. They buy non-potable water—they call it "dirty water"—to wash clothes and cook, and clean water to drink, in the five-gallon bottles.'

'They don't have running water?'

'Oh, no.'

'How do they take baths?'

'In the river. But it is contaminated, with raw sewage. That is what you smell.'

The air was as dry as dirt, and the stale breeze now carried a foul stench.

'Raw sewage? From Mexico?'

'From both sides. There is no sewer system in this *colonia*, so they dump the waste in the river. And many of the American-owned *maquiladoras*, the factories on the other side, they dump their industrial waste into the river.'

'But that's illegal.'

'In some parts of the world. But as I said, Mrs. Bonner, this is another world entirely. Cancer rates are quite high, and the children, they always have the open sores and many illnesses from the river—hepatitis, dysentery, cholera, tuberculosis, even dengue fever. You have had your shots?'

'My shots?'

Lindsay Bonner had seen poverty before, in the rural counties and the inner cities. But she had never before seen anything like this. *Colonia Ángeles* looked like a scene from one of those 'feed the children' commercials on Sunday morning television. But this wasn't Guatemala or Africa. This was America.

'How did all this come to be?'

'These *colonias*, they began appearing along the river back in the fifties and sixties. But during the eighties and nineties, the population exploded with the immigration boom, some say because Reagan granted amnesty and citizenship to the Mexicans already here, so more followed, also hoping for citizenship—if not for them, at least for their children born here. They know the law, too.'

'My husband, he calls those children "anchor babies." '

'Yes. He does. Anyway, this is flood plain land, worthless for regular development. So the owners sold off small lots to Mexican immigrants, just pieces of dirt, with no roads or utilities. They built their homes with whatever scrap material they could salvage, piece by piece, what the sociologists call "incremental construction." Not exactly the American dream, as you can see. But it is all they can afford.'

'In Austin, these places would be bulldozed as unfit for human occupancy.'

'This is not Austin, Mrs. Bonner. This is the border. Travel up and down this river, and you will see nothing but *colonias* outside the cities, two thousand at last count. The state says four hundred thousand people live in the *colonias*, but I think there are many more, perhaps one million. How can the state know for certain when the federal government cannot even get an accurate count for the census?'

'So they live without running water, sewer . . .?'

'Electricity.'

'I thought the state had funded services for the *colonias*?'

'Yes, ten years ago, the state issued five hundred million in bonds to provide utilities to the *colonias*, and about half now have them. This *colonia* does not.'

'So when will these people get utilities?'

'They will not. The money has run out. Most of these

people will die without ever having turned on a light or flushed a toilet.'

'We need more money.'

'But, Mrs. Bonner, your husband vetoed more money for the *colonias*.'

'He did? Why?'

'He said the federal government should pay for the utilities since these people are illegal immigrants. Squatters, I think he called them.'

'They're human beings. And they shouldn't have to live like this.'

'Tell your husband.'

'I will.'

'But to be fair to the governor, we need billions, more money than the state of Texas can provide, to keep up with the people coming across the river and the children born here. The borderlands, it is both the poorest and the fastest growing population in all of America. That is why we must count them for the census, so the borderlands can get its share of federal funds.'

'But they're not citizens.'

'That does not matter. The census counts everyone living in America, legal or not. Funds and seats in the House are divvied up by population, not citizenship. If only these people will fill out the forms and be counted, Texas will get three, maybe four more seats in Congress and billions more in federal aid. Each of these residents is worth fifteen hundred dollars, if we can get them counted.'

'My husband wants to send these people back to Mexico, but he sends me down here to get them to fill out the census reports so Texas can benefit from their presence here?'

'Odd, is it not? But we need federal money to do what the

state cannot afford to do. The problem is, we are asking these people to come out of the shadows and be counted while ICE conducts raids right here on the border. They do not trust the government. And, of course, they did not receive the census forms.'

'Why not?'

'No mailing addresses. The *colonias* do not officially exist, at least as far as the Postal Service is concerned. So the Census Bureau must send workers in, to go door to door, to count the residents. But they are too afraid.'

'The workers or the residents?'

'Both.'

'We have boxes of forms in the back of the Suburban. We can give them the forms, and they can fill them out and mail them in.'

'Mrs. Bonner, these people do not go to the post office, and most cannot read or write.'

'The forms are printed in Spanish, too.'

'They cannot read or write Spanish or English.'

'But we've got to try!' Lindsay Bonner prided herself on being a positive person who never lost hope—not when volunteering at the food bank or the AIDS clinic or even the homeless shelter in Austin—but the heat and the stench and the filth now seemed to suffocate her spirit that day. She fought back tears. 'We can try.'

The congressman offered a grandfatherly squeeze of her shoulders and a sympathetic expression.

'Yes, Mrs. Bonner. We can try.'

They walked down the dirt road and stopped at a shanty with a covered contraption sitting above an open fire like a cookout. The congressman leaned over the pot and sniffed.

'*Tesguino*. Homemade corn liquor.' He called into the home. '*¡Hola!*'

A hand appeared and parted the blanket that served as the front door. A young Mexican woman peeked out; she held an infant in her arms. Lindsay smiled and spoke to her in Spanish.

'*Buenos días, Señora*. I am Lindsay Bonner. We need you to be counted for the census.'

'*No habla, Señora. No habla.*'

The woman pulled the blanket shut in Lindsay's face. But, of course, she did *habla*. They walked down the dirt road, deeper into the *colonia*. Lindsay approached every woman she saw, but she received the same reception. *No habla, Señora*.

'I travel all over Texas, and people always want to talk to me. But not here.'

The congressman patted her shoulder as if consoling her.

'Do not be offended, Mrs. Bonner. These women, they do not know you are the governor's wife. They do not even know who the governor is. They have no television, no cable news, no English newspapers. These people do not live in our world. Here in the *colonias*, you are just another Anglo whom they fear.'

'Where are the men?' Lindsay said.

'Gone. For good or for the day. They come and they go, leaving pregnant women behind. The men who do stay leave before dawn and return after dark. And you do not want to be in the *colonias* after dark.'

'How do they get through the gate, with the Border Patrol?'

'They do not. They came to work construction in Laredo, but the wall prevents that. So now they work for the cartels in Nuevo Laredo.'

'Where do these people get food?'

'Across the river.'

'They work and shop on that side and sleep on this side . . . This is just a suburb of Mexico.'

The breeze blew stronger, and she gagged at the foul smell from the river. The congressman held out a white handkerchief to Lindsay. She took the handkerchief and covered her mouth and nose. For a moment, she thought she might throw up.

'Perhaps we should go back?' the congressman said.

'No.'

She removed the handkerchief from her face and marched down the dirt road to a shack constructed of old garage doors for walls, a black tarp for the roof, and a dirty blanket for a door. A clay flowerpot with a single yellow sunflower sat outside.

'*¡Hola!*'

A small brown face peeked out. A child's face. A haunting dirty little wide-eyed face. Lindsay smiled at her, and the child smiled back. Lindsay reached into her pocket and pulled out a peppermint from breakfast at the hotel. She stepped closer and leaned down and held the candy out to the girl. The child hesitated but took the candy. Then she was gone. Lindsay stood straight and faced the congressman.

'We've got to get these people counted, so we can get that federal money. So we can help them.'

'But I am afraid that they do not trust us.'

'Is there anyone here they do trust?'

'Yes. There is such a person.'

'Who?'

'The doctor.'

Chapter 4

' "Is your mama a llama?" I asked my friend Jane.

' "No, she is not," Jane politely explained. "She grazes on grass, and she likes to say 'Moo!' I don't think that is what a llama would do."

' "Oh," I said. "I understand now, I think that your mama must be a . . . Cow!" '

Bode Bonner felt about as goddamn stupid as a grown man could possibly feel, reading *Is Your Mama a Llama?* by Deborah Guarino, a story about a little llama named Lloyd looking for its mama llama. He hated these events, but reading to elementary school kids had become a ritual for politicians these days—a ritual usually performed by this politician's wife. But she had bailed for the border that day. So the governor of Texas found himself facing twenty-four kindergartners.

He'd rather be facing twenty-four Democrats.

He flipped the book around so the kids could see the picture. A collective 'Aah!' went up, and one boy said, '*Vaca,*' which Bode knew from his experience working cattle on the ranch with the *vaqueros* meant 'cow.' The kids started chattering in Spanish, which made him wonder if they even understood the words he was reading. Tacked to the wall were colorful posters with numbers and colors and shapes and explanations printed in English and Spanish, just like the state's official documents: *uno*/one . . . *dos*/two . . . *tres*/three . . . *blanco*/white . . . *rojo*/red . . . *azul*/blue . . . *círculo*/circle . . .

rectángulo/rectangle . . . *cuadrado*/square. He wondered how many of these kids had just come up from Mexico with their parents for spring harvest. Back when Bode was growing up in the Hill Country, Mexicans worked the ranches and farms, but their children did not attend public school. They couldn't. He didn't think about such things back then; that's just the way it was. But he thought about such things now.

Because he was the governor.

And the most difficult job for the governor of Texas—for any of the fifty governors, all of whom faced massive budget deficits in this Great Recession—was figuring out how to pay for public schools. Which is to say, how to pay to educate the state's poorest children. During his tenure in office, at his wife's relentless urging, he had doubled the K-12 budget to $50 billion—*$10,000 per student*—but SAT and achievement test scores still hovered near the bottom among the fifty states, just ahead of Mississippi, not exactly a bragging point at the annual governors' conference. Most politicians blamed the teachers for the failure of public education—the first rule for politicians being, *Blame someone else before the voters blame you*—but the statistics made the job seem utterly hopeless: five million students in Texas schools speaking a hundred different languages but almost two million unable to read, write, or speak English; the highest teenage pregnancy and dropout rates in the nation; the lowest literacy and graduation rates; and the fourth highest poverty rate. And fully one-half of the nation's child population growth over the last decade had occurred in Texas. All poor children.

How the hell was the state of Texas supposed to educate so many poor, pregnant, non-English-speaking kids?

But the law required the state try, so Texas schools didn't just employ 330,000 teachers; they also employed 330,000 cops, social workers, nurses, counselors, ESL (English as a second language) facilitators, tutors, administrators, school bus drivers, janitors, and cooks. Schools now served free breakfast, lunch, and dinner, administered achievement tests and flu shots, supplied textbooks and toothbrushes, offered classes in math and parenting, and provided pregnancy counseling and childcare. Public schools had become social agencies sucking billions from the state budget. But the education activists—including his wife—wanted even more money. 'Educate or incarcerate,' she always said, and he knew in his heart that she was right. But he also knew a harsh political fact of life: there was no more money for these children.

The state of Texas was broke.

He turned back to the book and read another passage—the little llama named Lloyd now thought a kangaroo might be his mama—then again showed his audience the picture, which evoked another loud 'aah' and 'canguro' from the kids. They were bright-faced and wide-eyed and seemed to be enjoying themselves, English-language skills notwithstanding. A few listened intently, but most were too busy eating peanut butter crackers and sucking on juice boxes to pay attention. At the back of the classroom, two cameras captured the moment; one was from a local TV station, the other from a private production studio. These kids didn't know it, but they would soon be starring in a 'Bode Bonner for Governor' commercial.

Mandy had arrived early to set up the event. She chatted with the TV reporter and checked the production camera to ensure the angle caught Bode in his best light; she looked incredibly sexy in a skintight knit dress, the perky blonde cheerleader-turned-political aide. He wondered if she had any underwear on.

Jim Bob stood in the corner, as if he'd been put in time-out with an iPhone. He seemed pleased. Because he had dreamed up another brilliant campaign photo op: the Republican governor reading to a bunch of kids. And not rich white kids in West Austin, but poor brown and black kids in East Austin. West of Interstate 35 was downtown, the state capitol, the Governor's Mansion, lakefront estates, and rich white people; east of the interstate was the city dump, crime, and poor black and brown people. Democrats. The Republican governor had a sneaking suspicion that his political strategist had intentionally sent the governor's wife out of town so he'd have to read to these kids. He looked back down at the book and read the final passage when the little llama finally found his mama llama.

' "*My* mama's a . . . llama! And this is . . . the end." '

Praise the Lord. Bode turned the book so the kids could see the picture of the mama llama cuddling the little llama. One kid pointed and said, '*Un camello.*' The others nodded.

Un camello? A camel?

'No, no, it's not a camel,' Bode said. 'It's a llama.'

Their faces were blank.

'*Una llama,*' he said, even though he had no idea if that were the correct translation.

From his audience: 'Aah.'

'*¡Un libro más!*' one cute little girl with dangly loop earrings said.

Un . . . one . . . *más* . . . more . . . *libro* . . . book? She wanted him to read another book? Not only no, but hell no.

'Oh, I'd love to, kids, but the governor's got to take care of some real important state business.'

The teacher, a sweet-faced young woman named Ms. Rodriguez, stepped to the front of the classroom and said,

'Well, Governor, that was, uh . . . that was wonderful. Thank you so much for visiting our class today. Children, let us thank the governor with a big round of applause.'

The kids didn't make a move.

So she said, '*Niños, dénle un fuerte aplauso al gobernador.*'

Now they clapped—as if they'd been told they had to come to school that Saturday. The teacher forced a smile for Bode.

'Thank you, Governor. I am sorry Mrs. Bonner could not come today. She has adopted our school, as you know—'

He didn't know.

'—and spends entire days in my classroom, tutoring the children, trying to teach them English.'

So that's what she did with her days while he played golf with lobbyists.

Ms. Rodriguez's soft brown eyes took in her charges, now experiencing a collective sugar high from the juice: the boys, booger-farming, butt-scratching, crotch-grabbing, pushing and shoving and taunting—

'*¡Cabrón!*'

Ms. Rodriguez's eyes flashed dark.

'Ricardo!'

She glared at the boy and put a finger sharply to her lips.

—and the girls, twirling around in their fluffy dresses or colorful sweat suits and singing *Tejano* tunes and smelling of perfume.

'I love these children,' she said, her face back to sweet.

'You do?'

'Yes. In my classroom, they are my children.'

Ms. Rodriguez sighed, and her shoulders sagged. She seemed older now.

'Of course, I often think I am their mother. I have them

from seven in the morning until seven at night. They come for the free breakfast and stay for the free dinner. They are on welfare and WIC and CHIPS, but they have the manicured nails and the pierced ears and the new Nike sneakers and their parents have the iPhones and drive the fancy pickup trucks with the silver wheels and they all have the satellite TV. Most are undocumented, as my parents were, but my parents sacrificed so I could go to college and have a better life. I do not think these children will have a better life.'

She bit her lower lip, and Bode thought she might cry.

'Thank you, Governor, for caring about these children. Mrs. Bonner, she has told me how much you care. As she says, "If we do not educate them, we will certainly have to incarcerate them." I look at them each day and wonder who will be educated in twelve years and who will be incarcerated. I am afraid that more will be in prison than in college. That saddens me. I know it saddens you as well.'

She planted her face in his chest and wrapped her arms around him.

Bode felt terribly uncomfortable. The truth of the matter was, he hadn't thought about these kids in that way. He thought of them as a budget item—an item that was ballooning out of control, just like the defense budget at the federal level. And just as the president would be committing political suicide if he cut the defense budget, Bode Bonner would be committing political suicide if he cut the education budget. That would mean he didn't care. So, like every governor before him, he had thrown billions more at education to prove he cared. But for what? Half of these kids would drop out before graduation to get a job, join a gang, go to prison, or have a baby. He took one last glance around the classroom and wondered how the state of Texas could ever spend enough money to make the public schools work. How could any state? It was depressing, another aspect of the job he didn't much care for.

Ms. Rodriguez hung tight.

He patted her back but desperately hoped to escape her grasp and this classroom without her tears or the kids' peanut butter fingers all over his Armani suit. But when she finally released him, Mandy herded the little rugrats around him for the cameras.

'Come on, kids, we'll make a memory,' she said in her perky voice. 'I'll send your teacher a photograph for your classroom.'

The kids gathered close and put their sticky hands all over his suit, which now looked like an Armani peanut butter and jelly sandwich without the jelly. Memories were made, and Bode was brushing the peanut butter off his coat when a black boy, taller than the others and wearing brand new Air Jordan sneakers, low-slung pants, and a Kobe Bryant jersey when he still wore number eight, pushed forward and said, 'My mama says you don't care about poor folks like us.'

The kid was in kindergarten but looked like he should be in the penitentiary; his hair was braided into long dreadlocks in the fashion favored by black pro athletes. And he sported the same gangster attitude. Bode wanted to get down in the kid's face and say something like, 'Poor? How much did those sneakers cost your mama?' But the Professor cleared his throat like he was choking on a chicken bone and nodded at the cameras. So Bode forced a smile.

'Well, son, your mother's mistaken. I'm the governor, and I care about all Texans.'

'You sayin' my mama's a liar?'

'I'm saying your mother doesn't know me.'

'Unh-huh. Mama says only time you come east of the highway is when you wanting to get reelected. Rest of the time, we don't never see you.'

'Well, you're seeing me now.'

'Mama says she saw you play football on TV, says you wasn't no good, says—'

That did it. Now Bode got in the kid's face. He spoke through clenched teeth while smiling for the cameras.

'Yeah, well you tell your mama I was a two-time all-American and I got scars up and down my goddamn knees and anytime she wants she can come over to the Mansion and kiss my big white—'

'Okay, kids!' Jim Bob said, loudly enough to drown out Bode's voice. He stepped between Bode and the black kid like a referee breaking up a fight. 'Time for the governor to go.'

Bode gave the reporters his standard spiel about public education being the future of Texas then finally escaped the cameras. When they got out of microphone range, Jim Bob said, 'That'll make a nice commercial.'

The governor of Texas turned to his strategist and said, 'Next time, let's hire some kids.'

Tears ran down the child's dirty cheeks. She was perhaps five or six and looked like the girl who had run up to Lindsay when they had first arrived at the *colonia*, with the same stringy hair and gaunt face and dangling earrings. She whimpered softly; the doctor handed her a tissue.

'That is a nasty cut,' he said in Spanish.

Lindsay and Congressman Delgado had just entered a small clinic housed in a white modular structure situated at the northern edge of the *colonia* sporting the distinct scent

55

of disinfectant and a sign over the door: *Médico*. A golden retriever lay just inside the front door next to an unoccupied desk. The girl sat perched on a stainless steel examining table along the far wall. The doctor sat on a rolling stool in front of her with his back to them. But he glanced up at a mirror on the wall, apparently positioned so he could see who entered the clinic. The space was compact but orderly and well lit—

'The lights,' Lindsay said. 'How does the clinic have electricity?'

The congressman pointed to the ceiling. 'Solar panels on the roof. When he built this clinic, Jesse put in a solar-powered generator, small, but enough to power the clinic. There is much sun on the border.'

—but the shelves seemed too bare for a medical clinic. Fans sat propped in open windows and created a warm breeze. An office with a desk occupied one back corner, the examining table under a bright operating room light the other. A woman stood next to the child and patted her hand, more to soothe her emotions than the child's, it seemed. The doctor examined the girl's foot under the light and spoke to her softly. After a few moments, he held out a shard of glass with tweezers.

'You must wear shoes, Juanita.' She was the same child. To the mother, the doctor said, 'Does she have shoes?'

'No.'

He began cleaning and bandaging her foot.

'Jesse Rincón,' the congressman said to Lindsay. 'Our celebrity doctor. Inez, the doctor's assistant'—he glanced over at the unoccupied desk by the door—'is gone. She must be on an errand.'

The congressman stepped behind the desk and rummaged through papers as if he had done it before.

56

'Inez collects his press clippings in a book. Ah, here it is.'

The congressman picked up a thick binder and came back around the desk to Lindsay. He held the binder out as if he were a preacher reading scripture from the Bible. The pages were filled with newspaper clippings.

' "Harvard Doctor Returns Home to the Colonias" – *Laredo News.*' He turned the page. ' "Doctor Trades City Practice for Colonia Poverty" – *Brownsville Post.* Jesse graduated from Harvard Medical School, then surgical residences at Boston Mass and Johns Hopkins. He could be getting rich performing heart surgeries in Houston or giving Anglo women the large new breasts in Dallas, but he came home to work in the *colonias.*' He paused a moment then looked at her. 'Who does that sort of thing these days?'

He flipped the page. The clipping showed a grainy photo of a young man speaking at a podium.

'When he came home, Jesse spoke to civic groups to raise funds to build clinics in the *colonias* up and down the river. The local papers picked up his story. You have not heard of him in Austin, but from here to Boca Chica, everyone knows of Jesse Rincón.'

He held the book out to her. She took it and turned through more pages and read of the doctor's early life in Nuevo Laredo and his education at Jesuit in Houston and Harvard in Boston, her concentration interrupted by the girl's sudden cry. The doctor had given her a shot, no doubt tetanus.

'Juanita,' the doctor said, 'look in that box and find a pair of shoes.'

He lifted the child with her freshly bandaged foot down from the table. She wiped her eyes and limped over as if the bandage were a plaster cast and then leaned so far over she almost fell into the box. He glanced over at Lindsay and the congressman while the girl rummaged then emerged with a pair of pink sneakers and a broad smile.

'You like those?'

'*Sí.*'

The doctor hefted her onto the examining table again then slipped the shoes on her feet as if he were the prince putting the glass slipper on Cinderella.

'You must wear these always.'

He lifted her down again then reached into his coat pocket and gave her a yellow sucker. The child grabbed a naked doll off the bed then gave the doctor a quick hug. Her mother said *gracias* many times. The girl limped toward the front door with her mother following but noticed Lindsay and stopped. She ran a hand across her snotty nose then turned her wet brown eyes up to Lindsay.

'*Qué bonito el cabello.*'

'*Gracias.*'

She and her mother walked out the door past the dog. Lindsay turned back to the binder and a black-and-white photo from the *Laredo News* of the doctor standing outside the clinic. The caption read: 'Dr. Jesse Rincón, 33, home from Harvard.' The story was five years old. He wore a black T-shirt under a white lab coat over jeans and boots. His dark hair was long for a doctor and combed back, but strands fell onto his angular face. His smile was soft, his teeth brilliant white. He was Latino and—

'He is handsome, no?' the congressman said.

'He is . . . Yes.'

Lindsay stared at the photograph a moment longer then looked up and found herself staring at the doctor himself—at his eyes just a few feet away. They were as blue as the sky.

'My father,' the doctor said, answering her unasked question.

He peeled off the latex gloves and tossed them into the trash basket then removed his lab coat and hung it on a rack. He was again wearing a black T-shirt. He was lean and muscular with silky black hair. He appeared not to have aged since the photo five years before.

'He was American, my mother was Mexican. She fell hard for his blue eyes.'

He spoke with a soft Latin accent, not as pronounced as the congressman's, but with the same formality of one for whom English was not his native tongue. He stuck a hand out to the congressman.

'So, Ernesto, what brings you to the *colonias* today?'

'The census.'

The doctor grunted. 'Good luck with that.'

He looked Lindsay up and down.

'I see you have suffered the wind and the dirt.'

Her cream linen suit now appeared gray.

'Jesse,' the congressman said, 'I would like to introduce the governor's wife. Mrs. Bonner, this is Dr. Jesse Rincón.'

'It is a pleasure to meet you, Mrs. Bonner.'

He took her hand. She had shaken thousands of strangers' hands as the governor's wife, but never as a woman. He held her hand and stared into her green eyes. It had been a long time since a man had stared at her. The congressman broke the spell with a chuckle.

'Jesse can seduce money from misers, which would make him a very successful politician. We had a charity auction in Laredo, and a rich divorcée paid five thousand dollars for a date with him.'

The doctor released her hand.

'I built a clinic in the Boca Chica *colonia* with that money.'

'Five thousand dollars built a clinic?' Lindsay said.

'I used illegal Mexicans.' He held his serious expression a beat then smiled. 'The residents volunteered their labor.'

He had not taken his eyes off her. Lindsay felt her face blush like a teenage girl, so she broke eye contact, stepped over and placed the binder on the desk, then returned as the governor's wife.

'Dr. Rincón, the congressman says the residents here trust you. We need them to be counted for the census, so the state can get federal funds to help them.'

'And do you think that will happen?'

'That we'll get federal funds?'

'That the state will help these people?'

'If you will help us.'

'I will help you, but I will wait to see if the state will help them. Leave the forms here with Inez . . .' He glanced around. 'Where is Inez now? Well, leave the forms on her desk, and she will help the people complete them.'

'Thank you.' She paused then said, 'Doctor, may I ask you a question?'

'Certainly.'

'Why did you come back? Does working here make you feel useful?'

'Useful? Yes, I suppose it does.'

'He is a role model for the children,' the congressman said.

The doctor shook his head. 'No, Ernesto, I am no role model. The girls want to be *madres*, and the boys want to be *soldados*, making a thousand dollars a day with the fancy pickup trucks and young women on their arms. That is the life they want.'

'A short life it is,' the congressman said.

'Yes, but they would rather live one day as a king than fifty years as a peasant. But one day is often all they have.'

The door behind them suddenly swung open, and two large Latino men burst in carrying an unconscious teenage boy and the harsh smell of sweat and gunpowder. The boy's head and limbs hung limp; blood soaked his white T-shirt. The bigger man carried a handgun in his waistband. The congressman pulled Lindsay back. The dog by the door stood.

'Stay, Pancho,' the doctor said to the dog. To the men, he said in Spanish, 'On the table.'

'Mrs. Bonner,' the congressman whispered in her ear, 'we must leave. For your safety. These men, they are cartel *soldados*.'

He tugged on her arm, but she held her ground. The adrenaline had kicked in.

'Gunshot?' the doctor asked.

'*Sí*,' the smaller man said.

The men lay the boy on the examining table. The doctor pulled on latex gloves then grabbed a pair of scissors and cut the boy's shirt down the center. He took a towel and wiped blood from the boy's chest. He spoke to the men in Spanish.

'What kind of gun?'

'*Cuerno de chivo*.'

'*¿Aquí?* In the *colonia*?'

'No. *Allí*. Across the river.'

The doctor did not look up from the boy.

'The *federales* shot this boy?'

'*Sí*,' the man without a gun said.

'An AK-47 is a high-velocity projectile,' the doctor said. 'It usually causes severe internal damage. There is not much hope for this boy. Get that gun out of my clinic.'

The big man glared at the doctor a moment then said, 'Do not let him die, Doctor. It would not be good for any of us.'

The doctor's eyes met his for a long moment, then the man turned and walked out the door without so much as a glance at Lindsay and the congressman. She inched closer to the examining table. The doctor checked the boy's breathing and listened to his heart with a stethoscope.

'You should have taken him to the hospital.'

'You know we cannot take him there.'

'How old is he?'

'*Diecinueve.*'

Nineteen.

'What is his name?'

'Jesús.'

Hay-zeus.

'Is he your son?'

'No.'

The doctor jerked his head at the door. 'His?'

'No.'

The doctor examined the boy's chest.

'Entry wound through the right chest wall . . .' He rolled the boy onto his left side and checked his back. '. . . but no exit wound. The bullet is still in him. I do not see any other entry or exit wounds.'

The man nodded. '*Uno.*'

The doctor put his ear close to the boy's chest. With each breath, Lindsay could hear a sucking sound. A sucking chest wound, also known as a penetrating thoracic trauma. He needed a chest tube stat.

'I must insert a chest tube,' the doctor said.

The boy coughed violently and spit up blood. The doctor

put his finger in the entry wound. He pointed with his free hand to a nearby table.

'Hand me that scalpel.'

The man glanced from the doctor to the table and then to his own bloody hands. He did not move.

'*¡Bisturi!*' the doctor said again.

Lindsay stepped over, picked up the scalpel, and held it out to the doctor.

'I'll start IVs,' she said.

The doctor gave her a puzzled look.

'I was an ER nurse in San Antonio. We had a lot of gunshot wounds.'

'Coat and gloves.'

He took the scalpel.

Bode Bonner held a giant pair of two-handed fake scissors with the blade open over a wide red ribbon stretched across the front entrance of an organic grocery store in North Austin. Thirty minutes after leaving the elementary school, cameras clicked and store employees applauded as Bode cut the grand opening ribbon. The governor of Texas reduced to opening a grocery store, like Michael Jordan doing underwear commercials. Why?

'Smile, Bode,' Jim Bob whispered so close that Bode felt his hot breath in his ear. 'They gave half a million bucks to your campaign.'

Governor Bode Bonner smiled.

Chapter 5

The adrenaline energized Lindsay Bonner's body. An emergency room offered a rush like no other nursing experience. She had been a certified trauma nurse. She had kept her license current, perhaps in the hope that one day she might again be a nurse. That she might again be useful.

'Mrs. Bonner,' the congressman said, 'all the blood . . .'

She removed her suit coat and tossed it to the congressman. He stood alone by the front desk with the dog; the doctor had sent the other man outside to wait. She grabbed a lab coat hanging on a rack and put it on. She pulled on latex gloves then checked the boy's pulse and took his blood pressure.

'Pulse is one-forty-two, blood pressure is seventy over forty. He's in shock from the bleeding.'

She found two saline bags and attached them to a stand. She searched the shelves and found two sixteen-gauge needles and antiseptic. She wiped the boy's left wrist with antiseptic then inserted a needle into his vein. She connected the IV. The doctor opened the entry wound in the boy's right chest wall; blood spurted out.

'He is hemorrhaging. We must open him up.'

'A thoracotomy, here? Without a CT first? To see what's inside him?'

'We must work blind. If we do not, he will surely die.'

'Mrs. Bonner,' the congressman said. 'Please, I must take you back to Laredo.'

The doctor looked at her.

'I'm staying,' she said.

'Jesse, please,' the congressman said.

'Ernesto, I cannot do this by myself. I need her help.'

The congressman made the sign of the cross. The doctor turned back to the boy and performed an endotracheal intubation as if it were a daily routine. He walked over to a small refrigerator and removed yogurt and peanut butter and a blood bag.

'O-negative.' He tossed the bag to the congressman. 'Ernesto, please take this outside and hold it in the sun for a few minutes, to warm it up.'

The congressman held the bag as if holding a live human heart. He disappeared through the door. Lindsay started another IV for the blood transfusion.

'Help me get him on his left side,' the doctor said.

The doctor pushed and she pulled until the boy was propped up on his side. She held him while the doctor ran gray duct tape around the boy's waist and then around the table until he was securely in place. The doctor positioned the boy's right arm above his shoulder, then picked up a clean scalpel and leaned over the boy. He felt down the boy's side to locate the fourth and fifth ribs. He placed the scalpel between the two ribs and slid it down the boy's side. Blood appeared along the incision.

Blood gushed from the receiver's nose.

The scent of testosterone and the sound of large young men colliding with great force filled the bowl of the stadium. Grunts and groans, whistles and cheers, tubas and drums pounding a deep bass rhythm. The rhythm of football. And life.

At least for Bode Bonner.

The receiver tried to stand, but his legs wobbled like a newborn calf. The defensive back had tried to take his head off with a forearm across the face and had damn near succeeded. Two trainers ran over, wiped away the blood, and helped the player to his feet. His eyes were dazed and confused; he didn't have a clue. He had a concussion.

'A few more hits to the head,' the Professor said, 'and that boy will be drooling the rest of his life.'

The trainers escorted the player off the field, and a fresh body replaced him in the line-up. There was always a replacement body. The Professor shook his head.

'Why do they do it?'

'Same reason I did it,' Bode said. 'Same reason I'm in politics.'

'The girls?'

'The testosterone.'

'You're in politics for the testosterone?'

'I'm in politics because I *have* testosterone.' Bode pointed to the field. 'Takes testosterone to play out there, and when you're too old to play football, there's politics. It's the last American blood sport, Jim Bob. Hell, a political debate's the next best thing to knocking a wide receiver unconscious . . . *mano a mano*. Man to man.'

'I think it means "hand to hand." '

'Winning in football or politics requires testosterone. A lot of it.'

The Professor pondered that a moment. Then he turned back to Bode.

'What about Bachmann? She doesn't have any testosterone.'

'And she won't win.'

Bode turned back to the game. The state of Texas could not afford to educate its children, but the University of Texas had money to burn on football. It was just before noon, and Bode and Jim Bob stood on the sideline at the one-hundred-thousand-seat Darrel K. Royal–University of Texas Memorial Football Stadium on the UT campus just north of the state capitol. He watched the replay on the 'Godzillatron,' the massive HDTV screen above the south end zone. UT's athletic department grossed more money than any other college in the country—almost $150 million annually from tickets, merchandising, even its own cable sports network—and spent more money on football than any other college in the country. Consequently, UT was perennially ranked in the top ten in football, if not academics. Which meant that the most powerful man in the state was not the governor of Texas—the state paid him $150,000 a year—but the head coach of the Texas Longhorns—the university paid him $5 million. The team was playing an orange–white spring practice game before fifty thousand fans; ESPN was broadcasting the game live on national TV.

'They want to interview me at halftime?'

'Uh, no,' Jim Bob said. 'They've already got the head cheerleader lined up.'

'Figures.'

Football in Texas wasn't a sport; it was a religion. Twenty-five years before, Bode Bonner had preached the gridiron gospel on that very field, and his congregation had joined in the chorus: 'Bo-de! Bo-de! Bo-de!' He would give anything to hear that chant again, to be out there on that field again, to be young and strong with his entire life ahead of him. But it was all behind him.

Youth.

Football.

The good part of life.

The sideline camera swung his way, so he flashed a politician's smile and the UT Longhorn hand sign: a fist with the index and pinkie fingers extended to fashion horns. Bode's smiling face was now displayed on the Godzillatron, but the crowd did not cheer, as if they didn't know that the governor of Texas had once been a star player on that very field—or even that he was the governor. The camera swung over to Mandy; her bouncing breasts now filled the huge video screen.

The crowd cheered.

Bode shook his head. Once a cheerleader, always a cheerleader. All she needed were pompoms.

'You think it's gonna last forever,' he said. 'But you blink an eye, it's twenty-five years later and you realize those times out there on that field, those were the best times of your life.'

Bode flexed his right knee, the one that had suffered four surgeries in four years of college ball, surgeries that precluded a professional career for number 44 on the Texas Longhorns. His knee always hurt, but he'd do it again in a heartbeat.

'I was a college football hero. Now I'm the governor of a broke state. That's a long fall.'

'You're a hero to lobbyists.'

Jim Bob chuckled; Bode didn't. He felt his spirit spiraling down into that dark place called middle age again. Jim Bob slapped him on the shoulder.

'Maybe killing something would improve your spirits.'

Bode responded with a weak shrug. 'Might.'

'Sure it would. Let's fly out to John Ed's ranch, take the horses out for a free-range hunt . . . smoke cigars, drink whiskey, sleep under the stars. Last time I talked to John Ed, said he was stocking the place with exotics from Africa. Hell, Bode, you could kill a water buffalo.'

'A water buffalo? That'd be like shooting a fucking elephant.'

'How about a blackbuck?'

'Been there.'

'Impala?'

'Done that.'

'Bison?'

'Boring.'

'Zebra?'

'Please. It's a pony with stripes.'

'Yak?'

Bode faked a yawn.

'Lion?'

'Mountain?'

'African.'

'An *African* lion? John Ed's got African lions on his ranch?'

'One.'

'How the hell did he get an African lion into Texas?'

'Don't ask, don't tell.'

'Damn. I always wanted to go on safari.'

'Well, now you can. Without leaving Texas.'

'Is that legal? Shooting an African lion if you're not in Africa?'

Jim Bob shrugged. 'You're the governor. And John Ed's ranch is twenty-five square miles in the middle of nowhere. It's like Vegas: what happens out there stays out there.'

The action came their way, a swing pass to the running back. The strong safety launched his body at the receiver and knocked him to the turf right in front of Bode.

'Good hit, number twenty-two!' Bode shouted.

He grabbed the safety by the shoulder pads and yanked him up then slapped his butt—not something one man should do to another man anywhere except on a football field. Still, the player gave Bode a funny look before retaking the field.

'Damn,' Bode said, 'his butt's hard as a rock. My butt used to be that hard.'

'Thanks for sharing.'

'You know, a lion's head up on the wall of my office, that'd look pretty damn nice.'

'Real nice.'

'But if it's illegal, I can't put it up in the office.'

'Sure you can. We'll just say you killed it in Africa a few years back, just now got it mounted and shipped over.'

'Will the press buy that?'

'They bought that lame-ass story about you killing a wolf while jogging the greenbelt—who carries a gun while jogging . . . even in Texas?' He snorted. 'Local press ain't exactly *60 Minutes*.'

Jogging with a high-powered handgun had earned Governor Bode Bonner an A-plus rating from the NRA, the only A-plus he had ever gotten in his life. He turned to his strategist.

'Let's kill that lion.'

'I'll call John Ed, set something up, early next month. April in the Davis Mountains, that'd be nice.'

Professor James Robert Burnet, Ph.D., stepped away from the football field and pulled out his iPhone to call John Ed Johnson, billionaire and generous Republican donor, but he shook his head. Excitement. Challenge. Adventure. The thrill of victory. The agony of defeat. He often felt more like the activities director at a fucking summer camp for kids than the chief political advisor to the governor of the great state of Texas.

He hit the speed dial and waited for the call to ring through. He turned back to his political benefactor whooping and hollering at the play on the field. They were like brothers and had been since fifth grade. Jim Bob was the smart brother; Bode was the handsome, popular, athletic brother who always got the girl. Girls. Voted most likely to succeed, homecoming king, and class president (Jim Bob ran his campaign), he was the big brother who saved his little brother from bullies. Without Bode Bonner, Jim Bob wouldn't have survived middle school; he couldn't have afforded college at UT without Bode getting him a job tutoring football players; he wouldn't now be the resident political genius in Texas, he wouldn't be making $500,000 a year, he wouldn't be getting calls from millionaires and billionaires and lobbyists and legislators seeking favors from the governor, he wouldn't be working in the Governor's Mansion . . .

But still.

No man wanted to be co-dependent on another man. It wasn't—

Manly.

But Bode Bonner had cornered the market on manly in the state of Texas.

A gruff voice came over the phone, and Jim Bob said, 'John Ed, you still got that lion?'

Chapter 6

'Boys like him,' the doctor said, 'they die by the dozens each day in Nuevo Laredo, in cartel gunfights with the *federales* or with each other. This boy, he is very lucky. He will not die this day.'

The boy's chest wall and ribs on his right side were held open by a retractor, exposing the thoracic cavity. The doctor was now searching for the bullet with a small flashlight. He inserted a pair of forceps into the boy's chest, then retracted the forceps to reveal a small piece of lead.

'AK–47. What the *soldados* call the *cuerno de chivo* . . . the goat's horn, because that is what the weapon resembles. But it has only a single purpose: to kill human beings.'

Across the rotunda, a tall, lean man with a shaved head shook hands with Jim Bob; his coat opened enough to reveal a pistol in a belt holster. He didn't look like a cop, but anyone with a concealed-carry permit could pack a gun into the Texas State Capitol, no questions asked. Bode waited by the white marble statue of Sam Houston for the Professor to finish his conversation. He glanced up at old Sam and wondered how he had looked back on his life at Bode's age—and what a life that man had lived. Living with the Cherokees, fighting the War of 1812, being elected a member of Congress and governor of Tennessee, leading the Texas revolution against Mexico, capturing Santa Anna at San Jacinto, and being elected the first president of the Republic of Texas—all before his forty-third birthday. And he went on to be elected the first U.S. senator from Texas after statehood and then governor of the state of Texas. Every day of that man's life had been an adventure.

Men today didn't get to live such lives.

The state capitol sat quiet, the silence broken only by the subdued voices of a middle-school field trip gathered in the rotunda, their fresh faces turned up to gaze at the star on the dome two hundred and eighteen feet above them. The legislature came into session every other year, in odd-numbered years, and this was not such a year. During even-numbered years, the capitol hosted field trips. But during the sessions, lobbyists took over the place and students stayed at school. No parent wanted their children watching the state legislature in action.

Jim Bob shook hands again with the tall man then dodged the field trip and came over to Bode. His heels clacked on the terrazzo floor embedded with the seals of the six nations whose flags had flown over Texas: Spain, France, Mexico, the Republic of Texas, the Confederate States of America, and the United States of America.

When he arrived, Bode said, 'Who's that?'

'Eddie Jones. He works for you.'

'He does?'

'He does now.'

'What does he do?'

'Odd jobs.' Jim Bob shrugged. 'Glorified gopher.'

'A gopher with a gun?'

'Shit, Bode, my newspaper boy carries a gun. This is Texas.'

They had stopped off at the capitol for the governor's weekly press conference. Standing in the rotunda lined with portraits of the governors of Texas from Sam Houston to

William Bode Bonner now brought all the burdens of office back into his thoughts. He gestured at the portraits.

'Jim Bob, Texas prospered under every one of those governors. I don't want this state to fail on my watch. What are we going to do about this budget deficit?'

'What budget deficit?'

'The twenty-seven-billion-dollar deficit.'

'There's no deficit.'

'What are you talking about? The comptroller's revenue projections show we're going to be twenty-seven billion short over the next two years.'

'Bode, read my lips: there—is—no—deficit.'

Bode exhaled heavily. 'Jim Bob, that's not gonna fly. Everyone knows we're looking at a big deficit. There's no denying it. That'd be like you denying you're bald.'

'I'm not bald. I have a beautiful head of thick, curly brown hair just like when I was a kid—'

'Wearing those thick glasses.' Bode laughed. 'You're a fuckin' nut . . . or a goddamn genius, I'm not sure which.'

'I'm an optimist. And you'd better be one, too. That's what voters want to hear. And that's what you're going to tell them right up to election day: there is no deficit. We'll deal with reality come January when the legislature convenes. Nothing we can do till then anyway.' He shrugged again. 'Denial ain't a river in Egypt—it's our campaign theme.'

Bode turned and stared at his own image. How many times had he stood there and imagined his portrait on the wall of the majestic rotunda of the Texas State Capitol? How proud had he felt standing there when his portrait was hung? Life had been exciting eight years ago when he had first been elected governor. The adventure was upon him, the economy was booming, and his wife loved him. Now—

74

'I'm hiding a twenty-seven-year-old mistress from my wife and a twenty-seven-billion-dollar deficit from the voters.'

He glanced up again at Sam and felt the sharp stab of shame; would they erect a statue of William Bode Bonner in the capitol one day?

'What kind of man am I?'

'You're not a man,' the Professor said. 'You're a politician.'

Mandy arrived to retrieve the governor. They walked across the hall and into the press room. Bode stopped at the door and regarded the nearly empty space.

'That's it? Two print reporters? And one's from the UT student paper? Where's the Austin paper? The TV reporters?'

Mandy gave him a lame shrug. Jim Bob checked his iPhone.

'Oh, there's a big wreck out on the interstate. They sent the camera crews to cover that instead.'

'Figures.'

Mandy whispered: 'The girl is Kim, the guy is Carl.'

'Kim and Carl. Got it.'

Bode stepped to the podium and again became the governor seeking reelection. He put on his politician's face.

'Kim, Carl, good to see y'all today. What'd you think about the primary?'

'What primary?' Carl said.

He was being a smart-ass because he was a Democrat.

'Oh, you mean the Republican general election?'

'Well, Carl, when you get tired of losing, let me know, and I'll put in a good word for you with the state Republican Party chairman, maybe he'll let you join up.'

Bode chuckled; Carl did not. He had a liberal's sense of humor, the kind that worked only when they won.

'I'm announcing today that after numerous requests by me,

the federal government has finally deployed a Predator drone to the border to assist in drug and immigrant interdiction.'

Kim, the UT student reporter, stood.

'Governor, is it true that the drone will be armed with missiles to shoot Mexicans?'

Bode could tell from the tone of her voice that she was being sarcastic. She was a Democrat, too.

'Don't tease me, Kim.'

She rolled her eyes and sat.

'I'm also deploying the Ranger Recon unit to the border. Ranger Recon is an elite unit of the Texas Rangers. They will engage in covert operations to secure our border since the president refuses to do so.'

Kim stood again.

'What kind of operations, Governor?'

'I can't tell you.'

'Why not?'

'Because they're covert operations. Covert means secret. If I told you, it wouldn't be a secret anymore.'

'A secret?'

'You know, something you don't want everyone to know.'

'I know what a secret is, Governor, but why are the Ranger Recon operations secret?'

Bode turned his palms up.

'Because they're covert operations.'

That shut her up. She sat down, and Carl stood. He reported for the alternative newspaper in Austin. His column ran between ads for sex partners and sex toys.

'Governor, you're campaigning on a "faith, family and schools" theme.'

'That's correct.'

'So where do you go to church?'

He didn't. But he couldn't say that in public in Texas.

'A church.'

'Which church?'

'I can't tell you.'

'Why not?'

'Security.'

'*Security?* Who the heck would want to shoot the governor of Texas? Maybe someone important like the speaker of the House, but—'

'Funny.'

Carl thought he was.

'Governor, projections are that we're facing a twenty-seven-billion-dollar deficit in the next biennial budget.'

'Who told you that?'

'The comptroller.'

'Well, that's not true, Carl.'

'We're not looking at a big deficit?'

'Nope.'

'But the comptroller is—'

'Wrong. We're fine. No deficit.'

'No deficit?'

'No deficit.'

Carl frowned. Bode cut a glance at Jim Bob, who nodded as if to a student who had correctly answered his question. The reporter retreated from the budget.

'Governor, you're the tea party's favorite son here in Texas. Have you thought about testing the national waters for a presidential run?'

'You trying to get rid of me, Carl?'

'Well . . .'

'Heck, if I moved to Washington, I wouldn't get to see you every week.'

'We could text.'

'I've got the best job in the country.'

'Well, Governor, your Democratic opponent says you're not doing your job, says you're a part-time governor, says that you work less than ten hours each week.'

'But I sing better than him.'

'Perhaps, but we've obtained your bodyguard's official log for the last month under the Open Records Act and found that you worked out at the downtown YMCA and jogged around the lake twenty-nine times, played golf thirteen times, had lunch with your daughter four times, and—'

'You don't want me to have lunch with my daughter?'

'I think your opponent wants you to work a little more.'

'My opponent wants my job. Look, when you're the governor of Texas, everything you do is for the people of Texas.'

'Playing golf?'

'Talking state business.'

'With lobbyists?'

'Don't they have a right to be heard?'

Bode had been around Carl long enough to know that he was building up to his big question of the day—'Carl Crawford's scandal of the week.'

'Governor, the Board of Pardons and Paroles has opened an investigation to determine if the state of Texas executed an innocent man on your watch.'

'Who?'

'Billy Joe Dickson.'

'Dickson? That the ol' boy convicted of burning his house down with his kids in it?'

'No, that's the ol' boy convicted of murdering his mother with an ax.'

'Down in Houston?'

'Up in Dalhart.'

'Oh, yeah, I remember now. He was guilty.'

'You're sure?'

'Yep.'

'So why is the board conducting an investigation?'

'Politics.'

'They're all Republican. You appointed them.'

'I did?' He grunted. 'Oh, then they're just mad.'

'About what?'

'We're gonna cut their budget.'

'Why? If there's no deficit?'

'There's no deficit because we cut spending before there is a deficit.'

'But—'

Bode sighed. Democrats. He answered four more questions then called it a day. He walked out the door followed by Jim Bob.

'We'll replace the entire Board of Pardons and Paroles,' the Professor said. 'That'll derail the investigation.'

'Can we do that?'

'It's one of the few things the governor can do.'

Bode threw a thumb back at the press room.

'Won't the press bitch?'

The Professor shrugged it off.

'So? Voters won't hold it against us if we execute the wrong guy every now and then. No one's perfect.'

Chapter 7

The boy's heart stopped.

'Doctor, he coded!'

The boy named Jesús had come through surgery fine—until now. Cardiac arrest. The doctor sat on the stool suturing the boy's chest wall. He dropped the sutures then took the stethoscope and listened to the boy's heart. He grabbed a portable defibrillator. He applied the electrodes to the boy's chest but didn't yell 'Clear!' as the doctors had in the ER. He just looked at her. She held up her hands to show that she was clear of the patient. She didn't need a seven-hundred-fifty-volt shock. The boy's body twitched with the electric shock. She put the stethoscope to his chest.

Nothing.

Lindsay recalled the big man's words: *Do not let him die, Doctor. It would not be good for any of us.* She felt sweat beads on her forehead. She said a quick prayer. The doctor shocked him again. The boy's body twitched harder this time, then he coughed. She checked his heart.

'He's back!'

Lindsay let out the breath she had been holding. The doctor resumed his suturing, as calmly as if he had been interrupted only by a phone call from a pharmaceutical rep.

'Where's Mom?'

'Laredo. Probably having a margarita with lunch right about now.'

'What's she doing in Laredo?'

'Trying to get Mexicans counted for the census.'

Bode gave Becca, his eighteen-year-old daughter, a big bear hug. He had wanted a boy—William Bode Bonner, Jr.—but he had gotten a girl—Rebecca Bodelia Bonner. She couldn't play football, but she was tall and athletic like her old man, she was tough and fiercely competitive like her old man, and she liked girls like her old man. His daughter was a lesbian.

'You feeling okay, honey? You look a bit peaked.'

In fact, she looked like hell.

'Oh, we're just hung over. We went to the music festival last night, over on Sixth Street. It was wild.'

Every March the South by Southwest Film and Music Festival took over downtown. Thousands of young folks from across the country descended upon Austin hoping their band or film might get discovered by a record or movie studio. Best Bode could tell, they spent most of the nine days getting drunk and stoned and raising hell on Sixth Street. No event did a better job than SXSW of promoting the city's official slogan: 'Keep Austin Weird.'

'You're not supposed to tell your old man you're hung over.'

'Oh.' She giggled. 'Then we stayed in our dorm and studied.'

'You're also not supposed to act like your old man's a moron who didn't go to the same college.'

'You're a hard man to please.'

'That's what I hear.' He gave her a little kiss on her fore-head. 'You might be in college now, but you're still my little gal.'

She kissed him on the cheek. Then Darcy kissed him on the other cheek.

'And I'm your gal's pal.'

Becca had brought Darcy Daniels over to the mansion for Thanksgiving dinner and announced during dessert that she was a lesbian and Darcy was her lover. Bode damn near spit out his pumpkin pie. He hoped the lesbian thing was just a college fad, like voting Democrat, and she would grow out of it, so he hadn't made a big deal about it, especially after the Professor said it would help with the Independent voters. She made a face.

'Daddy, you gotta lose the hair spray. Go natural, like me and Darcy.'

'You don't use hair spray?'

'Or shave.'

'Your legs?'

'Our girl parts.'

'Your girl parts?'

'All the sorority girls, they get Brazilian wax jobs. Not us. We go natural.'

'And I needed to know that because . . .?'

She giggled again, which Bode liked, and they sat. They'd always had more of a father–son relationship where they could talk about anything, but Brazilian wax jobs were a bit much even for this father. The waitress came, and Bode ordered the peanut butter pancakes.

'Oh, Daddy, congratulations.'

'For what?'

'*Duh* . . . Winning the primary.'

'Oh. Yeah. Thanks.'

'You don't seem happy about it.'

Bode shrugged. 'Uncontested.'

'And you like a contest.'

'So do you.'

'Like father like daughter.'

They fist-bumped.

'So what've you been doing this morning?' she asked.

'Reading to kindergartners.'

Becca laughed. 'Why?'

''Cause your mother bailed for margaritas on the border.'

They were having lunch at Kerbey Lane Cafe on the Drag right across from the University of Texas campus. It was noisy and busy and colorful with college kids and body art. Kerbey's was an institution in Austin, known for the tattooed wait staff and great pancakes. They had lunch together every week—same day, same time, same place—a standing reservation for the governor of Texas at the same table on the raised section fronting the plate glass window and Guadalupe Street just an arm's length beyond. The sidewalk ran right outside the window, so students walking by could see him and wave at him, although most waved with only one finger. Democrats—at least until they graduated, got a job, and started paying taxes. Becca sniffed the air and made a stinky face then leaned in and whispered.

'Hank's wearing that yukky aftershave again.'

'At least he showered this morning—and *shaved*.'

Hank Williams, Bode's Texas Ranger bodyguard, stood at attention behind them. His daddy had named him after the country-western singer. Senior, not Junior. Hank was even bigger than Bode and wore the khaki western-style Texas Ranger uniform complete with a cowboy hat and boots and a wide tan leather holster packing a nine-millimeter handgun, cuffs, Mace, and a fifty-thousand-volt Taser—and his sunglasses so he could check out the coeds without appearing obvious. Not much else for the governor's bodyguard to do. It wasn't as if a UT sophomore was suddenly going to jump up from her booth, pull an AK-47 from under her Spandex short-shorts, and shoot the governor of Texas dead. A loud crash of plates and glasses and silverware caused Hank to slap leather. Bode chuckled.

'Easy there, Hank. No need to draw your weapon. Waiter just dropped a tray.'

Jim Bob sat at the next table. His head was down, and his fingers were fiddling with that fucking phone again. Mandy never came to Bode's lunches with Becca. Call him old-fashioned, but it just didn't seem right to bring his mistress to lunch with his daughter, particularly since his daughter was the spitting image of his wife. Becca had inherited her mother's looks and red hair and Bode's height and athletic ability and penchant for rebellious acts in college, like turning lesbian her first semester.

Which reminded him.

'Jim Bob, give me that photo.'

Without looking up from the phone, the Professor reached inside his coat and pulled out a newspaper clipping then held it out to Bode. He took it and unfolded it on the table and gave his daughter a look that said, 'Well, what do you have to say for yourself?' She glanced at the photo and giggled.

'Daddy, they're just boobs. And it's legal.'

The photo was of Becca and Darcy sunning topless at Barton Springs Pool, which was in fact legal in Austin. They were not named in the caption: 'An Austin tradition.'

'No. They're the governor's daughter's boobs.'

'And the governor's daughter's partner's boobs,' Darcy said. 'They're nice, don't you think, Governor?'

Darcy was being a smart-ass, but Bode had to admit it, her boobs were nice. In the photo and in person. Both girls were wearing biker shorts and tube tops with no bras. Bode pulled his eyes off Darcy's boobs and regained his derailed train of thought.

'Becca, I'm trying to get reelected. If someone recognized you, I might've lost the evangelical vote.'

'Oh, so it's not about me going *nekkid* in public, it's just about politics.'

'*Just?* Honey, when you're the governor of Texas, *everything's* about politics.'

She abruptly jumped up with a big grin, as if she had a straight-A report card to show her dad.

'Look what we did.'

Having a lesbian daughter wasn't nearly as traumatic as Bode thought it would be when she had first broken the news. At least he didn't have to worry about her getting knocked up by some dope-smoking hippie. Sitting across the table from these two girls, both young and beautiful, tall and lean, you'd figure them for athletes, not lesbians. But they were both. Athletes and lesbians. They played on the UT girls' volleyball team. They were now pulling up the legs of their shorts to display their muscular buttocks and matching heart tattoos—which didn't elicit even a raised eyebrow in Kerbey's, except perhaps from Ranger Hank.

'You're not supposed to show your butt tattoo to your old man.'

But he smiled. She was a chip off the old block. She had been hell on a horse, and she would've been hell on a football field, if she'd been a boy. Bode Bonner had wanted a boy but had gotten a daughter. And he loved her with all his heart, even if she was a lesbian.

Chapter 8

'Boys marrying boys and girls marrying girls and both having babies and joining the PTA. They think that's just fine and dandy because that's their lifestyle—but what about the kids? Aren't they entitled to a choice in the matter? Would you have wanted two daddies or two mommies growing up? Heck, growing up with acne is tough enough without also being a social experiment. Vote for the children. Vote for the sanctity of marriage. Vote Republican. Vote for Bode Bonner.'

'Cut!'

The director flashed a thumbs-up to Bode. They had stopped off at the studio to shoot a few campaign commercials hitting the hot-button topics: gay marriage, abortion, immigration, and gun control. 'In times of economic despair,' the Professor always said, as if lecturing a class on politics, 'divert the voters' attention to the emotional social issues.'

Hard to argue with success. Still, Bode wondered if he would rather have a grandson with Becca and Darcy or no grandson at all.

'We're ready, Governor!'

Bode faced the camera and read his lines on the teleprompter: 'Since *Roe v. Wade* was deemed the law of the land, fifty million abortions have been performed in the United States. Fifty million children didn't get their chance at life. Because six Supreme Court justices—six *lawyers*—decided that their lives didn't count. Because those six lawyers think they're entitled to dictate the law to three hundred million

Americans. That's not a democracy—that's a dictatorship. Choose democracy. Choose life. Vote Republican. Vote for Bode Bonner.'

'Cut!'

Bode was standing in front of a green screen. The young director came over wearing a fluffy hairdo and a big smile. He looked like a college kid.

'We'll fill in the background later, put you in front of an abortion clinic.'

Mandy arrived with an armful of clothes and a cowboy hat on her head. She reminded Bode of his big sister, Emma, when she was a teenage queen of the Kendall County Rodeo. Then she died. Bode removed his Armani coat and silk tie and put on a denim rancher's jacket and the cowboy hat. The director positioned Bode against the green screen again.

'It'll look like you're standing right on the border above the Rio Grande.'

Bode recited his lines. 'Juan Galván, a Mexican national, crossed the border into Texas, traveled to Houston, and robbed and murdered Sarah Brown, a thirty-eight-year-old mother of four. He was convicted and sentenced to death. The Mexican government appealed to the State Department for a stay of execution. The Feds agreed. I didn't. The state of Texas executed Juan Galván last month. But ten thousand other Mexican nationals still sit in Texas prisons, some on death row, all convicted of violent crimes against Texans. And more Mexican criminals cross our border every day. Because the president refuses to finish the wall and secure the border. Vote for Bode Bonner, and I'll secure our border. I'll make sure Mexican criminals stay in Mexico.'

'Cut!'

One take. He was that good.

'We'll intercut shots of the dead woman and her kids,' the director said. 'Guaranteed tear-jerker.'

'That was a bad crime.'

Bode had signed the death warrant. Mandy returned with a .357 Magnum handgun. It looked like a cannon in her small hands.

'Where'd you get this from?'

'Cabela's,' Mandy said. 'I never knew how many women buy guns. I charged it to the campaign account.'

Bode held the gun like Marshal Rooster Cogburn charging the bad guys in *True Grit* and read his lines: 'Romero Polanco, a Mexican national, entered the U.S. illegally and traveled to Amarillo to work in a meat-packing plant. A month into the job, he was fired for showing up drunk. He left the plant and went directly to the home of Edna Smith, a sixty-six-year-old grandmother. He broke into her house and tried to rape her. But Edna had lived in the harsh Panhandle of Texas all her life, and she was as crusty as the land. She pulled her .357 Magnum and shot Romero six times in the chest. Mr. Polanco's criminal days are over but Edna's days are not—because she owned a gun. Guns don't kill—only bad people with guns kill. But liberals in Washington want to take your guns away and let your grandmother get raped by illegal Mexican immigrants. As your governor, I won't let that happen. Vote to keep your guns. Vote for your grandmother. Vote for Bode Bonner.'

'Cut!'

The director came over to Bode.

'You like that one, Governor? We combined immigration *and* gun control.'

'I never heard about this Polanco case.'

'That's because it didn't exactly happen.'

'It didn't?'

The director shook his head.

'Well, what did happen, exactly?'

'A grandmother shot a burglar.'

'Illegal Mexican?'

'White boy on meth.'

'So how the hell did he become an illegal Mexican?'

'The Professor. Literary license, he said.'

Bode grunted then gestured to his political strategist. When Jim Bob arrived, Bode said, 'This Polanco case is fiction?'

Jim Bob glanced at the director, who offered only a lame shrug in response.

'It's a good spot,' Jim Bob said. 'It'll play with the tea partiers.'

'It's a lie.'

'Riding the wave, Bode.'

Lindsay had bandaged the boy's chest and was now checking his pulse and studying the intricate tattoo on his left arm—a large *LM* in fancy script—when the boy's eyes abruptly blinked open. The doctor had removed the ET tube, and the boy coughed as if he had a sore throat, which he surely had.

'Doctor, he's awake.' She wiped sweat from the boy's face and said in Spanish, 'How do you feel?'

'Tired,' the boy said. 'Where am I?'

'The clinic, in *Colonia Ángeles*. Your friends brought you here.'

'Where are they?'

'Outside.'

'I must speak to them.'

The doctor went to the front door and stepped outside. The two men soon entered and came over to the boy. But they looked at Lindsay.

'Uh, I'll leave you alone.'

She walked over to the congressman, who was sitting at the doctor's desk in the corner eating yogurt. The doctor returned and joined them.

'Jesse, I stole a yogurt,' the congressman said. 'I missed lunch, which is not good for my low blood sugar. Will the boy be all right?'

'Yes. With rest, he will live.'

'You're a very good doctor,' Lindsay said.

'I worked the ER during my residency at Boston Mass—I handled many gunshot wounds. As you did. I had forgotten how valuable a skilled nurse is—and you are a skilled nurse, Mrs. Bonner. Do you still work?'

She shook her head. 'I'm the governor's wife now.'

'Ah.' His eyes turned down. 'I am afraid you have ruined an expensive suit.'

She looked at herself for the first time since the boy had arrived; blood stained her linen skirt.

'Would you like to clean up? The restroom is there.'

'You have a restroom?'

He nodded. 'I installed a septic system and a two-hundred-gallon water tank, when I built the clinic. Electricity, water, a toilet—all the comforts of home.'

The congressman wiped sweat from his forehead with a handkerchief.

'Except air conditioning.'

Lindsay glanced over at the boy, who was pointing a finger at the men, as if he were giving orders. She turned back to the doctor.

'You don't have a nurse?'

'No. Inez is helpful, when she shows up. But she is not a nurse. And I cannot afford one. Of course, what nurse would work in the *colonias*?'

The congressman stood. 'It is late, Mrs. Bonner. We have been here four hours.'

'*Four hours?* Oh, my gosh—my Ranger will be frantic.'

'Do not worry. While you and the doctor worked on the boy, I went back and told them what you were doing. And that you were safe. Of course, Ranger Roy, he wanted to come in after you, but the local police assured him that would not be a wise move.'

She nodded. 'He really hopes to shoot someone before he retires.'

'Well, who would not?'

They all smiled, and she said, 'Thank you, Congressman.' She turned back to the doctor. 'And thank you, Dr. Rincón.'

'For what?'

'For letting me be useful again, if only for a day.'

They shook hands, and he seemed to hold her hand longer than necessary.

'Uh, Jesse,' the congressman said, again breaking the spell, 'should they be doing that?'

He nodded at the men, who were attempting to lift the boy from the bed.

'*¡Todavía no!*' the doctor said.

He released her hand and went over to them. Lindsay and the congressman followed.

'What are you doing?' the doctor said in Spanish. 'The boy must rest.'

'He will rest across the river,' the big man with the gun said.

'Driving him across the river will rip the sutures out.'

'No drive,' the man said.

'He still has a chest tube in him—it must come out in a day or two.'

91

'Do not worry, Doctor,' the smaller man said, 'we will bring nurses in for Jesús.'

'*Gracias*, Doctor,' Jesús said.

The big man slid his arms under the boy like a forklift and raised him as if he weighed nothing. The doctor surrendered, but grabbed two bottles of medicine.

'Here, give him one pill every twelve hours. It is an antibiotic, to prevent infection. And this pill is for the pain, it is morphine. He is going to hurt. And move his legs, so he does not get a blood clot.'

The smaller man took the pills and said, 'Okay, we will do that. *Muchas gracias*, Doctor. We will not forget this.'

They followed the men outside; Pancho trailed them. The man with the pills got into a black Hummer. The doctor shook his head.

'I told them, driving him across the river will tear the sutures.'

'How do they get through the gate in the border wall?' Lindsay asked.

'They do not. They cross upriver. With the drought, they can drive that Hummer across.' The doctor scratched his chin. 'I would note in the file that his check-out was against medical advice, but then, I do not have a file for the boy. I do not even know his last name.'

The Hummer abruptly drove off—without the boy. The big man carried the boy around to the back of the clinic where the land was open. They followed, and now Lindsay heard a WHUMP WHUMP WHUMP sound overhead. In the blue sky appeared a sleek black helicopter flying in low from across the river, the kind of helicopter often used by corporate executives who came to Austin to lobby her husband; its nose lifted and the helicopter landed in the desert a hundred feet behind the clinic, blowing up a cloud of dust. The big man carried the boy to the helicopter. The pilot opened the back door and helped load the boy. The big man climbed aboard, the pilot shut the door, and the helicopter then rose from the ground in a gush of wind that threatened to blow her over. They stared as it banked south and flew back across the river.

'Well,' the doctor said, 'you do not see that every day in the *colonias*.'

'See, Mrs. Bonner,' the congressman said. 'On this side of the wall, it is another world entirely.'

Chapter 9

Bode Bonner's body teemed with testosterone and endorphins, hormones and morphine-like brain chemicals that magically washed away the pain and twenty years from his body and guilty thoughts of his wife and budget deficits from his mind.

He felt good.

It was the end of another day in the life of a Republican governor up for reelection in a red state: easy, if not exciting. At least his schedule allowed him plenty of free time to stay in shape. He had just finished pumping iron at the YMCA fronting the lake; now he was running five miles around the lake. Blood still engorged his arms and chest; consequently, he was running without a shirt—not a recommended practice for most middle-aged men and certainly not for a politician up for reelection.

But Bode Bonner wasn't like most middle-aged politicians.

First, for all intents and purposes, he had already won reelection. And second, he didn't look middle-aged. His belly was still tight and his abs still sharply etched. His shoulders were still wide and his arms still thick with muscle. His legs were still strong, even if his right knee burned with each step. So he ran with Ranger Hank but without a shirt.

'Hank, don't fill out your daily logs anymore. Reporters can get hold of them. Damn nosy bastards.'

The state capitol sat on a low rise at the northern boundary of downtown Austin. Eleven blocks down Congress Avenue, the Colorado River marked the southern boundary. In town, the river was called Lady Bird Lake, in honor of President Lyndon Baines Johnson's beloved wife, Claudia Alta Taylor Johnson, known to the world as Lady Bird. A ten-mile-long hike-and-bike trail looped the lake. Bode jogged the lake almost daily. He wasn't alone. The trail was crowded with walkers, joggers, bikers, dogs, and especially—

'Praise the Lord,' Ranger Hank said.

—young, hard-bodied, barely dressed women.

Bode glanced back at the girl who had just jogged past. She wore Spandex shorts that appeared painted on her tight buns and a tube top that barely constrained her prodigious chest.

'Amen, brother.'

Running the lake was the part of living in Austin that Bode enjoyed the most, even if he and Hank were the only

Republicans on the trail that day. Or any day. Point of fact, a Republican living in Austin was lonelier than a white guy in the NBA. Texas was Republican, but the capital of Texas was Democrat. Austin was the liberal, leftist, loony blue hole in the bright red donut that was the state of Texas. The newspapers, the UT faculty and students, the residents, even the homeless people—everyone in the whole damn town was a Democrat. The only Republicans in town lived in the Governor's Mansion or worked at the capitol.

Which drove the Democrats in town nuts. They couldn't stand the fact that Republicans outside Austin—which is to say, every Texan who didn't live in Austin—kept sending Bode Bonner back to the capital. To their city. To live among them. To govern them. So they vented their anger by writing scathing letters to the editor of the local left-wing rag that masqueraded as a newspaper and scathing messages posted on blogs no one read, so desperate to be heard—the Internet gave everyone a voice, but no one was listening. At least not to Democrats in Texas. So they consoled themselves with their abiding faith that they were morally and intellectually superior to the vast majority of Texans who pulled the Republican lever, assured that they voted Republican only because they weren't smart enough to vote Democrat. *That's it! We're not wrong! They're just not smart enough to know that we're right!* Satisfied with that explanation to this perplexing human condition, they patted each other on the back and got stoned. But they couldn't deny a simple fact: they lost. They always lost.

Which made jogging among Democrats in Austin considerably more enjoyable for the leader of Republicans in Texas.

'Sweet *femále*,' Ranger Hank said.

He pronounced *female* as if it rhymed with *tamale*. Ranger

95

Hank wore jogging shorts and the massive leather holster packing his gun, cuffs, Mace, and Taser. He sounded like a car wreck with each stride. He gestured at the firm bottom of the girl jogging just a few strides in front of them. With the buds inserted into her ears and connected to the iPod strapped to her narrow waist, she was oblivious to their conversation.

'What do you figure?' Bode said. 'Junior?'

'Sophomore.'

Since Democrats constituted your nonviolent offenders for the most part, Ranger Hank served more as Bode's personal driver, caddie, jogging partner, and fellow appraiser of the female anatomy than his bodyguard. Hank likened their jogs around the lake to an episode of *American Idol*, except the girls weren't singing.

'Damn, she's only a year older than Becca. I kind of feel bad for staring.'

'But she's not your daughter.'

'Good point.'

He stared. She was a brunette with deeply tanned skin. Her tight buns were mesmerizing. Hypnotic. Bode's concentration was so complete that when she abruptly pulled up to tie her shoe, he almost plowed into her. He grabbed her by the shoulders to prevent knocking her down. He lifted her up, and she turned to him, close, almost as if she were in his arms. He inhaled her scent. She smelled of sweat and estrogen and youth and vitality and animal urges that ignited his male body. She looked even better from the front. But she wasn't tanned; she was Hispanic.

'You okay, honey?'

She removed one ear bud and gave him a once-over—the fine March day had turned warm so sweat coated his chest and no doubt made him look younger than his forty-seven

96

years—and he saw the recognition come into her eyes. He expanded his chest and tightened his arm muscles and waited for the expected, 'Oh, my God—you're Bode Bonner!' But it didn't come. Instead, she pulled away as if he had a poison ivy rash. Her eyes turned dark.

'You're a fucking Nazi!'

She replaced the ear bud, pivoted, and jogged away. Bode watched her tight buns bob down the trail.

After a long moment, Ranger Hank said, 'You want I should arrest her?'

'For what?'

'Being a Democrat.'

Bode exhaled and felt all the hormones and endorphins drain from his forty-seven-year-old body.

'If only it were a crime, Hank. If only it were a crime.'

Ranger Hank drew the Taser from his holster.

'Can I at least Tase her? Fifty thousand volts, she won't speak in complete sentences for a week.'

Eleven blocks north, Jim Bob Burnet sat in the Governor's Mansion watching *Fox News*, which ran 24/7 on the television in his office. He pointed at the screen.

'You want to go national in the Republican Party, that's the ticket.'

Eddie Jones slouched on the couch.

'You can't get the boss on?'

'Another governor from Texas is the last thing the party wants at the top of the ballot.'

Consequently, Jim Bob did not encourage Bode Bonner in that direction. What was the point? Just as he had wondered when his father had encouraged chubby little Jimmy Bob Burnet to play football at Comfort High.

'So this is it for him?' Eddie said. 'Governor of the great state of Mexico?'

'If he were governor of Montana or Colorado or even Okla-fuckin'-homa, he'd be the leading presidential candidate. He's a regular Roy Hobbs.'

'Who?'

'From that baseball movie, *The Natural*. Bode Bonner's a natural. He's got it all. The looks, the style, the voice—the man was born for the White House. But he was also born in Texas. And after George W., that disqualifies a candidate.'

'That don't seem fair.'

'This is politics, not preschool.'

But it wasn't fair. Jim Bob Burnet had long ago accepted the fact that he would live and die in Bode Bonner's considerable shadow. But he could not abide the fact that he would also live and die in Karl Rove's shadow. Rove took his man to the White House; Jim Bob would not. When people spoke of politics and the making of presidents, Rove would always be the man from Texas. It seemed so unjust. Jim Bob had a Ph.D. in politics; Rove had never even graduated college. But Rove had George W. Bush—a candidate with a pedigree—and in politics that was a hell of a lot more important than a college diploma. A political strategist was just a jockey—he was only as good as the horse he was riding. Rove rode George W. from the Governor's Mansion all the way to the White House where they proceeded to make LBJ look good when it came to presidents from Texas, and that was full-time work. When media types asked Jim Bob about Rove's political genius, he always wanted to say, 'Well, Rove proved his genius advising one American president—how'd that work out for America?' But Rove still cast a dark shadow over Texas, so Jim Bob kept his mouth shut. And his dreams shuttered.

There would be no White House for Jim Bob Burnet.

So, even though his candidate regularly repeated his desire to jump into the national political waters, Jim Bob talked him down from the ledge every time. Because the only thing worse than not taking your candidate national was taking him national and watching him fail spectacularly. Consequently, Jim Bob had resigned himself to a career of getting the Republican governor of Texas reelected every four years for the rest of his life—not exactly the work of genius—and teaching a class on politics at the LBJ School of Public Affairs. State politics. Not federal politics. Texas, not Washington. Minor leagues, not the majors. He often felt like a baseball pitcher with a ninety-eight-mile-an-hour fast-ball stuck in the minors his entire career. Sure, he was playing baseball, but . . .

'So, Professor, what exactly is my job description?' Eddie said.

'Odd jobs.'

'Odd jobs?'

Jim Bob nodded. 'Your skill set uniquely qualifies you to handle certain tasks for me during the governor's campaign for reelection.'

Eddie Jones was not educated or refined or possessed of a particularly pleasing personality, but he was handy to have around when it was dark out.

'Like what?'

'I don't know yet. But things always come up during the course of a campaign that require special attention. Unforeseen things. Unexpected things. Unpleasant things that require an unpleasant man.'

Jim Bob Burnet would never get his candidate into the White House, but he sure as hell wouldn't have his candidate kicked out of the Governor's Mansion. So he had hired Eddie Jones as an insurance policy of sorts. The sort of insurance seldom needed but which could prove career-saving if needed. A stop-loss policy. The business of politics was often unpleasant and often required an unpleasant man. He turned to the TV. The news returned from commercial break to a female Yale law professor arguing in favor of ObamaCare. They listened for a minute, then Jim Bob pointed the remote and muted her voice.

'Damn,' Eddie said, 'that bitch's voice sounds like the brakes on an old Ford pickup I had back in high school. And she's ugly as sin to boot. Hope to hell for her sake she can suck a tennis ball through a garden hose, otherwise she's gonna have to pay a man to screw her. Cash money.'

Yes, Jim Bob thought, Eddie Jones was the right man for the job.

'The governor, he is a very lucky man,' Congressman Delgado said, 'to have such a wife as you. And that I am not thirty years younger, for I would take you away from him.'

'You're very sweet, Congressman. And thank you for the late lunch.'

Lindsay Bonner was still high on adrenaline when she and Ranger Roy followed Congressman Delgado into his downtown Laredo office situated on the north bank of the Rio Grande. The receptionist took one look at the blood on her suit and jumped up.

'Mrs. Bonner—are you okay?'

'I'm fine.'

She was more than fine. She was a nurse again. At least for a day.

'She saved a boy's life,' the congressman said.

100

'The doctor saved his life. I helped.'

'You were amazing. Awesome, as the young people say. It was very exciting—would the boy live or die?'

'What boy?' the receptionist asked.

'Mexican boy,' the congressman said. 'He works for a cartel, probably Los Muertos. The *federales* shot him. They could not take him to a hospital, so they brought him to the clinic. Jesse and Mrs. Bonner, they opened the boy's chest right there in the clinic—oh, Claudia, you should have seen all the blood. Yes, it was quite a day.'

Ranger Roy's eyes had lit up at the sight of the congressman's pretty receptionist. So, like a good mother, Lindsay left her son to his awkward attempts at romance. She followed the congressman into his office. They had come back to retrieve their overnight bags. The state jet would be at the airport in an hour, and she would be back in the Governor's Mansion in two. Back in her prison, as if she had been given a twenty-four-hour furlough. She had escaped for a day and remembered how much she missed her old life. She had helped save a boy's life.

'Why would he work for a drug cartel?'

The congressman gestured her to the floor-to-ceiling window facing Mexico.

'Because on that side of the river, there is no one else to work for. The two main sources of income for Mexicans are money sent home by relatives working in the U.S. and drug money. The sad truth is, Mrs. Bonner, the Mexican economy would collapse without drug money. Even here in Laredo and other border towns on our side, the economy is driven by drug money. The cartel lieutenants, they pay cash to buy big homes over here because the neighborhoods are safer and the schools are better. They raise their families and

101

coach their kids' soccer teams in Laredo and commute each day to work in Nuevo Laredo.'

'They're here, in America?'

'Oh, yes. They are here, the money is here, and so the corruption is here, too. The cartels bribe law officers on this side to look the other way when shipments cross the river. And with such money comes violence. It will be here, too. And it will change our lives, just as it has changed theirs.'

He flipped through newspaper clippings on his desk.

'Twenty men killed in Acapulco . . . seventy-two in Hidalgo . . . one hundred sixty in Durango . . . one hundred eighty in San Fernando . . . They set fire to a casino in Matamoros and killed fifty-two. They murdered twenty-two journalists and ten mayors last year and the leading candidate for governor of the state of Tamaulipas, which includes Nuevo Laredo. They hang people from overpasses— imagine driving the interstate through Austin and seeing bodies swinging in the wind. We do not do that sort of thing in America. But in Mexico, governors, mayors, judges, prosecutors, police chiefs, they all get killed. The last chief in Nuevo Laredo was killed the same day he started. And just last week, guards at the state prison in Nuevo Laredo opened the gates and allowed the prisoners to walk out.'

'Why?'

'*Plata o plomo*. Silver or lead. The cartels tell politicians and police they must take the money or they will take a bullet. They pay one hundred million dollars in bribes every month . . . and they kill a thousand people every month.' He shrugged. 'At least in Mexico it is easy to know which politicians took the money.'

'How?'

'They are still alive.'

He gestured south across the river.

'The cartels engage in street battles in broad daylight. The city posts alerts on Facebook and tweets on Twitter to warn the citizens, and the schools have shootout drills to teach the students to lie on the floor until the gunfire stops, just as we once had nuclear bomb drills in our schools. Imagine if there were running gun battles in downtown Austin or Houston or Dallas every day—that is what Mexicans in Nuevo Laredo live with. Because of us. Would we live with that because of them? What if today the mayor of Denver were assassinated and tomorrow the governor of Oklahoma and the next day the police chief in Los Angeles? And all by Islamic terrorists? What if the Saudis were sending thirty billion dollars each year to those terrorists, which they used to kill forty thousand Americans the last four years? We went to war over three thousand American deaths. But that is exactly what we are doing to Mexico. Each year we send thirty billion dollars to the cartels for illegal drugs. And they are terrorizing Mexico—with our money. And our guns.'

He waved a hand up and down the river.

'Four thousand gun shops line the Texas side of the river, from Brownsville to El Paso. Sixty thousand guns in Mexico have been traced back to U.S. dealers, guns that killed Mexicans.'

'Why doesn't our government stop it?'

'The gun lobby is very strong, Mrs. Bonner. The Congress, we cannot even ban the assault weapons. Gunrunners pay straw purchasers to buy ten, twenty AK-47s at one time—the gun shops know those guns are going to the cartels. Obama proposed to ban such multiple purchases, but the gun lobby scared him off.'

'He didn't stand up to them?'

'He wants to be reelected.' The congressman exhaled. 'We arm and fund the cartels, but we blame the Mexicans for the violence on the border. Just as we blame the illegal Mexican immigrants for all that is wrong in America, even though we are to blame for much that is wrong in Mexico. But to blame is easier than to accept responsibility.'

'I thought the cartels were fighting each other?'

'Yes, they are fighting for the right to sell dope to the *gringos*. If we would stop buying their drugs, the violence on the border would end. Mexicans would live in peace—and in Mexico. The best way to stop illegal immigration is to stop the drug trade. But the flow of drugs across the border is relentless, like the wind.'

He pointed down at the bridge spanning the river.

'That is International Bridge Number One. Interstate 35 begins right there at the bridge and ends at the Canadian border. That is the drug super-highway. Half of all drugs smuggled into the U.S. travel up I-35. That is what the cartels in Nuevo Laredo fight for, and that is what Mexicans die for. What that boy today almost died for.'

'You said he worked for a cartel?'

'Yes. Most likely Los Muertos.'

'The Dead.'

'It is the most powerful cartel in Nuevo Laredo. And El Diablo is the most dangerous drug lord in all of Mexico.'

The congressman now motioned at the Mexican side of the Rio Grande.

'See the white building there, and the tall wall, just across the river? That is El Diablo's compound. He is young, only forty-six, handsome and quite charismatic, something of an icon among his people. He takes money from the rich *gringos* and gives to the poor Mexicans, like Robin Hood.

Or perhaps Pancho Villa. He is the *de facto* government in Nuevo Laredo. He funds everything—schools, hospitals, the church . . .'

'The church takes drug money?'

'Everyone in Mexico takes drug money.'

'Why?'

'Because it is the only money in Mexico. El Diablo, he gives away one billion dollars each year. The Justice Department labels him an international criminal and puts a ten-million-dollar bounty on his head, but the people of Nuevo Laredo, they view him as a hero. He is beloved by his people. They say he is an honorable man.'

'A drug lord?'

'Or he was . . . until we killed his wife.'

'We?'

'FBI, CIA, DEA . . . who knows?'

'How?'

'By mistake. Five years ago, they had the surveillance on his compound, and they thought it was him in the caravan, so they tried to kill him. Only they killed her.'

The congressman blew out a breath.

'They say it changed him.'

'In what way?'

'Before he was just a businessman, selling drugs to Americans just as we sell weapons to the world. He did not take our attempts to kill him personally. He understood it was just business. But after his wife, that is when he became El Diablo.'

Lindsay Bonner stared south across the Rio Grande at the white compound.

'The devil.'

★ ★ ★

105

Enrique de la Garza stared at the woman's image on the seventy-two-inch flat-screen television mounted on the wall of his office in the white compound on the south bank of the river. The high definition made her seem to be standing so close to him that he could almost inhale her scent. Her creamy smooth skin, her sensual green eyes, and most of all, her wild red hair. He liked the red hair on an Anglo woman. And she was a very alluring woman, the governor's wife.

'Counting all residents of Texas will determine the future of Texas,' she was saying on the television. 'And the future of the border.'

The Laredo station had interviewed her that morning in Congressman Delgado's office just across the river from Enrique's compound. She was in town to encourage *Mexicanos* in the *colonias* to complete the census reports. Of course, she would not venture into the filthy *colonias* herself; she was just a pretty face to attract the media.

A very pretty face.

He picked up the high-powered binoculars from his desk and walked to the bulletproof plate glass wall facing north and peered across the river at the top floor of the building in Laredo where the congressman kept his office. Was she still there? Just a few hundred feet away from him? He would like very much to meet her, the governor's wife.

'Mr. de la Garza, you still there?'

The voice on the speakerphone brought Enrique back to the moment. He dropped the binoculars from his eyes—but not before noticing the two Border Patrol agents down on the far riverbank, peering through binoculars at him—then replaced the binoculars on his desk and picked up the remote; he pointed it at the screen and froze the frame on the image of the governor's wife. He then said to his New York broker on the phone, 'Yes, *Señor* Richey, I am still here. Waiting for an answer.'

'I gave you an answer.'

'I am waiting for a better answer.'

Enrique's spacious office occupied the fourth floor on the north side of the compound, which was built around a court-yard with a pool. He walked to the courtyard side and gazed down at the pool, where Carmelita, his ten-year-old daugh-ter, sat on a chaise in her school uniform and texted on her iPhone, and Julio, her seventeen-year-old brother, played the grand piano. He opened the louvered windows slightly to allow the music in . . . ah, Bach. Enrique straightened the Monet on the wall then picked up the gold-plated AK-47 from the credenza.

'Mr. de la Garza,' the voice on the speakerphone said, 'I told you. The subprime market tanked. We didn't see it coming.'

'Then why did your firm bet that it would tank? You put one billion dollars of my money in subprime mortgages, and then your firm bet against those same subprime mortgages, did you not? Is that an honorable way to conduct business?'

'*Honorable?*' His broker chuckled. 'No, no, no, we don't do honorable on Wall Street. We do "legal and illegal," at least some of the time. And our actions in this instance were completely legal, according to our legal department.'

'Perhaps. But not very wise. You bet against me and now my account is worth half its original value.'

'I had nothing to do with that. I'm not responsible for what our trading division—'

'*Señor* Richey, I did not amass a seven-billion-dollar fortune by allowing others to act dishonorably toward me.'

Enrique slid open the sliding glass door and stepped out

onto the balcony overhanging the Río Bravo del Norte, what the *gringos* call the Rio Grande. He inhaled the lovely spring day then pointed the AK–47 down at the Border Patrol agents standing on the other side of the river next to their green-and-white vehicle parked on the river road and pulled the trigger. The bullets splashed into the water just in front of the agents. They dove behind their vehicle. He emptied the clip. He was not trying to hit them, just to make a point.

But one agent did not appreciate Enrique's point.

He walked to the rear of his vehicle and opened the tailgate. He emerged with a shoulder-mounted grenade launcher. He aimed it toward Enrique, but the other agent grabbed the weapon. The two agents got into a heated argument. Apparently, the Border Patrol frowned on its agents firing missiles into *México*.

Which amused Enrique de la Garza.

He stepped back inside and heard a frantic voice on the speakerphone: 'What's happening? Is that gunfire?'

Enrique's office door opened, and Hector Garcia, his second-in-command, entered with a bound-and-gagged man in tow. Julio followed, albeit reluctantly.

'Excuse me one moment, *Señor* Richey,' Enrique said to the speakerphone. 'I must terminate an employee.'

Enrique placed the AK–47 on his desk then stepped to the far wall and removed from a rack his prized four-foot-long handcrafted machete with the razor-sharp carbon steel black blade and the engraved mahogany handle. The employee's eyes got wide, and he tried to scream, but only a muffled sound came from his gagged mouth. Enrique and Julio followed Hector as he pulled the employee out onto the balcony and over to the railing then pushed his head down. But the employee struggled against Hector.

'Remove the gag,' Enrique said.

Hector removed the gag.

'Felipe, look at me.'

He turned his face to Enrique. Felipe Peña was only twenty-two, but he had lived a full life. A full, mean, cruel life. Four years before, Enrique had taken the boy into the cartel, hoping to save his soul. But it was not to be.

'You came to me, did you not?'

Felipe nodded.

'You swore allegiance to God, to me, and to the honor code, did you not?'

Another nod.

'You understood that violating the code is a crime punishable by death, did you not?'

Another nod.

'And what does the code state? Please tell me, Felipe Peña.'

As if reading from the scripture: 'We do not kill women, children, or innocents. We do not sell the drugs to *Mexicanos*, only to *gringos*. We do not ourselves use the drugs. We tithe twenty percent to charity and church.'

'Now, Felipe, have you lived your life by the code?'

He pondered a moment, then his shoulders slumped.

'No, *jefe*.'

'Did you use the drugs?'

'Yes.'

'Did you sell the drugs to *Mexicanos*?'

'Yes.'

'Did you kill an innocent?'

'Yes.'

'A ten-year-old girl you raped?'

'Yes.'

'Why? Why, Felipe Peña?'

The boy now cried.

'*Jefe*, it was the drugs.'

Enrique shook his head and sighed.

'The drugs. That is why we do not ourselves use the drugs we sell to the *gringos*. It is a filthy habit that blackens the soul with hate and cruelty, that does not allow one to live an honorable life. Felipe, if you were a *soldado* with another cartel, I would send Hector to put a bullet in your brain. But you are my *soldado*, you are my responsibility, your acts are my acts . . . so I must personally dispense justice to you. That child's parents have demanded justice, and I must give them justice. They look to me for justice because there is no other justice in Nuevo Laredo. Only me, Enrique de la Garza. I am the law in Nuevo Laredo. Felipe, I too have a ten-year-old child. If you raped and killed my Carmelita, would I not demand justice? If a man raped and killed your child, would you not demand justice?'

'Yes, I would.'

'Yes, Felipe, you would. You would demand justice. And I would give you justice. Now you must give justice to that child's parents.'

Enrique de la Garza now rendered his judgment.

'Felipe Peña, you have not lived your life with honor—will you now die with honor?'

Felipe blinked hard to clear his eyes of the tears, then he stood tall.

'Yes, *jefe*, I will.'

He turned back, bent his head over the railing, and awaited his fate with honor.

'Felipe, would you like to pray?'

'No, *jefe*. I am not worthy enough to pray to God.'

'Felipe, your family will never go hungry or homeless.'

'*Gracias, jefe.*'

110

Enrique held the machete out to Julio.

'Take it, my son, and dispense justice.'

His son now appeared nauseous.

'Father, I cannot.'

'Son, this is not a pleasant task, I know, but it is a necessary one. If the people of Nuevo Laredo are to one day look to Julio de la Garza for justice, you must be strong enough to dispense justice. Man enough.'

He saw the hurt in his son's soft face. He was not strong like his older brother. He was shy and sensitive, like his *madre*. Since his mother's death, Julio had never been the same. Sometimes Enrique worried that his son was homosexual, but he quickly put such thoughts out of his mind.

'I am sorry, Julio. You are your mother's son, with the gentle soul.'

Enrique turned back to Felipe Peña, grasped the handle with both hands, raised the blade above his head, and then swung the machete down with great force, cutting Felipe's head off cleanly. His head fell the hundred feet to the river below. Blood spurted from his open neck. Hector grabbed Felipe's legs and flipped him over the railing. His body now joined his head in the Río Bravo.

Enrique exhaled and suddenly felt tired. Dispensing justice in an unjust world always made him feel weary. He carried every judgment with him like a cross. But justice was his burden to bear. And he had learned that nature disqualified some men from honorable lives. He now heard a gagging sound and turned to see Julio throwing up over the rail. He handed the boy his silk handkerchief.

'Run along now.'

Julio walked quickly inside but stopped when Enrique called out to him.

'Oh, Julio, your Bach—it was very nice. *Muy bueno.*'

'*Gracias, padre.*'

'Did the tutor arrive for your sister?'

'Yes, Father, she is here.'

'Tell her I want to discuss Carmelita's progress in reading the *inglés*. Last night, when she read to me, she did not understand many of the words.'

'I will tell her, Father.'

'Also talk to your sister about spring break—where would you children like to go? Perhaps Cancún? We will make plans over dinner with your brother.'

They used to take family vacations to Europe, but with the international warrants for his arrest and apprehension and the $10 million bounty on his head, their vacations were now restricted to friendlier venues. Cancún was always nice. And California, of course.

'Yes, Father.'

Julio made a hasty exit. Fortunately, Enrique's first-born son would one day be man enough to dispense justice in Nuevo Laredo. Julio would never be man enough.

'He is a good boy.'

Hector said nothing, but Enrique knew he thought his second-born son weak. Enrique decided not to address the matter again. Not now, at the end of the day. The sun would soon fade into the Río Bravo; the breeze had turned cooler and held the promise of a fine evening. He pointed the machete up to the clear sky.

'Hector, I saw on the *Fox News* that the *gringos* have deployed a Predator drone over the border.'

'That is correct, *jefe*. From the Corpus Christi Naval Air Station.'

'I do not like it in my sky over Nuevo Laredo. Please shoot it down.'

112

Hector gazed skyward.

'They will not be happy if we do.'

'Who?'

'The *gringos*.'

'Hector, I did not ask if it would make the *gringos* happy. I simply asked that you shoot it down.'

Hector was a former captain in the Mexican Army's special forces. He had been trained in counterinsurgency tactics and advanced weapons systems by the U.S. Army, to fight the very cartel that now employed him. Enrique had offered him a substantial raise. 'If you are a paid killer,' he had said to Hector, 'why not be well paid?'

'The drone, it flies at an altitude of over seven thousand meters.'

'What would it take?'

'A missile.'

Enrique grunted. 'Then let us purchase a missile. Surely the Russians have what we require.' He gazed skyward again. 'I would very much like to shoot that Predator down.'

Hector shrugged. 'Okay. I will shoot it down.'

'*Bueno*.'

He handed the bloody machete to Hector for cleaning then waved to the Border Patrol agents who had witnessed the termination of Felipe Peña from the far riverbank. Hector exited the office, and Enrique returned inside and to his phone conversation with his broker.

'I have returned, *Señor* Richey. Terminating employees is a difficult affair.'

'Tell me.'

Enrique checked his clothing—a Tommy Bahama silk camp shirt over silk slacks and leather *huaraches*—for blood. A few droplets had splattered his trousers.

'Do you use baking soda or ginger ale for blood stains on silk?'

His broker's voice on the speakerphone: '*What?* Blood stains? Silk what?'

'Trousers. No matter, there are more where these came from. So, where were we?'

'I asked if that was gunfire.'

'Oh, yes, it was. Just a little target practice.'

'Skeet?'

'*Gringos.* So, *Señor* Richey, to resolve this dispute honorably, you must restore half a billion dollars to my account within three business days or I will be forced to file a complaint.'

There was laughter on the phone.

'Mr. de la Garza, you can file a complaint with the SEC or the FBI or the NFL, I don't give a shit. But it'll be a cold fucking day in hell before my firm refunds half a billion dollars to anyone. You don't know who you're dealing with—we're connected in D.C. The Feds don't fuck with us. So you can file your complaint with God Himself, but you ain't getting your money back.'

Enrique chuckled.

'Oh, no, *Señor* Richey, I file my complaints with Hector Garcia.'

'Who the hell's Hector Garcia?'

'He is the head of my complaints department. When a customer fails to pay his account timely or the government interferes with my business or a business associate acts dishonorably toward me, Hector Garcia resolves my complaint. And he will resolve my complaint with you by walking up to you one dark night there in New York City and putting a gun to your head and saying, "You should not have dishonored

Enrique de la Garza," and then he will put a bullet through your brain.'

There was no laughter now.

'Who the fuck—? You can't threaten me! This is America!'

'No, *mi amigo*—this is Nuevo Laredo.'

Enrique disconnected his broker and shook his head in amusement.

Gringos.

They think we are just the stupid Mexicans to be taken advantage of by the smart Americans. We run a thirty-billion-dollar-a-year enterprise, but we are stupid? We transport fifteen thousand metric tons of marijuana, cocaine, and heroin north across the border annually—despite fifty thousand *federales* on this side and twenty thousand Border Patrol agents on that side—but we are stupid? We launder thirty billion U.S. dollars through banks in America, Panama, Ecuador, and Europe each year, but we are stupid? And now the *gringos* open their roads and highways under NAFTA to Mexican trucks—*even though they know the cartels now own the Mexican trucking companies!*—thus allowing us to ship our dope directly to every town and city in America, but we are stupid? Ah, but the *gringos* must believe that we are just the stupid Mexicans because that allows them to feel better about themselves—*allows them to feel superior to the rest of the world*—even though they are the ones smoking, snorting, and shooting all that filthy dope into their bodies.

Oh, to be so stupid.

Enrique de la Garza employed American brokers and bankers, lawyers and accountants, financial planners and investment advisors; none asked too many questions, such as 'Where do you get all this cash from?' He was one of three hundred individuals identified as off-limits to U.S.

banks under the Foreign Narcotics Kingpin Act, so the U.S. government can say they are doing something to stop the drug trade, but their government does not enforce their own law because the banks want their profits. Just as the *gringos* want his products. Oh, the appetite they have for the marijuana and the heroin and the cocaine! Insatiable. And extremely profitable. Enrique's empire had grossed over $5.5 billion U.S. last year and was on track to gross $6 billion this year. His personal net worth now exceeded $7 billion; he had billions invested in U.S. real estate, stocks, and bonds. He ranked one hundred thirty-four on the *Forbes* list of billionaires. Twenty-four years ago, he had started with nothing but a Harvard degree, and now he had an empire that spanned the globe. Markets in North America, South America, and now even to Europe he transported his products via a fleet of 747s—there was no radar over the Atlantic Ocean—something no other cartel had even imagined. By land, by sea, by air, even by tunnels two miles long he transported his products north, always one step ahead of the *gringos*. Innovation, that was the key to staying ahead of the competition and foreign authorities. Enrique de la Garza possessed vision—he saw what others could not even imagine. And now, at forty-six years of age, he had it all—wealth, power, respect, the admiration of his people, good children—everything a man could desire . . . everything except the love of a woman. His eyes returned to the image frozen on the television.

A woman like her.

He often found himself longing for a woman again. For love. For romance. His wife had always said he was a hopeless romantic, and perhaps he was. But he had been without romance since her death five years before. Five years he had mourned for his beloved Liliana. He still loved her; he would always love her. But he wanted to love and be loved again, to feel a woman close to him—not a woman who wanted his money; those women he could have any day—but a woman who wanted him, as Liliana had.

Perhaps a woman like the governor's wife.

He stepped to the full-length mirror on the wall and examined himself. He was well mannered and well groomed, educated and sophisticated, still lean and fit from his *béisbol* days, but . . . gray streaks now marred his jet-black hair and goatee and made him look old. As old as he often felt. Older than his years. When he watched American baseball on the cable channels, always the advertisements were for the erectile dysfunction drugs and hair color for men. Enrique had no need for Viagra, not yet, but . . . He ran his fingers through his hair and stroked his goatee just as the door opened and Hector appeared.

'*¡Jefe!*'

Enrique raised an open hand.

'Hector, do you think I should use that "Just for Men"?'

'Just for what?'

'The hair color. To wash away the gray.'

'Oh.'

Hector was bald.

'Uh, I do not know, *jefe.*'

'Do you think she would find me more attractive?'

'Who?'

Enrique gestured at the television screen.

'The governor's wife.'

'Oh, yes. Definitely.'

'You are not just saying that?'

'No, no.'

'Hector, I need a woman—'

'I will go get you one.'

'No, not that kind of woman. A wife. A mother for Carmelita.'

It was very difficult these days to be a single parent with all the bad influences on children—the Internet, cable TV, violent video games, iPhones—he had caught Carmelita texting a boy at her school the other night. She was only ten! He wished their mother were still alive. She knew how to raise children. And how to be firm. Sweet Carmelita, she knew how to wrap her father around her little finger.

'Make a note for Hilda. Next time she comes to cut my hair, have her bring that hair color.'

'*Sí*.'

'Now what is it that you need, Hector?'

'*¡Jefe! ¡Esto es urgente!* Your son needs you!'

Enrique de la Garza—known to the rest of the world as El Diablo—turned from the mirror and took one last long look at the woman's image on the television screen.

'She is a very beautiful woman, no? I should like very much to meet her one day, the governor's wife.'

FIVE MONTHS
BEFORE

Chapter 10

The governor's wife stifled a yawn.

The heat and her county fair lunch of fried chicken, fried okra, fried ice cream, fried Twinkies, fried butter—every four years the governor's wife had to prove to the voters that she was still a country girl who ate country food—had conspired to make her drowsy. But she fought her heavy eyelids. It would not do her husband's campaign any good for the cameras to catch her yawning during his speech. Standing at the podium a few feet away, Governor Bode Bonner bellowed sound bites in his booming campaign voice.

'We got boys marrying boys and girls marrying girls and kids having kids and Mexicans having Americans and . . .'

Of course, it was difficult not to yawn when she had heard the same speech a hundred times, maybe more. She knew every crowd-pleasing phrase, every pause for effect, every applause line . . . and she hated every word of it.

She wanted to scream.

She always put her mind somewhere else during his speeches, tried not to listen to her husband's words and hoped he didn't believe them, that he was just an actor on a stage reciting his lines. But was he? Had he come to believe his own speeches? She feared he had. That he had bought into his own ambition.

He wanted to be president.

A faint hint of smoke from the wildfires out west and a stronger scent of farm animals filled the stock show arena at the Lubbock County Fairgrounds where that very morning the governor's wife had presented the prize for the Grand Champion Bull. The governor now stood before ten thousand registered Republicans gazing up at him like a flock of sheep, waving little American flags, and eating up his red-meat stump speech, the one in which he railed against the federal government, Washington, deficits, taxes, global warming, gay marriage, ObamaCare, liberals, and illegal Mexican immigrants.

'What part of *illegal* don't they understand? They don't need a path to citizenship—they need a path to the border!'

Amarillo on Tuesday, Midland on Wednesday, and Lubbock on Thursday. A campaign swing through the rural counties of West Texas—the Bible Belt of Texas. The brightest red counties in a bright red state. Tea party country. Bode Bonner country. Cattle ranches, cotton farms, and oil wells. Where the people loved their governor and hated their government—except the government that gave them farm and ranch subsidies and tax breaks for oil. They liked that part of government. But her husband was a politician, so he told them what they wanted to hear.

'They want to pick your doctor and indoctrinate your kids . . . They took Christ out of Christmas and prayers out of school . . .'

And she now wondered, as she often wondered when out on the campaign trail: How did she get from a cattle ranch in Comfort to a stump speech in Lubbock?

The first day of April had Lindsay Bonner longing for home. Not the Governor's Mansion—that had never been home to her—but their ranch in the Hill Country north of

San Antonio. Her family had moved to Texas when she was five and Comfort when she was fifteen. At twenty-two, she had married Bode Bonner and moved to his family's five-thousand-acre ranch. That had been her home until eight years ago when they moved into the mansion. She missed the ranch. She missed the small hacienda-style house with the courtyard and the flowers and the shade trees. She missed spring when the days were warm and the nights cool, when the green returned to the pastures, and the bluebonnets and Indian paintbrush covered the hills like a blanket of blue and red and yellow. She missed riding with Ramón and cooking with Chelo. She missed spring roundup with the *vaqueros*. Lindsay Bonner much preferred working cattle than working crowds. She was a reluctant politician's wife.

Her husband was not a reluctant politician.

'When it's hot and dry, they say it's global warming. When it's cold and wet, they say it's global warming. Hell, in Texas we call it summer and winter.'

The crowd cheered. They loved him. And Bode Bonner loved them. He craved attention, whether from football fans or registered Republicans. She did not. He had always been the star; she had always lived in his sizable shadow from that day in ninth grade when Bode Bonner, senior football star, had walked up to her in the hallway and asked her to the homecoming dance. The moment she said yes, she had taken up residence in his shadow. And there she had lived the past twenty-nine years. But now she needed more. Not more attention. Not more from a man. But more from life.

Her own life.

Politics had destroyed their lives. Her life, anyway. Bode had gone on to the University of Texas and majored in football. By the time she arrived at UT in his senior year,

123

his shadow consumed the entire campus. When the NFL passed on Bode Bonner due to the four knee operations, he returned to the family ranch. After she graduated with a nursing degree, she had become Mrs. Bode Bonner. He ranched cattle; she worked in the emergency room at a San Antonio trauma hospital. She was happy then; she had her own life and the life they shared. Then Becca came into their lives, and they were happier. She would never forget Bode lifting the little girl up onto his horse, sitting her in the saddle in front of him, and the two of them galloping off. It was a glorious moment. Becca Bonner was Bode Bonner's daughter, as beautiful as he was handsome, tall and athletic, at home riding horses and roping cattle.

Bode Bonner loved his daughter more than life itself.

Lindsay Bonner loved those years. She was content. Happy. Useful. But Bode needed more. More excitement, more adventure, more competition. He needed politics. Men needed three basic things in life: sex, food, and competition. Politics provided two out of three. So he ran for the state legislature to champion rural interests as Texas became more urban. He lost his first election as a Democrat, but he won his second election as a Republican and every election since. But it wasn't enough. It was never enough.

He always yearned for higher office.

'Texas was once an independent nation—and if Washington keeps messin' with Texas, we just might be again!'

She suddenly snapped out of her thoughts—the Lubbock Republicans sitting on either side of her were applauding the governor and glancing suspiciously at his wife. She was late with her applause. Again. She now clapped for her husband. He basked in the applause.

Bode Bonner had fallen in love with politics. It filled a

need inside him. It fed his competitive instincts and enabled his ambition. It stole the romance from their lives. He had found something he loved more than her. It was painful enough for a woman to lose her man to another woman, always a risk when her man is in politics, but to lose her man *to* politics, that bordered on cruel. But seduced by politics he was. So he ran for the governorship. Texas had turned red and Republican, but Bode saw that it had also turned green, as in money from big business, that the state capitol was no longer the seat of government, but instead a shopping mall where laws, rules, and regulations were bought and sold—and the people were sold out. But Bode Bonner had been different. He was a populist. A man of the people. He wanted to change things.

Now he wanted to get reelected.

She had campaigned with him that first election, criss-crossing the state of Texas in a pickup truck. It was romantic, it was fun, and it was important: Bode Bonner was going to make a difference. He promised change, and the voters put him in the Governor's Mansion. Election night was glorious, standing next to her husband, the governor of Texas.

But once elected, they descended upon him. People vested in state government: people doing business with the state, seeking money from the state, buying from the state, selling to the state, lobbying the state, controlling the state. People vested in the status quo. People who didn't want their world to change. The power brokers and lobbyists and lawyers entered their lives, and they changed Bode Bonner. He became what he had hated. He sold his soul for four more years in the Governor's Mansion. And she had aided and abetted him, the dutiful and loyal governor's wife.

And she was still living in his shadow.

He now grabbed the microphone and stalked the stage, no notes, no teleprompter, just Bode Bonner and a microphone, quoting chapter and verse of tea party politics.

'Washington is giving America away to Wall Street, to multinational corporations that outsource your jobs and in-source their profits . . .'

He could've been a preacher. The *Bode Bonner Hour* on Sunday morning television. So tall, so handsome, so articulate—an ex-football player, imagine that—but he wasn't real. He was just an image in a campaign commercial in his cowboy boots and hair sprayed in place. He was a cut-out cardboard figure you stood alongside to have your photograph taken. That was not the man she had married. That was the politician Jim Bob Burnet had created.

She blamed Peggy.

Jim Bob had met and married Peggy at UT; Lindsay had been her maid of honor and Bode his best man. But Jim Bob had changed when Peggy left him five years later and ran off to California with their daughter, when she had decided that Jim Bob Burnet would never give her the life she wanted. Peggy was like that. Politics—winning elections—became Jim Bob Burnet's life. His obsession. As if he needed to prove to himself and to Peggy that she was wrong about him. But he couldn't do it alone. He needed Bode Bonner. So he took her husband and changed him.

Jim Bob made her husband a politician.

'But your voice isn't heard in Washington because you live in a red state and vote Republican, because you read the Bible and not the *New York Times* . . .'

Bode pulled out the pocket-sized Constitution he always carried and waved it in the air like Moses waving the Ten Commandments, a signal that he was building to the big finale, whipping the crowd into an anti-government, tea party frenzy.

'Because you believe in Jefferson and Madison, not Marx and Lenin, free enterprise not freeloading, America not ObamaCare . . .'

He could fire up a crowd. He always said it was no different than firing up the football team before a game. This crowd was ready to play for Bode Bonner. To vote for Bode Bonner.

'This is our America! This is God's country! God bless Lubbock! God bless Texas! God bless America! And never ever forget: Bode Bonner's got your back!'

The crowd broke into wild applause and that familiar chant—'Bo-de! Bo-de! Bo-de!'—just as the crowd had chanted when he had starred on the Longhorn team. Back then, she had joined in the chant from the spectator seats. But not today. For two terms, she had accepted her role as the dutiful loyal spouse. She had played her role, perfected her role.

But that had all changed now.

Her trip to the border had changed her. A month had passed, a month of public appearances and photo ops and volunteer work—but something was missing. Or now she noticed what had been missing for so long. That day in the *colonias* had made acting a role unacceptable, living in someone's shadow intolerable, cheering from the sideline unbearable. She wanted to live her own life again. She wanted to be useful again.

She no longer wanted to be the governor's wife.

One man in the crowd did not clap or cheer or chant the governor's name, for he hated Bode Bonner with every fiber in his being. He was the state Democratic Party chairman, which is to say, the longest losing coach in the history of the game of politics. Twenty years he had gone without winning a statewide race in Texas.

With no end in sight.

Clint Marshall pulled out his cell phone and hit the speed dial for the mayor of San Antonio. Jorge Gutiérrez had first won political office before Clint was born. He was the leading Latino in Texas, which meant he was the leader of the Texas Democratic Party. He answered on the second ring.

'Clint, how are you this day?'

'Terrible. I'm in Lubbock.'

'Yes, well, that was your first mistake.' The mayor chuckled. 'What are you doing in Lubbock?'

'Stalking the governor.'

'Ah. And what have you learned?'

'That our boy's gonna get his ass kicked in November.'

'You just figured that out?'

'No—but I'm always hopeful. Or I was.'

'There is no reason to hope, my friend, not for the Governor's Mansion. Not this election. But be patient. Our time will come. The governor-for-life will surely die one day.'

He chuckled again.

'Maybe, but I'll be out of a job before then.'

'Do not fret, Clint. No one in the party expects you to beat Bode Bonner.'

'Jorge, the guy is fucking Teflon. We've got a twenty-seven-billion-dollar deficit, but no one blames him—hell, they don't even believe we have a deficit. We're suffering the worst economy in decades, and they don't care as long as they can keep their guns and watch *Fox News* on cable.' He paused. 'God, what I'd give for a good sex scandal in the Governor's Mansion.'

The mayor laughed. 'Clint, would you cheat on the governor's wife if she were your wife?'

'No.'

'Even a Republican governor is not that stupid. Search for another scandal, my friend.'

'Mrs. Bonner! Look this way!'

The cameras took aim at her like a firing squad, the photographers wanting a front-page photo called out to her, and the people reached out to her. She smiled for the cameras, but the crowds frightened her. The raw emotion. The mob mentality. The power her husband held over them. She eased closer to Ranger Roy, who towered next to her, protecting her, holding her door open and gently tugging her arm. One last wave, then she climbed inside the Suburban and breathed a sigh of relief.

She had escaped the crowd.

But her husband didn't want to escape. He loved the crowd. He thrived on the crowd. He needed the crowd as much as they needed him, cheering for him, touching him, taking photos with him, so desperate to breathe the same air he breathed. He shook hands and slapped backs and kissed babies—and a few women—until Jim Bob pulled him away and pushed him into the vehicle. But Jim Bob did not get in; he was not allowed in the same vehicle as the governor's wife. Ranger Hank shut the door and jumped in the driver's seat; Ranger Roy rode shotgun. They began a slow exit from the fairgrounds through a gauntlet of cheering Republicans. The governor of Texas had a big smile on his face and red lipstick on his cheek.

'Hell, I could win the White House on red states alone. They love me!'

Lindsay Bonner stared at her husband. Regardless of the many ways a man ages—hair graying and thinning and finally disappearing entirely; the sharp jaw line descending into floppy jowls; the V-shaped torso gradually turning upside-down until his waist possessed all the structural integrity (and allure) of a mud puddle—his wife still sees the man she fell in love with. She is blind to his physical diminishment.

But disillusionment—that was another matter.

Her husband's hair was still golden, his facial features still sharply etched, his body still remarkably tight and muscular, almost as if he hadn't aged at all the last twenty-two years. But he had changed. She no longer saw the man she had fallen in love with. She now sat next to a complete stranger.

'Who *are* you?'

His smile disappeared. He groaned.

'Don't start with me, Lindsay.'

Up front, Hank swapped an uneasy glance with Roy, as if to say, *Here we go again*. He turned up the volume on the radio.

'No. Really. Who are you?'

Her husband pointed at the cheering crowd outside the vehicle.

'Whoever they want me to be.'

'Do you really believe all that?'

'All what?'

'Boys marrying boys, girls marrying girls, Mexicans having Americans . . .'

'I'm just riding the wave.'

'What wave?'

He again gestured at the crowd.

'That wave. See, it's like investing—'

'Your daughter's a lesbian.'

'I'm hoping it's a college fad.'

'You really shouldn't encourage that.'

'I didn't tell her to be a lesbian.'

'Not her.' She now pointed at the crowd. 'Them.'

'I'm not encouraging anything. Jim Bob takes a poll then writes a speech saying what they want to hear. That's different.'

'That's following.'

'That's politics. Jim Bob says—'

'Jim Bob says . . .'

She shook her head.

'He's tweeting for me now, on that Twitter.'

'He was already thinking for you. Pretty soon, he'll be breathing for you. I guess I should have sex with him.'

She shuddered at the thought.

'Well, you sure as hell ain't been having sex with me.'

The Rangers grimaced, like kids when their parents argued. Their heads seemed to sink into their shoulders; Hank turned the air conditioning on full blast. She fought the urge to bring up Mandy Morgan—*as if I don't know!*—but she did not need that gossip running through the Ranger ranks across the state of Texas. Or did they already know? She stared west at the distant haze of the fires and took a long moment to calm herself; she turned back to her husband.

'Can we talk about the *colonias*?'

Another groan from the governor. 'No.'

'Bode, we need to help those people.'

'We're broke and they're Mexicans.'

'They're still people.'

'And we're still broke.'

'If you saw how they live—'

'I've been to Mexico.'

'But they live in Texas—without running water, sewer, or electricity.'

He exhaled loudly, a sign he was annoyed.

'Jesus, all you've talked about the last month is the *colonias*. I wish to hell Jim Bob hadn't sent you down to the border. Incited your liberal Boston breeding.'

She felt the heat rise within her.

'Bode Bonner, I'm not a Texan by birth or by choice. But after forty years living in this state, I am a Texan. And by God, it's high time you native Texans got over the Alamo and quit hating Mexicans!'

'I don't hate Mexicans. Hell, I was raised by Mexicans, I worked cattle with Mexicans, I dated . . . Never mind.'

'You don't hate particular Mexicans, just Mexicans in general.'

'I hate Democrats in general, not Mexicans.'

They cleared the fairgrounds and headed north on the interstate. The wind rocked the Suburban, as if they were driving a billboard up I-27. A pickup truck sped past with a gun rack in the rear window and a bumper sticker that read: O LORD, PLEASE GIVE US ANOTHER OIL BOOM, AND WE PROMISE NOT TO SCREW IT UP THIS TIME. She braced herself to make another run at her husband's humanity—or to find it again.

'Bode, the poverty in the *colonias* is staggering. We need to do something.'

'What? What can government do? We spent trillions fighting the war on poverty, and we lost. All we got for our money are more poor people. I got news for you, Little Miss Colonia—Texas is broke! But you want me to give more money we don't have to Mexicans so they can have more babies they can't afford? We can give those Mexicans all the money in the world, Lindsay, but they're not suddenly gonna start wearing J. Crew and shopping at Whole Foods. The solution isn't more money, it's better behavior. But government can't change human behavior. Government can't make people stop smoking or eating fast food or using drugs or having babies they can't feed. So government can't solve poverty.'

'Government can try.'

'It did. It failed. Government has never solved a single social problem, and it's never gonna solve a single social problem. You liberals cry for more money and more government, but the truth is, government can't make a difference in people's lives. Only people can.'

Her husband's words jolted her—and she knew at that very moment what she had to do. What she would do.

'You're right.'

'I am?'

'Yes. And I'm going to make a difference.'

'Good. You go make a difference while I govern a goddamn bankrupt state.'

'How bad is it?'

'Twenty-seven-billion bad.'

'On TV, you said we don't have a deficit.'

'I lied.'

'Why?'

'Voters don't want to hear it.'

'What are you going to do?'

'Cut the budget.'

'What?'

'Everything.'

'Schools?'

'Education and Medicaid eat up three-fourths of the budget.'

'Raise taxes.'

He laughed, but not as if it were funny.

'In an election year? You sound like a Democrat. Raise taxes. That's their answer to every problem.'

She didn't think this was the time to tell him she was a Democrat.

'Use the rainy day fund. What is it now, nine billion?'

'Nine-point-three.'

'Then use it. At least for schools.'

'The tea party will raise holy hell.'

'Do they control you?'

'No. They control the voters who control me.'

They rode in silence for a few miles through land that lay as flat as a table top and was as dry as cement. The drought had turned Texas into another Dust Bowl. When she again spoke, her voice was soft.

'Bode, you don't want to be the governor who gutted public education. You saw the children in Graciela Rodriguez's kindergarten class. They need our help.'

'How many of those kids will graduate in twelve years?'

'Half. Maybe. But she's their only hope. And you're her only hope. I told her you cared. Please don't make me a liar.'

He sighed and stared out the window at cattle searching for grass on the plains.

'Bode, please do the right thing.'

'You mean lose the election?'

'You used to want to do the right thing.'

'I used to lose. Now I win.'

'Is that all that matters?'

'Better than losing.'

'But why do you want to win?'

He looked at her as if she were crazy. 'Because I'm a politician. That's what we do.'

'But *why*?'

'To keep this state out of Democrats' hands, so they don't screw up Texas like they screwed up the rest of the country.'

'We're pretty screwed up if we've got a twenty-seven-billion-dollar deficit.'

'Don't ever say that in public.'

'Bode, I've been the governor's wife for eight years. I know what to say and not to say in public.'

'Well, if you want to be the governor's wife for another four years—'

'I don't.'

'You don't what?'

'Want to be the governor's wife.'

She could feel the Rangers' muscles tense up front. The governor turned fully to his wife.

'What the hell does that mean?'

There were two Bode Bonners: the public politician and the private man. She still loved the private man, but there was less of him to love. With each passing year living in the Governor's Mansion—with each election—the man seemed to merge into the politician. Or the politician consumed the man. Like a cancer. She had seen cancer eat away at patients in the hospital until they were just a shell of their former selves. The cancer that afflicted her husband—political ambition—had had the same effect on him. Ambition had eaten away all that was good inside Bode Bonner and left him a shell of a man. She had hoped he would recover, but she knew now that he would not survive. He wasn't fighting his cancer. He had become his cancer. She could no longer bear to look at him, this man she had loved and lain with and looked upon as her hero. She now averted her eyes so he could not see her tears.

'Bode, I'm not happy. With my life.'

'Lindsay, this *is* our life. I'm the governor, and you're the governor's wife.'

'I'm forty-four years old. Becca's in college. She doesn't need me, you don't need me—what am I supposed to do the rest of my life? Smile for the cameras? Shop? Play tennis and do lunch at the country club? That's not me. I didn't sign up for that.' She wiped her eyes and turned to him. 'Bode, I can't do this anymore.'

His expression changed. She saw fear in his eyes.

'You want a divorce?'

'I want to be useful.'

'You are. You're the governor's wife.'

'I'm used, not useful. Bode, I don't want to just breathe oxygen and fill the space inside my clothes. I want my life to have meaning. I want to make a difference.'

'You do. You volunteer at the homeless shelter, the food bank, the elementary school—'

'I want to be a nurse again.'

'A *nurse*?'

'Yes.'

'You can't be a nurse.'

'Why not? I kept my license up to date.'

'Where are you gonna work? In the ER at Austin General Hospital? Everyone knowing who you are? It'd be a goddamn fiasco.'

It would.

'Look, Lindsay, we'll talk about all this when I get back, okay?'

'Back from where?'

'Hunting. Me and Jim Bob, we're flying out to John Ed's ranch, tomorrow morning.'

'How long will you be gone?'

'Just for the weekend. I'll be back Sunday evening.'

'I don't want to wait that long.'

He patted her knee as if putting off a child. She hated when he did that.

'Come on, honey, this can wait till then, give you time to think it through. When I get back, we'll talk this out, okay?'

She knew they wouldn't. He just hoped she'd move on to something else. Another 'do-good deal,' as he referred to her volunteer work. But this was her life.

'Bode, I have thought this through. I'm going to be a nurse. I'm not asking your permission.'

His jaw muscles clenched, and she felt his blood pressure rising.

'Where? Where are you gonna be a nurse? You're the governor's wife, and everyone in the state of Texas knows you on sight, that famous red hair. So you may want to be a nurse, Lindsay, but you ain't gonna be—not unless you can find some place in this whole goddamn state where no one knows you're the governor's wife!'

But there was such a place.

'*¿Nombre?*'
  'Tendita Chavarria.'
  '*¿Cuál es la edad?*'
  '*Veinticuatro.*'
  '*¿Cuál es el sexo?*'
  '*Sí.*'
  'No. *Femenino.*'
  'Oh. *Sí.*'
  '*¿Niños? ¿Número?*'
  '*Cinco.*'
  '*¿Marido?*'
  'No.'
Five hundred miles south of Lubbock, Inez Quintanilla

137

sat at her desk in the clinic in *Colonia Ángeles* across from a resident, completing another of the census forms left by the governor's wife. Jesse Rincón sat at his desk, thinking of the governor's wife. A woman such as her had never before come into his clinic. The women who came into his clinic were like the woman Inez now interviewed, twenty-four years old with no husband for herself or father for her five children, women who no longer dreamed of a life beyond the wall, women who would live and die in this *colonia*. But twenty-nine days ago she had walked into his clinic—into his life—and now he could not get her out of his life. Out of his head. Each day he thought of her; each night he dreamed of her. A married woman. The governor's wife.

Was there truly such a thing as love at first sight?

He had no romance in his life, and no prospects for any. Women did not come to the border; they fled from the border. They desired a life in the cities, not a life in the *colonias*. So he had long ago abandoned all thoughts of love. Marriage. Family. He had resigned himself to a solitary life, as if he were the priest his uncle had wanted him to be.

Then she walked into his clinic.

In the month since, he had searched her on the Internet, read about her and stared at her image on the computer screen, as if he were a smitten schoolboy back at the Catholic school in Nuevo Laredo. He followed her daily schedule in Austin as the photographers caught her coming and going, entering an elementary school and leaving a coffee shop, entering the food bank and leaving the AIDS clinic, entering the homeless shelter and leaving the gym. He went with her on campaign swings to Houston and Dallas and West Texas; she was in Lubbock that day. He knew that this was not what a doctor would call 'healthy,' for him to know the governor's wife's itinerary, but the governor's official website posted it there for all the world to read.

For him to read.

He was sure that her memory would fade from his mind, and his behavior, so out of character for him, would return to normal. But twenty-nine days had passed, and neither had. Each night his heart drove him to the computer screen, to gaze at her image, to know what she had done that day. But in his head he knew that she would never again walk into his clinic, that he would never again see her face, that he would never again speak to her. Yet still he thought of her. The governor's wife.

'Dr. Rincón.'

Jesse looked up to Inez standing there. The resident had left, and Inez was now pulling on yellow rubber gloves to conduct the first of her twice-daily disinfectant scrubs of the clinic. He looked past her to two strangers standing at her desk, a man and a woman. The man held a professional camera.

'They are from a Houston newspaper. They want to interview you.'

Another interview. He had tired of telling the story of the *colonias* because few people listened and those who did had a short attention span for other people's problems in this bad economy, particularly Mexicans living illegally in America. He wanted to tell them to go away, but when he looked back down at the order forms for medicine and supplies he could not afford, he was reminded how much money he needed. Perhaps a few people in Houston would read the story and see the photos and send money. Jesse sighed then stood and walked over and greeted the strangers like close friends.

'*Bienvenido*. I am Jesse Rincón.'

The reporter stuck her hand out to him.

'Kikki Hernandez.'

Another woman who did not belong in the *colonias*. But she was not the governor's wife. She was a young and very pretty Latina dressed as one would expect a female from Houston. Her fingernails were red, her scent was intoxicating, and her cameraman was named Larry; he was a middle-aged and overweight Anglo dressed as if he were going to a pro wrestling arena.

'So, Ms. Hernandez—'

'Kikki.'

'So, Kikki, what brings you all the way from Houston to Laredo? Do you want to see the *colonia*?'

'Actually, Doctor, I wanted to see you. I was in Brownsville for a story last month, and a local reporter—Alexa Hinojosa, do you remember her?'

'Yes, I remember Alexa.'

'She certainly remembers you.' Kikki's eyes twinkled like the stars on a clear night. 'She said I should tell your story to Houston. She said she met you when you built a medical clinic in Boca Chica.'

'Then I shall tell you my story. Come, let me show you *Colonia Ángeles*.'

He took his guests for a tour and watched their expressions change as the *colonia* confronted them fully. Kikki Hernandez seemed to age before his eyes. Larry the cameraman took many photographs of the *colonia* and the children, photos that would shock the wealthy people of Houston next Sunday morning when they opened their newspaper, photos that might bring money for medicine and supplies. When they returned to the clinic an hour later, Kikki Hernandez drenched her manicured hands with the gel sanitizer sitting on Inez's desk and rubbed her hands forcefully, as if trying to rub off a tattoo she now regretted. He knew she was think-ing, *Get me back to civilization!* Jesse gave them cold bottled water. After she had gathered herself, Kikki Hernandez sat before his desk and fanned her face.

'It's only April, but it feels like summer.'

'It is always summer on the border.'

'Doctor, why do you do this?'

'Someone must.'

'Surely there's more to it.'

Perhaps his melancholy mood and his thoughts of lost love made him vulnerable to her soft eyes, but Jesse now told Kikki Hernandez what he had never told anyone.

'My mother lived in Nuevo Laredo. She was very beauti-ful. When she was twenty-one, she had a brief romance with a handsome American and became pregnant. He did not stay around, perhaps he did not even know she was pregnant. But she wanted her child to be an American citizen, as the father was. So when she was ready to deliver, she came across the river, to the midwife in this *colonia*.'

He felt his emotions rising.

'And?'

'There were complications.'

Kikki stared into his eyes.

'She died.'

'Yes. In childbirth.'

She stared again.

'Yours.'

'Yes. She died giving me life.' He fought his emotions. 'No woman has died in childbirth in the *colonias* on my watch.'

'So this is your mission in life?'

'I suppose it is.'

'Does that make you happy?'

141

'It makes me useful.'

'Is that the same as happy?'

'One must be useful to be happy, I think.'

'Do your patients pay you?'

'Not in money.'

'How do you make a living?'

'A few heart surgeries at the Laredo hospital each month. My specialty.'

'Heart surgeons in Houston make millions and live in mansions. They seem happy . . . and useful.'

She had very nice legs. He spread his arms to the clinic.

'You think I should give up all this for such a life?'

'Do you think you will get married and live happily ever after here?'

Jesse caught Larry the cameraman rolling his eyes.

'Happily ever after? No, no, no, Kikki—we do not do happily ever after on the border.'

She smiled. She had a very nice smile as well.

'So you will live out your life in obscurity?'

'No. In this *colonia*.'

'Alone?'

'Apparently.'

'You don't want children?'

Jesse Rincón leaned back in his chair and studied Kikki Hernandez. He and she, they would make handsome babies.

'That would require a wife.'

She offered a coy smile. She did not wear a wedding ring.

'Certainly you have prospects?'

'I am afraid not.'

'A handsome doctor with no romantic prospects?'

'A poor doctor with no romantic prospects.' Jesse again spread his arms to the clinic. 'What woman would want

142

to share this life with me? How about you, Ms. Kikki Hernandez—would you like to marry me and have my babies and share this life with me?'

The smile left her pretty face. But Larry now smiled, as if Jesse had made a fine joke.

Chapter 11

'You've got to stop using that "Texas was once a nation and we might be again" line in your stump speech,' the Professor said.

'Why? The people love it.'

The Professor sat across the aisle from Bode with his face in the *New York Times*, not recommended reading before breakfast, even for a Ph.D.

'I told you—it's a myth. It's not true.'

'Sure, it is. Texas can secede from the Union anytime we want.'

'No, we can't.'

'Why not?'

'The Civil War.'

'Other than that?'

It was the next morning, and the governor of Texas was flying out to West Texas. Of all the perks of office, Bode enjoyed the Gulfstream the most. Jetting around the two hundred sixty-eight thousand square miles that was the state of Texas at three hundred miles per hour beat the hell out of being tailgated by eighteen-wheelers running eighty-five on the interstate. They were over the High Plains, but his thoughts were still in Austin, where he had left his wife.

Was their marriage over?

Lindsay Byrne had been part of his life for almost thirty years. Could he live without her? Did he want to? He still loved her, but did she still love him? He had stepped out on her with Mandy, sure, but their troubles had begun long before Mandy. Because of politics. Like most voters, she took politics seriously, more so than politicians, just as football fans took the games more seriously than the players. Players and politicians understand that it's just a game. You win some, you lose some, but the goal is to survive to play the next game or compete in the next election. But voters seemed to think that politicians could do good.

More particularly, his wife seemed to think that *this* politician could do good.

She had been so excited when he had first been elected governor. He—they—were going to do good. He had believed it, too. But reality crashed the party like a SWAT team: politics is all about money. Who pays it to the government; who gets it from the government. Politicians are money-brokers, and money rules everything and everyone in politics. Even Bode Bonner. Consequently, he had disappointed his wife. Which was a hard thing for a man, disappointing the only woman he had ever loved.

'What's wrong, honey?'

Mandy Morgan sat next to him, but her fingers were tiptoeing up and down his thigh. He took her hand and put it in her lap. She pushed her lips out.

144

'I'm not in the mood,' Bode said.

'Really? There's something about flying that puts me in the mood.'

'Girl, breathing puts you in the mood.'

That familiar twinkle came into her eyes, as if he had laid down a challenge. She unbuckled her seat belt and hiked her black leather miniskirt high enough to climb onto his lap and reveal her red lacy thong. She was wearing a low-cut top that exposed a good portion of her impressive breasts, which she pressed against him as her lips went to his ear. She moved her bottom against his lap.

'I'm not sure, Bode, but I think you might be getting in the mood.'

He was.

His mind might be elsewhere, but his body was present and at full attention. Funny how men could separate the mind and body when it came to sex. Women always talk about sex being more of a mental exercise than a physical one; for men, it was just the opposite. It was strictly a physical act. A man could have sex while wondering how the Longhorns were playing; in fact, a man could have sex while watching the Longhorns play and figuring out how to bet the over-under. Jim Bob noticed the commotion in seat 3B.

'Jesus, get a room.'

He folded the newspaper, stood, and headed up front to join Ranger Hank and the pilots.

'I'll be in the cockpit.'

'Me, too,' Mandy said with a little giggle.

She slid down his lap and unbuckled his cowboy belt. He leaned his head back and closed his eyes—

'Bode, honey, are you a member of the Mile High Club?'

—and listened to the engines humming outside while inside Mandy—

'Oh, baby.'

Two hundred fifty miles due south of the governor's Gulfstream, Jesse Rincón said, '*El bebé viene de pies.*'

'What does that mean, Doctor?' the woman cried in Spanish.

'Your baby is coming out the wrong way. Feet first. That is not good. Inez!'

Over six thousand men, women, and children lived in this *colonia*, many more children than women or men. He had never met this woman named Alma until she had walked into the clinic an hour ago fully dilated and experiencing contractions. She had awakened that morning in Mexico, but when contractions began she had waded across the Rio Grande; she wanted her child to be an American citizen. She knew the doctor in *Colonia Ángeles* would deliver her baby. There were now Mexican businesses that arranged tourist visas and stateside vacations for wealthy pregnant Mexican women—often wives of drug lords—offering a stay at a luxurious resort, facials and body wraps at a spa, shopping sprees, and delivery of an American citizen at a private hospital with a birth certificate to evidence that fact.

Poor women just waded across the river.

Alma should be admitted to a hospital for an emergency C-section, in case complications arose, such as the umbilical cord compressing or wrapping around the baby's neck and depriving the child of oxygen; and an anesthesiologist should be on stand-by. But Jesse did not even have a receptionist standing by.

'Inez!'

Of course, the hospitals would turn her away. She was a Mexican without money. He might have to perform a C-section there in the clinic. Alone, if Inez did not return soon.

'Inez! Why is she always gone when I need her?'

The woman named Alma screamed with pain.

'*¡Ay, Dios mío!*'

'Oh—my—God!' Mandy said. 'Is there any place to shop?'

Bode chuckled. Okay, she wasn't Phi Beta Kappa, but she had skills. She was buckled in, applying lipstick, and staring out the window as they landed at the private airstrip on John Ed Johnson's ranch outside Fort Davis, population 1,000, in far West Texas. Located four hundred miles west of Austin, one hundred seventy-five miles east of El Paso, and eighty miles north of the Rio Grande, the deserted, desolate land might seem a perfect drug-smuggling route for the Mexican cartels. But wolves and mountain lions and even black bears roamed the land and made the journey north tricky if not deadly. From the air, the land seemed as barren and drought-stricken as the rest of Texas. But on the ground, in the Davis Mountains, hundreds of springs kept the land alive. Bode felt a sense of excitement surge through his body. He couldn't wait until the next morning when he would saddle up a horse and ride the land.

And shoot a lion.

The woman cried at the pain as if she had been shot.

'Inez!'

The clinic felt like a steam bath. Jesse wiped sweat from his face. He sat on the stool between her spread legs and crouched close to the birth canal, waiting and hoping the child would deliver without complications. He put his hand inside her vagina and spread his fingers, trying to create room. One tiny foot appeared. Now the other. And the legs. The buttocks emerged next, then the back, and then . . . the head did not follow.

The baby was stuck.

Jesse did not pull. He waited. But he could not wait long because the baby's head would compress the umbilical cord against the birth canal. The baby could suffocate. Jesse slid his fingers deep into Alma's vagina and along the baby's face. He found the nose then pushed his hand back against the canal to create space so the baby could breathe. He waited. And sweated. Alma screamed. He heard the clinic door open, but with his hand inside Alma, he could not raise his head enough to see in the mirror on the wall.

'Inez, where have you been? Wash your hands and put on gloves. Hurry.'

He heard the water running. But neither the scent he now inhaled nor the voice he now heard belonged to Inez Quintanilla.

'Is it breech?'

Jesse froze. Was it his imagination or was it really her voice? He slowly turned to the voice . . . to the governor's wife, standing there in full, pulling on a white coat and latex gloves. The first thought that entered his mind as he sat there with his hand in one woman's vagina while he stared at another woman was, *She changed her itinerary*. The second thought was, *Yes, there truly is such a thing as love at first sight*. Alma screamed again.

'Yes.'

'We need to get her to a hospital.'

'No money and no time—the baby is here.'

A few minutes later, he breathed in the scent of birth. Dr. Jesse Rincón delivered his 1,164th baby. He still had never lost a mother or child during birth.

John Ed Johnson carried himself with the bearing of a man accustomed to getting his way. He was seventy-one years old and stood six feet three inches tall just as he had when he played defensive end for the Longhorns back in the late fifties and early sixties. He sported a bald head that was covered by an LBJ Stetson; he wore a plaid flannel shirt, khaki pants, and brown round-toed boots. He boasted a net worth of $5 billion. Often.

'Governor.'

John Ed greeted Bode with a big smile and a strong hand-shake as soon as he got out of the Hummer his host had sent to pick them up at the airstrip.

'Damn, John Ed, you're still strong enough to break a half-back in two.'

'Those were the days.'

John Ed had led his team in tackles, sacks, and opponents' broken bones. He could have gone pro, but the pay back then didn't merit his time. He had majored in oil: how to find it, drill it, produce it, sell it, and get rich off it. For the last fifty years, he had done exactly that. He slapped Bode on the back but his eyes went to Mandy.

'And who's this little gal?'

She stuck out a manicured hand and offered her perky professional pose.

'Mandy Morgan, the governor's aide.'

'And what exactly do you aid him with?'

'Whatever he requires.'

'I like the sound of that.'

John Ed greeted Jim Bob and Ranger Hank then led them into the lodge. John Edward Johnson's hunting lodge was not a rustic cabin with Spartan accommodations. It was a twenty-room log structure with an indoor hot tub, swimming pool, sauna, billiards room, bowling alley, tennis court, skeet range, concierge, private chef, and Hummer driver.

Oil had been good to John Ed Johnson.

'This here's Pedro,' he said by way of introducing the middle-aged Latino who greeted them at the front door. 'Anything you need, Governor, you tell Pedro, he'll take care of it.'

'Lunch is served, *Señor* John Ed,' Pedro said.

'Hope you folks are hungry,' John Ed said. 'Rosita's cooked up a mess of Mexican food special for the governor of Texas.'

They followed John Ed through the foyer and into a great room with a two-story wall of windows offering a majestic view of the Davis Mountains. The room featured a manly aroma from the wood and leather and animal heads on the wall and a full-grown grizzly bear stuffed and standing there as if about to pounce on its prey.

'Shot that big bastard up in Montana,' John Ed said. 'Right between the eyes.'

The Johnson ranch comprised twenty-five square miles, the entire perimeter of which was surrounded by a twenty-foot-tall game fence. Inside the fence exotic game roamed freely. Outside the fence Mexicans tended to the grounds, cleaned the lodge, and cooked the food.

'Here's the menu,' John Ed said.

They sat at a dining table made of mesquite and set for lunch. Bode scanned the menu expecting to read his choice of entrées and desserts. Instead, he read—

'Alpine Ibex?' Mandy said. 'For twenty thousand dollars? That's an expensive lunch.'

John Ed threw his head back and laughed.

'Where'd you find this gal, Bode? I like her.' He turned to Mandy. 'Honey, that ain't the lunch menu—that's the hunting menu.' John Ed read from the menu. 'Addax Antelope, six thousand . . . Dama Gazelle, ten thousand . . . Roan, twenty thousand . . . Bongo, thirty-five thousand . . . Cape Buffalo, fifty thousand . . .'

Bode scanned down the menu: American Bison, Arabian Oryx, Nubian Ibex, Sable, West Caucasian Tur, Wildebeest.

'You raised your price on the wildebeest since I bagged mine,' Bode said.

'Yep,' John Ed said. 'Course, it didn't cost you nothing then, and it ain't gonna cost you nothing now.'

'Appreciate that, John Ed.'

'Least I can do for good government.'

Jim Bob held up his iPhone.

'John Ed, you still don't have cell phone coverage out here?'

'Hell, Professor, there ain't no cell towers from here to El Paso.'

Hank's eyes lit up when a pretty young Latina wearing a colorful peasant dress and carrying a serving tray entered through swinging double doors. She placed platters of beef-and-cheese enchiladas, refried beans, tortillas, and guacamole on the table then returned with cold bottles of Dos Equis beer. When she leaned over the table, John Ed swatted her bottom. Bode caught her grimacing on the way out, and a disturbing thought shot through his mind: Did Mandy grimace when he wasn't looking? But he quickly drowned that thought with a long drink of the Dos Equis.

151

'Rosita, she's a fine little cook,' John Ed said. 'Found her down in Lajitas, working in a little *cantina*. Figured she was too pretty to waste away there, so I brought her up here. She's a cute little gal, just turned twenty-one.' He lowered his voice and leaned into Bode. 'She'll even do room service.'

He winked.

The thought of a seventy-one-year-old man with a twenty-one-year-old mistress made Bode a bit nauseous. Then he thought of himself, a forty-seven-year-old man with a twenty-seven-year-old mistress. Was the only difference between John Ed Johnson and Bode Bonner twenty-four years and five billion dollars?

Four hundred miles down the border, Lindsay Bonner cradled the newborn child. She had given birth once and assisted in many emergency childbirths and had never ceased to be amazed by the miracle of life.

'*¿Esperanza es americana?*' Alma the mother said.

'Yes, she is an American citizen,' the doctor said in Spanish. 'I will sign the birth certificate to prove it.'

Alma smiled through her pain.

'You did a wonderful job, Doctor,' Lindsay said.

He wiped sweat from his face.

'I could not have done it without you, Mrs. Bonner.'

They regarded each other a long moment, until the clinic door burst open, and three brown and armed men entered. One was bald; they were dressed in black outfits, like soldiers. Their expressions were hard.

'Turn away, quickly,' the doctor whispered, 'so they do not see your face.'

She sat on the stool next to the examining table and faced the wall. In the mirror, she saw another man enter the clinic. His expression was not hard. He carried himself in a manner that combined elegance and personal authority; from the way the others regarded him, he was an important person here on the border, perhaps a politician. He was tall and handsome with a goatee and jet-black hair even though he appeared middle-aged. He wore a loose shirt and slacks that draped like silk. His cologne scented the clinic. He recoiled at the sight of the blood on the doctor's lab coat and gloves.

'What happened?' he asked in Spanish.

'Breech birth.'

The doctor apparently knew the man, but he kept his distance. He removed the latex gloves and tossed them into the trash basket.

'Are they okay, mother and child?' the man asked.

'Yes.'

'*Bueno.* I have a girl and two boys. Born in the USA. Houston. The poor *gringos*, they come south to *México* because they cannot afford American doctors. Rich *Mexicanos*, we go north to America for better healthcare. Odd, is it not?' He seemed to have amused himself. 'So, Dr. Rincón, I have heard much about you. It is an honor to finally meet you. You went to Harvard?'

'Yes.'

'Go Crimson.' He smiled; his teeth were perfect and white. 'I grew up poor and dreamed of escaping poverty by playing American *béisbol*, but I could not hit the curveball. So I went to Harvard on a minority scholarship. I am no longer poor.'

'What brings you to my clinic?'

'To thank you.'

'For what?'

'For saving my son's life.'

153

'Your *son*?' The doctor frowned. 'The boy? A month ago, with the gunshot?'

'*Sí*. My first-born, Jesús.' He shrugged. 'The boy was careless.'

'How is he?'

'Oh, he is fine. I sent him away.' He gestured to the north. 'To *Tejas*. To become a man.'

'No complications?'

'No. I had nurses with him twenty-four/seven. He is a strong boy. He recovered quickly. I have been shot three times myself. We are a hardy breed, *Mexicanos*.'

'Then what do you need from me?'

'*Nada*. It is what you need from me.'

'And what is that?'

The man held a hand out to his men; the bald soldier slapped an envelope into his hand, which he then held out to the doctor. He took the envelope, opened it, and removed a stack of green bills.

'One hundred thousand dollars,' the man said. 'Is that a fair compensation?'

The doctor stared at the money, then sighed and handed it back to the man.

'You know I cannot take your money.'

The man's expression seemed pained, almost as if his feelings had been hurt.

'I understand, Doctor. Perhaps you will accept these gifts.'

He snapped his fingers. The armed men went back outside and returned moments later with their arms full of large boxes. They stacked the boxes on the floor and returned for more. After several trips, a dozen boxes sat on the floor of the clinic.

'What is all this?' the doctor asked.

154

The important man pulled a switchblade from his back pocket and released the blade. He cut the tape sealing a box and opened the top. The doctor looked inside then reached in and held up a stethoscope.

'Supplies, surgical instruments . . .'

'Medicine.'

The man sliced open more boxes. The doctor pulled out cartons of medicine.

'Penicillin, amoxicillin, tetracycline . . . *Botox?*'

The man shrugged.

'How did you acquire all this?' the doctor said.

'That is of no concern, Doctor. This is payment for my son's life. *Gracias.*'

In the mirror, Lindsay saw him turn to her. She ducked her head.

'And thank you, Nurse. Jesús said you treated him with much kindness. I will not forget.'

She did not acknowledge him. But she looked into the mirror in time to catch the man winking at the doctor. He lowered his voice.

'I like the red hair on a woman, too.'

He snapped his fingers again, and he and his men headed to the door; but the man turned back.

'*Hasta la vista.*'

Until we meet again. He disappeared through the door. Lindsay stood and carried the child over to the doctor.

'Who was that?'

The doctor hesitated a moment before he said, 'That was El Diablo.'

'You devil.'

Mandy was in a naughty mood. Two girlie drinks and that

gal turned randy. She performed a little striptease, dropping her thong and flinging it across the room with her foot, then stepped down into the hot tub holding her piña colada aloft. The warm water made her skin flush pink, which rendered her even more attractive. She slid over to Bode and sat on his lap then kissed him. She tasted of coconut and rum and smelled of his teenage years. She sipped her drink with one hand and reached down with her other hand and stroked him. It was too late to shoot anything that day, so he had swallowed a Viagra pill with his third Dos Equis. Now, between Mandy's skilled hands and the little blue pill, Bode had a pretty fair erection working when someone knocked on the door.

'¿*Señor gobernador?*'

Pedro.

'Yes?'

Pedro cracked the door and spoke without entering the room.

'A phone call has come for you. Ranger Roy? He is on line five.'

Bode searched the room and found the phone on a small table between a chair and a towel shelf.

'*Gracias.*'

Pedro shut the door. Bode climbed out of the hot tub and walked the few paces to the phone. The lodge was too isolated for cell phone service, so it was either landlines or satellite phones. Bode grabbed a towel and wiped sweat from his face then put the receiver to his ear and punched the blinking light.

'Yeah, Roy?'

'Uh, Governor, we, uh . . . we can't find your wife.'

'The hell you mean, you can't find my wife?'

'She took off in your Suburban soon as you took off in the Gulfstream. We haven't seen her since. It's almost dark. We can't get her on her cell phone.'

'Aw, hell, she's probably down at the homeless shelter.'

'We checked.'

'Food bank?'

'Nope.'

'AIDS clinic?'

'*Nada.*'

'Oh, I know—she's probably at that elementary school in East Austin.'

'It's closed.'

'Goddamnit, Roy, you're supposed to be her fucking bodyguard!'

'Yes, sir.'

'Which requires that you know her whereabouts at all times, in order to guard her body.'

'Governor, you know I'd never let nothing bad happen to Mrs. Bonner. They'd have to kill me first.'

His voice cracked. Bode sighed.

'I know, Roy.'

'But don't worry, Governor, we're pretty sure she wasn't kidnapped.'

'*Kidnapped?* Why the hell would you think she's been kidnapped?'

'We don't.'

'Then why'd you bring it up?'

'Uh, in case you were thinking it.'

'I wasn't. But I am now.'

'Oh.'

'Find her, Roy.'

Bode hung up and looked down. He wasn't really worried

about his wife being kidnapped, but he had lost his erection just the same.

Lindsay Bonner felt terrible. No doubt Ranger Roy was frantic by now, the governor's wife disappearing without a trace. He had probably already called the governor. That would have been a difficult call for Roy. She'd call him later that night when she returned to Laredo. There was no phone service in the *colonias*.

'We would celebrate with a caramel macchiato,' the doctor said, 'but there is no Starbucks here in the *colonias*. Can you believe that?'

The doctor smiled at his own joke. He poured her a cup of the coffee he had brewed at home and brought to the clinic in a tall thermos.

'When the helicopter took the boy away that day, I knew he was special. But El Diablo's son? I would never have dreamed that.'

'Would you have saved him if you had known?'

'Of course.'

'Will you keep the medicine and supplies?'

'Of course. I did not make a deal with the devil, Mrs. Bonner. The devil simply made a gift—and not to me. To the people in the *colonias*.'

'The congressman said he gives away a billion dollars every year.'

'Yes, that is what they say.'

'So you didn't know him before today?'

'Everyone on the border knows of El Diablo. But I had never met him or even seen him. The Justice Department put a bounty on his head, so he does not often venture to this side of the river.'

He sat back and studied her. She knew the question he wanted to ask.

'Well, Mrs. Bonner, if you have come back for the census forms, Inez has helped over one thousand residents fill out the forms, but I have already mailed them in.'

'I didn't come back for the census forms.'

'Then for what?'

Now she studied him.

'Did you always want to be a doctor?'

He sipped his coffee.

'Yes. My uncle raised me in Nuevo Laredo. When I turned sixteen, he secured my admission to the Jesuit School in Houston. He told them I would make a good priest. But I wanted to be a doctor.'

'I wanted to be a nurse.'

'You are a fine nurse.'

'No. I'm the governor's wife.'

'Yes. You are indeed.'

'But I want to be a nurse again. Your nurse.'

'*My nurse?* Here, in the *colonias*?'

'Yes.'

'Why not in Austin?'

'Because in Austin, I'm the governor's wife. Everywhere in Texas, I'm the governor's wife. Everywhere except here.'

'You want to work in the *colonia*? The governor's wife?'

'No one knows me here, and no one will know me.'

'I will know.'

'But only you. No one else will know. Not even your assistant.'

'Inez seems never to be here anyway. But your red hair— Mrs. Bonner, everyone in Texas knows the beautiful governor's wife with the red hair.'

She tried not to blush.

'What if El Diablo had recognized you just now?'

'I'll cut my hair short and hide it under a scarf. I won't wear make-up.'

'But one day, someone will recognize your name if not your face.'

'I won't be Lindsay Bonner. I'll be Lindsay Byrne. My maiden name. An Irish nurse from Boston. I'll even speak with an accent.'

'You were born in Boston? How did you end up in Texas?'

'My father was a doctor at the VA hospital in San Antonio.'

'And is he still?'

'No. My parents are both gone now.'

'I am sorry. I am also broke. I cannot afford to pay you.'

'I have money. I need a purpose. Doctor, I can help you.'

He drank his coffee and considered her plan. He frowned.

'Have you had your shots?'

'Yes . . . I think.'

'Mrs. Bonner, a life on the border is a harsh life indeed. Have you truly thought this through?'

'I have.'

'And where will you live?'

'Oh. I hadn't thought about that.'

'If you go to a hotel in Laredo, you will have to show your ID, give them your credit card. Word will get out fast that you are living here on the border. If you rent a house or apartment, someone will recognize you. You cannot live here in the *colonia*, it is not safe.'

'You live here.'

'No. I live on the other side of Laredo, on fifty acres over-looking the river. My uncle had no children, so he left that land to me, and the small houses on it.'

'Houses?'

'The main house and a guesthouse.'

'Is anyone living in the guesthouse?'

'No, but—'

'Would you like a tenant?'

'The governor's wife, living in my guesthouse?'

'No. Your nurse.'

She had been certain he would readily agree to her plan, but he did not. He stared at her, and she knew he was asking himself if she was just a rich woman running away from her boring life.

'Doctor, I'm not running away from my life. I'm trying to have a life.'

'In the *colonias*?'

He stood and wandered about the clinic. He dug into one of the boxes El Diablo had brought and raised up with a carton of scalpels. He placed the carton on an empty shelf. He then went over and opened the front door and stood in the doorway.

Jesse Rincón gazed out upon *Colonia Ángeles*. Six thousand patients. One doctor. A nurse would be a godsend for the patients. And for the doctor.

The governor's wife had come back.

But for how long? How long could she tolerate the harsh life of the *colonias*? How long before the wind and the dirt and the death and the hopelessness crushed her spirit like that empty beer can lying in the dirt road? How long before 'I can help' became 'I can't take it anymore'? How long before she called it quits and ran home to her old life in the Governor's Mansion? To the governor?

Those questions he asked himself. But the answer to each

161

question was the same, and he already knew the answer: one day she would leave. About that he had no doubt. But there was one question that Jesse Rincón could not answer, a question that would not be answered until that day came, when the governor's wife left him: Was it truly better to have loved and lost than never to have loved at all?

'Doctor?'

His shoulders rose and fell with a deep breath. He turned and walked back to her.

'Go home, Mrs. Bonner.'

He sat down behind his desk and began packing his bag.

'But I thought—'

'This is not a Junior League project, Mrs. Bonner. This is life on the border.'

'I'm not here for that. I'm here because I care.'

'About these poor people? Why?'

'Because someone has to.'

'I do.'

'You can't do this by yourself.'

'I have for five years.'

'I can help you.'

'For how long? A day? A week? Maybe a month? Then the stink and the dirt and the death will beat you down, and you will run home to Austin, back to the Governor's Mansion where you belong. Go home, Mrs. Bonner.'

'You need a nurse . . . and I need to do this.'

'Why? Because you had a fight with the governor and now you need to prove something to him?'

'Because I need to prove something to myself.'

'And what is that?'

'That my life can still have meaning. That I can still make

a difference.' She fought back the tears. 'That I'm not too old to be useful.'

He stared at her, as if trying to see into her soul. He finally stood.

'Okay. Are you hungry?'

Bode bit into the thick juicy steak. He chewed with the intensity of a man still pissed off at his wife for ruining a sexual encounter with his mistress—and harboring a nagging worry that his wife had been kidnapped. After Ranger Roy's phone call—and despite Mandy's best efforts—he could not recapture the erectile moment. He chased the steak with a swallow of bourbon. Pedro entered the dining room with a portable phone in hand.

'*Señor gobernador*—Ranger Roy, he has called again.'

Bode took the phone and answered.

'Well?'

'We found your wife, Governor.'

Lindsay Bonner wrapped the green scarf around her head and tucked her red hair underneath. She then put on a wide-brimmed straw hat. She checked herself in the mirror and smiled.

She was no longer the governor's wife.

They had stopped off at an outdoor market in Laredo on the way to the doctor's homestead on the other side of town. She shopped for clothes to wear as Nurse Byrne; he shopped for groceries. He said he cooked. Latino music played and Spanish was spoken; it reminded her of their vacation to Acapulco years before. She held a yellow peasant dress against her body and looked in the mirror. She turned at the sound of girls giggling; the doctor stood surrounded by several pretty

163

young Latinas. They flirted and took cell phone photos with the handsome doctor. He really was something of a celebrity on the border. Lindsay now appraised herself in the mirror. She sighed. She was still lean and slim and even considered the glamorous governor's wife; but she was not a beautiful young girl anymore. She was a forty-four-year-old woman.

Her cell phone rang.

'What the hell are you doing down on the goddamn border?'

Bode had stepped out of the dining room. Waiting for the call to ring through, his blood pressure had jacked up to mini-stroke levels. Still, he felt relieved when his wife answered—but his anger and the alcohol quickly took over.

'Are you drinking?'

'No . . . yes.'

He could never lie to her, except about Mandy.

'How'd you find me?'

'GPS. Your cell phone.'

'My *phone*?'

'Cell phones are just tracking devices that make calls.'

'You tracked my phone?'

'The Rangers did. So what do you think you're doing?'

'I'm nursing.'

'Who?'

'No. I'm going to work as a nurse.'

'In Laredo?'

'In the *colonias*.'

'Oh, for Christ's sake, Lindsay, that's crazy!'

'Maybe to you, Bode. But not to me.'

'You're the governor's wife.'

'Not down here.'

'Go home, Lindsay. Now.'

'No. I'm staying here. Give my best to Mandy.'

The line went dead. He stared at the phone. Shit.

Lindsay stared at her phone a long moment then looked up at the doctor looking at her. His arms were full with two bags of groceries and his face with the awkward moment.

'She's twenty-seven. Mandy.'

Which made the moment even more awkward.

'So,' he said with a forced smile, 'let us have dinner.'

'I hope you bought wine.'

The governor of Texas downed his bourbon. His third. He needed hard liquor after learning that his wife knew about his mistress.

'That sonofabitch can carve up a cow faster'n those raptors in that dinosaur movie,' John Ed was saying. 'I get Manuel to run a dried-up cow inside the game fence every week or so. That big ol' lion sniffs her out in no time, hunts her down, pounces on her, rips her apart. Damnedest thing I've ever seen.'

Mandy, Ranger Hank, and Jim Bob had gone upstairs. Mandy needed her beauty sleep, Hank needed his sports fix on satellite TV, and Jim Bob needed to plug his laptop into a landline like a patient on life support. Bode and John Ed had gone into the study to drink Kentucky bourbon and smoke Cuban cigars.

'You sure you want me to shoot your lion?'

'There's more where he came from. Course, you gotta track him down and get close enough to put a bullet in him. Maybe two.'

John Ed puffed on his cigar.

'Manuel, he'll have the horses saddled and your guns

packed, ready to ride at dawn. He's a good tracker. He'll find that lion for you. Used to be the foreman on a game ranch outside Guadalajara, big place catering to Americans. Then the cartels took over the country, so Americans stopped going south to hunt—they became the hunted instead of the hunter. I needed a place to hunt, so I turned this land into a game ranch, hired Manuel. Been with me five years now.'

'He legal?'

'Hell, no. None of my Mexicans are legal.' John Ed chuckled. 'While back, me and Manuel, we're riding the range in the Hummer, he asks me, "*Señor* John Ed, is Obama going to make me a citizen?" I said, "Why the hell do you want to be an American citizen?" He says, "I want to vote." You believe that? I bring him up here, give him a job, place to live . . . now he wants to vote. How's that for gratitude?'

John Ed Johnson had come of age back when men were men and women were cheerleaders and Mexicans did the hard work and kept their mouths shut.

'Life was simple back then,' John Ed said. 'Oil, cattle, and Mexicans doing what they were told and didn't expect us to educate their kids or make them citizens.'

Bode knew better than to get John Ed started on Mexicans, so he diverted the conversation.

'You riding out with us in the morning?'

'Nope. Man my age, I sleep in. You and Jim Bob have fun. Me and Mandy, we'll have a long breakfast.' He winked. 'You know, I never lost my testosterone. Most men my age, they need a pill to get it up, if they can. Not me. You?'

'*Me?* Hell, no.'

Bode said it with such conviction he almost believed himself.

'I still wake up every day with a hard-on,' John Ed said,

'which is why I sleep in . . . usually with Rosita. I enjoy sex in the morning.'

John Ed Johnson had a reputation for being a horny old bastard, chasing skirts all across Texas and plowing through four wives. He was currently between wives if not skirts. But being a self-made billionaire—and not in computer code that no one understood, but in cattle and oil that everyone understood—he had achieved that larger-than-life legendary Texan status, the kind of man kids would read about in their Texas history class one day, like LBJ and H.L. Hunt. A Texas politician could never have a better friend—if you always said yes—or a worse enemy—if you ever said no. You did not want to be on his bad side. As Jim Bob said, 'That's a dark place indeed.' John Ed had contributed $20 million to each of Bode's last two campaigns—there was no limit on campaign contributions by individuals in Texas—and Bode was waiting on his $20 million check for the current campaign. John Ed Johnson had put Bode Bonner in the Governor's Mansion.

And he could take Bode Bonner out.

Like Bode, John Ed had grown up on a cattle ranch; unlike the Bonner family's modest five-thousand-acre spread, the Johnson family's land in West Texas spread over three counties and was measured in square miles rather than acres. His granddaddy had taken a hundred thousand head of cattle on the long trail drives north to the railheads in Kansas back in the 1800s. By John Ed's time, the trains had come to Texas.

But if his old man had been the Bick Benedict of his time, John Ed was the Jett Rink of his. After his dad died, he turned production on the ranch from Angus beef to black gold. Oil. Just as Texas had produced the beef the nation needed during his old man's time, Texas produced the oil the world needed during John Ed's time. Texas had so much oil that from 1930, when the great East Texas field was discovered, and for the next forty years, the Texas Railroad Commission controlled the price of oil—in the entire world—by controlling the amount of oil Texas produced. Texas sat on a sea of oil.

But the Middle East sat on an ocean of oil.

In 1960, the Arabs formed OPEC, modeled after the Railroad Commission. By 1973, Texas no longer controlled the price of oil; OPEC did. Americans stood in gas lines during the oil embargo because Texas no longer supplied the world's oil or even America's oil; the Arabs did. For the last forty years, the Arabs had controlled the price of oil in the world. Even in Texas.

'Took a lot of the fun out of the oil business,' John Ed always said, 'not being able to control prices.'

So John Ed moved on to the next big thing: water. Just as a landowner in Texas owns the oil under his land, he also owns the water. And he can sell that water.

'Ninety percent of Texans live in the city now, and they're fast running out of water because they want their pools full and their grass green. They'll be drinking spit in twenty years, ten if this drought don't let up. Then they'll pay an arm and a leg for drinking water. My water. I bought up groundwater rights all across West Texas, figure I can pump that water out of the ground, pipe it to the cities, and turn a nice profit. Water's more valuable than oil these days. If you control water, you control Texas.'

'I thought you already controlled Texas.'

'Not all of it.'

'What'll happen to West Texas without water?'

'Who cares? Ain't much to look at now.'

'How you figure on piping the water to the cities?'

'I've got to build the pipelines, hundreds of miles. Problem is, I've got to acquire the rights-of-way from landowners. I can negotiate with a thousand owners and buy the rights-of-way, but that gets expensive and time-consuming. Or I can condemn that land . . . well, I could if I possessed eminent domain power as a common carrier, like my gas company.'

His expression told Bode that he was about to ask the governor of Texas for a small favor.

'I need a special bill, Bode, that grants my water company common carrier status. I need the power to condemn land for my pipelines. I need you to twist a few arms—the speaker's and the lieutenant governor's—and get my bill passed.'

'There'll be some political heat, if this gets out.'

'Maybe. But the Professor said your latest poll numbers are high enough to weather some heat.'

'You already talked to Jim Bob about this?'

'Yep. When he called about you boys coming out. He's your political advisor, isn't he?'

Bode nodded.

'So—can I count on you, Bode?'

Bode didn't like it—giving John Ed Johnson the power to take people's land for his water pipeline—but he needed John Ed's $20 million.

'You bet, John Ed.'

'Appreciate that, Bode. I won't forget. Oh, tell Jim Bob I'll wire my twenty-five million campaign contribution over Monday.'

'Twenty-five?'

John Ed shrugged. 'After seeing your gal Mandy, I figured you could use a little extra spending money.'

'Thanks.' Bode drank his bourbon. 'You know, John Ed, I appreciate the support you've given me as governor. If I made a run for the White House, would you back me?'

'Why the hell would you want to do that?'

'An adventure.'

'Cheaper adventures to be had . . . Like your gal Mandy.'

John Ed drew a breath on his cigar then exhaled sweet smoke.

'Buying the Governor's Mansion, that's a forty-million-dollar deal. Buying the White House, that's a billion-dollar deal. And turning a profit on that kind of investment is damn hard 'cause you got to buy Congress, too, and those bastards don't come cheap. Wall Street pays billions for Congress, every election cycle. Even I can't fund that for long—five billion don't go as far as it used to. You want to move up to the White House, you gonna have to get the big boys behind you. They write those kind of checks every four years without blinking an eye.'

John Ed drank his bourbon.

'Hell, son, was me, I'd stick to being governor-for-life.'

'I just think I could win, riding the wave.'

'Wave? What wave?'

'The tea party.'

John Ed snorted. 'Pissin' in the wind. The money always wins in politics.'

'I don't know, John Ed. The middle class is pretty fired up about the social issues—abortion, gay marriage, immigration.'

'That's why they're stuck in the middle class.'

'What do you mean?'

'I mean, politics ain't about none of that social crap. It's about money. Rich people and poor people, we vote for the money. Poor folks vote for anyone promising to give them more money, rich folks for anyone promising to take less of our money. But the middle class, they take their Bibles into the voting booth—and that costs them money.'

'How so?'

'Because while they're fretting over girls getting abortions and boys screwing boys, the politicians are stealing them blind. See, rich folks like me, we've got a lot of money individually, but not as a group. Hell, Obama could take every penny from every billionaire in America, and it wouldn't fund the government but for a few months, not when the Feds spend ten billion dollars every day. The big money's in the middle class. A hundred million folks working their butts off every day to put Junior and Sissy through college, that's where the income's at, that's the mother lode of taxes. Only way the government can spend four trillion a year is to tap the middle class. So the politicians keep the middle class occupied with that social crap—'

'While they steal their money.'

'Exactly.'

'Never occurred to me.'

''Cause you're middle class. No offense.'

Bode swallowed his bourbon. John Ed Johnson didn't pull his punches, and he wasn't a billionaire for nothing. Bode wouldn't turn his back on the old man, but he learned something every time they talked. It wasn't exactly a father son relationship, but it was a relationship of sorts nonetheless.

'How 'bout another bourbon, Governor?'

The governor's wife sipped her wine. She and the doctor were sitting on the back porch of his house in rocking chairs. Pancho, the golden retriever, lay on the plank wood floor. Soft music drifted out through open windows. Mexico beyond the river seemed serene and peaceful at night. She had settled in to the guesthouse and cut her hair then showered and dressed in her new clothes for dinner. The doctor did cook.

171

They ate grilled fish and drank wine. She had awakened that morning in the Governor's Mansion in Austin; she was now staring at the stars over the Rio Grande.

'This is my retreat from the reality of the *colonias*,' the doctor said. He pointed up. 'Look, see the eagle.'

The bird glided on the currents back and forth between Mexico and America.

'Does the reality ever make you question your choice to work in the *colonias*?'

'Sometimes. But it is a useless question to ask. This is where I belong. My life will play out on this river.'

They were silent for a time, just the sounds of the river and the night. Then the doctor spoke.

'Back before the Mexican War—what the Mexicans call the American Invasion—steamboats ran up and down the Rio Grande.'

'It doesn't seem deep enough.'

'It is not now. The river often runs dry before it reaches the Gulf of Mexico. But before the dams and the droughts, the river was deep and swift and wide. Ferries and steamboats ran the river. I often sit here and imagine what life on this river was like back then, when all of this land was Mexico, before the history of the border turned bloody. And wrongs beget wrongs.'

He stared toward the river a long moment before he spoke again.

'History runs deep here on the border. Much deeper than the river.'

That night in South Texas, the governor's wife went to bed happy. In West Texas, the governor went to bed with his mistress. Neither knew that their lives were about to change forever.

Chapter 12

From two hundred fifty yards out, Bode Bonner sighted in a feral hog. A big one, at least three hundred pounds, feeding at dawn. One of three million roaming wild in the state of Texas. Nasty creatures, a nuisance to ranchers and farmers, rutting up pastures and crops. Consequently, the state authorized year-round hunting for feral hogs, even from helicopters. Feral entrepreneurs trapped and sold them to the Japanese, who considered wild boar meat a delicacy. Texans considered it coyote bait. Bode exhaled and squeezed the trigger. The hog dropped like a sack of potatoes when the .375-caliber bullet impacted its head.

'Good shot,' Jim Bob said.

The Professor was smoking one of John Ed's Cuban cigars and spotting for Bode through high-powered binoculars. Ranger Hank stood behind them, as if on the lookout for a Comanche war party. Manuel held the horses.

'Easy shot, with the wind down and this rifle. Even with a hangover.'

Bode had drunk too much bourbon with John Ed the night before. But Rosita's strong coffee and breakfast of *migas* and spicy *salsa* had slapped his mind clear. Not as clear as the blue sky, but sufficient to hunt. He leaned the rifle against a rock and drank more coffee from the thermos Rosita had filled. April mornings a mile up in the Davis Mountains still got down to freezing, so Bode wore a hunting jacket over a denim shirt and a western-style leather holster packing his matched set of Colt Walker .44-caliber six-shooters just like

Captain Augustus McCrae carried in *Lonesome Dove*. He couldn't strap on the six-shooters in the city, so he couldn't pass up the opportunity in the country. He loved being out of the city and in the country and on the back of a horse, only the smell of gunpowder and cigar smoke in his nostrils. They had gotten up at five, eaten breakfast, and met Manuel out back with the horses saddled and their guns loaded. Mandy was sleeping in.

John Ed Johnson wore only a bathrobe when he quietly opened the door to the guest bedroom. Across the spacious room he saw a mass of blond hair emerging from the comforter on the king-sized bed. He walked over and dropped his bathrobe then lifted the comforter and climbed aboard. He sidled close to the naked backside of the governor's aide. She stirred.

'Bode?'

'Guess again, honey.'

She jumped back against the headboard and clutched the comforter to her body.

'Mr. Johnson!'

'John Ed.'

'Mr. Johnson—what are you doing?'

'I thought we might play while the governor's away.'

'I'm not a plaything, Mr. Johnson!'

'Aw, I doubt Bode would mind.'

'I mind. I love Bode, and he loves me. I would never cheat on him.'

'Not even for a million dollars?'

'Not even for a million dollars!'

Odd. That usually worked.

'Well, hell, guess I'll go climb into Rosita's bed.'

John Ed slid out of bed and put on his bathrobe.

'The governor's in a helluva lot more trouble than he knows, having a woman who's not his wife in love with him.'

Lindsay Bonner opened her eyes onto a different world. She was waking up alone again, but not on the day bed in the sitting room in the Governor's Mansion in downtown Austin. She lay in a soft bed in a small guesthouse situated among a stand of palm trees only a few hundred feet from the Rio Grande and Mexico beyond.

Had she really done this?

She was a forty-four-year-old woman. She was the mother of an eighteen-year-old college student. She was a married woman and had been for the last twenty-two years. She was the governor's wife.

Whose husband was probably fit to be tied right about now.

But she had done it. She had escaped the crowds and cameras, the press and politics, the Governor's Mansion and the governor's wife. All of that was her husband's adventure. She had embarked on her own adventure. Her own life. A life that would have meaning.

Lindsay Bonner would make a difference.

She jumped out of bed and showered in the small bathroom. Then she dressed in her new clothes: the yellow peasant dress, green scarf, wide-brimmed hat, and pink Crocs. But no make-up. She looked at herself in the mirror. She barely recognized the woman looking back at her.

Here on the border, she was not the governor's wife.

Jesse Rincón ran the river, as he and Pancho did each morning. But that morning was unlike any before.

The governor's wife lay asleep in his guesthouse.

Five years now, he had resigned himself to a life without fame or fortune or love. He had never sought fame or fortune. Love was a different matter. He had often hoped for love. And now love was upon him. But for how long? How long would she sleep in his guesthouse? How long would she work with him in the *colonias*? How long before she left him? These questions threatened to darken his mind, but he refused them entry.

He stopped short.

Jesse Rincón vowed at that moment, standing in Texas and staring at Mexico as the sun rose over the Rio Grande, that he would not look beyond each day. He would live each day he had with her as if it would be his last, because one day it would be.

Bode slid the rifle into the leather scabbard secured to his saddle. They mounted their horses and rode off. They would leave the hog for the vultures that were already circling overhead. Hank and Manuel took the lead twenty yards ahead. Manuel Moreno was a short, wiry man, perhaps forty but possibly fifty. He carried a two-way radio linked to the lodge. Jim Bob carried a satellite phone. Bode Bonner was the governor of Texas, and he sure as hell didn't want to be lost and stranded on this ranch, twenty-five square miles of the most beautiful and brutal land in Texas.

'John Ed ambushed me with that eminent domain bill last night, said he talked to you about it.'

'Yep.'

'You knew he was gonna ask me for help getting it through the legislature?'

'Yep.'

'Why didn't you tell me?'

'Would you have told John Ed no and forgone the twenty million if I had?'

'No.'

'That's why I didn't tell you.'

'He's giving us twenty-five.'

'That'll put us over forty-five million. Good work.'

'Still, Jim Bob—next time, tell me.'

They rode on in silence. The air was cold, and the wind was down. The sky was big and blue, the mountains brown and low. Hawks and peregrine falcons soared on the currents above, and cool spring water bubbled out of the earth below. Named in honor of Jefferson Davis, the president of the Confederate States of America, the Davis Mountains were part of the Chihuahuan Desert that extended up from Mexico. The lower elevations were in fact desert, hot and dry and dotted with prickly pear and cholla cactus and creosote bush and giant yuccas and enough agave plants to supply several tequila factories. But the climb into the higher elevations brought blue grama grass and clear spring creeks and forests of ponderosa and *piñon* pine and even silver aspen. They called this land a 'sky island.' Bode had made the journey to these mountains many summers; while the rest of Texas suffered the hundred-degree heat, the mountains offered a cool oasis. The clean air soon eased his irritation at his political strategist. He could never stay mad at Jim Bob Burnet. They had been inseparable since fifth grade. Bode had rescued Jim Bob from bullies, and Jim Bob had saved Bode from math and science. They needed each other back then, and they still did today.

'I asked John Ed if he'd support me if I made a run for the White House.'

'And?'

'Said he couldn't afford it.'

'He didn't lie. Supreme Court threw out the campaign finance law, so the next presidential campaign's going to cost each party a billion dollars, and that's real money, even for John Ed.'

Jim Bob inhaled on his cigar and seemed to ponder the mountain sky. When he spoke, he was the Professor.

'A presidential run, Bode, it's brutal. Physically and mentally. Campaigning every day for two years, studying policy like you're cramming for a world history final so you don't come off an idiot in the debates, getting demonized by the left-wing media searching for every woman you ever dated to see if they'll claim sexual harassment . . . They're pit bulls with press passes. Why subject yourself to that?'

'It'd be a hell of an adventure.'

'Could be a hell of a disaster.'

'The thrill of victory or the agony of defeat . . . That's why we play the game.'

The Professor puffed on his cigar.

'You're a full-blown type-T personality, you know that? T for thrills.'

'Never denied it.'

'We did a research study at the school, why men go into politics.'

'So why do we?'

'Power, fame, money, thrills . . . and younger women, of course.'

'Politics offers a man the complete package without the need for post-season knee surgery.'

'If you win.'

'One big play, Jim Bob.'

The Professor exhaled cigar smoke.

'Bode, you've got a good thing going, governor-for-life. Don't fuck it up.'

Bode responded with a grunt.

'Hell,' the Professor said, 'look at the upside. You couldn't shoot an African lion if you were president.'

'True.'

'And you sure as hell couldn't bring Mandy along, the press corps follows the president everywhere.'

'Which would be a definite drawback, especially on the longer flights.'

The Professor chuckled.

'I told her we'd drive into Marfa for lunch at the Paisano Hotel,' Bode said. 'She's dying to see where Elizabeth Taylor slept when she was out here to film *Giant*. And she wants to shop, says she gets the shakes if she goes more than twenty-four hours without buying something.'

'Women.' Jim Bob shook his head. 'See, Lindsay's like us, that's why she went down to the border.'

Bode had informed Jim Bob that Lindsay had gone down to the border to work as a nurse in the *colonias*—and that she knew about Mandy.

'But Peggy, she was just like Mandy . . . well, except for the looks . . . and liking sex.'

Jim Bob and Peggy had married at twenty-five and divorced at thirty. She lived in California with their daughter. Bode's daughter was a lesbian who would never give him a grandson, but it could be worse: Jim Bob's daughter was a Californian.

'I tell you Fran got accepted to Stanford and Caltech? I'm trying to talk her into coming to UT. Be nice to have her around again. I miss that girl.'

'Why the hell would she go to Stanford or Caltech if she can go to UT?'

Jim Bob shrugged. 'An education?'

'But their football teams suck.'

'She doesn't play.'

'She could be a cheerleader.'

'She wants to be an engineer.'

'Train?'

'Environmental.'

'See, that's what living in California does to kids.'

Bode hoped for a laugh or at least a smile, but got neither. The Professor's expression turned down, as if he'd been denied tenure, and Bode knew that if he didn't get Jim Bob's mind off Fran, the melancholy would set up camp and dog him for days.

'So you were saying about Peggy?'

Jim Bob had loved Peggy with the desperation of a man who had had few opportunities for love, but she had left him for a richer man, a man who could give her the life she wanted. Bode knew that talking about Peggy would only get Jim Bob pissed off, a more favorable mood on a hunting trip than melancholy.

'Oh, yeah. So I asked Peggy one day—this was back when I was in grad school and already plotting the Republican takeover of Texas—before Rove beat me to it—and we were living in that little rent house just off campus—I said, "Honey, what do you want to do with your life?" She said, "I want a big house on the lake, a Mercedes coupe, a country-club membership, a . . ." I said, "No. That's what you *want* in life. But what do you want to *do* with your life?" Well, she looked at me like I was fucking crazy, and she said, "That *is* what I want to do with my life. I want to live in a big house on the lake, drive a Mercedes coupe, play tennis at a country club . . ." '

'What's your point, Jim Bob?'

'My point is, that's the basic biological difference between men and women: Men want to *do* things. Women want to *have* things. Which is why men and women don't understand each other, don't get along with each other, and don't stay married to each other. For us, it's all about the *doing*. Achieving something. Leaving our mark on the world. For them, it's all about the *having*. Acquiring something. Making their girlfriends jealous.' Jim Bob puffed on his cigar and blew out smoke rings like a fucking Indian sending smoke signals. 'We want to kill a big furry creature; they want to buy a fur coat.'

'So what's that got to do with Lindsay going down to the border?'

'She's not a normal woman like Peggy or Mandy. She's more like a man than most men. She doesn't give a damn about having things, she wants to do things. She wants her life to have meaning.'

'What, you're an expert on my wife?'

'I've known her as long as you have.'

Jim Bob pointed his cigar to the distant sky.

'Look—an eagle.' He stared a moment then said, 'Still, I can't believe Lindsay went down to the border by herself. That's fucking crazy. And nursing in the *colonias*, shit, she might bring something back.'

'What, like a Mexican?'

'Like a disease.'

'She's got all her shots.'

'She ain't a heifer, Bode.'

'She's a stray.'

181

'You knew that when you married her, a liberal from Boston.'

'Why can't she be happy shopping at Neiman Marcus like other women?'

'Because she's not like other women.'

'Most women want desperately to escape the border,' the doctor said. 'But you come to work here.'

'I don't shop,' Lindsay said.

'Ah. That explains it.'

'I could never go out in public like this in Austin—these clothes, no make-up, no Ranger Roy.'

'But why? You look very pretty. And your clothes, it will be nice to have some color in the *colonia*.'

'The cameras. They're my constant companion, so I have to look perfect. The press thinks everything I do is for the cameras, that my life is scripted for a political purpose, that I'm not just getting coffee or going to the gym or teaching kids to read. I'm campaigning. Most politicians' wives live for the cameras. But I hate the cameras.'

'There are no cameras in the *colonias*.'

They had eaten breakfast tacos—scrambled eggs, refried beans, and *salsa* wrapped in wheat tortillas—in the doctor's kitchen and were now driving to *Colonia Ángeles* in his old pickup truck. Pancho rode in the back. It was Saturday.

'Doctor—'

'Please. If we are going to work together, you must call me Jesse.'

'Jesse. And I'm Lindsay Byrne from Boston. So you work weekends?'

'I do not play golf.' He smiled a moment but the smile didn't last long. 'The truth is, I have nothing else to do.'

They soon turned off Mines Road and onto the dirt road that led to the border wall. When they arrived at the big gate, no Border Patrol agents were in sight.

'They're not here to let us in,' Lindsay said. 'How will we get through?'

'Key code.'

Jesse got out. She fought the wind and followed him to the gate. On the wall was a key pad.

'Wait,' she said. 'An American citizen has to enter a key code to travel from this side of the wall to that side? From this America to that America?'

'Uh . . . yes.'

'How does that work?'

'It is easy. See, I punch in the code—six, three, one, nine—'

'No. How does it work when the police need to come to the *colonias*? They have to get out and punch in the key code?'

'Oh. The police do not come to the *colonias*.'

'What about ambulances?'

'They also do not come.'

'Fire trucks?'

'No.'

'Oh. Well then, I guess a key code works just fine.'

'You love her?'

'I'll always love Lindsay.'

'Mandy.'

'*Mandy?* I'm old enough to be her . . . It's not like that.'

'She know that?'

Bode assumed she did. Why would a gorgeous twenty-seven-year-old girl fall in love with an older man? An older man had an affair with a younger woman for one reason.

'My wife doesn't want to have sex with me.'

'Hell, Bode, if you wanted sex, why'd you get married?'

Jim Bob was amused by his own words.

'When I vetoed that children's health insurance program,' Bode said, 'she moved out of our bedroom, sleeps on the day bed in the sitting room.'

'Yep, that was a mistake. She's got a blind spot when it comes to kids.'

'You told me I had to veto it, to stand up to Washington's unfunded mandates.'

'True, but it was a mistake if you wanted sex with Lindsay. Course, Mandy's not a bad replacement player.'

'I had lots of opportunities, but I never cheated on her, till she left our bed. Now I can't stop.'

'It is habit forming.'

'My wife stops having sex with me because of politics, but I'm not supposed to have sex with anyone else because I'm married? Why's that fair?'

'It's not.'

'Why should I feel guilty?'

'You shouldn't.'

'Then why do I?'

'Because that's what women do to men. But, hell, Bode, you don't have to feel guilty anymore—she knows about Mandy.'

The man's twenty-seven-year-old mistress had been discovered by his wife, and she had run off to the border. What would happen when the politician's twenty-seven-billion-dollar budget deficit was discovered by the voters? Would they run off, too?

'Why would she do that over politics?'

Jim Bob puffed on his cigar. 'It's the hero syndrome.'

184

'The what?'

'Hero syndrome. You've been her hero since high school. Now you're not.'

'I'm not?'

'Hate to be the one to break the news.'

'Helluva lot easier to be a hero on the football field. Now she wants me to fix up the *colonias* for a bunch of Mexican squatters.'

'You can't do that. You gotta take a hard line on immigration or that tea party wave will drown you.'

'That's what I told her. She said it's not about politics, it's about the children. Can you believe that?'

'She's always been a bit naïve.'

'What if she doesn't come back?'

'She'll be back. She'll get tired of the border and come crawling back home.'

'What if she doesn't come back because of Mandy?'

Jim Bob didn't answer for a time. Then he said in a soft voice, 'Peggy had an affair . . . I still would've taken her back.'

Bode did not look at his old friend. Instead, he felt old.

'My dad got prostate cancer at my age, died at fifty-five. Every year I get my physical, I sweat out the PSA results.'

'All men do. I had a biopsy two years ago.'

'On your prostate?'

'PSA was elevated. Turned out to be a false alarm.'

'You never told me.'

'Did you want to know?'

'Well, hell, yeah, I wanted to know. You're my best goddamn friend.' He shook his head. 'Shit, Jim Bob, you don't tell me nothing anymore—John Ed's bill, your biopsy . . . What was it like?'

185

The Professor puffed on his cigar.

'It wasn't the most fun I ever had.'

'That's how it is for men—a finger up your butt, an elevated PSA, and all of a sudden you're pissing your pants and holding a limp dick the rest of your fucking life. Or the cancer kills you.'

The two middle-aged men rode in silence, pondering life and death, mistresses and wives, budget deficits and deceived voters, past infidelity and future impotence . . . until Jim Bob Burnet finally said, 'Shit, let's kill something, see if that'll perk up our spirits.'

The children stood in a circle in the middle of the main dirt road in the *colonia*. Lindsay and Jesse got out of the pickup and walked over. The children parted to reveal a coiled-up rattlesnake hissing and shaking its tail.

'*¡Águas!*' Jesse yelled. '*¡Quítense de la víbora!*'

He herded the children back. The snake slithered around on the hot dirt.

'There are many snakes in the *colonias*,' he said. 'I really hate snakes.'

'We must kill it,' Lindsay said. 'Before it bites the kids.'

'Yes. We must.'

He put his hands on his hips and studied the snake, which hissed and spat at its tormentors.

'If I had a gun, I could shoot the snake, but I do not have a gun. Perhaps I could drop a cinder block on the snake, that would certainly kill it. Or perhaps I could drive the truck over it several times. Or perhaps I could . . .'

Lindsay looked around. She spotted a shovel leaning against a nearby shanty. She walked over, grabbed the shovel, and picked up a brick. She returned and threw the brick at the snake, striking it and giving her just enough time to raise the shovel and slam the sharp edge down on the snake, cutting its head off. The children squealed with delight. Jesse gave her a look.

'Yes, well, I suppose that is also an effective method.'

'I grew up in the country.'

Bode sighted in the African lion. It was a majestic creature, four hundred pounds of muscle and mane. He almost hated to kill it. Almost.

'What do you figure?'

They sat positioned on a ridge overlooking a low valley set against a tree line where a spring creek ran. Bode had propped the rifle on a rock formation; Jim Bob had the binoculars on the beast. Ranger Hank stood guard. Manuel again held the reins to the horses.

'Six hundred yards. We need to get closer.'

'We'll spook him. With this scope, I can see the fly on his nose from here.'

'But can you shoot him from here?'

'Reckon I'll find out.'

Testosterone and adrenaline and the anticipation of the kill coursed through Bode Bonner's body. Hunting was almost as exciting as sex, and he never pulled the trigger too soon. He ran his hand over the smooth custom-fitted English walnut stock of the AHR Safari 550 DGR (Dangerous Game Rifle) as if it were Mandy's smooth thigh. He fingered the bolt then worked the controlled-feed action and chambered a 270-grain, .375-caliber H&H Magnum cartridge from the four-round magazine. He flicked off the safety. He touched his left index finger to the single-stage trigger set at exactly 3.5 pounds. When he squeezed the trigger the hammer would release and drive the firing pin into the back of the cartridge igniting the primer which in turn would ignite the gunpowder inside the cartridge which would create sufficient gas pressure to propel the bullet down the barrel, turning to the right two full twists before exiting the twenty-four-inch barrel, and through the air at 2,690 feet per second, closing the distance to the lion before Bode could blink, and, if his aim were true and the lion didn't move, slamming into the beast's head and boring through its brain and blowing out a chunk of skull on the other side, killing the creature instantly. The taxidermist would patch up the lion's skull and mount the head—or maybe Bode would get the entire lion stuffed, as if it were about to pounce on anyone entering the Governor's Office. That'd give a lobbyist a fucking heart attack. Bode inhaled then exhaled slowly and gently squeezed the trigger and—

'What the hell?'

—the lion bolted—because something had bolted from the tree line. Bode looked up from the scope then back through the scope. He found the something in the cross hairs . . . only it wasn't a something . . . it was a someone . . . a young barefooted girl, her short dress ripped and torn, her face filled with fright, running across the open range.

'What's she doing out here?' Jim Bob said, the binoculars still to his face.

'Hauling ass,' Bode said. 'Like someone's after her.'

'Someone is.'

Bode swung the scope off the girl to three men on dirt bikes riding hard and fast behind her. After her. Chasing her as if they meant to catch her. The girl glanced back but kept running as if her life depended on it. But she wasn't fast enough. The men ran her to ground. They stopped and dropped the bikes then surrounded the girl. They looked Mexican and mean. They kicked the girl, grabbed her hair and yanked her up, then slapped her face, knocking her back down to the ground.

'Bad *hombres*,' Jim Bob said.

'She's just a kid.'

The men now pointed guns at her. She held her hands up, pleading to them.

'*Shit*. They're gonna kill her.'

Bode put his finger on the trigger.

'Not on my watch.'

He aimed center mass and fired four times.

The doctor's assistant screamed—'Aah!'—and grabbed at her heart when she entered the clinic. She recoiled from the rattlesnake hanging by the door.

'Where did this *serpiente* come from?'

'Inez,' Jesse said, 'this is *Señora* Byrne. She killed the snake, with a shovel. She is a very skilled snake-killer. And nurse. She will be working with us. She is Irish.'

Inez Quintanilla was a pretty young Latina about Becca's age. She wore too much make-up and perfume, she smacked her gum, and she seemed amused. She regarded the snake and then Lindsay.

'Why?'

'I didn't want the snake to hurt the children.'

Lindsay spoke in her Irish accent.

'No. Why does an Anglo want to work here, in the *colonias*?'

'I want to care for the people.'

Now Inez was more than amused.

'No one cares about us.'

Inez maintained eye contact with Lindsay for a long moment then dropped her eyes to Lindsay's pink Crocs.

'I like your shoes.'

They rode the horses down to the barefooted girl. Bode, Jim Bob, and Hank dismounted; Manuel held the reins. The girl sobbed hysterically on the ground and spoke fast in Spanish.

'*¡No me mate! ¡No me mate!*'

'You killed them, Governor,' Hank said.

Hank kicked the three men just to make sure they were dead. They were. The first one had a hole the size of a fist in his chest. The second one had returned fire, but they were out of range for his handgun; Bode had shot him in the chest as well. The third one had cut and run; Bode had shot him in the back. Twice. The blue grama grass turned red with the men's blood.

'Mexicans,' Hank said. 'Check out those tattoos. Gotta be a drug gang.'

'What the hell are they doing out here?'

'Ask her,' Jim Bob said.

'Like I know Spanish.' Bode turned to Manuel to get him to translate. 'Manuel—'

Manuel dropped the reins to their horses. He stared down at the dead bodies. When he looked back up at Bode, his expression had changed. In a quick movement, he yanked his reins then kicked his horse and galloped away as if the Border Patrol were chasing him.

'Manuel!'

Bode turned back.

'Think he knows something we don't?' Jim Bob said.

Bode pulled his Colt six-shooter and scanned the valley. There might be a more desolate place on the planet, but you'd have to search for it.

'Keep an eye out, Hank.'

Hank drew his handgun. Bode squatted next to the girl and touched her shoulder. She now turned her face to him. She was in fact just a kid.

'*¿Más hombres?*'

She shook her head.

'*No. No más.*'

'What's your name?' Her face was blank. '*¿Nombre?*'

'Josefina.'

Bode had exhausted his Spanish skills.

'What are you doing here?'

She shook her head again. '*No habla.*'

Bode tried to recall Lindsay's Spanish.

'*¿Qué . . . usted . . . aquí?*'

She jumped up and headed toward the tree line. She gestured for them to follow.

'*Vengan.*'

She led them into the trees and across a shallow spring creek and deep into a pine forest. Bode kept a keen eye out and his gun drawn, in case she was leading them into a trap. She wasn't. She led them into a clearing. They stopped and stared.

'Well, I'll be damned,' Jim Bob said.

Stretched out in front of them were neat rows of green leafy plants standing fifteen feet tall. Dozens of rows. Thousands of plants. A farm.

'Marijuana,' Hank said.

The girl nodded. '*Sí. Marihuana. Narcotraficantes.*' She called out, as if to the plants themselves: '*¡Salgan! ¡Ya estamos a salvo!*'

Brown faces slowly emerged from among the plants.

★ ★ ★

'Viagra?'

The doctor's assistant held up a carton of the medicine. Lindsay and Inez were unpacking the boxes El Diablo had brought the day before and stocking the shelves. Jesse was working at his desk on the other side of the clinic. He looked up with a smile.

'Erectile dysfunction, that is certainly not a problem in the *colonias*.'

'All this was donated?' Inez said.

'Yes. From, uh . . . from Houston.'

'That reporter, Kikki, she had the hots for you, Doctor.'

Lindsay glanced at Jesse; he shrugged innocently. Lindsay turned back; Inez had caught their interplay.

'So, *Señora*,' Inez said in a low voice, 'the wedding ring—you are married?'

'Yes.'

'That is a very unusual ring. May I look at it?'

Lindsay removed her wedding ring for the first time in twenty-two years. She placed it in Inez's open palm. The ring was one of a matched set handmade by James Avery in Kerrville, just up the road from the Bonner Ranch outside Comfort. The ring had two separate bands, one gold, one silver, with the ends twisted together to form a knot. A lovers' knot.

'It is beautiful,' Inez said. 'I dream of one day having such a ring. And a husband who will take me beyond the wall.'

She handed the ring back to Lindsay, reluctantly it seemed.

'So, *Señora*, why are you not with your husband?'

'We're separated.'

'But you still wear your wedding ring?'

'I'm still married.'

'Does the doctor know this?'

★ ★ ★

192

'We got an all-points bulletin out on Manuel Moreno,' DEA Agent Rey Gonzales said. 'He must've been the inside man on this operation. Mexican cartels, they're setting up these farms in isolated areas—national and state parks, Indian reservations, remote ranches—from here to California. They send men north to grow the dope here, so they don't have to smuggle it across the border. The men live on the land, tend the plants, harvest and ship to the dealers. Low overhead, high profits, so to speak.'

Hank had called in the Feds on the satellite phone. Federal agents from El Paso had arrived in helicopters and now swarmed the scene in black and blue windbreakers with white and yellow letters identifying their agencies: FBI . . . DEA . . . ICE . . . DHS. Federal Bureau of Investigation. Drug Enforcement Agency. Immigration and Customs Enforcement. Department of Homeland Security. Plus DPS troopers, Texas Rangers, and the Jeff Davis County sheriff. They interviewed the children, took photos and collected evidence, examined the dead men, chopped and stacked the plants, and gathered a cache of high-powered weapons.

'Americans think all this shit stays south of the river,' Agent Gonzales said. 'But the cartels, they're here now.'

'We should send the special forces into Mexico,' Jim Bob said. 'Kill the drug lords.'

Agent Gonzales shook his head. 'You kill one drug lord, another takes his place before the sun sets. Too much money to be made selling dope to the *gringos*. Last four years, we seized six thousand tons of dope coming across the river. But the DTOs—drug trafficking organizations—they shipped sixty thousand tons.'

'*Sixty thousand tons?*'

'Metric.'

'How?'

'How not? Trucks, trains, planes, automobiles, buses, boats, submarines, tunnels, ultralights . . . you name it, the DTOs do it. Even with all our interdiction efforts, they've got a ninety percent success rate.'

'Is the drone helping?'

'Border Patrol's grabbed a few immigrants with the drone, but the DTOs got radar tracking it, so the drone don't slow down their shipments.'

He waved a hand at the camp.

'Sophisticated operation—booby traps, tripwires, irrigation pipes running down from the spring, drip lines throughout the plants. Almost harvest time. The cartel won't be happy with you, Governor.'

'That I killed their men?'

'That you found their dope. Street boys like these, they're a dime a dozen in Mexico. But that'—he gestured at the agents cutting and stacking the plants—'that's two hundred million bucks fixin' to go up in smoke.'

'Two hundred million?' Jim Bob said.

Agent Gonzales nodded. 'I figure this grow site for a hundred acres in production, maybe fifty thousand plants. Commercial grade, from seed to harvest in four months. Each plant produces a pound of dope, each pound is worth four thousand dollars wholesale. Ninety-nine percent profit margin.'

'Money really does grow on trees,' Jim Bob said.

'Three times a year. And this is a small operation compared to the grow sites we busted out west. Last year, we eradicated four and a half million plants on federal lands. Do the math, that comes to eighteen billion dollars' worth of weed.'

'Should've been a dope farmer.'

'You and me both.'

'What about the children?' Bode said.

They had found twelve Mexican boys and the girl, Josefina.

'Abducted in border towns, brought up here to work the plants. The boys, they're ten, eleven, twelve years old. Been out here almost a year now.'

'What's going to happen to them?'

'ICE will take them into custody, try to locate their relatives.'

'And if they don't?'

Agent Gonzales turned his palms up and shrugged.

'How's the girl?'

'Not so good. She was their sex slave. The men raped her regularly. But the one you shot in the back, she said he came to the camp only a few weeks ago. He raped her twice a day. And beat her bad.' The agent's jaws clenched. 'She's only twelve. You did the world a favor, Governor, shooting those Mexicans full of holes.' The agent's face was stern and his skin brown. 'Americans want to smoke dope, figure it ain't hurting no one. But someone always gets hurt.'

A car horn interrupted them, and a black Hummer came crashing through the brush and over the creek and skidded to a stop. John Ed Johnson jumped out of the driver's seat and marched over, his head covered by a Stetson and his trouser legs tucked into tall boots, looking like LBJ himself pissed off at a congressman who had voted against him; Mandy followed behind, tiptoeing through the clearing in a dress and heels. John Ed arrived in a huff, glanced at the marijuana field, then addressed Agent Gonzales.

'These Mexicans growing dope on my land?'

'It was an inside job, Mr. Johnson. Your man Manuel.'

'*Manuel?*'

'He rode off,' Bode said. 'Heading south. Making a run for the border.'

John Ed seemed stunned. 'Manuel did this? To *me*?'

'We'll catch him,' Agent Gonzales said.

'Why the hell don't you people do your job and secure the goddamn border?'

Agent Gonzales held his ground.

'You want me to do my job, Mr. Johnson? Maybe I should check the immigration status of all the Mexicans working for you.'

'You do, and I'll have your job.'

'You don't want my job, Mr. Johnson.'

John Ed stomped off in search of another federal employee who might show more respect for a billionaire. Agent Gonzales shook his head.

'That says it all about our immigration policies.'

A WHUMP WHUMP WHUMP sound came from beyond the tree line and then over the trees came a half dozen helicopters, like a scene out of *Apocalypse Now*.

'Who the hell are they?' Agent Gonzales said.

'Network and cable TV,' Jim Bob said.

'Who called them?'

'I did.'

The DEA agent stared at Jim Bob as if he were nuts then walked off just as Mandy arrived and said, 'Shit.'

'What's wrong?'

She grabbed Bode's shoulder to steady herself then lifted her foot.

'I stepped in shit.'

Bode turned to his political strategist but pointed up at the helicopters.

'Why'd you call the media?'

'Because this is it.'

'This is what?'

'Your one big play. Your game changer. You wanted it—you got it.'

'What the hell are you talking about?'

The Professor aimed a finger in the direction of the three men Bode had killed.

'Those dead Mexicans . . . they're your ticket to the White House.'

Jesse held the dead rattlesnake high as they entered the small café.

'Luis! Look what I have brought for you.'

Luis Escalera, the proprietor, came around from behind the bar.

'Jesse! *Mi amigo*. What have you there?'

Jesse gave the snake to Luis. He would fry the rattlesnake meat and make a fine belt from the skin. Jesse had brought his nurse into town on her first day for lunch at his favorite café, a small colorful place with good food and a large television on the wall above the bar showing the Houston Astros baseball game on cable. They sat at a table near the bar. Pancho lay at their feet.

'This afternoon,' Jesse said, 'I will take you around the *colonia* and introduce you to the residents. And perhaps this evening you would like to go to a restaurant, a place with music?' He lowered his voice. 'We will leave Pancho at home.'

She smiled, and it was a nice smile.

'I would like that.'

The governor's wife gazed at him from across the table, but Jesse saw the governor's face. On the TV behind her.

'Look.'

She turned in her chair to see the screen. 'Breaking News' ran below the image of the governor standing in front of a clump of microphones and surrounded by Latino children. Lindsay stood and walked over to the bar. Jesse followed.

'Luis, please turn up the volume.'

Luis did, and they heard the governor speaking.

'I was sighting in a feral hog from up on that ridge when a young girl ran from this tree line, chased by three men on dirt bikes. I could see through the scope that she was just a kid. They ran her down, slapped her, pointed guns at her. I figured they were gonna kill her, so I shot them before they could shoot her.'

'He shot someone?' the governor's wife said.

The camera caught three other people standing off to one side of the governor: a bald pudgy man, a big Texas Ranger, and a young blonde woman. She was very pretty. The governor's wife pointed at the woman's image on the screen.

'That's Mandy. He's having an affair with her.'

Mandy Morgan gazed upon the governor of Texas. She had loved Bode Bonner from the first moment she had met him, in his office the day she hired on. He was tall, he was handsome, and he was twenty years older than her. All of her affairs had been with older men.

Was she seeking a father figure, as her therapist had suggested?

Her father had died when she was only seven. He was not there when she was crowned homecoming queen or prom queen. He was not there when she graduated high school or college. He would not be there to give her away at her wedding. She could not remember a father's love or his arms around her.

She felt safe in Bode Bonner's arms.

She loved him, and he loved her. He hadn't said it, but she knew it. She wanted to be his wife, but he had a wife. But his wife had moved out of their bedroom, so Mandy had moved in—at least when his wife was out of town or they were. The governor's wife refused him sex, so she had stepped in to give the governor what he needed. She thought of it as her civic duty.

The satellite phone she was holding rang. She answered.

'This is the governor's wife. Put Bode on.'

'Mrs. Bonner, he's giving a press conference. I'll have him call you back.'

'I'll hold.'

'Yes, ma'am.'

Lindsay covered the phone with her hand.

'*Ma'am*. She calls me ma'am, like I'm old enough to be her mother.' Lindsay sighed. 'Maybe I am.'

She turned back to the television. 'DEA Agent Gonzales' now spoke into the microphones.

'These dead Mexicans, they were just teenagers, throwaways south of the border. The cartels recruit them off the streets because they've got nowhere else to go, train them as smugglers and assassins. No one's gonna miss these boys.'

The camera captured close-up images of three bodies spread out on the ground like dead gunslingers in those old Western photos. They were young, with tattoos on their arms. The camera panned slowly over their vacant faces. The last face seemed vaguely familiar, as did the *LM* tattoo in fancy script on his left arm. Lindsay pointed at the screen.

'Oh, my God! Jesse, is that—'

Jesús.

Enrique de la Garza reached up to the big television screen on the wall of his Nuevo Laredo office and gently touched his dead son's image. He had sent his first-born son to *Tejas* to become a man—but not a dead man. Not a man shot down like an animal in a big-game hunt by the governor of Texas. To be stuffed and displayed on a wall. No, that was not what he had intended when he sent his son across the Río Bravo del Norte. Yet . . . there his son lay. Dead. Shot in the back. Twice. Like an animal. By the governor of Texas. Whose Anglo image now filled the screen. Who smiled broadly and held the rifle that he had used to murder Enrique's son. Who stood over the dead body of Jesús de la Garza for the cameras like a proud hunter showing off his trophy kill.

'I would very much like him dead,' Enrique said.

Hector Garcia rose from the sofa and came over to Enrique.

'You want to kill the governor of Texas?'

'Yes. Very much.'

'But, *jefe*, we have never before killed an American politician.'

'We have killed Mexican politicians. We have dispensed justice to corrupt mayors, governors, police chiefs, *federales* . . . Why can we not kill an American governor? Why can we not dispense justice north of the river?'

'Oh, we can kill him. That will be easy. But the *gringos*, they will send troops to the border. They will seek *venganza*. They will demand justice.'

'It is I who seek revenge. It is I who demand justice. They killed my wife, Hector, but I did not seek revenge then because it was a mistake. I did not kill the *gringos* then because that would not have been justice. But this . . . this was no mistake. He murdered my son.'

Enrique de la Garza now addressed the governor of Texas on the television.

'You murder my son, but I am not to seek revenge? The Muslims, they murdered your sons and daughters on nine/eleven, and you sought revenge. You invaded their countries and killed tens of thousands of their sons and daughters, brothers and sisters, mothers and fathers, spilling innocent blood to quench your thirst for revenge. Oh, but you are the Americans. You are the righteous avengers. The holy Anglos. They were only the unholy Muslims, and I am only the stupid *Mexicano* who feels not the sun on my back or the pain in my heart. Who is a manual laborer but not a man. Whose son's life is not worthy of revenge. Who does not deserve justice.

'Is that what you think, Governor?'

He stepped over to the wall rack and removed his prized machete. He returned and raised the blade to the governor's image on the screen.

'Am I not a father? Do I not love my son? Are your sons worthier of revenge and justice than mine? Because I am Mexican and not American? Because my skin is brown and not white? Because I speak Spanish and not English? Because I live south of the river and not north?

'Is that what you think, Governor?'

Enrique de la Garza, Mexican, father, dispenser of justice in Nuevo Laredo, and now seeker of *venganza*—the man known to the world as El Diablo, head of the notorious Los

Muertos drug cartel—said only two more words to Hector
Garcia.

'Kill him.'

· ·

Chapter 13

'Mandy! These kids are running around the mansion like
they're at a goddamned McDonald's.'

'Bo-*de*,' Mandy said, her face contorted in that familiar
pretend frown. 'Don't talk like that in front of the kids.'

The Mexican children had brought out the mother in
Mandy. She was prepping them for the cameras, smoothing
the boys' hair and fixing their clothes, wiping syrup from
their pancake breakfast off their faces, and generally having
one hell of a time corralling the kids into their positions on
the floor around Bode. She bribed them with donuts.

It was just after seven the following Monday morning,
and Bode Bonner sat on a stool in the living room of the
family quarters in the Governor's Mansion surrounded
by the thirteen kids. The last forty-eight hours had been
a whirlwind. They had remained in West Texas Saturday
night. Bode gave statements at the scene that ran on the
network evening news and cable outlets. With the majestic
Davis Mountains as the backdrop and the governor of Texas

holding a high-powered rifle and standing over three dead Mexicans—political candidates always established their manly *bona fides* by taking reporters on hunting trips, but they only shot ducks—his first national media exposure had garnered the Professor's approval.

'Hell of an introduction to America,' Jim Bob had said.

They wrapped up their post-shooting interviews at the scene with the FBI and the DEA and the Texas Rangers and even the Jeff Davis County sheriff, a good ol' boy named Roscoe Lee whose county morgue now held the three Mexican *hombres* on ice. The on-the-ground ruling was 'defense of a third person'; the killings had been justified in order to save another person's life, being little Josefina. No criminal charges would be filed against the governor of Texas. Point a gun at another human being and pull the trigger, and you're either a murderer or a hero. It's a fine line.

Bode Bonner was on the hero side of the line.

After the interviews, they transported the children back to John Ed's lodge in the Hummer like school kids on a class outing. Mandy the *madre* sat them around the big dining room table, and Rosita fed them beef tacos, refried beans, and guacamole. They ate as if they hadn't eaten in months—until federal agents with 'ICE' in bold white letters on black jackets and big guns on their hips arrived to take them into custody pending deportation. The kids—like every Mexican—knew ICE meant *Inmigración*, so the appearance of the agents threw them into a frenzy. They screamed—

'*¡Corren!*'

—then tossed their tacos at the agents and bolted from the dining room table and scattered about the lodge looking for hiding places; Bode later found little Josefina curled up in a small cabinet beneath a bathroom sink. He had tried to get the ICE agents to calm down, but refried beans and guacamole splattered across their black jackets didn't sit well with the Feds.

'We're taking these Mexicans into custody!'

Bode got in the head ICE-hole's face.

'The hell you are! I found them! They're in Texas—and I'm the goddamned governor of Texas!'

'I don't care if you're the fucking king of Canada! Those kids are coming with us!'

'Prime minister,' the Professor said. 'Canada has a prime minister, not a king.'

The ICE agent gave Jim Bob a 'fuck you' look then said to Bode, 'These kids belong to the federal government.'

'The hell they do,' Bode said.

Governors of the fifty states hate natural disasters like hurricanes and tornadoes and wildfires that tear a swath of destruction across the land, and man-made disasters like an offshore oil rig blowout that dumps millions of barrels of oil into pristine waters, and Wall Street gamblers who play high-risk games with the world's economy and lose, busting state budgets in the process; but they reserve their highest degree of hatred for the most arrogant, self-righteous, and overbearing bastards to walk God's green earth.

'Fucking Feds,' Bode said.

Texas Governor Bode Bonner and Texas Ranger Hank Williams put their big bodies between the Feds and the kids. They remained in a Mexican stand-off until Jim Bob made a few calls to Washington. The secretary of the Department of Homeland Security worked for a politician, so she sided with politics. The last thing her Democratic president (who wanted Latino votes in the next election) needed was thirteen Mexican kids shown on the national news being perp-walked out of the lodge like criminals by ICE agents under her command. She ordered the agents to stand down. They weren't pleased, particularly when Bode gave the head agent a parting, 'Fuck you and the horse you rode in on.' ICE departed in defeat, Bode, Jim Bob, and Hank shared high-fives all around, and Rosita and Pedro searched the lodge calling out to the kids in Spanish: 'Please come out, children. ICE is not going to take you away. The governor is going to take you on the airplane to Austin. You will live in the Governor's Mansion. *La mansión del gobernador de Tejas.*'

Legal custody of thirteen Mexican children was now vested in the governor of Texas.

The Professor's idea. He said the political lesson learned from Kennedy was that if you surround a handsome politician with cute children the voting public will form a favorable impression of him even if he's screwing Marilyn Monroe on the side. The man didn't have a Ph.D. in politics for nothing. So they had all flown back to Austin Sunday morning in the Gulfstream. They put the kids in the spare bedrooms in the mansion, but the boys kept running outside to pee on the south lawn. Turns out, they had never before used an indoor bathroom. Bode gave them a Toilet 101 lesson; fortunately, there were no bidets in the mansion. Once the boys discovered the kitchen—'*¡Cocina interior!*'—and learned that the chef would cook whatever they wanted upon request, they had eaten around the clock while watching Mexican *fútbol* on cable. Mandy signed on as camp counselor, and Lupe adopted them like the children she never had. They laughed and smiled and seemed like normal kids who didn't speak English, not kids who had been held captive for a year on a remote marijuana farm in West Texas.

Except Josefina. She did not laugh or smile.

They were now scrubbed clean and sporting new clothes from the Gap. Mandy and Hank had taken them shopping the day before and charged $3,000 on the campaign credit card. But the kids would look nice on national TV. Because the governor of Texas was about to do what you do in America when you win the lottery or lose a reality show or claim a politician sexually harassed you or get banned from the prom for being a same-sex couple or kill three bad-ass *hombres* in West Texas: you go on television and tell the nation how you 'feel,' that being critical information all of America needed to know before breakfast—along with that Kardashian girl's latest love fiasco, of course. Bode had always experienced the urge to puke his oatmeal at the pathetic people parading their emotions on the network morning shows, desperate for their fifteen minutes.

Now he was about to join the parade.

The local station's producer came over and said, 'George is wrapping up his interview with the couple that got kicked off *Dancing with the Stars* last night. You're up next.' He sized Bode up then turned and shouted, 'Make-up!' Back to Bode: 'New York will run a setup piece then you'll go live with George.'

The make-up lady arrived and gave Bode a once-over through her red reading glasses. She patted a powdery pad on his forehead.

'That'll keep the glare down. Not much I can do about the hair.'

Lupe had brushed and sprayed his hair to perfection that morning. The make-up lady stepped away, leaving Bode to stare at Jim Bob in the corner fiddling with his phone. Texting. Twitting. Tweetering. Whatever. Immediately after the shooting on Saturday, the Professor had commenced orchestrating a nonstop media blitz for the coming week. The shooting had made front-page headlines in every major newspaper in the country on Sunday—they called him an 'American Hero'—and the mansion switchboard had been overloaded with calls from media outlets across the country and around the world. Everyone wanted a piece of Bode Bonner. Jim Bob Burnet held the hottest news story in America in his hands, and he was using it to Bode's best advantage—because in the 24/7 news cycle that was life in America today, anyone could become someone in twenty-four hours.

Bode Bonner was now someone.

Jim Bob stepped over to Bode with the phone held high and said, 'You got over two hundred thousand followers now, more than Romney. Course, he's a Mormon. How exciting could his life be? Oh, you made the nationals.'

'I did?'

'You did. The Rasmussen tracking poll puts you at ten percent among Republican voters, Gallup at twelve. You're in the game now, Bode. America saw you for the first time this weekend and they liked what they saw—a rugged, hand-some, action-hero.'

He paused as if pondering the mysteries of the universe.

'What are the odds? We go out to John Ed's ranch that day, we're on that ridge and you're already sighted in at the exact moment the girl tries to escape—right place, right time, right gun. If I were a religious man, I'd say it was God's will. But I'm not, so I'd say you are one lucky SOB. And one thing I've learned from gambling in Vegas—when you're on a lucky streak, don't quit.'

'Ride the wave.'

'All the way to the White House. The "Bode Bonner for

President" campaign starts right now. I've plotted out a media tour for the next seven days, starting with the network morning shows. After that, we fly back out to John Ed's ranch for the *60 Minutes* profile. Tomorrow we fly to L.A., then Chicago, New York, and wrap up the week in D.C. on *Fox News Sunday*. One week from today, you'll be the presumptive Republican candidate for the presidency of the United States of America. If you don't fuck it up.'

'How?'

'By saying something stupid on national TV.'

'No. How will I be the Republican presidential candidate in one week?'

'Because you're fixing to catch the biggest wave in politics since Reagan in eighty. He was bigger than life, and you're about to be. This is a game changer, Bode. The sort of thing that can put a Texan back in the White House.'

'How do you know?'

'Because this is what I do.'

What he did was make Bode give up the Armani suits. 'Italian suits and French cuffs won't sell in Iowa and New Hampshire.' So the governor of Texas was wearing a starched, buttoned-down, long-sleeved, pearl-white shirt with the athletic cut to accentuate his impressive physique, jeans, a black cowboy belt with a sterling silver Great Seal of Texas buckle, and black cowboy boots. The Professor was frowning.

'Did Lupe spray your hair this morning?'

'Of course.'

'Well, don't do it anymore. Man using hair spray evokes vanity and femininity. Voters don't want their president to be vain or their commander-in-chief to have a feminine side.'

'You never complained before.'

'You never had a chance to be president before.'

His eyes hadn't left Bode's hair, and the frown hadn't left his face. He reached his hand up with his fingers spread wide to Bode's head—but he froze in midair.

'Where's Mandy?'

Bode nodded toward the back corner where Mandy stood with little Josefina, whose arms were wrapped tightly around herself. She was only twelve and slight of build and looked more like a skinny boy than a girl. When Mandy reached out to touch her shoulder, she recoiled. Jim Bob called out to Bode's aide and mistress.

'Mandy!'

She broke away from Josefina and arrived with a frown.

'Josefina's terrified of being touched by anyone. We need to get her a therapist. I'll ask mine if he counsels children.'

'You have a therapist?'

She shrugged a yes. 'I'm taking the kids to the pediatrician this afternoon,' she said.

'Check their eyesight. A couple of the boys sit two feet from the TV. And take them to the dentist, their teeth are terrible. Take Lupe to translate.'

'Can I use the campaign credit card?'

'Sure.'

The Professor's eyes had returned to Bode's head.

'Mandy, run your fingers through Bode's hair.'

She eyed his hair then Jim Bob.

'But his hair looks perfect.'

'Exactly.'

She shrugged and stepped close enough to Bode that he could inhale her scent. He felt a stirring, then he felt guilty. His wife knew about his mistress, but he still felt guilty. His mistress ran her fingers through his hair. Jim Bob observed the result in his professorial mode.

'Again.'

She repeated the maneuver. This time Bode felt strands of hair fall onto his forehead. Jim Bob framed Bode's face with his fingers.

'Audience for these morning shows is female, so you've got to appeal to women. Mandy, look at this man. As a woman—and God knows, you are a woman—do you want this man?'

'Every day. Every time I see him. In fact, right now. God, I love it when he wears those tight jeans.'

Her face flushed as her body temperature spiked, and she licked her red lips then took a step toward Bode as if to embrace him.

'Downshift your engine, girl,' Jim Bob said. 'We got cameras in the room.'

'Oh . . . yeah.'

She blew out a breath and shook her head at the opportunity lost then returned to the kids. Bode and Jim Bob looked after her—her firm bottom encased in the tight form-fitting knit dress—and Jim Bob said, 'Naturally horizontal.'

'We're live in ten seconds!' the TV producer said. 'Children, quiet down.'

They were chattering *muy rápido* in Spanish.

'I feel like I'm at a bullfight in Juarez,' Jim Bob said.

'Mandy, give them some more donuts.'

She passed out donuts, and the kids quieted down. Jim Bob went back to the corner, and Josefina took her place at Bode's feet.

'We're live!' the producer said.

On the monitor, Bode saw the anchor in New York addressing the camera.

'As all of America knows by now, this past Saturday Texas

210

Governor Bode Bonner went on what he thought would be just another hunting trip on an isolated game ranch in the desolate Davis Mountains of West Texas—but unbeknownst to him, he was about to stumble upon a scene straight out of an action movie.'

The setup piece played on the monitor, a rehash of the shooting with video of the ranch and the valley where he had shot the Mexicans, the dead bodies splayed on the ground, and the children looking filthy and pitiful in ragged clothes at the marijuana camp. The video lingered a long moment on Bode surrounded by the kids almost clinging to him, and then the screen switched to Bode surrounded by the kids in the living room of the Governor's Mansion.

'Now, live from Austin, Texas, we're joined by Governor Bode Bonner and the children he rescued. Welcome, Governor.'

Bode tousled the hair of the nearest boy—he thought that'd be a nice touch on national TV—then smiled into the camera and said, 'Morning, George.'

'Governor, you look like you're having fun.'

'Oh, we've kind of adopted the kids here at the mansion, fixing them pancakes in the kitchen this morning, playing out on the lawn . . . and, boy, they love cable TV. And donuts. Like Carlos here.'

He patted the boy's head again; the boy looked up and said, '*Soy* Miguel.'

'Oh, Miguel. Sorry.' To the camera: 'Thirteen kids, I haven't gotten their names down yet.'

George laughed. 'You know, Governor, I knew very little about you before this weekend, and all I had seen of you was a tough-talking, tea party Texan. But we're seeing a different side of you.'

'I'm the governor, George, but I'm also a father. I can only imagine how much these kids' folks back home are worrying about them. We're working fast to get them back to their mamas in Mexico.'

Bode's usual public voice was not twangy like a country singer or Deep South like the Mississippi governor, but just a soft drawl—of course, since Bush a Texas drawl had not proved popular anywhere but Texas.

The smallest boy turned to Bode and said, '¿*Mi madre?*'

'Your mama's fine, Flaco.'

'*Yo soy* Rubén.'

'Governor, you're a staunch opponent of illegal immigration, yet you risked your life to save those Mexican children. Why?'

'Saving these kids wasn't about being a politician, George, it was about being a man. I wasn't about to let those cartel thugs kill little Josefina here.'

Now it was time for the big question of the morning.

'Governor, when you shot those men, how did you feel?'

'Pretty damn good. They were dead and she wasn't.'

Josefina turned her sweet face to him as if on cue and said, '*Es el hombre.*'

'You're the man, Governor,' George said.

The scene was replayed on the other network morning shows. Little Josefina even repeated her '*el hombre*' line without prompting. On national TV. He needed to put her on the campaign payroll.

Two hundred thirty-five miles south, Jesse Rincón watched the governor's wife pack her black satchel with medicine and supplies and hard candy. He looked back down at the Laredo newspaper spread across his desk. On the front page was a photo of the governor surrounded by the Mexican children he had rescued from the marijuana farm. Jesse read about the governor then again looked up at the governor's wife. Three days she had been in his life. To see her, to breathe her in, to begin and end each day with her—she had brought hope back to him. Hope for love in his life. But she was married to the governor of Texas.

'El Diablo, he will not be happy with your husband.'

'Now he knows how I feel.'

They kept their voices low so Inez at her desk could not hear them.

'You do not understand. He will seek *venganza*. Revenge.'

'Against the governor of Texas?'

'They kill governors in Mexico every day.'

'But this is America.'

'Mexico or America, it is just a little river cutting through the land. El Diablo will not be deterred by such formalities.'

'But that probably wasn't the same boy.'

'No. That probably was not his son. But that was his marijuana.'

Lindsay Bonner finished packing her satchel for her morning rounds. The residents did not want to bother the doctor with minor injuries and illnesses, so the Anglo nurse would make house calls in *Colonia Ángeles*.

It was her third day on the job.

They had worked over the weekend. They had eaten out Saturday evening and in Sunday evening. They had sat on the back porch overlooking the river both nights, and Jesse had told her stories of the borderlands. They had watched the news reports about the governor of Texas killing the three men in West Texas. No mention was made that one of the men might have been the son of the most notorious drug

213

lord in Nuevo Laredo. The man had a Los Muertos tattoo on his left arm, just as El Diablo's son had; but so did the other two dead men, and so did thousands of other young men in Nuevo Laredo. The man's face had bloated after lying dead for hours in the hot sun, so she and Jesse hadn't been able to make a positive identification from the image they had seen on television or in the paper. But she had called Bode and warned him just the same; he was unfaithful, he was ambitious, he was a politician, but he was still her husband.

He had laughed it off.

She had put it out of her mind. What were the odds that the boy they had saved was the same man Bode had killed? What would El Diablo's son—the son of a billionaire drug lord in Nuevo Laredo—be doing at a marijuana farm on a remote ranch in West Texas? And even if he were the son of El Diablo, what could his father do? Bode Bonner was the governor of Texas, not a local politician in a small Mexican village. He lived in the Governor's Mansion in Austin behind a tall fence. He had a 24/7 security detail of Texas Rangers. He was safe.

But still . . .

The clinic door opened, and a pretty young woman and a burly man holding a video camera on his shoulder entered. Lindsay turned her back to them and pushed the wide-brimmed hat down on her head. Inez greeted the guests. She had dressed in her best clothes and done her hair and overdone her make-up. She hoped to be discovered and taken beyond the wall, like Cinderella of the *colonias*. She was a pretty girl, but not that pretty. She came over to Lindsay and Jesse.

'Doctor, she is Gaby Gomez, with the San Antonio TV station. They are here to tape your interview.'

214

A Houston newspaper had run a story about *Colonia Ángeles* that past Sunday, which had caught the attention of the San Antonio station. They had called Jesse at home and requested an interview, a human interest story for their morning show the following Sunday. Jesse agreed only because it would bring checks for the *colonias*.

'It is so exciting,' Inez said. 'The doctor, he is famous.'

'Perhaps in a few poor counties along the border, Inez.'

'I hope to be famous one day.'

The poor thing.

'They said it is a "day in the life of" profile,' Inez said. 'They will follow you around all day.'

'Guess I'll be gone all day,' Lindsay said.

She put two bottled waters and two granola bars in her satchel.

'Can I go with you?' Inez said.

'You want to come with me on my rounds?'

'Not with you, *Señora*. With the doctor and the cameras.'

'Pancho!' Jesse said.

The dog rose from his position by the front door and trotted over.

'He will go with you.'

Lindsay patted the dog's head and said, 'You want to go on rounds with me?'

Inez watched as the nurse threw the black satchel over her shoulder and slipped out the back door followed by Pancho. She turned back to the doctor.

'The *señora*, she is shy with the cameras.'

'Bode, you need a wife to win the White House.'

'I know.'

'It's a package deal. Voters size up the first lady candidates

215

as much as the presidential candidates. You've got to get her back.'

'I know . . . I just don't know how.'

It was just before noon, and Bode and Jim Bob were strapped into their seats aboard the governor's jet for the final approach to John Ed Johnson's private airstrip. Ranger Hank was again up front with the pilots. Mandy had stayed behind to play camp counselor at the mansion. Jim Bob fiddled with that fucking phone again.

'Your Twitter followers exploded after the morning shows. Over half a million now.'

Bode responded with a grunt.

'Now, listen, Bode, whatever you do, don't talk politics with this reporter.'

'Why not? It's an opportunity to share my political views with the American people.'

'It's an opportunity to screw up on national TV. We've got to find out how the shooting went down with the Independent voters first.'

'Why?'

'Because they're the swing votes. In a national election, the Independents decide who wins. So no politics until I get the poll results in.'

'You're the boss, Professor.'

'We'll meet the production crew at John Ed's lodge. They flew into El Paso from New York last night and were driving out this morning.'

'Why didn't they fly into Austin and out with us?'

'And have all of America see you flying in a private jet on *60 Minutes* when twenty million people are out of work?'

The Professor didn't have a Ph.D. in politics for nothing.

★ ★ ★

Back in the Governor's Mansion, Mandy Morgan walked into Jolene Curtis' office and shut the door behind her. Jo looked up. Mandy aimed a manicured finger at her.

'You stay away from Bode. He's mine.'

Jo smiled. She was very pretty. Which meant there was one too many pretty young women in the Governor's Mansion.

'He's married,' Jo said.

'Not for long.'

'And you figure you can keep him from straying again?'

'I can keep him . . . and I can get you fired. Which won't look good on your résumé. Which means you get to go back to pole dancing.'

Mandy opened the door then turned back.

'I want you gone by the time we get back from the media tour.'

Mandy left Jolene with a look of shock on her very pretty face.

Lindsay Bonner ducked her face against the dust blown by the dry wind and her nose from the foul smell of the river. The stench was savage when the wind blew from the south, and the wind always blew from the south. For an hour now, she had walked the narrow dirt roads accompanied by Pancho. She was the Anglo nurse, not the glamorous governor's wife. She wore a loose blue peasant dress under a white lab coat, the pink Crocs, a yellow scarf, and the wide-brimmed hat.

'*Hola*,' she said to each woman and child she encountered. They washed and cooked and played outside their residences. Life in the *colonias* was lived out of doors. 'I am the doctor's new nurse,' she said in Spanish. 'Are you ill? Are your children sick?'

'No, no,' was the standard response.

She introduced herself and said she would make rounds each day and would be available at the clinic as well. She urged them to come to the clinic if they or their children fell ill or developed sores or suffered injuries. She knew it would take time for them to trust her. But she wasn't going anywhere.

'*Señor gobernador*, it is very good to see you back again.'

John Ed Johnson had wired $25 million to the 'Bode Bonner Reelection Campaign' that morning as he had promised then had flown up to the Panhandle to buy more water rights, so Pedro greeted them at the lodge.

'Been pretty exciting around here the last few days.'

'*Sí. Mucho conmoción*. The cameras, they are here.'

Pedro grabbed their gear and led them inside. Jim Bob leaned into Bode.

'Okay, here's the deal. I negotiated an exclusive interview in exchange for another interview when your book comes out.'

'What book?'

'Your memoir.'

'What memoir?'

'The one I'm negotiating with publishers for right now. Every presidential candidate writes a book these days—Obama, Palin, Paul, Gingrich, Cain, even Bachmann . . . it's a campaign tool. Course, you've got to donate the money to charity.'

'I don't want to.'

'Give the money to charity?'

'Write a book.'

'You don't have to. I'm going to write it. I'm thinking about calling it. *Take This Government and Shove It*.'

'That has a nice ring to it.'

'By the time I'm through with your memoirs, you'll be a regular Teddy Roosevelt.'

'He was crippled.'

'That'd be Franklin.'

'Oh.'

Jim Bob Burnet sighed. The boy got hit in the head on the football field one too many times for his own good. But, it wasn't as if political success required a genius intellect. In fact, smarts often proved an impediment to a political career, Obama being Exhibit A that you can be too damn smart to be a good president. You don't want to over-think the job. Which was not a worry with Bode Bonner.

'*Buenos días*,' Lindsay Bonner said to the children gathered around a chicken as if considering how to pluck it and cook it for lunch. The children and the chicken instinctively withdrew from the Anglo nurse. She reached into the satchel and found the hard candies. She squatted and opened her hand to reveal the colorful candies. The children eyed them then debated with each other. She unwrapped a candy, put it in her mouth, and made a yummy sound, as if trying to get little Becca to eat pureed squash. At least the sweet dispelled the taste of dirt. She held the candies out to the children. One little girl in a ratty red dress stepped forward bravely and snatched a piece. She put the candy in her mouth and smiled broadly.

'*Dulce.*'

Sweet.

The others now stepped forward and took the candy. They did not withdraw. They gathered around her and petted Pancho. They smelled worse than the dog; they either bathed in the river or didn't bathe. Their hair appeared not to have been brushed in months; their faces were dirty and their feet bare. Open sores spotted their arms and legs. She reached into her satchel and pulled out a pair of latex gloves. She put them on then found the antibiotic cream and the 'Dora the Explorer' Band-Aids.

'This will help your sores,' she said in Spanish.

She squirted the antibiotic on a Band-Aid and applied it over one child's sore. The girl examined Dora and smiled.

'*Es chula.*'

'Yes, she is cute.'

Lindsay soon had applied a half dozen Band-Aids to each child. Their mothers had come to see what the Anglo nurse was doing to their children. They had been suspicious at first, but now they were smiling. Several of the women were pregnant, so Lindsay discussed their prenatal care and recorded their names and expected due dates in her journal. Inez kept a notebook with medical histories of every patient. She now sat at an old picnic table with half a dozen Mexican women discussing their medical issues and drinking Kool-Aid from tall plastic fast-food glasses—even the clean water didn't taste clean, so they made Kool-Aid to mask the taste—as if they were suburban stay-at-home moms drinking mochas at a Starbucks. She had decided not to focus on the living conditions in the *colonia* but instead on the living. She was here for the people. She was here to make a difference in their lives. And in her life.

She heard a scream from down by the river.

'Governor, that's a long shot.'

The network folks wanted to retrace Bode's every step that day, so they had driven out to the scene in John Ed's

Hummer. Bode sat perched on the same ridge with a camera focused on him. Jim Bob and Ranger Hank stood behind the camera. The female reporter sat next to him, close enough for him to catch the scent of her perfume. She was a good-looking broad with a twinkle in her blue eyes and her blond hair blowing in the breeze like she didn't give a damn. Like she'd be fun on a camping trip on a cold night, building a fire, eating meat seared on a stick, drinking a few shots of bourbon, then climbing into a double-wide sleeping bag and—

'You must have a really big one.'

'What?'

'Your rifle. It must be big.'

'Oh. Yeah. It's a big rifle all right.'

He unpacked the big rifle, loaded a cartridge, and sighted in through the scope. Down below, the valley was vacant. The FBI, ICE, DEA, DPS, Texas Rangers, and Border Patrol had collected the evidence, removed the bodies, cut and burned the marijuana, and cleared out. Only a feral hog rooting around showed any signs of life in the valley. But not for long. The camera was running when Bode put the cross hairs on the hog's head and pulled the trigger.

BOOM.

'Oh, my God, that's so loud!' the reporter said, sounding girlish in a sexy way. 'Did you hit the hog?'

Bode snorted. 'Of course I hit the hog.'

They drove the Hummer down past the dead hog and to the marijuana farm. The reporter set up the camera angle then gave an intro: 'I'm standing in the desolate but starkly beautiful Davis Mountains of West Texas with Bode Bonner, the swaggering former college football star and'—a coy smile—'the charming governor of Texas.'

221

She and the camera turned to him.

'So, Governor, the cowboy image isn't just an image?'

He wore the same jeans from that morning, but he had changed into a denim shirt and old work boots. He didn't want to clean crap off his handmade boots.

'I've been a cowboy all my life.'

'I like cowboys.'

'Do you now?'

Bode couldn't tell whether she was flirting with him or setting him up, but being male he naturally sided with flirting.

'Those poor children, living out here for a year. And the girl, getting raped and beaten.'

Bode thought, *Here it comes*.

'Governor, how did you feel when you shot those men?'

'Pretty damn good. They were dead, and she was alive.'

'Governor, it seems incredible that a Mexican drug cartel could operate a huge marijuana farm right here in Texas.'

'They're not just here in Texas. The cartels are everywhere in America now. The drugs are here, and the violence is coming. We're outmanned and outgunned. The GAO says we have operational control over less than half of the border. That's like saying the NYPD has control over only half of New York City—how safe would that make you feel?'

'How do we stop them?'

'Secure the border.'

'But the president went to El Paso just three months ago—he said the border is secure.'

'We're standing a hundred seventy-five miles east of El Paso and eighty miles north of the Rio Grande in a marijuana farm operated by a Mexican drug cartel for the last year—that seem secure to you?'

222

'Governor, you're not worried that the cartel might seek revenge?'

'Against me? I'm the governor of Texas.' He stood tall and aimed a finger at Ranger Hank. 'They'd have to come through that big Ranger to get to me, and then they'd find out that I'm not much fun in a fight.'

The reporter's eyes twinkled.

'Governor, the tea party sees this incident as supporting their anti-immigration position—do you agree?'

Bode stuck with Jim Bob's play.

'Look, I'm a politician, but everything I do isn't about politics. What I did out here two days ago wasn't about immigration policy—it was about little Josefina and those twelve boys. They didn't deserve to be abducted and held as slaves, whether they're Mexicans or Methodists. I'm the governor of Texas, and those cartel *hombres*, they were committing crimes in Texas. That made it my business, not my politics.'

Lindsay cradled the child and cried. She had heard a scream, and then a boy had come running to her. The nurse was needed at the river.

'¡*Apúrate!*'

She hurried. At the river, a small child lay next to the water. Blood drenched the dirt. Other children had gathered around. Lindsay slipped and stumbled and got muddy going down the low bluff to the river below. When she arrived at the child, she knew immediately that the child needed more than a nurse.

'¡*Llamen al doctor!*'

Get the doctor.

'That was a good line,' Jim Bob said. ' "My business, not my politics." '

They were back on the jet and drinking bourbon.

'I winged it.'

'Well, it worked this time. But don't do it again, okay? Makes me nervous.'

'You're the boss, Professor.'

Jim Bob drank his bourbon and felt the warmth inside him. Eight years he had begged the networks to interview Governor Bode Bonner; now they were begging him for interviews. It felt good, tables turning and all. It felt good to have a stud horse he could ride right through the front door of the White House. This was his chance to escape Karl Rove's shadow. To make his own shadow. To prove to his ex-wife that she should've stuck with him for better or for worse—because it was fixing to get a hell of a lot better for James Robert Burnet.

Jesse had taken the camera crew for a brief tour of *Colonia Ángeles*. They now stood at the farthest point from the river. The border wall was visible in the distance.

'We stand on land that America has abandoned in the drug and immigration war, a land that is neither here nor there, neither—'

A dog barked in the distance. Then he heard a boy's scream.

'¡*Doctor!*'

A boy ran toward them, trying to keep up with Pancho. They both arrived out of breath.

'Doctor,' the boy said in Spanish, 'we have been searching for you! Come quickly! To the river! The nurse, she needs you!'

Chapter 14

'How pathetic is that?' Jim Bob said.

The next morning at nine, Bode, Jim Bob, Mandy, Ranger Hank, and the thirteen Mexican children stood just inside the front entrance at the Austin-Bergstrom International Airport and stared at the mass of humanity waiting in line at the security checkpoint to be scanned, searched, patted down, felt up, and otherwise subjected to personal humiliation by employees of the Transportation Security Administration.

'Like sheep lining up to be slaughtered,' Jim Bob said. 'American citizens letting a government employee violate them, just because they're scared.'

'This is bullshit,' Bode said.

'*Caca de toro*,' Miguel said from behind Bode.

Not an exact translation, but close enough.

'It is indeed,' Jim Bob said. 'All a president has to do is promise to make these sheep safe and secure, and they'll hand over their constitutional rights. Just to fly on a plane.'

'Not that,' Bode said. 'That I've got to fly commercial, go through security like everyone else.'

'Oh. Yes, you do.'

'Why can't we take the state jet?'

'I told you, Bode, you can fly the Gulfstream all over Texas because Texans don't care. You're Republican, they're Republican, they're gonna vote for you no matter what. Democrats and Independents are irrelevant in Texas.'

His phone rang. He checked the caller ID—'MSNBC . . . as if'—then muted the ringer.

'But if you want to play politics on a national stage, we've got to change your game for a national audience. It's a different market. For some reason—mental illness, lack of education, bad parenting—not everyone in the other forty-nine states is Republican. So things that wouldn't raise an eyebrow in Texas go viral in other states.'

'What's that got to do with flying commercial?'

'Because that national audience got mad as hell when they saw Pelosi flying around the country on private jets at taxpayer expense and Boehner skirting the security lines at Reagan Airport. But Pelosi and Boehner did it anyway, because they're tone deaf to the people. Because they think they're better than the people. Bode Bonner doesn't.'

'I don't?'

'No. You don't. Bode Bonner is a populist, a man of the people. He flies commercial, he stands in the security line like everyone else, he goes through the scanner like everyone else, he gets felt up like everyone else . . .'

'He does?'

'He does.'

Bode sighed. 'Jim Bob, you sure about this?'

The Professor pointed at the security line.

'The path to the White House starts at the back of that line.'

'Are we at least flying first class?'

The Professor now regarded Bode as he would a D student.

'Hell, yes, we're flying first class. You and me. Mandy and the kids and Hank are back in coach. We'll go through security with this rabble, but we're sure as hell not sitting back in coach with them for four hours.'

But it was a long journey from where he now stood to a safe seat in first class. He had to go through security, walk down the terminal to the gate, loiter among the citizens for an hour, subject himself to possible verbal abuse—a Republican governor out among Democratic voters—and otherwise expose himself to enemy fire. This was his first public appearance since he had shot three Mexicans dead. How would the public react? More specifically, how would the liberals in Austin react? Would he again be greeted with 'You're a fucking Nazi!'? Would they toss the f-word and perhaps fast food at him? Would they shoot angry glares and middle fingers at him? And he couldn't exactly hide; he stood six feet four inches tall, and everyone in Texas knew Bode Bonner on sight.

'Jim Bob, you really think this is a good idea? This ain't Lubbock.'

'Trust me.'

Bode felt as if he were taking the field against Oklahoma—in Oklahoma. He took a deep breath and squared his shoulders.

'Let's do it.'

As soon as they took their place at the back of the security line, Bode knew why the Professor had earned a Ph.D. in politics. An obese woman smelling like McDonald's and wearing a stretch sweat suit—why do they do that?—just in front turned to Bode, stared up at him as if in disbelief, and then cried out in a shrill voice.

'Oh, my God! You're Bode Bonner!' She held up her cell phone. 'I'm one of your followers!'

The man in front of her turned and stared at Bode. His eyes got wide, and he cried out, 'Bode Bonner!' The woman in front of him turned and shrieked, 'Bode Bonner—in line with us!' Word ran up and down the serpentine security line and people turned to him like dominoes dropping—

'Bode Bonner!'

'He's in line with us!'

'Can you believe it?'

—until every person standing in line was staring at him and pointing at him and grinning at him with faces as bright as Becca's when he had surprised her with a pony for her fifth birthday. Their hands instinctively came up armed with cell phones. Hundreds of little lights flashed like machine-gun fire and voices called out to him.

'You the man, Bode!'

'Way to go, Governor!'

'We got your back!'

'Send all them Mexicans home in body bags!'

And then the chant rose up from the crowd.

'Bo-de! Bo-de! Bo-de!'

His worries evaporated like spit on the sidewalk in August. He stood there and took it all in and let the people's admiration wash over him like a star athlete who had just won the big game—or a war hero home with victory in hand. And maybe he was. Maybe this was a war. A culture war. The Second Mexican War. A war the American people wanted desperately to win. Maybe they had found their hero.

'Bo-de! Bo-de! Bo-de!'

Stubby arms suddenly clasped him around his waist and put him in a death grip.

'Take my picture, Earl!'

Aw, shit, the fat woman wanted her photo with him.

Bode cleared security first after enduring the full-body scan; he hoped his manliness made him proud on the screen. He put his boots and belt back on and pushed his wallet and other personal items into his pockets. Jim Bob emerged next, grumbling something about 'Russia and the goddamned KGB.'

'How'd you know these people would react like that?' Bode said.

'I didn't. I had a hunch. Now all those cell phone photos will be posted online, picked up by the news outlets. Bode Bonner, man of the people.'

Two of those people, round white-haired women, waddled over in their bare feet and wrapped their Michelin man arms around Bode and squeezed tight. They released him, and one said, 'You're even better looking than Regis Philbin.' They turned and went over to the conveyor belt to retrieve their personal items.

'Cat ranchers,' Bode said.

'Cat ranchers?'

'You go to their house, I guarantee you they got two dozen cats each.'

'You're a cattle rancher. You got what, five thousand head?'

'Yeah, but I can eat a cow.'

'Never know with those women.'

The kids trickled through next. Then Ranger Hank emerged. Even a Texas Ranger could not carry weapons onto a commercial flight, so he had to empty his holster and pockets. Out from the holster came the nine-millimeter handgun and two spare ammo clips, the Taser, the Mace, the cuffs, the flashlight (actually a sledgehammer with a light on the end), and the sap (an eleven-inch leather strap with a lead weight at one end); from one cowboy boot came a .22-caliber pistol; from the other boot came a compact serrated knife with a T-type push grip; and from his pants pocket came a rolled-up sleeve of quarters, a substitute for brass knuckles, which were illegal in Texas. Hank walked over in his white socks and carrying his cowboy boots and looking as if he had just undergone a body cavity search.

'Think you got enough weapons there, Hank?' Jim Bob said.

They all gathered around and waited for Josefina and Mandy, who was sticking close to the shy girl now. The TSA screeners waved Mandy through.

But they stopped Josefina.

They pulled her out for a pat-down. Her expression showed her confusion. Mandy stepped over to the screener and said, 'She doesn't speak English.' A Latino screener spoke to her in Spanish, and little Josefina now understood. She screamed.

'¡No, no, no!'

The security line froze. Screeners and armed TSA guards swarmed the scene like a SWAT team, surrounding the little Mexican girl. Her brown eyes turned to Bode. She was crying. He groaned.

'Aw, shit.'

Ranger Hank stepped forward, but Bode stopped him.

'I'll handle it, Hank.'

Bode hitched up his jeans for the turf battle he knew would ensue. He had fought many such battles in his years as governor, as all governors had, over education standards, air pollution permits, water quality, prison conditions, Medicaid, and taking Mexican kids into custody on a West Texas ranch. The Feds would fight you over anything and everything just because they could. Because they had the power to make your life miserable. To withhold federal funds. The EPA was perennially the worst offender, of course, but the HHS and HUD, DOJ and DOE, ICE and FEMA and OSHA and even the USDA weren't far behind. But since its creation, the DHS—Department of Homeland Security—and its airport stormtroopers—the TSA—seemed determined to take federal arrogance to levels never before seen outside the Supreme Court Building, treating airline passengers as suspects and patting down old folks, people in wheelchairs, and even young children.

'She's just a kid!'

Josefina's TSA screener was overweight and wore a United States badge, never a good combination. By the time Bode arrived and stepped between Josefina and the screener, Mandy was in her face.

'She's scared!'

'Ma'am,' the screener said in the way that let you know she wasn't saying 'ma'am' out of common courtesy but only because her work rules required her to, 'she either gets patted down or she don't get on the plane.'

'*Doesn't*,' Mandy said.

Correcting a federal employee's grammar was always a mistake, in Bode's experience. The screener leaned her massive body toward Mandy as if to intimidate the oh-so-lithe Mandy, but Bode's gal held her ground. Mandy Morgan was a tough little broad. Bode figured he'd better break this up before blows were exchanged.

'She's with me,' he said.

The screener's glare remained fixed on Mandy.

'Then you better get her outta my face so I can do my job.'

'Not Mandy . . . well, she's with me, too, but I mean the girl. Josefina.'

The screener pivoted like a politician after a bad poll and faced Bode. The realization of who was standing in front

231

of her came across her face, but not in a good way. Her expression changed from a woman itching for a cat fight to a Democrat still angry because four years ago her candidate had lost to the man standing before her.

'Governor, she can be with God Himself, but she's gonna get patted down.'

Great, a federal employee with attitude. But then, he was being redundant.

'Look, the girl suffered a traumatic experience, I'm sure you saw the story on TV.'

'I don't know what you're talking about.'

'Where have you been the last three days?'

'Here. Working overtime. People got the flu.'

That's the thing about disease that always frustrated Bode: those who should get it never did.

'Well, she's in a very delicate state right now, and your patting her down would not be good for her.'

'Wouldn't be good for the passengers on that plane if she's carrying a bomb.'

'A *bomb*?' Bode moved just enough to reveal Josefina hiding behind him. 'Does she look like a terrorist?'

'We're not allowed to engage in profiling.'

'Just in stupidity?'

That really didn't help matters.

'Step aside, Governor.'

'No.'

The armed guards stepped closer. The crowd in the security line had grown restless and vocal.

'You tell 'em, Governor!'

'They're supposed to be working for us!'

'This ain't Russia!'

'Don't worry, Governor—we got your back!'

232

As much as Bode enjoyed the thought of decking a federal employee, having the governor of Texas wrestled to the ground by armed guards on national TV—cell phone cameras rose above the crowd to record the moment—might not be the best political move, so he tried to defuse the situation.

'Would you please call your supervisor?'

She gave him a 'proceed straight to hell without passing GO' look then said into her shoulder-mounted microphone: 'Supervisor, Gate Eight security. A-S-A-P.'

It didn't take long for an older man to arrive in a golf cart. He stepped out with a two-way radio in his left hand and walked over with a slight limp. He assessed the situation then stuck his right hand out to Bode.

'Governor—what's the problem?'

Bode shook hands and checked the supervisor's name-plate—'Ted Jenkins'—then motioned Ted away a few steps. Josefina stuck close to him.

'Ted, you been watching the news, what happened this past weekend out in West Texas? The shooting?'

'Yes, sir. Good job.'

Thank God—a Republican.

'Used to work Border Patrol,' Ted said, 'till some border bandits shot me in the leg. Couldn't foot chase no more, so I transferred to TSA.'

'So you heard about the children being held captive—'

'Yes, sir.'

'—and that a girl was held as a sex slave for over a year?'

'Yes, sir.'

Bode leaned in and lowered his voice.

'Well, Ted, this little girl behind me—that's her.'

Ted's face registered his shock. He peeked around Bode at Josefina.

'She's just a kid.'

'Yes, Ted, she is just a kid. Who's terrified of being touched by anyone, especially strangers. If your screener pats her down, she's likely to have a psychotic episode, fall down to the floor screaming, probably start foaming at the mouth. Right here in your airport.'

'A psychotic episode?'

'And it'll all be caught on those cell phone cameras'—Ted glanced back at the crowd aiming cell phones their way— 'and shown on national TV tonight. A TSA screener touching a little girl's private parts, a little girl who was raped daily for a year by three men who worked for a Mexican drug cartel, a little girl I saved from being killed by those same men just three days ago. And this is how she's treated by the American government?'

'Shit.'

'Shit is right, Ted. And you and I both know that in politics shit rolls downhill. Fast. The press will jump all over the president and that ball of shit is gonna start rolling downhill from Washington and by the time it arrives at this airport in Austin and drops on your head, it's gonna be one big pile of shit, Ted.'

Ted considered the situation: he had his screener-with-attitude standing with her fists embedded in her wide hips and a scowl on her face; he had the governor of Texas offering him advice, man to man; he had little Josefina, terrified with tears running down her puffy cheeks, hiding behind the aforesaid governor; he had a crowd of angry citizens armed with cell phone cameras; and he had his government career.

He chose his career.

'Fuck it,' Ted said in a barely audible voice. He turned to his screener. 'LaShawna, the girl's good.'

LaShawna glared at her boss a long moment then pointed a fat finger at Bode.

'Then I wanna pat him down!'

Ted sighed heavily. 'Give it up, LaShawna.' To Bode, in a low voice: 'She washed out at the police academy, but we hired her. Go figure. Have a good trip, Governor. You got my vote if you run for president.'

Ted twirled a finger above his head as if to say, Move out! The crowd cheered.

'You the man, Governor!'

Bode nudged Josefina away from the checkpoint—'Let's go, honey.' When she realized she was free to go, the fear drained from her face. Her brown eyes lifted to him, and she tugged on his shirt. He leaned down to her. She tapped a finger on his chest and said through tears, '*El hombre.*'

'I need a bourbon,' Bode said.

They had survived security and economy-fare coach class and were now safely ensconced in full-fare first class. The flight to L.A. would take three and a half hours, with a sexy stew serving them bourbon and steak. When Bode went to the lavatory, she slipped him a card with her phone number. She was based in L.A. Mandy was back in coach.

Bode decided to check on the kids. He ventured into the crowded coach section and was again greeted like a war hero. Hands shot into the air for high-fives and autographs. Passengers stood for cell phone photos with him. The going was slow, so it was twenty minutes later before he arrived at the rear of the plane where Hank, Mandy, and the kids occupied the last three rows. Hank had crammed his six-foot-six, two-hundred-sixty-pound body into the coach-class seat; he looked like an unhappy teenager in a baby stroller. The kids were digging into box lunches. They were again decked out in Gap clothes, and their newly cleaned teeth gleamed bright in the cabin light. Alejandro and Vincente wore new glasses; both boys were as blind as bats. They'd all been given clean bills of health by the pediatrician. Josefina was neither pregnant nor infected with a sexually transmitted disease. She would see a therapist when they returned to Austin.

'Those sandwiches okay?'

'Bode, these kids have been eating squirrels cooked over a campfire for the last year,' Mandy said. 'Ham-and-cheese sandwiches, potato chips, and oatmeal cookies, this is gourmet for them.' She took a bite of her sandwich and shrugged. 'Actually, it's not that bad.'

Little Josefina sat in the window seat and stared out at the blue sky. She hadn't touched her lunch.

'Josefina.'

Her eyes turned to him.

'You okay? ¿Bueno?'

She gave him a shy nod.

'Hi, Governor.'

The coach–class stew had arrived.

'Hi'—he checked her nameplate—'Carol. I'm Bode Bonner.'

She grinned. 'Like I don't know? I'm a follower! I got your tweet that you'd be on our flight. The girls haven't been this excited since David Hasselhoff flew with us.' She held out a napkin. 'Would you autograph this for me?'

He signed the napkin.

'All these kids, they're with me.'

Her eyes got wide. 'These are the kids you rescued? Oh, my God!'

'I'd appreciate it if you'd take real good care of them.'

'Of course, I will—I got your back, Governor.'

She held up an open hand for a high-five; he obliged.

'And this is Mandy. She's watching them.'

Mandy mumbled a hello through a mouthful of ham and cheese.

'You need anything at all, you let me know,' Carol said.

Emilio raised his hand.

'What do you need, Emilio?'

'*Yo soy* Ernesto.'

'Oh, yeah . . . Ernesto. You need something?'

A blank face.

'*¿Qué necesita?*' Mandy said to him.

He made a gesture as if drinking and said, '*¿Leche de cabra?*'

'You want . . . *leche* . . . milk . . . *de* . . . of the . . .'

'Goat,' Mandy said then shrugged. 'It's like a Spanish immersion class.'

'Uh, we don't have goat's milk, Governor,' Carol the stew said. 'But we do have cow's milk.'

'That'll work. Bring thirteen.'

The milk run arranged, Bode returned to first class and his steak lunch. Jim Bob wanted to spend the flight time prepping for the upcoming television appearances, but Bode got the steak and a few bourbons down him and decided to enjoy the attention from the stewardess—her name was 'Su, without the e'—and the other passengers in first class asking for his autograph and photos with him. He enjoyed the moment—until a guy dressed like a CEO came up and ruined the moment.

'Governor, you've got to run for president. Business needs you. The country needs you.' He lowered his voice and leaned in. 'We need a white man in the White House.'

Bode Bonner had played football with black guys, showered

with black guys, roomed with black guys, and chased white girls with black guys. Many had been his friends back then and some still were today. They always greeted each other with man-hugs at team reunions. When you fought together on a football field, you didn't give a damn what color your teammates were, only that they wanted to win as much as you did. So Bode Bonner didn't take kindly to anyone assuming he was a racist just because he was a Republican. He got in the guy's face.

'Hey, bud, I don't like that racist crap. So you best get your butt back in your seat before I stick my boot up your first-class ass.'

First-class passengers departed first at L.A. International Airport. Bode hoped to avoid more commingling with the coach class at the baggage claim so he grabbed his carry-on baggage and hurried up the jet way and into the terminal and—

A flash of bright light momentarily blinded him.

He blinked hard and saw black spots. He raised a hand to shield his eyes from the lights—the bright lights of news cameras. Someone screamed, 'Bode Bonner!' and thunderous applause broke out. The crowd—*Californians!*—gave the governor of Texas a standing ovation. Bode recovered quickly and smiled broadly. He pushed forward; hands reached out to touch him. He signed autographs while men and women leaned close and took self-photos with cell phones. Voices called out to him from the crowd.

'You're the man, Bode!'

'Bode, you're our hero!'

'Run for president! Please!'

He felt as if he were in Lubbock instead of L.A. Jim Bob caught up with him.

'How'd they know we were coming today?'

'I tweeted. This'll be on the local news tonight, national in the morning.'

'You're good.'

'This is what I do.'

On the PA system, a deep voice announced: 'Governor Bode Bonner, arriving at Gate Four, your ground transportation is waiting outside baggage claim.'

Which had almost the same effect on the terminal as an announcement that George Clooney was standing buck naked at Gate Four. The crowd surged toward them. Mandy herded the kids off the plane, and they took a victory lap through LAX. Ranger Hank took point and cleared a path through the gauntlet of cell phone cameras. As they passed each gate, waiting passengers picked up on the applause that was washing through the terminal like a tidal wave and continued all the way to the baggage claim. They waited for their luggage—one bag for each kid, Hank, Bode, and Jim Bob, and four for Mandy—with his new fans who followed him outside to a waiting—

'Limo?' Jim Bob stood on the sidewalk as if horrified at the sight of the long black limousine. 'Mandy, you got us a limo?'

'For all the kids. We couldn't take five cabs.'

'You should've gotten a hotel van. Okay, let's get in before they take too many pictures.'

They all jumped into the limousine, safe from the cameras behind blacked-out windows. Hank rode shotgun, and the kids took seats down both sides; Mandy made sure they were buckled in, then joined Jim Bob and Bode on the rear seat. She squeezed tight and said, 'Gosh, honey, you're almost as popular as Kim Kardashian.'

* * *

It was eighty degrees in L.A., so they stopped on Rodeo Drive—Alejandro was disappointed; he thought they were going to a real rodeo—and bought swimsuits for the boys at Brooks Brothers and the girls at Ralph Lauren. While Bode signed autographs and took photos with the cute clerk and shoppers, he noticed Josefina staring at a yellow dress and touching it as if it were gold. The Bode Bonner Reelection Campaign bought the $600 dress for her.

They were now poolside at the hotel in Beverly Hills. Jim Bob's pale flesh glowed in the sun, so they found lounge chairs in a shady corner and ordered sodas and strawberry daiquiris. Ranger Hank stood guard, as if Bode Bonner were a movie star, Mandy stood by the pool, looking stunning in her new black bikini, and the kids stood at the water's edge, as if they had never before swum in a pool.

'They haven't,' Mandy said.

Bode dove into the pool then coaxed the children in. The boys finally jumped in, but Josefina sat on the ledge and dangled her feet in the water. Mandy sat next to her, and they shared a little girl talk. Jim Bob fiddled with his phone. Bode tossed Carlos into the deep end. He came up sputtering and splashing wildly—

'They can't swim!' Mandy cried.

—so Bode plucked him out of the water and carried him to the shallow end.

'Sorry about that, Carlos.'

'Bode!'

Mandy pointed at Filiberto. He had climbed the steps and was unzipping his swimsuit, apparently to pee in the pool.

'No, no, Filiberto!'

Bode waded through the water and over to the boy.

'No peeing in the pool.'

'*¿Que pasa?*'

'Mandy, what's the word for peeing?'

'I don't know.'

Bode motioned to the cabana with restrooms.

'Toilet.'

'Ah.'

Filiberto trotted over to the restroom. A Latino waiter approached their position; Hank blocked his path. He had been as jumpy as Jim Bob since the shooting.

'Hank, he's just bringing our daiquiris.'

Bode got out of the pool and grabbed a daiquiri and the lounger next to Jim Bob. But he noticed a group of women on the far side who didn't seem pleased to see brown-skinned kids in the pool, especially in light of the fact that they were probably peeing in the pristine water at that very moment. The Professor opened his black notebook.

'We had a good overnight. Your Twitter followers topped a million, and the CNN poll puts you at twenty percent among Republicans. The shooting went down "approve" with Independents, "strongly approve" with Republicans, and "holy shit, shoot some more Mexicans" with the tea partiers. It even polled positive with thirty percent of Democrats.'

'Good.'

'Except now you're in the cross hairs. Any Republican who looks like he could challenge Obama, the liberal media goes gunning for him, hard, because they want Romney. They know Americans will never elect a Mormon president.'

'Which means . . . ?'

'They'll try to make you look stupid, like they did with Bush and Palin.'

'It worked.'

'Difference is, you're sneaky smart.'

'Sneaky smart?'

'You're a lot smarter than folks figure.'

'Thanks . . . I think.'

'It's a good thing to be underestimated, Bode, especially in politics. Bush and Palin, they're sneaky stupid—they're both stupider than everyone figured and everyone figured they were pretty stupid. So making them look stupid on national TV was easy. You being a Texan, everyone's going to naturally assume you're just as stupid. But you're not. You're a helluva lot smarter. So they'll underestimate you and—BAMM!—you prove you're smarter than they thought. Which makes you look real smart.'

Bode nodded. 'It's like sneaky fast. I hated sneaky fast receivers. They look like they should be slow, then—BAMM!—they blow right past you and leave you holding your jockstrap.' He sipped his daiquiri. 'Sneaky smart. I like it, Professor.'

Bode checked on the boys; they were apparently trying a Mexican version of waterboarding on Miguel—'Hey, let him up!'—and then he checked on the women across the way. They waved the pool attendant over.

'Now, so you don't look sneaky stupid, we've got to prep for the talk shows.' The Professor launched into his positions . . . Bode's positions . . . on the political issues of the day. 'Remember, Bode, the federal budget is four trillion dollars, and there's a voter who's vested in every single dollar. You cut a dollar, you lose a vote. The calculation is that simple. And primary states depend on federal spending—'

Bode's attention drifted away from the Professor and over to the women across the pool. The attendant had come over and then departed. He now returned with a man in a suit. The women seemed quite animated. The suit listened, looked over at them, listened again, looked again. He headed Bode's way.

'—the entire state of Iowa is planted in corn to feed the ethanol plants not people, so you go there and tell those corn farmers you're cutting the ethanol subsidy, your presidential campaign ends in Des Moines.'

Bode felt his blood pressure ratchet up, and not because of the ethanol subsidy. He knew the hotel suit was going to tell him the kids must vacate the pool.

'So, Bode, your position on the federal budget and spending is, (a), you support a balanced budget amendment; (b), we need steep cuts in federal spending; and (c), we need to secure our border and deport those damn illegal Mexicans.'

Bode's eyes were locked on the hotel suit.

'Okay?'

Bode's thoughts returned to the Professor. He didn't want to confess to having checked out on his prep talk, so he said, 'You're the boss, Professor.'

The hotel suit arrived and stood over him and blocked out the sun. Bode didn't like being talked down to, so he stood and towered over the suit. Those snotty Beverly Hills women weren't going to keep his Mexican kids out of the hotel pool.

'Uh, Governor . . .'

'Look, bud,' Bode said, pointing at the children in the pool, 'those kids are guests just like those women over there—I'm paying for them, they're with me—and they're gonna swim in that goddamned pool as long as they want to, you understand? And no one's gonna—'

'Governor'—the suit held out a pen and hotel stationery—'the ladies just wanted me to ask you for your autograph . . . and if you'd take a photo with them.'

★ ★ ★

243

'Governor, after you killed those Mexican *hombres*, weren't you afraid there might've been more of them who could've come after you? With guns?'

'Aw, hell, Jay, I still had a hundred rounds of ammo and a fast horse.'

Twelve hundred miles away in Laredo, Texas, the governor's wife stared at the television in disbelief. Her husband was on the Leno show. And even more unbelievable, he wasn't wearing Armani and French cuffs, but instead a powder-blue Oxford shirt, jeans, and cowboy boots. His blond hair wasn't sprayed in place; it fell onto his forehead as if he could care less. He looked like the man she had fallen in love with in Comfort, not the politician who had cheated on her in Austin. He held a long rifle with the butt embedded in the chair seat next to his leg like a cowboy riding shotgun on a stagecoach through Comanche territory. The California crowd cheered Bode Bonner. But there was no cheer inside Lindsay Bonner.

'Does it get any better?' she said.

'The Leno show?' Jesse said.

'Being a doctor and a nurse in the *colonias*.'

The child down by the river had been killed by a stray bullet. She was only four years old. The doctor had explained to his nurse that men in Nuevo Laredo often fired their guns into the air, the same as she had seen men do in news reports from the Middle East, as if the bullets do not come down. But they do, often with great force. Enough force to kill a child. The girl was not the first such victim, and she would not be the last. Twenty-four hours later, they both remained shaken by her death. Holding the child on the riverbank and feeling the life that was no more, it had hurt her in a way she had never before experienced.

'No. It does not get better.'

She sighed.

'I wish he wouldn't do that.'

'Go on the Leno show?'

'Make jokes about killing those Mexicans. I have a bad feeling about that.'

Chapter 15

'*¿Está el médico?*'

A young girl had stepped into the clinic but spoke to Lindsay from the door.

'No.' Lindsay spoke Spanish. 'But he should be back soon. Can I help you?'

The girl dropped her eyes and shook her head. She wore too much make-up and a yellow tube top that revealed her torso and the top of a red lace thong above her low-slung jeans.

'What's your name?'

'Marisol Rivera.'

'That's a pretty name. How old are you?'

'Fifteen.'

'How old is your boyfriend?'

'What boyfriend?'

'The one who got you pregnant.'

'I did not say I was pregnant.'

'But you are.'

The tears came now.

'Why do you come to the doctor?'

'I want an abortion.'

Two hundred thirty-five miles north in Austin, Carl Crawford ate his wholegrain muffin and drank his Fairtrade coffee and watched the morning news and thought, *Bode Bonner is the luckiest son of a bitch on the planet.*

The governor's arrival at L.A. International Airport the day before was the feature segment. The crowd—*Californians, for Christ's sake!*—hailed him like a conquering king home from the crusades against the Mexicans. Sure, they were cartel gunmen, and yes, they were operating a marijuana farm, and true, they had raped the girl and held those kids as slaves, but . . . Carl sighed. Anyone else, and he might be cheering, too. But Bode Bonner? Carl had spent the last eight years of his professional life chasing down every scent of scandal emanating from the Governor's Mansion: shady land deals, state appointments to cronies and campaign donors, misuse of campaign funds, even the execution of an apparently innocent man. But nothing stuck to the governor of Texas.

And now he's an American hero.

The only silver lining in Carl's dark cloud of a mind was knowing that no one fell harder or farther than an American hero exposed by scandal. So Carl would continue his search for scandal in the Governor's Mansion, scandal that would drive Bode Bonner from office. The governor's staff was loyal to a fault—but there was always a fault line, a crack in the loyalty of every politician's entourage, one follower who stopped following. He would find that person. He would use that person. He would bring Bode Bonner down. Unless that Mexican drug cartel killed him first, as some drug war experts on the cable talk shows had suggested might happen.

Carl could only hope.

Jesse Rincón had never before had a *colonia* woman ask him to end a life. These women had nothing in life, yet they desperately wanted to give birth to life. But this girl sitting across his desk now pleaded for an abortion.

'If my employer learns I am pregnant, he will fire me,' Marisol Rivera said in Spanish.

'You work in a *maquiladora*?'

'Yes. Across the river.'

'What do you make?'

'*Un dólar la hora.*'

One dollar an hour.

'No. What kind of product do you make? Televisions, toasters, clothes . . . ?'

'Underwear for the *gringos*, panties and thongs.'

She stood and turned to show her backside. She reached back and pulled the top strap of her red thong up for him to see.

'I take a few from time to time. What they call a perk.'

'Not as good as health insurance.'

'I save my wages so that one day I might live beyond the wall, perhaps when I am twenty years old.'

She dreamed of living beyond the wall, but she was destined to be yet another pretty *chica* whose life is derailed by a child before she is sixteen. And Jesse had no doubt that in fifteen years, her daughter would be sitting before him begging for an abortion so that she might live beyond the wall.

'But that dream will not come true, Doctor, if I am fired for being pregnant or if I have this baby. Will you do it?'

'Marisol, I cannot.'

'Why not?'

'I am Catholic.'

'And I am fifteen and pregnant.'

'What are you going to do?'

Marisol Rivera had left. Jesse now shook his head.

'I do not know. It is easy to say a woman should have a right to an abortion, but it is something else to perform the abortion. To end a life. What if my mother had chosen an abortion?'

'She thinks the baby will ruin her life.'

'If I perform the abortion, one day she might live beyond the wall. If I do not, she will surely live out her life on this side of the wall.'

'Is there a doctor in Laredo who will do it?'

'No. There might be one in McAllen, perhaps as far away as Brownsville.' He exhaled. 'Two lives rest in my hands.'

She could tell he needed to think, so Lindsay went over to Inez's vacant desk and updated her medical histories. Jesse sat quietly for a long time. Finally, he stood and began assembling surgical tools by the examining table.

'Find her,' he said.

'Your dad's on *Oprah*,' Darcy Daniels said.

Becca Bonner lay sprawled on her bed in their dorm room. Asleep. They always napped after volleyball practice. Darcy rolled out of her bed, stepped over to Becca's bed, and gave her a shake. Her eyes opened.

'Your dad's on *Oprah*.'

Becca rubbed her eyes and said, 'I thought she quit?'

'It's a special.'

On the flat-screen TV mounted on the wall, Becca's dad stood on the stage surrounded by the thirteen Mexican children. Darcy and Becca had gone to the mansion the past Sunday to meet the kids. The audience gave the governor a standing ovation.

'He didn't spray his hair.'

'Josefina looks pretty in that yellow dress.'

On the television, her dad introduced the children, first the boys and then he turned to Josefina, who was almost hiding behind him.

'And this beautiful young lady is Joscfina.'

The camera captured her face as she slowly raised her brown eyes to him.

'¿Yo . . . Josefina . . . soy hermosa?'

'Yes, you are beautiful.'

Tears rolled down Josefina's cheeks. She hugged Becca's father.

'Bode Bonner . . . *el hombre* . . . *es mi héroe*,' she said on national TV.

Lindsay did not know where Marisol Rivera lived, so she and Pancho walked the *colonia* asking everyone she saw if they knew her. Up and down the dirt roads with the black satchel over her shoulder she trudged, stopping from time to time to tend to minor injuries and apply antibiotic to children's sores. The wind brought the smell of the river into her nostrils and the dirt of the desert into her mouth and inside her clothes. She spat dirt then retrieved her water bottle from the satchel and rinsed her mouth. But her thoughts were on this child so desperate to have a life torn from within her so that she might live beyond the wall. The sadness of the thought crushed her spirit that day.

It was just after five when Pancho barked.

Down a little dirt side path near the river she saw residents gathered around a small shack. A sense of fear enveloped her. She ran to the shack with Pancho at her side. The people parted for the Anglo nurse, and she ducked her head and entered the shack. She gasped at the sight of so much blood. She thought she might faint, so she went to her knees. A wire clothes hanger seemed to float in the blood. The girl lay in gray dirt made red by the blood.

Marisol Rivera would never live beyond the wall.

'I'm against abortion.'

'No, you're not.'

'I'm for abortion?'

'No, you're not for abortion either.'

'Then what am I?'

'A politician who wants to be president.'

They had flown into Chicago that morning and arrived at O'Hare to a hero's welcome. Jim Bob had tweeted ahead. They checked into the Ritz and then went to the studio. After taping the show, Mandy took the kids back to the hotel for a room-service dinner and a pay-per-view movie; Bode, Jim Bob, and Ranger Hank took a cab to Morton's for a thick steak. They now sat in a booth drinking bourbon; Hank drank a soda. He stood when a middle-aged couple came up to their table and held out a menu for Bode to autograph.

'Easy, Hank. We're fourteen hundred miles from the border.'

Bode signed the menu. The couple then leaned in and took a self-photo with their cell phone, as had strangers at the studio, on the sidewalks, and in the entrance of the restaurant. After they left, Bode turned back to Jim Bob.

'Abortion is a wedge issue the Democrats use to split Republicans and women.'

'It ain't the only issue splitting men and women.'

Two attractive young women wielding iPhones now stopped at their table.

'Governor, will you take a photo with us? We're followers.'

'Two pretty gals like you? You bet.'

He stood between them and wrapped his arms around them. They squeezed in tight and smelled intoxicating. He liked Chicago. They held out their phones and took a few photos then thanked him. Bode returned to his seat but he and Jim Bob watched the girls sashay off.

'Nice followers,' Jim Bob said. But his thoughts soon returned to politics. 'So your position on abortion is: You hate to see a life ended. You don't think the Supreme Court should make up the law to suit their politics. The people should. Democracy should. But we have more pressing national matters to deal with right now, like the economy and deporting those damn illegal Mexicans.'

'You sure that'll work?'

'This is what I do.'

Bode downed his bourbon.

'She reminded me of my mother,' he said.

'Which one?'

'Not the girls . . . Oprah.'

'You're mother was white and Irish.'

'She has a sweet face.'

Like his mother before the cancer. Once she died, his dad's days were numbered. The official cause of death was prostate cancer, but the real cause was loneliness. He couldn't

251

go on without her. Then it was just Ramón and Chelo to raise Bode Bonner the boy. But now Bode Bonner the man wondered: If his wife did not come back, would he die of loneliness, too?

Chapter 16

Boca Chica lay two hundred miles southeast of Laredo.

They left in the pickup truck just as the sun rose over the Rio Grande and drove south on U.S. Highway 83, the river road. The river ran south from Laredo for almost a hundred miles, then veered east on its zigzag journey to the Gulf of Mexico; the highway followed the river. Their journey would take them to *Colonia Nueva Vida*.

'You didn't kill that girl,' she said.

Marisol Rivera had died at five and been buried by sunset in the small *colonia* cemetery. There was no police investigation, no autopsy, no news report, no obituary in the local newspaper. There were only tears.

'Or your mother.'

Jesse did not speak for several long miles. She worried that she had overstepped with him, mentioning his mother. But he finally spoke.

'My father did not want me, and my mother died having

me. Dying is a way of life on the border, I know that. But I cannot understand why God made it so.'

'He didn't.'

He stared at the road ahead for a time before he again spoke. 'You are right. I forget. There is no god on the border.'

They rode in silence for many miles.

Jesse Rincón had made this journey many times during the last five years, only Pancho to provide company if not conversation. Driving the river road through the brown borderlands, he often contemplated his life and the choices he had made, and always he would revisit his choice to return to the *colonias*. His medical school classmates would be well into their private practices by now, well into families and financial success. What would his life be like now if he had made the same choice? Wife and children . . . a nice house in the suburbs of Houston or Dallas or perhaps Austin . . . vacations to the ocean or mountains twice each year . . . teaching soccer to his son or daughter . . . his sons and daughters, for he had wanted a big family, perhaps because he had only his uncle growing up. All those dreams he had envisioned as a child in Nuevo Laredo and as a student at Jesuit and Harvard, and he knew that was to be his life.

But then he came home when his uncle died.

He buried his uncle in Nuevo Laredo then drove back across the river and out to *Colonia Ángeles* to visit his mother's grave in the little cemetery. There he had cried for her and for himself. He felt alone in the world.

He stood to leave but heard a shrill scream from a shanty where women had gathered. They told him in Spanish that the woman inside was having a child, but the baby was stuck and the midwife could not turn the baby. The woman and

253

child would surely die. He ducked inside the shanty and saved mother and child.

He knew then that this was to be his life. Coming home to the *colonias* had not been a choice, any more than one chooses where to be born. But still he had questioned his path in life, this harsh life on the border.

But not that day.

That day the governor's wife rode next to him. Their paths in life had intersected on the border. And he no longer felt alone in the world.

'Do you make this journey often?'

Lindsay decided to break the silence.

'Once a week before. Now, perhaps twice a month. But never at night. Highway bandits.'

'Bandits? In America?'

'On the border, it is—'

'I know. An entirely different world.'

Pancho sat between them, the windows were down, and a hot breeze blew through the vehicle. Lindsay stared out at the desert landscape that seemed endless and vacant. Until she saw blue water.

'That is Falcon Lake,' Jesse said, 'where the American on a jet ski was murdered by the cartel. The Mexican government sent an investigator, but the cartel killed him, too. No more investigators came after that. The border runs down the middle of the lake, but Mexican pirates often cross over and rob American fishermen.'

'Bandits and pirates?'

He shrugged.

'But they say the bass fishing on the lake is very good.'

★ ★ ★

They drank coffee from a thermos and drove through border counties called Zapata and Starr and Hidalgo and small border towns named Rio Bravo and Roma where the river and highway both turned east—

'Back in the fifties,' Jesse said, 'Marlon Brando came here to film the movie *Viva Zapata*. I have never seen it. But these counties became famous when the votes of dead people here elected Kennedy and Johnson in nineteen-sixty.'

—and La Joya and Mission and Alamo and the landscape gradually changed from the scrub brush of the desert to the fertile delta land of the Lower Rio Grande Valley, lush and tropical with palm trees and bougainvillea, lemon and lime orchards, cotton and cane fields, orange groves and grape-fruit orchards, and humid air that seemed to stick to her skin. They followed the river all the way to Brownsville at the southernmost tip of Texas.

'The river wraps around three sides of this land and creates a peninsula. There are over one hundred *colonias* in the county, some completely surrounded by Brownsville, but the city will not annex them because they would not add to the tax base. Ah, we are here.'

Jesse braked to a stop in front of a small white structure that appeared identical to the clinic in *Colonia Ángeles*.

'Four hours, that is not a bad time.'

It was just before eleven.

'I trained a nurse/midwife to work here. Sister Sylvia, she is a nun.'

Lindsay wrapped a green scarf around her head to cover her red hair.

'Will she recognize me?'

'Who would expect to see the governor's wife in a *colonia* outside Boca Chica?'

255

They got out and went to the front door where a sign was posted: EL PROHIBIDO EL PASO. DANDO A LUZ.

'Yesterday there was death,' Jesse said. 'Today there will be life.'

Pancho found a shady spot outside. Inside they found a sparkling clinic offering an antiseptic scent, six women in labor, and Wayne Newton's voice on a boom box.

'Sister Sylvia, she likes Wayne Newton. I am not sure why.'

The clinic had been arranged like an old-time labor-and-delivery ward. Three women with bulging bellies lay in beds lined along one wall and three more along the opposite wall. There were no privacy curtains, but there was much moaning and groaning and occasional curses in Spanish. The joy of labor.

'No epidurals in the *colonias*,' Jesse said.

A round, gray-haired Anglo woman wearing blue latex gloves, a colorful scrub top, and a big crucifix hurried over to them. She had a stethoscope around her neck and a relieved expression on her face.

'Doctor, thank God you have come. Six women, I could not do this alone.'

'Sister Sylvia,' Jesse said, 'this is Nurse Lindsay Byrne. She works with me now. She is Irish.'

A reminder to use her accent. The women greeted each other.

'Sister Sylvia normally delivers two or three babies each week, but six in one day, that is a bit much even for her. That is why she called me.' To Sister Sylvia: 'Any breeches?'

'No, thank God.'

She made the sign of the cross.

'Okay, let us wash up and see what we have.'

Jesse and Lindsay went over to a sink in the back and scrubbed their hands with surgical soap then put on latex gloves. They followed Sister Sylvia to the first woman. In this case, child.

'I've arranged the mothers by age,' Sister Sylvia said. 'This is Delilah Morales. She is fourteen. She is expecting her first child.'

She did not look up from her iPhone. She was texting. Her nails were long and painted red. Her perfume overwhelmed the small space.

'We are close enough to town for cell phone service,' Jesse said. To the girl, he said, 'Hello, Delilah. I am Dr. Rincón. I will be delivering your baby today.'

Like a waiter at a fine restaurant.

'*Gracias.*'

She groaned against a contraction. After the pain had passed, she resumed texting. Jesse put his hands on either side of her belly and felt for the baby.

'Delilah, I must check your dilation, to see how close you are to delivery.'

She did not respond so Sister Sylvia put Delilah's left leg in a stirrup, and Lindsay did the same with her right leg. Delilah's full attention remained on the iPhone. Jesse put his hand between Delilah's legs. That got her attention.

'Hey! What are you doing?'

'I must check your cervix.'

'Well, don't do it down there!'

Jesse chuckled. 'That is where your cervix is. I have to feel it, to see how dilated it is, to know how close you are to delivery.'

'With your fingers?'

'I am afraid so. It will not hurt much.'

'I do not let men touch me down there.'

One of the other women across the room laughed.

'You sure let Gustavo touch you down there or you would not be here now!'

'*¡Cállate la boca!*'

'Girl, do not tell me to shut up!'

'Ruby,' Sister Sylvia said, 'she is Delilah's mother.'

'They're both pregnant?' Lindsay said.

'Yes. Ruby will become a mother and a grandmother today.'

'Okay, ladies,' Jesse said, 'no fighting. It is, uh, not good for your babies.' Back to Delilah. 'I am a doctor. I have delivered many babies. I know you are scared since this is your first baby, but trust me, I know what I am doing. Okay?'

She shrugged and went back to texting. Jesse inserted his fingers into her vagina.

'*Dos.*'

Two centimeters. Her cervix had opened only enough for him to slide one fingertip in. Delivery would occur at about ten centimeters. Delilah's labor would continue for some time. Sylvia recorded the information.

'Where are the fetal monitors?' Lindsay asked.

'We have no monitors, no sonograms, no incubators, no epidurals—'

'What do these women rely on?'

'Us. And prayer. Right, Sister Sylvia?'

She crossed herself again. They repeated the procedure with the other women. Rosie Ochoa was seventeen and having her second child; she was saying a rosary and was dilated six centimeters. Griselda Guzman was nineteen, dilated five centimeters, and crying silently through the contractions; this would be her first child. Marcela Vasquez was twenty-one, six centimeters, and having her third; her eyes were closed and an iPod was plugged into her ears. Luisa Chavez was twenty-eight and five centimeters; this was her sixth child. And Ruby Morales was thirty-seven and about to deliver her fifth child—soon. She was dilated eight centimeters.

'Okay,' Jesse said, 'Ruby will deliver first, and then Rosie, Griselda, Marcela, and Luisa will deliver close together, so let us move them to one side, in case we are delivering four babies at once. Delilah, she will be last and the most difficult.'

'Why?' Lindsay said.

'Big baby and small hips.' He blew out a breath. 'It will be a long day.'

They pushed Rosie and Griselda to the other side of the room and swapped them out with Ruby.

'No, no, no!' Delilah said. 'Do not put my mother next to me. I do not want to listen to her.'

'If you had listened to me, you would not be pregnant at fourteen.'

Delilah groaned with a contraction.

'Remember the pain, child.'

'Ladies,' Jesse said in mock reproach. 'Sister Sylvia, you watch that side, Nurse Byrne will watch this side. Let us eat lunch.'

The promise of new life seemed to lift Jesse's spirits. He went to the small refrigerator at the back.

'Sister Sylvia, did you bring me shrimp poor-boys?'

'Of course. Six, in case we are here into the night. With the red sauce you like.'

They checked that the mothers were comfortable then sat and ate lunch.

'Oh, Doctor,' Sister Sylvia said, 'Alexa Hinojosa, the newspaper reporter, she stopped in and asked me to have you call her the next time you are here. She is very pretty. She and you would make beautiful babies together.'

The moment turned awkward, so Lindsay changed the subject.

'Where are the husbands?' she asked in a low voice.

'Not husbands,' Sister Sylvia said. 'Fathers. Except Ruby, she is married.'

'The others aren't?'

'No. I am afraid that marriage is no longer a prerequisite to parenthood, in Hollywood or the *colonias*.'

Two thousand miles north, Bode, Jim Bob, and Ranger Hank stood on a sidewalk in Manhattan. They had flown into New York that morning and checked in at the Plaza. After lunch, Mandy took the campaign credit card and the kids to Macy's. Jim Bob, Bode, and Hank took a cab. The Professor now spread his arms to the building rising in front of them as if it were a cathedral.

'The country was on the brink of disaster, we faced the same fate as the Roman Empire, but this place single-handedly saved America.'

They were standing out front of the *Fox News* building.

'Tea party TV, Bode. Don't fuck it up.'

'Ruby, you were born to have children,' Jesse said.

'Yes, all you must do is catch. I have the wide hips. My mother, she also had such hips. Together, we have now made twelve children. And no epistle.'

'Episiotomy.'

'*Sí*. We are baby factories . . .' She grunted. 'Let me push this *bebé* out.'

She did. Jesse sat on a rolling stool at the foot of her bed.

260

Lindsay stood next to him. The baby's head crowned and emerged from the birth canal.

'Catch my baby!'

He did. He held the baby's head with his left hand. Lindsay handed him a rubber syringe. He inserted the syringe into the baby's mouth and suctioned mucous and water. The baby's shoulder emerged next, and then the baby just fell into Jesse's waiting hands. Lindsay held a sterile towel out, and Jesse placed the baby on the towel. He suctioned the baby's mouth and nostrils. The baby took his first breath of air and cried. His voice and the smell of new life filled the clinic.

'Ruby, you have a fine new son,' Jesse said.

Lindsay wiped the baby while Jesse clamped and cut the umbilical cord. Sister Sylvia came over with a warm blanket and took the baby. She wrapped him like a papoose and placed him in his mother's arms.

Three hundred fifty miles north, Eddie Jones sat slouched on the couch in Jim Bob's office in the Governor's Mansion, drinking a beer and watching the governor on a cable talk show on *Fox News*. Ranger Roy drank a root beer, the kind without caffeine. What a boy scout.

On the television, the boss was saying, 'If you subsidize corn, you'll get more corn. If you subsidize Mexicans, you'll get more Mexicans. If you tell Mexicans that babies born in the U.S. will be American citizens, you'll get more anchor babies. And we have—six hundred thousand in Texas the last decade.'

'So you were a merc in Iraq?' Ranger Roy said.

Roy was wide-eyed, like a kid talking to his baseball hero. Eddie nodded and gestured at the television. 'Hank's in

New York guarding the governor—why aren't you there guarding the governor's wife?'

'She's not in New York.'

'She stayed here?'

'She's not here, either.'

'You're here, and you're her bodyguard.'

Roy now looked like he might cry.

'She ran off.'

'Whoops.'

Roy drank his root beer like a man drinking whiskey to drown his sorrows. He swiped a Texas Ranger sleeve across his mouth.

'Guess you weren't around much, before she left.'

'Nope.' Eddie drank his beer. 'She got another man?'

Roy shook his head.

'She wants to be useful.'

'*Useful?* What the hell does that mean?'

Roy threw up his hands.

'How should I know? I've never been married.'

'Hell, I've been married, and I don't know.'

'Where's your wife?'

'Living with another man. I went to Iraq, she went to divorce court.'

Eddie Jones was ex-special forces when he had hired on as a 'private contractor' to the CIA in Iraq, which sounded better on the evening news than 'mercenary.' The pay was great, the work fit his skill set, and the independence refreshing after twenty years in the army. But one incident involving civilians, and Eddie found himself unemployed and unemployable. Hard to explain that sort of thing on a résumé.

'I'm worried about her,' Roy said.

'My ex-wife?'

'The governor's wife. I don't want nothing bad to happen to her.'

On the television: 'Governor, you're not at all worried that that Mexican drug cartel might seek revenge?'

Eddie pointed at the TV.

'Roy—you best worry about the governor.'

Jesse Rincón rolled on the stool from bed to bed, from birth to birth. Four babies were born within minutes of each other. Only the most difficult birth remained.

'*¡Hijo de la chingada!*' Delilah screamed with the pain.

The fourteen-year-old child was not ready to have a child. But have it she would. The baby was coming, ready or not. They gathered around her bed. The wall thermometer registered ninety degrees. The windows were open, and the fans were blowing, but only hot air. Everyone sweated.

'She is dilated eight centimeters,' Jesse said.

Delilah screamed as the next contraction began.

'It hurts!'

'Remember that the next time Gustavo wants to romance you,' her mother said.

'Not helpful, Ruby,' Sister Sylvia said.

'*¡Jodale!*'

'Listen to the mouth on her,' Ruby said.

'It is just the pain talking,' Jesse said.

'No, she talks like that all the time.'

The contraction passed, and Delilah breathed as if she had just run a sprint. Sylvia wiped her sweaty face with a wet towel and gave her ice chips to suck on.

'The first birth can be difficult,' Sister Sylvia said, 'but it will end soon.'

'When?'

'Soon.'

'Keep your legs tight together next time,' Ruby said.

'But, Mother, if I do, the baby cannot get out.'

'Not now. With Gustavo.'

Delilah screamed again. The next contraction had already begun. She shouted in Spanish, 'I will never have sex again!'

The three Texans stepped out onto the New York City sidewalk.

'That went well,' Bode said, 'until he brought up his bull-shit word for the day. He just wanted to prove he's smarter than me. Who the fuck knows what fatuous means?'

'Foolish or silly,' the Professor said.

'Who?'

'That's what fatuous means.'

'Oh.'

The Professor slapped Bode on the back.

'Don't worry about it. Palin makes up her own words, and tea partiers don't care.'

'*¡Empujón!*'

Jesse sat on the stool at her feet, Lindsay stood next to him, and Sister Sylvia stood at Delilah's head. The other mothers nursed their babies and watched.

'Crowning.'

The baby's head crowned but did not come out.

'Big baby, small hips,' Jesse said. 'Hand me the block. Time, Sister.'

Jesse had anticipated a difficult delivery, so he had prepared a Pudendal block. He took the hypodermic needle and injected the numbing medication into her vaginal wall. Wayne Newton was singing 'Danke Schoen.'

'Scalpel.'

Lindsay handed him a sterile scalpel. He performed an episiotomy.

'One minute, Doctor,' Sister Sylvia had said.

'Forceps.'

Jesse took the forceps and maneuvered them into the birth canal and tried to guide the baby out. Delilah dropped her iPhone.

'Two minutes, Doctor.'

'We have got to get this baby out.'

Delilah turned her head to Sister Sylvia and vomited.

'Doctor!'

'It is okay. Just make sure she is not choking. Delilah, I need you to push hard.'

'I cannot.'

'You must.'

'No.'

'Push!'

'Delilah,' Ruby yelled, 'you push that baby out or I am going to come over there and push it out for you. Now push!'

She pushed.

'*¡Carajo!*'

The baby's head cleared the birth canal.

'Good, Delilah,' Jesse said.

The amniotic membrane still covered the head, so Jesse tore it with his fingers, releasing the fluid onto the towel in his lap.

'The cord is around the neck . . . clamp.'

Lindsay grabbed two clamps and handed one to Jesse. He clamped the cord. She handed him the second clamp; he clamped the cord again. She handed him surgical scissors;

265

he cut the cord and unwrapped it from the baby's neck. Without looking at her, he held a hand out; she placed a ball syringe in his hand. He suctioned mucous from the baby's mouth and nostrils.

The baby did not breathe or cry.

Jesse suctioned again, but still nothing from the baby. The shoulders were stuck in the birth canal. Jesse rotated the baby enough to allow the shoulders to clear; the baby slipped out into his hands. It was a girl. Delilah breathed out as if her life had just been saved.

But her baby's life had not yet been saved.

Lindsay held out a sterile towel. Jesse put the baby on the towel then held her in his lap. He suctioned again then rubbed her back. She still did not breathe. He gently slapped the bottoms of her feet. Nothing.

He stood and kicked the stool away. It rolled across the clinic until it struck the far wall.

'Hold her.'

She took the child. Jesse leaned over and began mouth-to-mouth. He blew soft breaths into the child. Lindsay realized she was crying, and the clinic had fallen silent except for Wayne Newton singing and Rosie saying the rosary. Sister Sylvia crossed herself again.

'Breathe!' Jesse shouted.

The baby breathed. And cried. Loudly.

'Now I know that is my granddaughter,' Ruby said.

Sister Sylvia took the baby in a warm towel. Without thinking, the governor's wife embraced Jesse Rincón.

An hour later, Delilah said into her iPhone, 'Oh, Gustavo, our daughter, she is beautiful. I love you so much.'

'God help me,' Ruby said.

It was just after six.

'It is too late to drive back to Laredo tonight,' Jesse said. 'Border bandits. We will drive back tomorrow morning.'

'Jesse,' Lindsay whispered, 'I can't be seen in Brownsville.'

'We will go over to the island. There is a small motel I know.'

Jesse went to each mother one last time. Lindsay said goodbye to Sister Sylvia, who hugged her like a mother.

'I am sorry, Nurse Byrne.'

'For what?'

'For mentioning the pretty reporter to the doctor.'

'Why?'

'I did not know that he was already in love.'

'He is?'

Sister Sylvia patted her shoulder. 'Yes, he is. But you wear a wedding ring . . . and your husband is the governor.' She smiled. 'I like Oprah.'

'He was on *Oprah*?'

'Yesterday. But do not worry, I will keep your secret.'

Sister Sylvia wanted to say more.

'What is it, Sister?'

'He is a very good man, the doctor. Please do not hurt him.'

They drove east to Port Isabel where the smell of the sea came to them on the breeze.

'Why do these poor women have more babies?' Lindsay said.

Jesse sighed. 'I do not know. Perhaps because the church says it is God's wish. Or perhaps because the government will pay for the babies. Or perhaps they hope an American baby will keep them in America. Or perhaps they just think a baby will make life on the border better. Of course, it will not.'

Lindsay's spirits stayed low until the Gulf of Mexico came into sight. They drove over the Queen Isabella Causeway toward the tall condo towers and hotels on the distant island silhouetted against the blue sky.

'We are over the *Laguna Madre* . . . Mother Lagoon.'

They drove onto South Padre Island and along a palm-tree-lined boulevard past condos and hotels and restaurants and surf shops that fronted the beach. They turned into a small motel. Lindsay stayed in the truck while Jesse checked in. What if he took only one room? Would she insist on a second room? Or would she . . . ? She had been without romance for a very long time, since politics had seduced her husband. She missed it. Romance. Jesse returned, got in, and handed her a key.

'Our rooms are down at the end. Nothing fancy, but clean.'

They had brought overnight bags just in case. She cleaned up and changed into a white sundress. She had sweated through her green scarf so she pushed her red hair under a yellow scarf and topped it off with a sun hat. She went outside and found Jesse waiting; he wore jeans, sneakers, and a black T-shirt.

'There is a good seafood café down the beach. We can walk.'

She removed her sandals and walked barefooted through the wet sand where the tide died out. On the horizon shrimp boats returned with the day's catch. Surfers waited for one last ride, and a lone fisherman stood in the surf with a long pole. Joggers and fellow walkers passed them; a few took curious second glances at her. She almost didn't care. Pancho raced ahead, clearing the beach of seagulls and brown pelicans and blue herons that had lighted on the sand. The air was wet and filled with salt, the sea breeze fresh and cool on her face. The Gulf of Mexico lay smooth and blue before them, and the sun set in front of them in shades of yellow and orange. She felt like a girl on a first date. Like lovers without the lovemaking. But she was neither.

She was a forty-four-year-old woman married to the governor of Texas.

She very much wanted to kill this old man. She hoped each time that he would have the heart attack during sex. She wondered if she could fuck him to death. Was that possible? Rosita Ramirez did not know, but she was willing to try.

Six hundred twenty-five miles west of South Padre Island, John Ed Johnson rolled off Rosita. Seventy-one years old, and testosterone still oozed from every pore in his body. Always had. He sat up, grabbed his bourbon from the night-stand and then the remote, and turned on the television.

'Hey, look there, Rosita. The governor's on TV.'

On the television, the governor of Texas said, 'Hell, Dave, I shoot first and ask questions later.'

John Ed and the studio audience laughed.

'But you shot him in the back.'

The governor nodded. 'Twice. So he didn't file a civil rights complaint.'

John Ed bellowed with laughter.

'Why?'

'Because he wouldn't turn around so I could shoot him in the front.' After the laughter died down, the governor's expression turned solemn, and he said, 'Look, Dave, those men were armed and dangerous, they beat the little girl, and they pointed guns at her. That made them bad guys. And in Texas, we shoot bad guys.'

More applause.

'Now, Governor, did I read correctly that one of the bad guys got away? The guy that worked at the ranch? Aren't you worried?'

'Nah. That *hombre*, he's sitting in Mexico somewhere tonight, drinking a Corona.'

Fifty meters outside the bedroom window, Manuel Moreno squatted and peered through high-powered binoculars at *Señor* John Ed and Rosita.

Chapter 17

'*¿Es América?*'

Little Josefina stared up as cameras captured the moment. Bode felt a bit uneasy about this just being another photo op—this was the Statue of Liberty, after all—but how could he argue with the Professor when his poll and Twitter numbers continued their rapid climb into the stratosphere?

'Yes, honey. This is America.'

She turned to him and tapped her chest. She wore the yellow dress.

'*¿Ya soy yo una americana?*'

The American consulate had been working with the

Mexican authorities to locate the children's parents or next of kin. So far, they had found Javier's mother in Piedras Negras and Pablo's older sister in Ojinaga; they would fly home when they returned to Austin. And they had found the bodies of Josefina's mother and father in Chihuahua. They had known what the men would do to their pretty daughter, so they had put up a valiant fight. Which earned them each a bullet in the head. Josefina had no one back in Mexico. She knew it. Her eyes told him so.

They had returned to Laredo after noon, stopped off at the house to change, and then driven out to *Colonia Ángeles*. Lindsay made her daily rounds without major incident, welcome after the previous day in Boca Chica. Her worries about her husband's safety had eased with each day; and Austin seemed distant here in the *colonias*. Like another world. When she returned to the clinic, she found Inez at her desk but Jesse gone.

'Where's the doctor?'

'He went to the movies.'

'The movies?'

'*Sí*. He goes every other Friday. Unless it is raining, then he goes the following Friday. But that does not often happen here on the border. The rain.'

Bode and Lindsay Bonner had stood right there on their last trip to New York, for their twentieth anniversary. She had seemed happy that day. But when they had returned to Austin, he vetoed the funding for the children's health insurance program. And politics came between them.

'*¡Caramba!*' Carlos said.

They had brought the kids up to the observation deck at

the Empire State Building. The view from a thousand feet up was breathtaking. The kids pointed and spoke Spanish and seemed excited.

'*Bueno*,' Alejandro said.

Emilio threw up.

'Was the movie good?' Lindsay asked.

Jesse had returned to the clinic late that afternoon. Inez had gone out back.

'What movie?'

'The movie you went to see.'

'Oh. I did not go to see a movie. I went to get a movie. Tonight is movie night.'

'Where?'

'Here. Every other Friday, we show a movie, outside, on the side of the clinic. The white wall, it is a good screen. Come, I will show you.'

They went outside where Inez was setting up an old reel-to-reel movie projector aimed at the side of the building. A long black extension cord ran from a plug on the outside wall of the clinic to the projector. A few residents were already staking out places with blankets and lawn chairs, like Austinites gathering in Zilker Park for an outdoor concert.

'We have the only electricity in the *colonia*, so we pop corn and show movies twice a month. Instead of a drive-in, we are a walk-in. Tonight's movie is *Viva Zapata*. It is the story of the revolutionary Emiliano Zapata. He is a national hero in Mexico. As I said, Marlon Brando came to the border back in the fifties to film it.'

'How'd you get it?'

'The theatre in Laredo loans the movies to me. I spoke

272

to the owner's civic club, and afterward he asked how he could help.'

When the sun set and the *colonia* was plunged into darkness, Inez flipped the switch and the movie played. The Spanish sound track was scratchy, but no one seemed to care. The night air carried the smell of popcorn and *tesguino*. The residents of *Colonia Ángeles* ate and drank and laughed.

'Is this a comedy?' Lindsay whispered to Jesse.

'It is to them, an Anglo playing a Mexican hero.'

Just then a bright light streaked fast and high into the night sky followed by a brief explosion, like fireworks. The children clapped.

The crowd cheered as if he had just hit a walk-off home run.

Bode stood on the pitcher's mound in Yankee Stadium surrounded by the kids. They all wore Yankees warm-up jackets and caps. The boys held hot dogs, and Josefina a fluffy pink cotton candy. She wore her yellow dress. They had met the players and conversed with them in Spanish. You couldn't slap the smiles off their faces. Especially Ranger Hank's.

'*¡Béisbol americano!*' Miguel shouted.

Fifty-two thousand fans packed the stands. Yankees versus Red Sox with a national hero throwing out the first pitch on national TV. Bode reared back and threw a strike to the catcher. He smiled and waved his cap. The catcher handed him the ball and asked him to autograph one for him. Bode signed the ball then walked over to Jim Bob and Mandy with the kids. Mandy looked stunning in black tights and a black miniskirt and the baseball jacket; he hoped his wife wasn't watching his mistress on television. Jim Bob gestured to Bode's image on the big video screen in center field. Bode

273

squatted down to the kids and pointed at the screen. They all turned to the screen and waved to the crowd.

Bode Bonner basked in the cheers.

'They cheer him. He is a murderer, but the *gringos* cheer him. Because he murdered Mexicans.'

Two thousand miles south of Yankee Stadium, in the white compound in Nuevo Laredo, Enrique de la Garza stood in his office and stared at the image of the Texas governor on the television. It had been one week since that man had murdered his first-born son. One week knowing that he would never again see his son's face or hear his voice, never again laugh at his antics or teach him the family business, never again watch American baseball with him or play catch in the courtyard.

His son was dead.

His brother cried for him, and his sister cried for herself. She missed her big brother. As her father missed his son. The loss was unbearable. The pain unimaginable. The desperation he now felt seemed far worse than after his wife's death. Because her death was a mistake. But his son's death was murder.

He demanded justice for Jesús.

But there would be no justice in America. The governor would not be charged with murder; instead, he was hailed as a hero. Enrique had watched him on the morning shows and the news shows and the cable talk shows as he boasted of murdering his son: 'I shoot first and ask questions later,' he had said, and the *gringos*, they laughed. Now he was cheered as a hero at a baseball game. Regarded as a righteous savior instead of a cowardly murderer. A killer of Mexicans. Oh, how the *gringos* loved that. Remember the Alamo! Manifest

274

Destiny! Once again, Americans murder Mexicans as they did during the Invasion. Once again, they take what is ours. Once again, we have no justice.

Once again, the Americans steal life from the de la Garza family.

Two hundred ten years before, the king of Spain himself had granted sixty thousand acres of land straddling the Río Bravo to Juan de la Garza. Juan built a magnificent *rancho* with many cattle and *vaqueros*. Then the American president decided that God wanted the United States to extend from the Atlantic to the Pacific, so he sent the army to take this land from Mexico. And take it they did, from here to California. Half of Mexico they stole from Mexicans. Then the president signed a treaty that set the Río Bravo as the new border but granted continued title to Mexicans owning land north of the river. But the Americans wanted that land as well. They wanted it all. So the Mexicans were required to prove their title to land they had lived on for generations. 'Your titles must be approved by the Texas legislature in Austin,' the Americans said. 'But we promise to give the titles back to you.' The governor sent a commission to the border to collect the original land grants from the Mexicans. The commissioners put the titles in a trunk and the trunk on a boat for the trip up the coast; but the boat sank in Matagorda Bay. The commissioners, they survived, but the Mexicans' titles did not. An unfortunate accident, the commissioners said. Very sorry.

And then the Texas Rangers rode upon the Mexicans' land.

They put their guns to Juan de la Garza's head and demanded his signature on a deed—or his blood. Juan refused, and so he died on his land. As did many Mexicans. The river ran red with

275

Mexican blood for many years. And when the killing stopped, the Americans owned all of the land north of the river. They stole our land and, with it, our history and our future. The Americans sentenced the once wealthy de la Garza family to a life of poverty—until the great-great-grandson named Enrique de la Garza established the Los Muertos cartel to impoverish the Americans with the filthy drugs.

No, *gringos*, it is not about the money—it is about history and honor, *venganza* and justice, the past and the future. It is about *México* and *Mexicanos*.

The history of the borderlands has now come full circle. That which you so coveted now comes back to haunt your soul. To enslave you to the evils of heroin and cocaine and marijuana. To impoverish you with poor people. The governor stood at the Statue of Liberty where Enrique de la Garza had also stood and read the inscription: 'Send us your tired, your poor . . .' And we do. We will. We have. And more we will send north. Tens of millions more. To America. You once invaded us, now we invade you. You have impoverished us, now we will impoverish you. With our drugs and our poor. We will export our marijuana and cocaine and heroin and our hungry and illiterate and poor. Our poor will become your poor. Our poor will make you poor. Our poor will inundate your schools, your hospitals, your prisons, and your cities. This we have done to Texas. This we will do to America. Billions you spend on our drugs; trillions more you will spend on our poor. Drugs and poor people we send north that will impoverish you as you have impoverished us.

But there remains a balance due for what you have stolen from us—our land and our wealth, our history and our honor, our justice and our future. All that you took from us. And for that you owe a debt you will pay until the end of time.

Only when there is justice will that debt be paid in full. And as God was his witness, there will be justice. For *México* and *Mexicanos*. For Jesús de la Garza.

'*Ya lo hice, jefe.*'

Hector Garcia entered with a broad grin.

'What have you done, Hector? Have you killed the governor, as I asked? No, you have not.' Enrique pointed at the governor's image on the screen. 'See, there he is.'

'Uh . . . no. I have not done that.'

'Then what have you done that you think would please me so?'

'The Predator drone—I have shot it down.'

Enrique only grunted in response.

'*Jefe*, does that not make you happy?'

'My happiness, Hector, is now defined by a singular moment: when you walk into this office and drop the governor's head on my desk.'

Chapter 18

The Roman Catholic church constructed the San Agustín Cathedral in downtown Laredo in 1872. *La catedral* features a clock tower that rises five stories above the pavement and a stark white exterior that continues inside to a sanctuary with a tall arched ceiling and a white altar. Lindsay Bonner knelt in the back where the pews were vacant. Jesse had driven her to church but refused to enter the church. He believed in God and he was Catholic, but he understood neither God nor the Catholic church. Why had God abandoned this border and the church these people? She too had questioned her God and her church, but she needed to be in church and to pray to God that Sunday morning. Because she was contemplating sin.

The sin of adultery.

One hundred sixty miles north of the cathedral in which the governor's wife now prayed, San Antonio Mayor Jorge Gutiérrez took a bite of his *migas* which he chased with the strong coffee. He was watching *Fox News* on the flat-screen television mounted on the wall above the counter in the small café. Normally, the television would never be tuned to *Fox News* in this café in the Prospect Hill neighborhood, but given that the governor of Texas was on the national show that morning, an exception had been granted. When his face appeared on the screen, the patrons booed and made derisive comments in Spanish. San Antonio's Hispanics—which is to say, all of San Antonio—did not vote Republican.

On the TV, the host said, 'Welcome, Governor. It's an honor to have you on the show. You're a genuine American hero.'

'Aw, heck, I only did what any American male with a three-seventy-five-caliber safari rifle fitted with a scope would've done in the same situation.'

'I'm not so sure about that, Governor. I think a lot of Americans would have cut and run.'

The governor nodded. 'Democrats.'

The diners booed again, but Jorge chuckled. That was a good line, he had to give the governor that. Jorge sipped his coffee just as his phone rang. He checked the caller ID then answered.

'Clint, my friend.'

Clint Marshall, the state Democratic Party chairman.

'You watching this?'

'Yes, I am.'

On the television, the host took the governor through the hot-button issues of the day, like ticking items off a shopping list—spending and taxes, the debt and deficit, abortion and gay marriage, welfare and ObamaCare—and Jorge's attention alternated between the governor on the television and Clint on the phone.

The host, on the TV: 'Governor, you've railed against the stimulus, but you took the money to balance your state budget last year. Why?'

'Because the Feds took that money from us. Texas is a donor state—we pay more in taxes to Washington than we get back from Washington. Texans are funding New York and California, and we don't appreciate that.'

Clint, on the phone: 'Well, if Texas had voted for Obama, maybe he'd give us more federal money.'

'I think that is his point, my friend.'

The governor, on the TV: 'We're fifteen trillion dollars in debt. We're spending ten billion a day and charging four billion to our Bank of China credit card. Borrowing money and printing money isn't the same as having money.'

Clint, on the phone: silence. Jorge chuckled.

'Come on, Clint. That was a good line.'

'Jorge! You're just encouraging him.'

'He cannot hear me. He is in Washington.'

'Oh. Yeah. Still, it's the principle.'

'Ah, yes. The principles of politics.'

The governor, on the TV: 'It used to be a crime to charge more than ten percent interest, so only the mob engaged in loan sharking. But the big banks bribed Congress with campaign contributions to legalize loan sharking. Now credit cards charge thirty percent. How many trillions of dollars have been transferred from Main Street to Wall Street because of that one federal law?'

Jorge noticed a murmur of grudging approval from the crowded café. They were middle-class Hispanics who used credit cards.

Clint, on the phone: 'Okay, he's right about that.'

The governor, on the TV: 'Twenty million Americans are unemployed on Main Street, but Wall Street is making record profits. Where's Main Street's bailout?'

The murmur grew louder. Everyone in the café had a spouse, sibling, child, or friend who was unemployed.

'And what about that, my friend?' Jorge said.

Clint, on the phone: 'Yeah, yeah.'

The governor, on the TV: 'The government steals money from one citizen and gives it to another, but both citizens lose their freedom. One becomes dependent upon the government, the other a slave to the government.'

The murmur broke into Spanish . . . words of approval.

'He is very good,' Jorge said.

Clint, on the phone: 'Tell me.'

The governor, on the TV: 'I really don't care what two consenting adults do, as long as they do it inside. But, if it's okay for two men or two women to marry, then why not one woman and two men or one man and two women? . . . Well, actually, that should be illegal.'

The host: 'One man marrying two women? Why?'

The governor: 'No man should be forced to bear the shopping expenses of two women.'

The diners laughed heartily. And they applauded. The governor of Texas.

Clint, on the phone: 'Are they clapping? Hispanics?'

'Yes, my friend.'

The host, on the TV: 'Governor, the latest *Fox News* poll shows that you now hold a commanding lead among Republicans with forty-two percent. And while Obama beats every other Republican by double-digits in head-to-head matchups, he doesn't beat Bode Bonner. It's all square. Which means the Republican Party needs you. Question: Don't you want to be president?'

'I'm not running.'

'No way, no how?'

'Nope.'

'You're absolutely sure?'

The governor gave the camera a broad smile.

'Pretty sure.'

The *Fox News* show ended, and the café became noisy with animated political discourse. The proprietor changed the channel to a local Spanish station favored by his Hispanic clientele. Jorge waved to the waitress for the check.

'We've got to beat him,' Clint said.

'Next year? For the White House?'

'This year. For the Governor's Mansion.'

Jorge laughed.

'That will not happen, Clint. He is the governor-for-life.'

Clint launched into a profane narrative, so Jorge focused on the local Sunday morning show on the television. A pretty Latina reporter named Gaby Gomez introduced the lead story. That past Monday, she had journeyed to a *colonia* outside Laredo to tape a 'day in the life of' profile of a young Latino doctor named Jesse Rincón. Harvard-educated and born in Texas to a Mexican mother—one of those so-called 'anchor babies'—Dr. Rincón had returned to the border to care for his people. Jorge grunted. These human interest stories often proved not so interesting, but this story held promise. So when the waitress brought his check, Jorge held up his coffee cup for a refill. He would wait for the show to return from a commercial break.

'Jorge,' Clint said, 'I just got off the phone with the national party chairman. He wasn't happy. Shit, he got a standing ovation at Yankee Stadium.'

'The chairman?'

'No! The governor—by Yankees!'

'The baseball team?'

'The people! They fucking love him. You see how many followers he's got on Twitter?'

'Twitter? Uh, no, I did not see that.'

'Four million—that's more than Snoop Dogg.'

'Whose dog?'

'Another week like this, and he'll have more followers than 50 Cent.'

'Snoop Dogg, 50 Cent . . . these are people?'

'Jorge, this is no longer just about the Governor's Mansion. This is about the White House.'

'Oh, Clint, you worry too much. After George W., no Texan will again be elected president, not in our lifetimes.'

'Don't bet on it. He's a hero now, and heroes are hard to beat. Especially a hero who kills Mexicans . . . no offense. You see the latest tracking polls? He's in a dead heat with Obama. A couple of our internal polls put him ahead.'

282

'He will fade. They all do.'

'Maybe. Maybe not. No other Republican has a snow-ball's chance in hell of beating Obama—but Bode Bonner's got a chance. A damn good chance.'

Jorge heard heavy breathing on the line. He often worried about Clint's heart.

'We've got to stop him, Jorge.'

'How?'

'We've got to beat him here in Texas.'

'A Democrat beating Bode Bonner in Texas? That is not possible. Not now.'

'Not a Democrat . . . a Latino. Me and the national chair-man, we think a Latino could beat him.'

'Not this election. Four years from now, possibly. Eight years from now, probably. Twelve years from now, abso-lutely. But not this year. Bode Bonner will win this year.'

'We don't have twelve years or eight years or even four! We've got to win this year! We need a Latino candidate now! This election!'

'But who?'

'That's your job, Jorge. Find him. Find the candidate, and the national party will put all the money behind him that it takes to beat Bode Bonner in November. The chairman said we'll have a blank check. Texas is now a national election—because if we keep Bode Bonner out of the Governor's Mansion, we keep him out of the White House. And, Jorge, if a Latino is elected governor of Texas, you will have won what you've worked for all your life.'

Jorge Gutiérrez was seventy-six years old. He had served as a city council member, state legislator, and now mayor of San Antonio for the last fifteen years. He ran for governor once, but lost in the Democratic primary to an Anglo who was backed by the state party. Thirty years ago, the state party did not need Jorge Gutiérrez. But they needed him now. Because Texas was now a minority-majority state. Because Hispanics accounted for forty percent of the state's population—which number increased by the day. By the birth. Seven out of every ten babies born in Texas that day would be Hispanic. In ten years, we will be the majority population in Texas, in the U.S. in twenty years. We immigrate, we procreate, and we populate—with a purpose. A plan. To take political power. Over Texas. Over America. For Hispanics.

Know this, my Anglo friends: Every year, *six hundred thousand* Hispanics born in the U.S. turn eighteen and become eligible to vote. Every year. Year after year. Forever.

Of course, the Democrats think Hispanics will vote always for them. That Hispanics are beholden to them since they call for citizenship to all illegal Mexicans while the Republicans call for a bus to the border. The Democrats think we will vote as instructed, as if they remain our *patróns* as they were back in LBJ's day. They want to make us dependent on government so that we will be dependent on the Democratic Party. But we will not be beholden to either party. To anyone. Except ourselves.

Then we will have respect.

Jorge Gutiérrez was the leading Hispanic in Texas, even though few voters outside San Antonio had ever heard of him. But politicians knew him well. Because he headed the 'Mexican Mafia,' as he called the network of Hispanics who had infiltrated the Anglo power structure in business, law, media, academics, and politics. Hispanics who long to see Texas and the nation turn from red and blue to brown, who stand ready to use their power to promote a Hispanic candidate for governor of Texas. Jorge had once dreamed that he would be that candidate. But, alas, it was not to be. He was too old and too tired. The people needed a new face, a new voice, a new leader. Someone who inspired them. Someone handsome and charismatic, educated and smart, someone who had one foot in *México* and one foot in Texas, someone like—

Jorge noticed now that the café had fallen silent. He had been lost in his thoughts. He glanced around. All eyes were turned up to the television. Dr. Jesse Rincón commanded their full attention. On the screen, the doctor wore a white lab coat over a black T-shirt and jeans. He stood in a shantytown surrounded by half-naked brown children. He squatted next to a little girl with a dirty face and a runny nose.

'And this beautiful little *niña* is Bonita. She is four years old. I delivered her right here in the *colonia*, as well as her two little brothers. Say hello to San Antonio, Bonita. *Salúdales a los ciudadanos de San Antonio, Tejas.*'

The girl smiled for the camera and said, '*Hola, San Antonio.*'

The doctor flashed a bright white smile, and the screen came alive with his face. He was handsome, more handsome than any TV doctor, as the women in the café would attest. His black hair was thick and silky and fell onto his forehead. He was tall and lean and photogenic. The children crowded close around the doctor like sinners to—

Jorge sat up. He said into the phone, 'Clint, I will call you back.' He disconnected the call. On the TV, the doctor stood and led the reporter through the *colonia*. The camera captured the desperate living conditions. The doctor gestured at a patch of bare dirt, where a few barefooted boys kicked a soccer ball.

'This is our *fútbol* field.'

The ball came to the doctor; he stopped it with his foot

then kicked it back to the boys as if he knew how. They continued through the shanties and to a small white structure. The doctor pointed to the blank side wall.

'This is our movie theater. We show movies on the clinic wall every other Friday night.'

He walked on until the *colonia* became the desert. The doctor pointed to a distant shadow that stretched across the land.

'To the north is the border wall.'

He now pointed in the opposite direction.

'To the south is the river. These people are caught between the border wall and the border, between America and Mexico, between the future and the past. We stand on land that America has abandoned in the drug and immigration war, a land that is neither here nor there, neither—'

'*¡Doctor!*'

The doctor turned at the sound of a loud voice off-camera. The camera now caught a young boy and a dog running to the doctor.

'Doctor,' the boy said in Spanish, 'we have been searching for you! Come quickly! To the river! The nurse, she needs you!'

The doctor said not another word. He broke and ran after the boy and the dog, as if in a race for his life. The camera followed, the image bouncing up and down as the cameraman ran to keep up with the doctor, deep into the *colonia*, cutting between shacks and across dirt roads, ducking under clotheslines and running around water tanks, dodging pigs and goats and squawking chickens and finally arriving at the river. A crowd had gathered on a low bluff above the river. The boy pointed down.

The camera captured the scene.

Down below, a solitary woman wearing a white lab coat over a blue dress and a wide-brimmed hat sat on the riverbank. The hat blocked her face from the camera, but she seemed to be cradling something. She rocked back and forth, as if rocking a baby to sleep. Or was she sobbing? The doctor slid down the dirt bank and ran to her; he dropped to his knees. The camera zoomed in for a closer shot, and Jorge could now see that the nurse was not cradling something. She was cradling someone. A child.

A child in a bloody white dress.

The doctor took the child and placed her on the ground. He leaned over and blew into the child's mouth, then pressed on her little chest. Again and again and again. He finally stopped. He sat on the riverbank a long moment, and his head hung so low it seemed that it might fall to the dirt. Finally, he lifted his head, and then he lifted the child. He held the child in his arms. From off-camera came a child's voice in Spanish.

'She was playing beside the river, and we heard gunfire from Nuevo Laredo. And then she fell. She was only four.'

Down below, the doctor stood with the child clutched in his arms. The child's arms and legs hung limp. He left the nurse behind on the bank and walked to a spot where he could step up onto the bluff; hands from the crowd helped him up. He walked toward the *colonia*. The camera caught his face. He was crying.

Jorge realized that everyone in the restaurant had fallen silent. And like the doctor, they were crying.

Back on the screen, the doctor in the white lab coat now stained red with blood carried the child into the *colonia*; the crowd and the camera followed at a respectful distance. They walked down dirt roads, past residents who stopped what they were doing and stood frozen in place, as cars on a high-way when a funeral procession passed, and who then joined the procession. The doctor finally came to a little travel trailer half sunk into the ground. He stepped to the door. The crowd and the camera stayed back. The doctor knocked on the door. After a moment, a woman appeared. Her eyes found the child. She screamed. She took the child into her arms and went inside. Her wailing could still be heard. The doctor turned and wiped tears from his face then walked down the dirt road. Alone. Neither the crowd nor the camera followed this time, but the camera remained focused on Dr. Jesse Rincón.

It was one of those moments Jorge Gutiérrez would never forget. Like where he was when he first heard that President Kennedy had been assassinated. And then Martin Luther King. And Robert Kennedy. Like watching the television as Neil Armstrong stepped onto the surface of the moon. Like seeing those planes fly into the twin towers on 9/11. Like witnessing a black man inaugurated president of the United States of America.

This was such a moment for Jorge Gutiérrez.

Jorge wiped the tears from his own face then pulled out his cell phone and hit the call back for the state Democratic Party chairman. Clint Marshall answered on the first ring. Jorge Gutiérrez's voice was solemn.

'I have found the candidate.'

Chapter 19

He was the leading Republican candidate for the White House.

The last week had been a blur of interviews and cameras and cheering crowds from L.A. to D.C. And with each television appearance, his poll numbers and Twitter followers had increased exponentially. Bode Bonner had ridden the tea party wave all the way across America.

But his wife was still in Laredo.

The whirlwind media tour was over, and Bode Bonner was back in Austin—back to budget deficits and a runaway wife who knew about his mistress. She had only been gone nine days, but he found that his thoughts turned to her more each day. He wanted her back. But did he want her back because he loved her or because he needed a first lady to win the White House? He didn't know. He couldn't know. He could no longer separate his political ambition from his personal life. What he wanted from who he was. Ambition burned hot inside Bode Bonner. It always had, as a football player and as a politician. It drove him to win the next game and the next election. But with each win, he wanted more. He needed more. And now, it drove him to become president.

But a president needed a first lady.

'You call her yet?'

'Nope.'

'Afraid?'

'Yep.'

Jim Bob fiddled with his iPhone then said, 'Your followers jumped again after the *Fox News* appearance yesterday morning and the *60 Minutes* segment last night—six million, more than Ryan Seacrest.'

'Who?'

There was a knock, and the door swung open on a stout middle-aged woman.

'Mr. Burnet, here are the latest poll results you asked for.'

She walked over, handed a stack of papers to Jim Bob, and said, 'Good morning, Governor.' Then she left.

'Who's she?'

'Helen. My new aide. Mandy hired her.'

'What happened to Jolene?'

'She quit while we were out of town.'

'Why?'

Jim Bob's focus had turned to the polls. He answered with a shrug.

'Damn, Jolene was a helluva lot easier on the eyes than Helen.'

Jim Bob flipped through the pages.

'You pulled ahead of Obama in the Bloomberg poll. In one week you've gone from not even being in the game to leading the game. Hell of a week.'

'You were right, Professor. You said I'd be the presumptive Republican candidate for president. I am.'

The Professor turned the pages but shook his head.

'No. I was wrong.'

'But I'm leading the Republican pack.'

'Not about that. About the wave. I said you were just riding the wave. You're not.'

'I'm not?'

The Professor looked up at Bode.

'You *are* the wave.'

★ ★ ★

290

Lindsay Bonner stood outside the small shanty in the least populated part of the *colonia*. A young girl had darted inside when Lindsay had spotted her from down the road. As she came nearer, she heard hushed voices from inside. Pancho barked.

'*¡Hola!*'

No response. Lindsay walked around the outside of the shanty and tried to peek inside. She heard whispers. She stepped to the front door—a piece of sheet metal pulled across an opening—and pushed the door open enough to see inside.

'No, John Ed, I don't have the speaker and lieutenant governor on board yet. We're flying down to Houston later this week, I'll talk to them then.'

'Goddamnit, Governor, I need to move on my water deals, before it rains.'

'Hell, yeah, you don't want to let a good drought go by without making some money.'

John Ed Johnson launched into a profane narrative, so Bode held the phone out with his left hand and made the universal masturbation gesture with his right fist. Jim Bob muffled a laugh from his spot on the other side of the governor's desk. After John Ed had tired of his tirade, he hung up without saying goodbye or go to hell. Bode shook his head.

'Man expects a lot for twenty-five million.'

Jesse Rincón was at his desk in the clinic when his nurse arrived in a sweat. Inez was gone. Again.

'What is wrong?'

Lindsay caught her breath. 'I found eleven girls . . . young girls . . . a man kidnapped them in Guadalajara, drove them north to the border . . . they said he's taking them to Houston to be—'

'Sex slaves.'

Jesse stood and went to the shelves. He found two large syringes.

'The cartels have branched out into human trafficking. They smuggle thousands of girls across the border, stash them in safe houses on this side until they can transport them north to the cities, where they force them to work as prostitutes. When is he coming back for them?'

'Soon.'

He grabbed a vial, inserted the needle, and filled the syringe. He then took a vial of Botulinum toxin and inserted the needle. Lindsay read over his shoulder.

'Botox?'

'Vacuum dried. I am reconstituting it with sodium chloride.'

He injected sodium chloride then rotated the vial. He then filled the syringe with the liquid Botox. Then he filled the second syringe. Just in case.

'Should be enough to paralyze, at least temporarily.'

'You sure?'

'I hope.'

The caravan arrived at East Austin Elementary. Bode and Jim Bob rode in the lead Suburban with five of the kids; Mandy and the other six kids followed in the second Suburban. Javier and Pablo were on the state jet at that moment, flying to Brownsville to be reunited with their families in Matamoros. Saying goodbye was harder than Bode had expected.

'Jim Bob, I told you to hire kids.'

'This isn't a commercial. And I didn't set it up. Lindsay

did, before she went to the border. You're giving out learning awards.'

They exited the vehicle. Bode walked up the sidewalk with the kids and into the school expecting to be greeted by Ms. Rodriguez, the kindergarten teacher. Instead, they were greeted by the Austin school superintendent and the entire board of trustees, as well as the principal and teachers. Bode leaned into Jim Bob and whispered.

'What the hell's going on?'

'Beats me.'

The superintendent stuck her hand out. Her nameplate read IRINA RAMIREZ, so he figured her for a Democrat. But she smiled like a Republican.

'Governor, it's an honor. Oh, how wonderful—you brought the children.'

He shook her hand, but he knew that wasn't going to be enough for her. She moved in for a full-body hug.

'Governor, what you did—saving these children—I cried.'

She released him, and Ms. Rodriguez wrapped her arms around Bode.

'Governor, you made us so proud.' She pulled back a bit and looked up at him. 'You made me proud, because you care.'

The tracking polls showed that the shooting was admired almost as much by Hispanics as tea partiers because the cartels terrorized Mexicans who had relatives in America—because Bode Bonner had stood up for Mexicans when Mexican lives were on the line. Twenty-six percent of Hispanics polled said they would vote for Bode Bonner for president. A Republican. Ms. Rodriguez introduced Bode to the others in English and then to the children in Spanish. She then led them down a corridor.

'Which grade today?' Bode asked.

'All of them.'

'What?'

'We've set up in the auditorium. You're addressing the entire school. Everyone wants to meet *el hombre*.'

Two beefy guys who looked like PE coaches yanked open the double doors that led into a vast auditorium filled with students, teachers, and cameras. The place looked like a pep rally before a football game. They walked down the center aisle, and a woman on the stage yelled into a microphone.

'*¡El gobernador de Tejas! ¡Y los niños!*'

The students stood and applauded then bolted from their seats and hugged him. Signs on the walls read 'BODE BONNER— MI AMIGO' and 'MI HÉROE' and 'MI GOBERNADOR'. The big kid in the Kobe Bryant jersey gave Bode a high-five. The students then greeted the kids like rock stars, mobbing them and reaching out to touch them. Joscfina wore her yellow dress and stuck close to Mandy; her face said she didn't know whether to smile or scream in fright. The boys enjoyed the moment, high-fiving and slapping hands with the students. They all took the stage, and the superintendent introduced the governor of Texas—in Spanish.

'Children, we are honored to have with us today the governor of our great state of Texas—Bode Bonner!'

The students screamed his name. The superintendent handed him the microphone. He spoke English; she translated in Spanish.

'Good morning. I'm so happy to be back at your school. Since I was last here, I met some wonderful kids, and I'd like you to meet them now. I'll introduce the children and let them tell you a little something about themselves. First up is Miguel Martinez.'

Bode figured each kid would say his favorite food and *fútbol* team. He handed the microphone to Miguel then sat next to Ms. Rodriguez. She would translate for him as Miguel spoke in Spanish. After the media tour, the boy seemed right at home in front of a crowd.

'I am Miguel. I am eleven years old. I lived in San Fernando with my mother and my father. We were very poor but we had a nice life. I was happy. Each year men would come to town and hire us to go north into Texas to pick the fruit in the valley of the Río Bravo. It was hard labor but also an exciting adventure. So when two men drove into town one day in a big truck with the cover, we thought they had come to hire us. We came outside to greet them, my father and my mother and me. One man walked up and put a gun to my father's head and shot him. Then he shot my mother. Then he pointed the gun at me and told me to get in his truck or he would shoot me, too. I got into the truck. That was my last happy day for a long time.'

Ms. Rodriguez's voice cracked. The auditorium was silent.

'We drove to other small towns along the river and the men, they took other children just as they took me. Thirteen in all. We went far into the desert where the river had run dry and the men drove us across. Into Texas. We drove north to the mountains where the men met another man named Manuel, who took us onto a ranch with strange animals, such as the buffalo and the antelope and even the lion. The Americans would come to the ranch and hunt for the animals. We often heard loud guns. They took us to a camp, which became our home for many days. They forced us to clear a field deep in the trees and plant the marijuana for the *gringos*, they said. If we did not work hard enough to please them, they would hit us and not give us food. They drank the alcohol every day.

We were very afraid. Until one day the men tried to get on top of Josefina but she fought and they slapped her and tore her dress and she ran into the trees to make the escape. We again heard the big guns and we thought the men had shot Josefina so we hid in the tall plants. Then we heard her voice, telling us to come out, that we had been rescued. We saw the big man with the yellow hair. He said he was the governor of Texas. And I felt the happiness in my heart once again.'

Jesse drove his pickup to the shanty where the girls had been stashed. Lindsay rode next to him, and Pancho rode in the back. When they arrived, he saw a truck parked outside the shanty, so he parked down the dirt road.

'Shouldn't we call the police?'

'As I said, the police do not come into the *colonias*.'

'What about the Border Patrol?'

'There is no time. If he takes these girls out of the *colonia*, they will disappear forever.'

Jesse handed one syringe to his nurse.

'If the man does not go down with the first needle, stick that in him.'

'How will I know?'

'You will know.'

He got out of the truck and uncapped the other hypodermic needle. He walked toward the shanty. He felt his heart racing. He was a doctor, not a hero. But if he did not act now, eleven girls would be lost. Lindsay got out and followed. As they came closer, he heard a man's voice from inside. He took a position just outside the metal door. He looked at Lindsay and put a finger to his mouth. They waited.

But not for long.

The metal door opened, and a large man backed out. Jesse

stabbed the needle into the man's neck and emptied the Botox into him. But the man did not go down. He was a big *hombre* and very strong. He swung around and grabbed Jesse by the neck. Jesse tried to knock his arms off, but it was as if he were hitting tree trunks.

Lindsay knew. She held the syringe like a knife and stabbed the needle into the man's neck and emptied the Botox. Then she jumped on his back and wrapped her arms around his neck and choked him. He swung around with her clinging tight and Jesse fighting him. He was strong, but she soon felt his body slowing. Weakening. Finally he collapsed to the ground.

'You are a tough woman,' Jesse said.

'Like wrestling a calf at spring roundup.'

'Well, he will not have wrinkles for some time,' Jesse said. 'Bring the truck.'

She drove the truck over. The girls came out and helped them load the big man into the back. Jesse covered him with scrap wood and metal.

'What are you going to do?'

'He is a *coyote*. That is what they call men who bring Mexicans north. I would like very much to kill him, but I cannot. Hippocratic Oath. So I will drive him far into the Chihuahuan Desert and dump him. There he can live among real coyotes. Or not.'

'What about the girls?'

'Take them to the clinic and feed them. When I return, we will take them to the Mexican consulate in Laredo. They will reunite them with their families. Come on, Pancho.'

He got into the truck and drove off.

The governor's last press conference in the state capitol had drawn two local print reporters and no cameras.

But that day he walked into a press room crowded with twenty-five reporters and a dozen cameras; it was the first opportunity for the local media to question Bode Bonner, American hero.

'Governor—are you going to run for president?'

'No, I'm happy being governor.'

'Oh, give it a shot, Governor.'

Carl Crawford, being funny again.

'I told you, Carl, I can't bear to leave you.'

'Really, it's okay.'

'Nope. Won't do that to you. Heck, if I weren't governor, what would you write about? What would you do with your life if you weren't searching for scandals about me?'

'Well, now that you mention it, Governor, I did want to ask you about your last campaign expense report, which shows several questionable charges.'

'Such as?'

'Such as a seven-hundred-dollar charge at Cabela's for a three-fifty-seven Magnum handgun and'—he read from a document—'a camo cami with matching thong.'

A camo cami?

Bode glanced over at Mandy. She winked. He turned back to Carl.

'We used the gun in a commercial.'

'What about the camo cami?'

'I expect I'll see that camo cami pretty soon.'

The other reporters laughed. Who could begrudge a hero a little fun with a camo cami?

'Anything else today, Carl?'

'Yes. There was also a three-thousand-dollar charge at the Gap here in Austin and a six-hundred-dollar dress at Ralph Lauren on Rodeo Drive in L.A.'

Bode pointed at Josefina standing by the door with Mandy. She was wearing the yellow dress.

'I bought that yellow dress for her. And clothes for the kids. And I paid for glasses and dentists and doctors for them. You got a problem with that?'

'Uh . . . no.'

Carl shut up and sat down. Kim, the student reporter, stood.

'Governor, can we talk to the children?'

'Sure.'

He motioned to Mandy. She led the kids into the room then Bode introduced them. Cameras flashed, and reporters gathered close to the children. The reporters asked no questions about the budget deficit or mistaken executions or even the governor's work schedule this time. All of their questions were directed at the children. Josefina called him '*el hombre*' and '*mi héroe*' again.

These Mexican kids were the best thing that had ever happened to Governor Bode Bonner.

'*¿Fútbol?*' Rubén said.

'No. Football *americano*.' Bode pointed out to the field. 'See?'

'*Sí.*'

'No. See. Watch.'

They had stopped off at the UT stadium. The Godzillatron showed a clip of Bode Bonner, number 44, running an interception back for the winning touchdown against Oklahoma. That was a hell of a game. ESPN wanted to interview him at halftime.

'Governor!'

The star quarterback ran over to Bode and gave him a high-five and a football signed by the entire team. The scene played out on the massive HDTV screen. The crowd cheered. The quarterback jogged back onto the field. The head coach hurried over to Bode and stuck his hand out.

'Governor! Good to see you! Thanks for stopping by. So what do you think about the team?'

They were playing another orange–white spring practice game. The Mexican boys were excited even though they didn't have a clue what was going on. Mandy was bouncing like a cheerleader, but the attention that day was on the governor of Texas.

'They look like national champions.'

The coach said something into his mike then turned to Bode.

'Third and one. What do you think, Governor?'

'Play action. Go long, Coach.'

The coach called the play, and the quarterback threw the ball. Long. For a touchdown. The coach high-fived Bode.

'I better watch out,' the coach said, 'you might take my job.'

'Don't worry, Coach. I've got an even bigger job in mind.'

'Hidi, Governor!'

'Looking good, Gov!'

'We got your back, Bode!'

'I'm a follower!'

Even Democrats were not immune to celebrity. And Bode Bonner was now a certifiable celebrity in Austin, like Lance Armstrong and Sandra Bullock. So he received no 'You're a fucking Nazi!' greetings that day while jogging the lake with Ranger Hank.

'Hi, Governor,' a young woman said with a coy smile as she jogged past.

300

Bode glanced at her and saw her glancing back at him. Damn. The other runners greeted him with big smiles and high-fives as they jogged past. They asked him for autographs and cell phone photos. Democrats! Even the local newspaper called him a hero.

'Everyone loves a hero,' Ranger Hank said.

Maybe Democrats weren't all left-wing lunatics. Maybe living in the capital city wasn't that bad after all. Maybe he'd build his presidential library in Austin.

'The boss really gonna run for president?'

Jim Bob looked over at Eddie Jones sitting on his couch as the sun set over Austin.

'Yep.'

'Can he win?'

'Yep.'

'Can I help?'

'You will.'

'I feel like I'm not earning my paycheck.'

'You're like the fire insurance policy on my condo, Eddie. I pay the premium every month and hope to hell I don't need to make a claim. But if my condo catches fire, I'll damn sure need to then.'

'Huh?'

'I'm happy to pay you, and I hope I don't need your services. But I might. Especially once we get the "Bode Bonner for President" campaign in full gear. A national campaign always has a lot of unforeseen, unexpected, unpleasant moments.'

The governor of Texas could be dead in a matter of days.

Five hundred seventy-five miles due west of Austin,

DEA Agent Rey Gonzales sat in his El Paso office and stared out the window at Mexico. On his desk lay the results from the investigation of the shooting in the Davis Mountains. Specifically, the fingerprint results. Two of the men the governor had shot and killed were exactly who Rey figured they were: throwaways. Street boys recruited by the cartel in Nuevo Laredo. Their prints were in the system due to prior detainment in the U.S. and deportation to Mexico. No one cried for them.

But the third man was not a throwaway.

His prints were in the system for a different reason: he was an American citizen who held a U.S. passport. Born in the USA. Houston, to be exact. His name was Jesús de la Garza, the first-born son of Enrique de la Garza, alias El Diablo, head of the Los Muertos cartel.

The governor of Texas had killed the son of the most dangerous man in Mexico.

Now, if a politician in Mexico had committed such a foolish act, he would be dead before the sun again rose over the Rio Grande. As would be his wife, his children, his parents, his relatives, his neighbors, and his dog. After being cut into pieces, beheaded, and burned beyond recognition. Every politician in Mexico—every person in Mexico above the age of six—knew this fact well.

Consequently, such a politician would immediately gather his family and drive as fast as possible to the nearest border crossing, throw himself and his family on the mercy of America, and beg for asylum and protective custody from the United States government. In the likely event that his request was denied, he would commit suicide. At least then he could control the manner of his demise.

But politicians in America do not understand such harsh

302

facts of life and death. They have lived under the rule of law all of their lives. They have lived under the protection of police and state troopers and the FBI and the DEA. They have not lived in constant fear of abduction, death, and dismemberment by drug cartels. They do not have tracking chips implanted in their bodies so they can be found with GPS if the cartels abduct them. That is not an American politician's life.

They don't have a clue.

The governor of Texas didn't have a clue. So what did he decide to do after killing the son of El Diablo? Did he decide to lay low until the media frenzy died down? Did he decide to stay out of the public eye? Did he decide to update his last will and testament and get his affairs in order? No, he did not decide to do that. He decided to go on a nationally televised victory tour, like a football team returning home after victory in the Super Bowl.

He decided to flaunt his foolish act to cheering crowds.

Which, of course, was not the most prudent course of action. In fact, the most prudent course of action would be to sign up for the Witness Protection Program and move to the middle of Alaska. If Rey Gonzales knew his Mexican drug lords—and he did—El Diablo would come after the governor. Hard. Even as Rey sat there in El Paso that Monday evening, *sicarios* might already be tracking the governor, waiting for the opportune moment.

To kill him.

So Rey had taken the information to his station chief and suggested 24/7 security for the governor. The chief laughed.

'You want me to call headquarters and ask for round-the-clock security for the same Texas governor who's hammering the boss over border security?'

'Yes!'

'No!'

'Why the hell not?'

'Politics.'

'Because he's Republican?'

'Because he's gonna run against the boss.'

'So?'

'So how you figure that's gonna play in D.C.? The president himself came here to El Paso and stood right by the river and declared to all the world that the border is safe and secure. Three months later, the governor of Texas kills three Mexicans running a cartel marijuana farm and holding thirteen kids captive eighty miles north of the border. How's the president gonna explain that in the debates? Now you want the president to admit that we can't stop a Mexican drug lord from sending hit men across the border to kill a U.S. governor?'

'But what if they kill the governor?'

The chief shrugged. 'He won't be running against the boss.'

'But—'

'But nothing, Rey. That information doesn't leave this office. Fact is, we've got no credible leads, no evidence of a plot, no information leading us to believe that the governor is in imminent danger . . . we got nothing except your vivid imagination.'

The chief paused a moment then almost pleaded.

'Rey, I'm up for a promotion . . . to headquarters. That promotion is my ticket off this fucking border—and I'm gonna punch it.'

DEA Agent Rey Gonzales now stepped to the window and gazed down at the Rio Grande. That sliver of water served as an international border. But a line on a map would not stop El Diablo. Rey sighed. The governor was hoping to be elected president next year. He should be hoping to survive the next day.

Six hundred miles downriver of El Paso, the governor's wife sat on the back porch of the doctor's house. When Jesse had returned from the desert, they had taken the girls to the Mexican consulate. The girls had hugged her, then Jesse had taken them inside. She had waited in the truck with Pancho. They had saved eleven Mexican girls' lives that day. She now pointed up at a group of birds, like ducks flying south for the winter. But these were flying north. And they were too big to be ducks.

'Are those eagles?'

Jesse stared into the night sky.

'Drug smugglers, flying ultralights.'

Lindsay now heard a low buzzing noise as they came closer. She saw the flying machines. Six of them, flying in formation.

'Together they carry about a ton of dope, probably heroin or cocaine. They drop their loads in the desert. Their *compadres* on this side track them with GPS. Sometimes they fly too low and are decapitated by power lines.'

He paused.

'Drugs, money, guns, girls—it all comes and goes across the river.'

Chapter 20

'Killing Mexicans has been an effective strategy for Texas politicians since the Alamo,' the lieutenant governor said.

The jet engines hummed and ice tinkled in glasses filled with bourbon as the Gulfstream ferried the governor of Texas, the lieutenant governor, the speaker of the Texas House of Representatives, and Jim Bob Burnet down to Houston for the biggest Republican political gathering of the year. Ranger Hank rode up front with the pilots.

'Made Sam Houston a legend. Looks like it's doing the same for you.'

The lieutenant governor downed his bourbon. His second, and they weren't even over La Grange. Mack Murdoch was seventy years old and had served in the state senate for forty years and as lieutenant governor for the last twenty-four. When he got drunk, he recited Barry Goldwater like other people recited Walt Whitman.

But even Jim Beam couldn't improve the speaker's mood.

'We're twenty-seven billion in the hole,' the speaker said, 'but all my House members want to talk about are Mexicans and abortions.'

Bode groaned. 'What now?'

'Voter ID and sonograms.'

'Sonograms?'

'They want to make a woman getting an abortion see a sonogram of the baby.'

'Before or after the abortion?'

'Before. And make the woman listen to the fetal heartbeat.'

'Shit, that's creepy.'

'They want to force girls to have babies they don't want and can't afford,' the speaker said, 'but they don't want to pay more taxes to support and educate those kids once they're born.'

Speaker of the House Richard Warren was forty-three, young to hold the most powerful elected office in Texas—hence, he had not outgrown his nickname 'Dicky'—and considered far too liberal to be a Republican in Texas because (a) he didn't believe abortion was murder, (b) he didn't believe in the death penalty, (c) he didn't believe the Second Amendment applied to assault weapons with thirty-round clips, (d) he didn't hunt, and (e) he didn't cuss. And worst of all, (f) he had chosen college at Yale over UT or A&M, always a subversive act in Texas.

'An abortion is a helluva lot cheaper than funding twelve years of school and ten-to-life in prison,' the lieutenant governor said.

Bode shook his head. 'Sonograms. Do these abortion folks just sit around all day dreaming this shit up? Don't they have jobs?'

'Governor,' the speaker said, 'I need you to declare the voter ID and sonogram bills emergency legislation so we can ram them through in the first week after opening gavel, then I can get my members to focus on the budget. House Bill One is going to be ugly.'

The Texas legislature met every other year for one hundred forty days. The first bills introduced each session in the House and the Senate were the general appropriations bills, traditionally designated House Bill 1 and Senate Bill 1. The speaker presided over the House of Representatives, the lieutenant governor over the Senate.

'State constitution requires a balanced budget,' the

307

lieutenant governor said. 'No exception for when Wall Street assholes screw up the world's economy.'

'Only two ways to balance the budget, Governor,' the speaker said. 'Raise taxes or cut spending.'

'Dicky . . . it's an election year.'

'So we cut spending.' He opened a notebook. 'I figured that, so I've taken a shot at the cuts. First, we fire ten thousand state employees.'

'Hell,' Jim Bob said, 'we got two hundred forty thousand. Fire a hundred thousand.'

'And we gut the public health programs. Twelve million to prevent teen pregnancies—'

'Like that worked,' the lieutenant governor said. 'Our teen pregnancy rate is the highest in the nation. Cheaper to give away condoms at school.'

'Abstinence-only, Mack,' Bode said. 'That's official state policy.'

'That's official state bullshit. TV ran a story the other night about high school girls in East Austin, showed them kissing their babies goodbye before they went to their senior class prom. They ain't abstaining, Governor.'

'—ten million for the *colonias*—'

'Shit.'

'—two billion from higher ed—'

'Christ, the UT president's gonna be over to the mansion crying in his beer—he's sitting on a fifteen-billion-dollar endowment and he bitches every time we cut a dollar from his appropriations.'

'If he's got a hundred million to spend on the football team,' the lieutenant governor said, 'he can pay his own fucking way. Hell, if we spent that much money on our team, we'd beat UT like a redheaded stepchild.'

Mack Murdoch wore his Texas A&M class ring as if it were a Purple Heart.

'Dicky, is the House on board with the "guns on campus" bill? My boys at A&M are chomping at the bit.'

'Mack,' the speaker said, 'I'm a little concerned that a kid who gets a B on a term paper might pull his piece and drop his professor.'

The lieutenant governor shrugged. 'One less Democrat in Texas.'

Bode gestured at the speaker's notebook. 'What else is on your list?'

The speaker had taken notice of Bode's grim mood.

'It's fun to talk about cutting spending out on the campaign trail, Governor, not so much actually doing it. And we haven't even gotten to the big budget items, K through twelve and Medicaid.'

Bode exhaled. 'Tell me about Medicaid.'

'Bottomless hole and getting deeper by the day. Fifteen billion a year, a third of the budget. Six out of ten births in Texas are Medicaid babies, we're adding two hundred fifty thousand more people to the rolls each year. Just to keep up, we need three billion more. Every year. Forever.'

'Why do poor people keep having kids they can't afford?' the lieutenant governor said. Then he answered his own question. 'Because they don't have to afford them. We do. Problem is, won't be long before there ain't enough working people to pay for all the poor people.'

Bode stared out the window at Texas twenty thousand feet below. Mack Murdoch was a cantankerous old fart who drank too much bourbon, but that didn't mean he was wrong. The great state of Texas was poor and getting poorer by the day. By the birth. Texas' population had exploded by 4.3 million during the last decade—twenty-five percent of the total U.S. population growth—and ninety percent of those new Texans were poor. They were making a poor state desperately poor. The future of Texas was not bright and shining. It was Mississippi.

'I'm telling you, boys,' the lieutenant governor said, 'this is the end of civilization as we know it. And with our demographics, Texas will be the first to go.' He sighed. 'This used to be a great goddamn state.' He held up his glass as if to toast. 'To Texas.'

Bode and the speaker didn't join him in the toast. The lieutenant governor shrugged then downed his bourbon. Bode turned to the speaker.

'Tell me about K through twelve.'

'Ten billion.'

'*Ten billion?* Shit, Dicky, that's, what, thirty percent of the education budget?'

'Thirty-seven. And another two billion for pre-K.'

'We're gonna cut twelve billion from public schools?'

The speaker turned his palms up. 'That's where the money's at.'

'What's that mean?'

'We cut art and music classes, PE, libraries, band . . . we'll try to save football and coaches. We won't be able to save the teachers. We'll have to fire thousands. Tens of thousands.'

'Tens of thousands?'

'Fifty, sixty, some projections say a hundred. Thousand.'

'A hundred thousand teachers?'

The speaker gave a grim nod. 'A third of the work force. And they won't take it lying down. They'll march on the capitol. You piss off a middle-aged woman, you're in big trouble.'

'I know. I'm married to one.'

'We'll have to amend the law to permit larger class sizes, maybe twenty-five kids per class, maybe thirty-five. Maybe fifty-five.'

'Fifty-five kids per class?'

'Governor, we net eighty thousand new students every year. So we need a billion more each year just to tread water. Even with this budget, we'll still be drowning before the next biennium.' The speaker blew out a breath. 'It's what they call unsustainable.'

'Twelve billion, that'll gut public education.'

'We could cut football,' the speaker said, 'stop building those fancy high school stadiums.'

'Cut football? In Texas?'

'We could drain the rainy day fund.'

'The tea partiers would go apeshit, vote us out.'

'We could apply the sales tax to services. We've got law firms in Houston and Dallas grossing a billion a year and not paying a dime in taxes.'

'Then they'll go apeshit,' the lieutenant governor said.

'So?'

'So it'll never get out of the Senate.'

'Why not?'

'Every one of my senators is a lawyer.'

'Can't school districts raise their local property taxes?' Bode said.

The speaker shook his head. 'Everyone's already maxed out the tax rate, and home values keep falling. Taxes are plummeting and costs are skyrocketing. Not a good scenario for the future of education.'

'We've already got the highest dropout and lowest graduation rates in the country.'

'First in executions, last in graduations,' the lieutenant governor said. 'The state motto.'

Bode ignored him. 'What else can we do?'

'Reform the property tax,' the speaker said. 'Eliminate the exemption for private country clubs and ag. We've got ranchers and farmers sitting on land worth millions, but paying a few hundred bucks in taxes. Urban taxpayers are subsidizing rural taxpayers.'

Bode shook his head. 'Not politically doable. Those ranchers and farmers would torch the capitol.'

'We could pass that real-estate sales reporting bill, make the closing agents report the price of all property sales.'

'Which does what?'

'Right now, there's no reporting, so there's no comps for commercial property. Buildings worth a hundred million in Dallas and Houston are on the tax rolls for a fraction of that, so developers are paying only a fraction of what they owe in property taxes. Across the state, we're talking billions in lost school taxes.'

'The business lobby will say we're raising taxes,' Jim Bob said.

'We're collecting taxes due. Homeowners are paying at one hundred percent market value, but developers are paying at twenty-five percent. That's not fair.'

'This is politics,' Jim Bob said. 'Not preschool.'

The speaker looked to Bode; he just shrugged, as if to say, The Professor's the boss on all things political.

'Then we fire teachers and close schools.'

'How many schools?'

'Hundreds.'

'Any in Austin?'

The speaker nodded. 'My wife's on the school board. They're talking five hundred teachers and nine schools.'

312

'You know which ones?'

'Matter of fact, she sent me an email yesterday, begged me to raise taxes and save our schools.'

'Wives are naïve like that,' Jim Bob said.

The speaker opened his laptop and tapped the buttons.

'They'll have to close Oakwood, Barton, East Austin—'

'Shit. That's Lindsay's school. She volunteers there. I read to those kids.'

'You read to kids in East Austin?'

Bode nodded. 'Ms. Rodriguez—she's the teacher—she's working her butt off, trying to educate those kids. They close her school, what happens to the kids?'

'Bused to another school.'

'What about the teachers?'

'Fired.'

Bode downed another shot of bourbon.

'Christ, closing schools, firing teachers, making women get sonograms to have an abortion—if a mistress wasn't enough, this'll make Lindsay divorce me for sure.'

'Oh,' the speaker said, 'we can all forget about conjugal visits next session.'

'Hell,' the lieutenant governor said, 'I ain't had a hard-on since nineteen-eighty-nine. June.'

'Thanks for sharing,' Jim Bob said.

'Prostate?' Bode said.

'Yep. They yanked it out, left me insolent.'

'Impotent,' Jim Bob said.

'That, too.'

'You miss it?' Bode said.

'My prostate?'

'Sex.'

The lieutenant governor sighed. 'Every day.'

'Can we focus here?' Jim Bob said.

'Hell, Governor,' the lieutenant governor said, 'might be a good time to jump ship and make a run for the White House. Course, going from governor of a broke state to president of a broke country ain't exactly a promotion.'

'You gonna do it?' the speaker said.

'Thinking about it.'

'Can you beat Obama?' the lieutenant governor said.

'I beat Oklahoma.'

'Governor,' the speaker said, 'you'd be leaving us at a bad time.'

'Texas wasn't broke when George W. was in the White House,' the lieutenant governor said.

'Now we're broke because he *was* in the White House,' the speaker said.

'If Bode gets elected president, our budget problems are over. We'll be rolling in federal funds.'

'I'll give all of New York's money to Texas.'

'That ain't cheap,' the lieutenant governor said, 'running for the White House. It ain't like here in Texas where one John Ed Johnson can fund your campaign.'

'Can you say Super PAC?' the Professor said. 'Supreme Court threw out the limits on contributions to political advocacy groups. Freedom of speech. So all the candidates are forming Super PACs, shadow campaigns collecting hundreds of millions. This election, money's gonna decide who wins.'

'Money can't vote,' the speaker said.

'The hell it can't. We're going to round up twenty billionaires contributing fifty million each.'

'Twenty times fifty,' the lieutenant governor said. 'That's a hundred million.'

'A billion. You gotta carry the one.'

'Oh.'

The speaker shook his head. 'The country's broke, but rich folks are still willing to bankroll a presidential campaign.'

'Money's made in Washington, Dicky, because that's where the laws are made.'

'Still, twenty billionaires . . .'

'Nineteen. John Ed is number one.'

'He's in?'

'He is if he wants his condemnation bill signed by the governor. Speaking of which, we need you boys to get behind John Ed's bill, push your members to pass it next session.'

'Jesus, Professor,' the speaker said, 'a special bill giving a billionaire the power to condemn folks' land?'

'You want to tell John Ed no?'

The speaker sighed in the face of political reality.

'No.'

'Good.'

'Well, Governor, until you move into the White House,' the speaker said, 'we've got to find some way to balance the budget.'

'We raise taxes, Dicky,' the lieutenant governor said, 'we'll be looking for jobs with those teachers.'

'Then we cut twenty-seven billion from the budget,' the speaker said.

'Damn, Dicky,' Bode said, 'there's no other way to balance the budget?'

'Only one.'

'What's that?'

'Five-dollars-a-gallon gas.'

'What do you mean?'

'When gas spiked to four dollars back in oh-eight, our oil and gas taxes spiked, too, generated an extra five billion for the

315

rainy day fund. I figure five bucks a gallon for a year, maybe two, we could balance the budget without taxes or cuts.'

'You run the numbers on that?' Jim Bob asked.

'Yeah. Five bucks would do it.'

'Like the good old days when oil and gas paid all the bills in Texas,' the lieutenant governor said. He raised his glass again. 'Extremism in the defense of liberty is no vice. And moderation in the pursuit of justice is no virtue.'

He was drunk.

'Goddamnit, Mack, no Goldwater quotes. We're trying to save our fucking state.'

Bode drank his bourbon.

'God, I hate this.'

'What—governing?'

'This economy gets any worse, we'll be shutting the state down. Last one out, turn off the lights.'

He poured another bourbon.

'We've got to keep this quiet until after the election,' Jim Bob said. 'Word gets out we're going to gut the budget, voters will be marching on the Governor's Mansion. Now is no time for the truth.'

'Amen to that,' the lieutenant governor said.

'Sam Houston came to Texas in eighteen-thirty-two because he saw Texas as the land of promise. It was. It is. There is still a place where freedom reigns and government does not— that place is called Texas. My fellow Republicans, welcome to Texas!'

Governor Bode Bonner stood on the dais framed by Texas and U.S. flags and two huge video screens on which his image was displayed for the ten thousand conservatives crammed into the Houston Civic Center. He was giving the opening

316

speech at the Republican political action committee conference, the best opportunity for Republican political candidates to audition for votes and money. Donors, fundraisers, bundlers, PACs, politicians, billionaires, and corporate executives had come to buy and sell political favors. Bode walked off the stage to thunderous applause. Of course, most of the audience were drunk by now.

A political event held in Houston, Texas, meant country-western music and money. Lots of money. And liquor, of course. And cowboy boots and ten-gallon hats. Texans 'playing Texan,' as Edna Ferber called it, twanging and drawling and spitting out 'y'all' and 'howdy' like they were getting paid by the 'y'all' and 'howdy.' Ranger Hank stood to the side of Bode and fit right in wearing his cowboy uniform. Jim Bob leaned into Bode from the other side and whispered, 'Ralph and Nadine,' just before a heavy-set, middle-aged couple arrived. The man stuck his hand out to Bode.

'Howdy, Governor. Good shooting.'

Bode shook his hand and slapped his back.

'Ralph, how you doin', buddy? And Nadine, you're looking as pretty as ever.'

She outweighed Bode by fifty pounds.

'Governor,' Ralph said, 'I sure like what I heard on *Fox News* last Sunday. You've got my full support.'

Jim Bob pulled out a small notebook and a sharp pen. He looked at Ralph.

'How much?' he said.

'How much what?' Ralph said.

'How much support?'

'Oh, well . . .'

'We need fifty million, Ralph.'

'Damn, Jim Bob, that's real money.'

'You've got three billion.'

'Well, sure, but . . .'

'We're forming a Super PAC. We have room for only twenty donors, Ralph. Buy-in is fifty million.'

'And what do I get for my money?'

'What do you want?'

'Hell, I got everything I want.'

'Must be something . . . a law, a regulation, an environmental waiver . . .'

Ralph glanced at Nadine then across the room.

'Honey, look, that gal over there, is that one of the Kardashian sisters?'

Nadine's head shot around.

'Where?'

'At the bar.'

'Oh, my gosh. It might be.'

'Better go check it out.'

Nadine scurried off. Ralph turned back.

'I want to have sex with my mistress in the Governor's Mansion, in the same bed Sam Houston slept in.'

'But that's my bed,' Bode said.

'Done,' the Professor said.

He jotted in his notebook.

'I got you down for fifty million, Ralph. I'll get back to you with wiring instructions and a date for your sleepover.'

They all shook hands.

'Thanks, Ralph,' Bode said. 'Have fun.'

'Long as the whiskey holds out,' Ralph said.

He left. Bode watched after Ralph.

'Ralph is so damn ugly, when he was a kid his mama took him everywhere with her so she didn't have to kiss him goodbye. Can you imagine what his mistress looks like?'

He turned to Jim Bob.

'Make damn sure to burn the sheets.'

A tall, white-haired man arrived next. Paul Saunders, the senior Republican senator from Oklahoma. His breath was ninety proof.

'Senator, good to see you,' Bode said.

'Governor. You've had an interesting couple of weeks. Reckon shooting those Mexicans will be enough to get you into the White House?'

'Maybe.'

'Maybe not. Obama got Osama, but his pop in the polls lasted one news cycle. Even so, that's an expensive journey. We can help you.'

Senator Saunders headed the Republican reelection committee. He held the purse strings to the Establishment money.

'We're forming our own Super PAC,' Jim Bob said.

The senator exhaled heavily.

'Goddamn Supreme Court. We get the law all fixed so we can control the flow of campaign money, then they toss the law out like yesterday's newspaper. "Unconstitutional," they said. "So fucking what?" I said. Never stopped us before. Hell, damn near every law we pass is unconstitutional if you want to get technical about that sort of thing.'

'Why are you coming to me?' Bode said.

The senator sipped his drink.

'Palin.'

'She scares the hell out of you boys, doesn't she?'

A senatorial groan.

'More than you can imagine. She refuses to play ball by our rules. She thinks she doesn't need us, that she can tell us to go to hell. You know what would happen if every Republican politician started thinking like that?'

'Democracy?'

'Chaos. The two political parties keep order in this country. This isn't some banana republic with fourteen fucking political parties. This is America. Voters have to choose: Democrats or Republicans. A or B. Not C, D, or E, none of the above.'

'What about the tea party?'

The senator smiled. 'Oh, they're a little full of themselves and feisty, but one tour through the budget process, and they'll fall in line.'

'So you need me to make sure Palin doesn't win the Republican nomination, force herself on you.'

'Like having to take a fat cousin to the prom.'

'What if I don't play by your rules?'

The senator chuckled.

'You might figure you're a wild horse, Governor, don't need to run with the herd, but you'll learn just like every other politician has learned—you want to make a career out of politics, you need the protection of the herd.' The senator shrugged. 'And, hell, Governor, when it's all said and done, it doesn't matter all that much if we control the Congress or the White House, as long as we control one or the other. Both is better but one is enough.'

'For what?'

'Gridlock.'

'Senator, how long have you been in office?'

'This term will make it an even forty-two years.'

'Back at the beginning, when you first ran . . . did you want to do good?'

The senator did not seem offended.

320

'Course I did. I grew up in the coal mines of Oklahoma, where men worked hard and died young. Like my dad. He wanted more for me, paid my way through law school. I was gonna change things, by God, make those folks' lives better . . . but six months in Washington and reality set in. All I was doing was collecting campaign contributions to get reelected and passing earmarks, because the voters demanded I bring the pork home. Or they'd find someone else who would. Forty-two years later, it's only worse. People might talk limited government, but they want government money.'

He drank again.

'But that's not the worst part.'

'What's that?'

'Worst part is, you start hating your own voters. Like you do the homeless, their hands held out when you walk down the sidewalk, always wanting more, more, more.'

He downed his drink and walked off.

Buying control of the U.S. government is man's work, like coaching football and destroying the economy. White men wearing custom suits and holding the purse strings of political action committees and multinational corporations. Such white men approached the governor of Texas throughout the night.

'Fifty million,' Jim Bob said to the CEO of a major defense contractor.

'What do I get in return?'

'What do you want?'

'More jets, ships, tanks, missiles, weapons—more everything. And no restrictions on our overseas sales.'

'Why?' Bode said.

'War is profitable. Iraq and Afghanistan, three-point-seven trillion so far—that's real money. And we arm the world.

Our weapons systems are currently employed in every major military conflict in the world, and most of the minor ones. No one kills anyone in this world without an American-made weapon.'

'Sounds like a slogan.'

'It is.'

'Your missiles kill innocent people all over the world.'

'Missiles don't kill—only bad people with missiles kill.'

'Fifty million,' Jim Bob said to the Wall Street banker.

'What do I get?'

'What do you want?'

'Control of the Fed.'

'Why?'

'Because the American people want to believe someone is smart enough to hold the reins on this economy, that a Greenspan or Bernanke can keep the economy rolling along without ever experiencing a recession. Fact is, no one's that smart. But the people don't want to hear that. They want a guaranteed life. They want their 401(k) and home values to go up, they want to live beyond their means in big houses they can't afford and watch TVs the size of a goddamned movie theater, they want their lives to be profitable and care-free. They want someone—the government, Wall Street, their fairy fucking godmother—to guarantee that they'll live happily ever after. Well, it can't be done.' He pondered his words a moment. 'But, it does give us some money-making opportunities.'

'Such as?'

'By controlling the Fed, we control interest rates and money supply. Which allows us to move the markets. We can make money long or short, if only the markets move.

322

So we raise the interest rate and tighten the money supply, which depresses stock and real-estate values, and we buy up both. Then we lower the interest rate and loosen the money supply, which sparks inflation, and we ride the bubble up.'

'Until it bursts.'

'We sell out before that happens, stick the middle class with the losses in mutual funds and subprime mortgages. Buy low, sell high.' He shrugged. 'It's not finding the cure for cancer, but it's a living.'

'More drilling,' the CEO of an oil company said. 'More domestic drilling, more offshore drilling, more Alaska drilling . . . more drilling everywhere.'

'Tough sell today.'

'We're sending eight hundred billion dollars every year to the Middle East for their oil, money to Muslims who want to destroy America. Would you rather drill at home or get killed at home?'

'Done,' the Professor said. 'But we need more from you.'

'More than fifty million?'

'We need some help on gas prices.'

'We're not gonna lower gas prices!'

'I don't want you to lower them. I want you to raise them.'

'Raise them? Why?'

'Because the governor's got to balance the state budget during the next legislative session, and the press is going to beat us up once it gets out that we're looking at a twenty-seven-billion deficit and demand we raise taxes.'

A smile.

'I understand.'

Bode didn't.

'What are you talking about, Jim Bob?'

'Higher gas prices at the pump mean higher gasoline taxes and severance taxes. Bode, we jack up the prices enough, we can balance the state budget on oil alone.'

'So what price did you have in mind?' the CEO said.

'Five bucks a gallon would be nice.'

'We can do that.'

'Five bucks?' Bode said. 'Folks won't be able to fill up their pickups.'

The CEO chuckled. 'One thing we learned, Governor— people will pay any price to fill up their SUVs and pickup trucks.'

'How are you going to justify five bucks a gallon?'

The CEO rubbed his chin and grunted.

'Well, we can't use the "tight world supplies" line this time—we used that back in the summer of oh-eight.' He grinned. 'World was awash in oil, but we raised prices to four bucks a gallon and consumption didn't drop a barrel. Press picked up on the shortage line and ran with it. Public bought it. Record profits that year.'

He paused and sighed. A wistful look came over his face.

'Boy, that was a fun summer.'

Jim Bob cleared his throat to get the CEO's attention back to the present.

'Okay, so let's see . . .' His expression showed that his mind was scheming. He suddenly snapped his fingers. 'I got it. You're gonna love this. We'll jack up the prices and say, "Demand is increasing because the economy is improving, so higher gas prices are actually good for America." '

'That's bullshit,' Bode said. 'The economy sucks.'

'So? The people are desperate for the economy to improve, Governor, so we'll tell them what they want to hear. Doesn't have to be true. You're a politician, you know that.' He smiled. 'Hell, time we're through, the people will actually be happy to pay five bucks a gallon.'

'You guys are good,' Jim Bob said.

'We've been at this game a long time.'

And so the night went. Before last call at the bar was announced over the public address system, Jim Bob Burnet had locked in $650 million in pledges to the Super PAC. He gestured at the vast hall.

'Two weeks ago, these people wouldn't have given you the time of day. Now they're lining up to write you a check for fifty million. Because you killed a few Mexicans.'

It was Friday night, but not movie night. Jesse and Lindsay had worked late at the clinic then stopped at Luis Escalera's café for dinner. On their way home, they picked up the mail at the post office. Jesse went inside and returned with a handful of letters, which he handed to her.

'What's all this?'

'Open them.'

She opened the first letter. There was a check inside for ten dollars made out to Jesse Rincón, M.D. She opened another; inside was a check for twenty-five dollars. The next was a check for fifteen dollars.

'They're all checks,' she said. 'From San Antonio.'

'That profile must have aired. We always get checks after an interview or article runs. Perhaps there will be enough money to buy a fetal monitor.'

They stopped off at the market then drove home. The phone was ringing when they walked into the kitchen with the groceries. Jesse answered.

'Jesse Rincón.'

'Doctor. This is Jorge Gutiérrez. I am the mayor of San Antonio. I have been calling you all week.'

'There is no phone service in the *colonia* where I work.'

'Ah. Well, I have you now. Doctor, I would like to meet with you.'

'About what?'

'Being the first Latino governor in the history of Texas.'

'You want to run for governor?'

'No. I want you to run.'

Jesse laughed. 'I am sorry, Mayor. I am a doctor, not a politician.'

'Oh, you are much more than a doctor, Jesse . . . May I call you Jesse?'

'Yes, of course.'

'Please call me Jorge. Jesse, I have read all the articles about you, in the border newspapers and in the Houston paper. And I saw the profile this past Sunday on the San Antonio television station.'

'Checks came in the mail today.'

'I can make many more checks come in the mail, Jesse.'

'How can you do that?'

'By spreading the word among my Mexican Mafia.'

'Your what?'

'My network of Hispanics in business, law, the media . . . Hispanics who want to help. Jesse, you could do much good for Latinos in Texas.'

'I am doing good for Latinos right here.'

'You could do more good in Austin. In the Governor's Mansion. Jesse, you could be the one.'

'The one what?'

'The one who leads Latinos to power in Texas. *El salvador.*'

'I am sorry to disappoint you, Mayor, but I am neither a politician nor a savior. I am just a doctor.'

326

'We've been waiting a long time for our savior.'

'I am afraid you must wait a while longer.'

'Jesse, you are the only man who can save America from Bode Bonner.'

The governor of Texas flew back to Austin late that night. They dropped Jim Bob off at his downtown condo then drove to the mansion. Bode climbed the stairs to the family quarters and entered the master bedroom. Mandy Morgan lay asleep on the bed. In a camo cami with matching thong. She was young, and she was beautiful, and she was sexy. He felt young.

Alive.

Vital.

Relevant.

But not because of Mandy. Because the great adventure was upon him. Because he was the man who would be president. Because he had the polls, the Twitter followers, the Super PAC, and the testosterone to win the White House. Because he had everything.

Except a first lady.

'Mayor Gutiérrez wants you to run for governor?'

Lindsay had overheard Jesse's conversation.

'That is what he said.'

They were sitting on the back porch overlooking the river. The stars were out, and the night was quiet.

'But that would be a conflict of interest,' he said.

'What?'

'Running for governor while loving the governor's wife.'

'Are you?'

'No. I will not run.'

'No. In love with me?'

'Yes. I am.'

He reached over and took her hand. Maybe it was the wine she had had with dinner, but she did not pull away. She held the doctor's hand and thought of her husband. He wanted to be president; a president needed a first lady. She wanted to be a nurse; a nurse needed a doctor. She felt herself drawn to Jesse Rincón—but as a doctor or a man? Or both?

Lindsay Bonner was not a complicated woman. She had never had issues. She had always known who she was and what she wanted.

Now, she wasn't so sure.

FOUR MONTHS
BEFORE

Chapter 21

'General Zaragoza defeated Napoleon's forces at Puebla on May the fifth, eighteen–sixty–two,' Jesse said, 'and brought democracy back to Mexico. That is what the Mexican people celebrate on this day, *Cinco de Mayo*.'

They stood before the general's statue in the San Agustín Plaza in downtown Laredo. Palm trees surrounded the plaza, as if they were the general's sentries. Street vendors sold Mexican food and margaritas, beer and bottled water. Mariachis strolled the plaza singing Mexican ballads, and Mexican flags flew from every light pole and storefront. Girls clad in old–style costumes performed traditional dances. The plaza looked and sounded and smelled like old *México*. Lindsay and Jesse had gone into town for lunch at the *Cinco de Mayo* festival. The local newspaper and television station had cameras capturing the crowd. Lindsay wore her scarf, hat, and sunglasses to avoid being recognized. But everyone recognized Jesse Rincón. Young girls flirted with him and asked for photos with him, and old men came to him and shook his hand. He had been interviewed on camera twice when a young man stuck a hand out to him.

'Doctor. Ángel Salinas from Austin. With *Texas Journal*. Mayor Gutiérrez said I should come to Laredo and interview you.'

Lindsay quickly averted her face. She knew Ángel, and he knew her. She walked to the far side of the plaza where the girls were dancing. Where her picture would not be taken and she would not be recognized.

'*Mrs. Bonner?*'

She turned to the familiar voice—to Congressman Ernesto Delgado. He held a long *churro* like a kid holding a popsicle. His face evidenced his astonishment.

'Is that really you?'

'Yes. It's me.'

'What . . . what are you doing here? Dressed like that?'

'I'm Jesse's nurse.'

'*No.*'

'Yes. For a month now.'

'I heard he had an Anglo nurse, but they said she was Irish.'

'I am.'

She demonstrated her accent.

'I would not have known it was you.'

'No one can know. You mustn't tell a soul. Please.'

'Your secret is safe with me. But why?'

'I need to be useful.'

He gave her a knowing nod. 'Ah, yes. At my age, I under-stand that need. But how will this work, when the governor is the president?'

'My daddy the president!'

Bode hugged his daughter and inhaled her fresh scent; she had showered (if not shaved) that day.

'You're like, a celebrity now.'

'Hell, if I'd known shooting a few Mexicans was all it took, I'd've done it a long time ago. Jim Bob, how many followers I got on Twitter?'

Jim Bob fiddled with his phone.

'Eight million.'

'Wow,' Darcy said, 'that's more than Selena Gomez!'

'I thought she died?'

'That was the singer. This is the actress.'

'Oh.'

Becca hugged him again.

'I'm so proud of you, Daddy.'

She seemed as excited as on her sixteenth birthday when Bode had surprised her with a new Ford pickup truck. Darcy hugged him, then they sat at their regular table on the raised seating section at the front window at Kerbey's on the Drag. UT students walked past on the sidewalk just on the other side of the plate glass and waved at the governor of Texas—with all five fingers. Jim Bob sat at the adjacent table and played with his phone. Ranger Hank stood at attention behind them.

'How are the kids?' Becca said.

Becca and Darcy had come over to the mansion and played with the Mexican children several times in the last month.

'Good. It's been fun to have kids around the mansion again, like when you were growing up.'

'How many are still with you?'

'Six. We found the others' relatives, but we've still got five of the boys and Josefina. The cartel killed her folks.'

'What are you going to do with her?'

'I don't know.'

'Why don't we keep her?'

'She's not a stray puppy, Becca. And without your mom here . . .'

Their waitress, a cute gal with tattooed arms and a nose ring, arrived to take their order. Bode went for the cinnamon peach pancakes. The girls went for salads.

'She still down on the border?'

Bode nodded. 'I figured on waiting her out, that she'd get bored and come back. She hasn't.'

'You know how she is when she's on a mission.'

The waitress returned with their drinks. Becca emptied two sweeteners into her tea and stirred.

'She'll have to come back, Daddy, if you're elected president. Only problem is, if you guys are living in the White House, we won't be able to have lunch together.'

'Sure we will. I'll just fly down every week.'

'No, I mean, the Secret Service won't let you eat here, with this big window right on the street. Someone might shoot you.'

'Well, no need to worry about that now.'

Becca laughed. 'Yeah, who would want to shoot the governor of Texas?'

She dropped her teaspoon.

Ranger Hank heard the spoon hit the floor and watched the governor and his daughter duck under the table at the same time to retrieve it, but his attention was diverted by a cute coed with long legs in a short skirt off to his left; he glanced her way just in time to catch a shot of her neon pink underwear as she sat down. Damn, that's a sweet *femále*. He turned back just as a black SUV skidded to a stop on Guadalupe Street directly in front of their window and two men jumped out and pointed high-powered automatic weapons at them. His right hand went for his gun, but he was too late. The first bullet hit him in his right eye, shattering his sunglasses and the back of his skull after boring a hole through his brain. He was dead before the next six bullets hit his body and his body hit the floor.

★ ★ ★

334

'*Daddy!*'

The plate glass window above them exploded. Bode lunged for Becca and covered her under the table as glass and bullets sprayed the restaurant. Diners in the lower section screamed and cried out and dove under their tables and booths. Waiters dropped serving trays and scrambled out of the line of fire; dishes and glasses crashed to the floor. It sounded like a war movie. But Bode knew it was real. Because Hank lay next to them, blood streaming from bullet holes in his face and chest. He was gone. But the gunfire was not. Bullets bit into the walls and sliced through light fixtures and cut wood support posts into splinters. Jim Bob was unhurt and under his table, punching 911 on his phone. But the police wouldn't arrive in time.

'Stay down!'

Bode reached over and yanked Hank's weapon out of his holster. It was a nine-millimeter semiautomatic pistol with a fifteen-round clip. He grabbed Hank's spare clip then clicked the safety off and chambered a round and waited for a pause in the shooting, when the men had run through their clips and had to reload. The gunfire lasted less than fifteen seconds, but it seemed like an hour. Then it stopped.

They were reloading.

Bode knelt up and saw two men standing in the middle of the street holding assault weapons. They were no more than twenty feet outside the restaurant. They had ejected spent clips and were inserting new ones. He stood and aimed the pistol center mass and fired. He hit both men in the chest three times each, dropping them.

'Don't move, Becca!'

He climbed through the blown-out window and walked to the men; broken glass crunched under his boots. One man moved; Bode shot him again. Twice. Bode approached a black SUV angled across Guadalupe Street; a dark figure moved in the driver's seat. He aimed and fired through the windshield. Five times. He ejected the spent clip and snapped in the spare just as a man fell out of the vehicle with an AK-47; Bode shot him six times before he could fire his weapon. He heard sirens in the distance. He checked that the SUV was empty then walked back through air thick with gunpowder. He looked through the open window at Becca.

'Are you hurt?'

She shook her head, but she wasn't looking at Bode. She was staring at Darcy, who lay motionless on the floor with her eyes open and a bullet hole in her forehead.

Ángel Salinas was a charter member of Mayor Gutiérrez's Mexican Mafia. He had driven the two hundred thirty-five miles from Austin to Laredo just to interview Jesse Rincón.

'Doctor,' Salinas said, 'you could beat the governor—'

His cell phone rang. He checked the number.

'It's my office.' He punched the button and answered. 'Ángel . . . *What?* . . . *When?* . . . *Shit!* . . . I'm leaving now.'

He disconnected but stared at his phone a moment. Then he looked up at Jesse.

'They killed the governor. His daughter, too.'

He ran off. Jesse turned in a circle searching for the governor's wife.

'They missed. We're both okay.'

Lindsay Bonner breathed a sigh of relief.

'Thank God.'

She had called Bode's cell phone. Her husband and her daughter had survived an assassination attempt. But Bode did not speak. There was more.

'What is it?'

He exhaled into the phone.

'They killed Hank and Darcy.'

She felt her legs start to give way.

'Oh, God. No.'

'I'm sending the jet to Laredo. You're coming home, Lindsay.'

'*Sicarios*,' DEA Agent Rey Gonzales said to the governor of Texas. 'Hit men.'

Austin police, Texas Rangers, state troopers, and FBI and DEA agents now swarmed Guadalupe Street outside the restaurant called Kerbey's. The street was blocked off from traffic, and police barricades and cruisers cordoned off the crime scene from the reporters and cameras. People shouted, emergency lights flashed, and blood stained the governor's clothes.

'Hit men?'

Rey nodded. 'Each cartel has a *sicario* unit. In-house assassins. Ex-military and law enforcement, hired out to the cartels.'

'And they're here in America?'

'FBI's got an entire task force devoted just to Mexican *sicarios* working in the U.S. They just killed a stockbroker up in New York named Ronald Richey.'

'He was into drugs?'

'Investment banking. Enrique de la Garza—we tagged him "El Diablo"—he's the head of Los Muertos, he invested a billion with Richey, blamed him for losing half in subprime mortgages.'

'So he killed the guy?'

'Bullet through his brain.' Rey gestured at the dead Mexicans sprawled across Guadalupe Street. 'Standard payment for a U.S. assassination is fifty grand cash plus two kilos of cocaine, worth three hundred grand on the street. We found two hundred grand cash and ten kilos of coke in their vehicle. El Diablo, he put a premium on your head. He wants you dead, Governor.'

'Because we found his marijuana?'

'Because you killed his son.'

'*His son?*'

'One of those Mexicans you killed on the ranch, he was El Diablo's first-born son. Jesús de la Garza, nineteen years old.'

Rumors had been percolating on the border that El Diablo had sent a team of *sicarios* into Texas. Rey knew the target had to be the governor. So he had taken it upon himself to come to Austin and warn the governor. He had arrived in town that morning, too late to save the Ranger and the girl. The governor and his daughter were just lucky.

'Who does this guy think he is, the godfather?'

'Governor, El Diablo makes the godfather look like a middle-school bully. The broker, that was business. This is personal.'

The governor turned to the bodies of the Texas Ranger and the college girl and his daughter sobbing in Mr. Burnet's arms. Then he turned back to Rey.

'You're goddamn right it's personal.'

The governor of Texas stood in front of a cluster of microphones set up in the parking lot. He faced a dozen television cameras but pointed at the crime scene.

'This is what happens when a sovereign nation can't control its own borders. When it won't control its own borders because of politics. People die.'

'Governor,' a reporter said, 'the FBI says these men were professional killers. They staked you out, knew your daily routine. They knew where to find you. Aren't you afraid El Diablo will make another attempt on your life?'

Bode Bonner stared into the cameras.

'I'm not afraid of the devil himself.'

'Oh, you should be, Governor. You should be very afraid.'

Enrique de la Garza once loved the game of *béisbol* more than life itself. He loved the smell of the grass and his leather glove and the feel of the wood bat in his hands. He had the glove and the arm but not the bat to play in the American majors. So his playing days had ended but not his love for the game. On the shelf in his office, he maintained a costly collection of baseballs autographed by the legends of the game. He often imagined autographing baseballs for fans before games in Boston; he went to many Red Sox games while at Harvard and often dreamed of playing shortstop at Fenway Park. He now picked up the Ted Williams ball and threw it as hard as he could at the image on the television of the Anglo he now hated more than any man before. He turned to Hector Garcia but pointed a finger at the shattered screen.

'I want that man dead. I want his head on my desk.'

He took a deep breath to get his blood pressure under control. He calmed and assessed the damage.

'Ask Julio to go online and order another television.'

Chapter 22

Hank Williams was buried two days later, and Darcy Daniels three. Governor Bode Bonner stood between his wife and daughter as Darcy's casket was lowered into the ground. Becca buried her face in his chest and cried until his shirt was wet. Roped-off barricades manned by Texas Rangers and state troopers kept the crowd back. Security was tight, but television cameras captured every moment. Lindsay Bonner wore a black dress, a black hat, and a black veil.

Enrique de la Garza watched the funeral on the television. Even in the veil, something about the governor's wife seemed vaguely familiar, as if he had seen her before. But like a dream he could not fully recall, he could not place her. He turned back to his *abogado* but pointed at the screen.

'They bury their people. I want to bury my son.'

'Enrique,' his lawyer said, 'during the last month I have exhausted every possible avenue—diplomatic channels through the American consulate, every political connection I have here and in the U.S., the church . . . I even called the local sheriff in Fort Davis and offered compensation. But he refused. The Americans, they will not release his body. And they probably have moved the body by now, to El Paso or perhaps Austin.' He gestured at the television. 'And trying to kill the governor, that did not help matters.'

Felix Montemayor had once served as attorney general of *México*. Born into an aristocratic family in Guadalajara, he had attended college at Stanford and law school at Yale. He had pursued a political career long enough to become connected and then a lucrative career in private law; he now enjoyed a more lucrative career as Enrique's personal lawyer. The press had dubbed him *el abogado del Diablo*. The devil's advocate. Enrique slid the satellite phone across the desk to his lawyer.

'Get him on the phone.'

'The governor?'

'The sheriff.'

Felix found the number in his briefcase then dialed. He put the phone to his ear. After a moment, he said, 'Sheriff Roscoe Lee, please. Felix Montemayor calling.'

Enrique gestured for the phone. He took it and waited for the sheriff to answer. A slow Texas drawl came across the line from four hundred miles away.

'This here's Sheriff Lee. Mr. Montemayor—'

'No, Sheriff. This is Enrique de la Garza.'

The phone went silent, but he could hear breathing.

'You know who I am, Sheriff?'

'I do.'

'And you know what I want?'

'I reckon so.'

'One million dollars, Sheriff. Cash. For my son's body. I can wire the money anywhere in the world you would like.'

'But I live here. In Fort Davis, Texas.'

'Then I will give you the money there.'

There was a long pause and then a heavy sigh.

'Well, I don't know what the hell I'd do with a million dollars anyway, Mr. de la Garza. Guess I'll pass.'

'Sheriff, are you a father?'

'I am.'

'Then you must understand my desire to bury my son in a proper Catholic service?'

341

'I do. But I can't let go of the body without the state boys and the Feds giving their okay, and that just ain't gonna happen, 'specially after you just tried to kill the governor. Some folks take offense at that sort of thing. So your boy is just gonna have to sit in my freezer a while longer.'

Enrique ended the call and looked at his lawyer.

'His body is still there.'

'This one of those unforeseen, unexpected, unpleasant moments?'

Jim Bob turned to the insurance policy named Eddie Jones and nodded.

'But not the kind I figured on.'

'You want me to bodyguard the boss from now on?'

Jim Bob shook his head. 'From what I hear, you're a little quick on the trigger.'

'Maybe. But I never lost a client.'

'We brought in more Rangers, SWAT guys carrying more than pistols.'

'Good. 'Cause they'll be back.'

'Bode killed them.'

'There'll be more.'

'I knew that was his son,' Lindsay said. 'Now he wants revenge.'

'Which is why you can't go back to the border. It's not safe, Lindsay. He might come after you.'

'No one down there knows who I am. In the *colonias*, I'm just a nurse.'

'What about Becca? This hit her hard.'

'I'll stay until she's ready to go back to school. She needs a bodyguard.'

The Governor's Mansion looked like a scene out of *The Godfather* after the war between the Mafia families had begun; armed guards patrolled the perimeter and spotters with rifles stood on the roof. Ranger Roy loitered thirty feet away. He apparently had decided not to let the governor's wife out of his sight this time, and he hadn't since she had returned to Austin. She had been gone a month, the longest she had ever been apart from her husband. She had embraced Bode when she had first returned to the mansion, but not since. She still slept on the day bed. Even nearly getting killed couldn't bring his wife back to their bed. Even though he had banished Mandy to the Governor's Office in the state capitol. They now sat outside on the bench facing the south lawn. They had returned from the funeral but had not gone inside the mansion. They sat close, but he knew better than to touch her.

'It's good to have you back.'

'I'm not back.'

'You ever coming back? For good?'

'I don't know.'

'You're leaving your family for a bunch of Mexicans in the *colonias*?'

'You left me for Mandy.'

'After you moved out of our bedroom.'

'I don't want to do this, Bode. Not now.'

Bode stared out at the green grass and the blue sky above. Hank and Darcy were gone, and his wife wanted to be.

'I need you, Lindsay.'

She sighed heavily, almost a cry.

'You don't need me, Bode Bonner. You just need a first lady.'

* * *

343

'When will the *señora* return?' Inez said from her desk by the door.

'I do not know.'

'But she will return?'

'I do not know.'

But he knew she would never return.

Jesse had driven her to the airport three days before. When she got out of his truck, he knew he would never see her again. That day had come. She had left him. And he had learned the answer to his question: It was better never to have loved than to have loved and lost.

'I miss her,' Inez said.

'I loved her.'

Lindsay embraced her daughter.

'I know, honey.'

'Why didn't he save her? Daddy.'

'He would have if he could. He would have stood in front of her, taken the bullet himself. Your father is a lot of things, Becca, but he's no coward.'

'I'm scared.'

'You don't have to be, not with your father here. He'll protect you.'

'I wish we were back on the ranch.'

'I wish we had never left the ranch.'

'Mom . . . are you guys getting a divorce?'

'*A divorce?* No . . . I don't think so . . . I don't know.'

'Do you have someone else?'

'No.'

Jesse didn't count as someone else, did he?

'Does Dad?'

Yes.

'No.'

She couldn't do that to her daughter.

'Then why are you living down on the border?'

'To do something good with my life.'

'He's going to be president.'

'That's his life, not mine.'

'You won't be able to work on the border when he's president. You won't be able to hide your face anywhere in the world then.'

For the first time in five years, Jesse Rincón contemplated leaving the *colonias*. His time with the governor's wife opened up all the possibilities of life for him. Perhaps the time had come for him to live beyond the wall. Perhaps the time had come for him to make a different choice in life. The thought of being alone the rest of his life now seemed unbearable. He wanted a woman in his life. He wanted the governor's wife in his life. But it was not to be.

'She is gone, Mother.'

Jesse brushed dirt from the small flat stone that marked his mother's grave in the *colonia* cemetery. GRACIANA RINCÓN . . . 1952–1973.

'But it is for the best. This border is no place for such a woman. Dirt and death, that is all the borderlands has to offer. A woman such as her, she belongs in Austin, or perhaps Washington. Yes, she will make a fine first lady.'

'When Governor Bode Bonner shot and killed three Mexican cartel *soldados* in West Texas and rescued thirteen Mexican children from a marijuana farm, he became an American hero. But when he grabbed his dead Texas Ranger bodyguard's gun and shot and killed three Mexican hit men—*sicarios*, they

345

are called—saving his daughter's life and the lives of dozens of diners in this restaurant in the middle of Austin, Texas, he became an American legend. A living legend. The only question is, with a Mexican drug lord gunning for him, how long will he remain living? Reporting from Austin, Texas.'

Jim Bob switched channels from network to network to network to catch the evening news reports. One reporter stood in the middle of Guadalupe Street just outside Kerbey's restaurant; another stood just across the street on the UT campus; and a third stood in the parking lot. All were reporting live from Austin, Texas, as they had for the last three days. The national media had descended on the capital of Texas.

'How did the hit men smuggle the weapons into the U.S.?' the reporter asked DEA Agent Rey Gonzales.

'They didn't. The gun laws in Mexico are very strict. So they crossed into the U.S. at Laredo, drove up I-35 to San Antonio, and bought the guns and ammo at a gun show last weekend. The cartels buy all their guns in Texas.'

'Fully automatic AK-47s with thirty-round magazines?'

'You can buy a bazooka at a gun show.'

'Without a criminal background check?'

The agent nodded. 'The "gun show loophole." Big enough to drive a semi through. The bad guys buy their guns at gun shows and missiles on the black market.'

'Missiles?'

'El Diablo, he bought a Russian-made missile and shot down our Predator drone.'

'A drug lord shot down our drone? I can't believe that.'

'You'd better believe it.'

'Agent Gonzales, do you think the governor's life is still in danger?'

Another nod. 'The governor killed El Diablo's son. He won't quit.'

'How can you ensure the governor's safety?'

'We can't.'

Jim Bob muted the news and turned to Bode with a big grin.

'Do you know how lucky you are?'

'Not getting killed?'

'Getting this kind of press coverage? Favorable pieces on the networks for a Republican?'

The Professor opened his black notebook.

'This poll was conducted after the assassination attempt. The more Mexicans you kill, the higher your poll numbers go. Seventy-six percent total favorable . . . unbelievable. White males, ninety-one percent. White females, eighty-four. African-Americans, forty-three percent. Hispanics . . . get this . . . thirty-nine percent.'

'In Texas?'

'In the U.S. This is a national poll. I've never seen anything like it. You're blowing everyone else away across the entire socioeconomic spectrum. The other Republicans are road kill in your rearview. And you're up on Obama by a million Twitter followers and twelve points in the polls. We're talking Reagan-over-Carter landslide.'

'Jesus, Jim Bob, they tried to kill my daughter.'

'No. They tried to kill you. She was just there.'

'Still.'

'Are you a "glass-half-full" kind of guy or a "glass-half-empty" kind of guy?'

'What the hell does that mean?'

'It means, you and Becca survived an assassination attempt. You can sit back and pout about it, or you can move forward and make the best of it.'

'Darcy and Hank are dead.'

'You didn't kill them. The Mexicans did.'

Jim Bob's phone rang. He answered.

'John Ed . . . yeah, he's right here. Hold on, I'll put you on the speaker.'

Jim Bob activated the speakerphone.

'You're on with Bode.'

'Governor,' John Ed Johnson's voice boomed from the speakerphone, 'glad you ain't dead.'

'Well, thanks, John Ed. I appreciate your—'

''Cause I need your help on my bill.'

'—concern.'

'So where do things stand? You got the votes lined up?'

'Goddamnit, John Ed, I've been a little fucking busy lately, shooting Mexican assassins, burying my daughter's roommate and my Ranger bodyguard. I told you I'd work your bill, and I will.'

'No reason to get testy.'

Bode exhaled. 'Sorry, John Ed, it's been a little stressful around here.'

'Yeah, okay. You boys have a good day.'

The line went dead. Jim Bob chuckled.

'John Ed ain't exactly the touchy-feely type.'

'He ain't exactly the human being type.'

The Professor leaned back in his chair and smiled.

'No one can stop you now.'

'There's a Mexican trying to.'

'Kill the governor for me, *por favor.*'

'We could kill his wife and daughter very easily,' Hector Garcia said.

'No. His wife and daughter did not murder my son. We

348

do not kill women or children or innocents. We have already killed one innocent, the college girl.'

'And the Ranger.'

'Rangers are not innocents.'

'My men, they were careless, with machine guns.'

'Yes, careless and now dead.'

Enrique looked Hector in the eye.

'Will you do that small favor for me?'

'*Sí, mi jefe*, I will send—'

'No. Do not send anyone. I want you to go north of the river. I want you to go into *Tejas*. I want you to kill the governor.'

'*Sí, mi jefe*. I will leave tomorrow.'

'*Bueno*. But first, Hector, bring my son home.'

Chapter 23

'You gave me no father, you took my mother, and now you take the only woman I have ever loved. You should not be so cruel. But then, why do I talk to you? You are not here to listen. There is no god on the border.'

Jesse and Pancho ran the river at dawn. He tried to run out his anger and his disappointment, his sadness and his longing, his loneliness and his broken heart. The sun just now peeked above the horizon and brought light to the borderlands. It had been one week since the governor's wife had left. It seemed as if forever.

Pancho barked.

He faced south as the river flowed. In the distance, two black objects appeared in the sky. They quickly grew in size. They came closer. Fast. And then that same WHUMP WHUMP WHUMP sound became louder and louder until two sleek black helicopters flying low and fast just above the river blew past in a rush of wind, weaving left and right with the course of the river.

Hector Garcia glanced out the window of the helicopter at the man and his dog. He once had a dog. Back when he was a captain in the special forces. A commando. Employed by the Mexican Army and trained by the U.S. Army. To fight the drug cartels. But his entire unit had hired out to the Guadalajara cartel as enforcers. Everyone except Hector Garcia.

He had hired out to Enrique de la Garza.

El jefe was different than the other cartel heads. He was educated and sophisticated. Religious and generous. A faithful husband and a family man. He even had a code of honor: Los Muertos do not use drugs, do not sell drugs to Mexicans, do not kill women, children, or innocents, and always tithe twenty percent to charity and church. They never initiated gun battles with other cartels; they only killed in self-defense or in the pursuit of justice; they killed corrupt politicians or *policia* only as a last resort, preferring instead to put them on the payroll; they were not wanton killers who hung corpses from overpasses to frighten the people or rolled heads into nightclubs or set fire to casinos to kill innocent Mexicans. They were not animals like the other cartels. They were civilized, like their leader. Hector had been twenty-five at the time, and after six years in the corrupt Mexican military, he yearned for order and discipline and honor. He had been Enrique de la Garza's right-hand man for seven years now. He would give his life for *el jefe*. He owed that much to him.

Because Hector had killed his wife.

Women were his weakness, and Liliana de la Garza made him weak. Her beauty was breathtaking and unparalleled among women. When Hector hired on and first met her, the lust ignited inside him. Over two years the fire grew and grew until his desire burned out of control. Until he thought he would go insane if he did not have her. One night, when *el jefe* was out of town, he drank the whiskey then went to her suite. He knocked on her door. When she answered, he pushed his way in.

He raped her.

She said Enrique would kill him when he returned. Hector knew his fate. The machete. He also knew that Liliana would attend mass at seven the next morning. She would travel in a caravan of Mercedes-Benzes to the cathedral. So he tipped off the *gringos* at the DEA in Laredo; he told them El Diablo would be in the caravan.

They killed Liliana de la Garza instead.

The Italian helicopter cruised at one hundred seventy-five miles per hour. They hugged the Río Bravo, running below radar; and with the Predator drone gone from the sky, the U.S. Border Patrol could not see the two helicopters flying west along the border.

They were invisible.

They cleared Laredo and Nuevo Laredo and the *maquiladoras* where the *gringos* enslaved the *Mexicanos* and the wretched *colonias* that lined both sides of the river on the western outskirts and veered northwest over the vast Chihuahuan Desert. They would cut the corner and pick up the Río Bravo again where it made the big bend. They flew low enough to see the jackrabbits and the roadrunners and the peasants heading north across the desert; they would most likely die before they reached the river. They soon passed over Sabinas and Nueva Rosita and the impressive Río Conchos. Hector sat up front with the pilot as he did back in the military. But this chopper was not as it had been flying old Hueys in the army. *El jefe* had spared no cost when he purchased the fleet of six helicopters. So they traveled in air-conditioned comfort, and the men sat in the back cabin in leather seats and played video games on the flat-screen monitor; their AK-47s lay at their feet on the carpeted cabin floor.

Hector's thoughts returned to *el jefe*. He had always viewed killing as part of the business. He did not take it personally. Not even when the *gringos* killed his wife. But his son's death—that he had taken personally. Jesús de la Garza had been a mean, cruel, undisciplined boy. Of course, his father could not see the true boy. He saw only the boy he wanted his son to be. Hector had not been disappointed when the governor of Texas had killed him. But *el jefe* had become obsessed with *venganza*.

So Hector Garcia would seek *el jefe*'s revenge.

They rejoined the Río Bravo at the big bend. They dropped down to just above the river surface and followed its course, veering right and left, through the steep rock canyons the water had carved into the rugged land over millions of years. The rock walls rose five hundred meters on both sides; brown water lay below and blue sky above. They flew so low that when they came upon two rafts of *gringos* floating down the river, the rafters bailed out for fear the helicopters would hit them. Hector and the pilot shared a laugh. It was a magnificent journey, but a short one. They soon emerged from the big bend and turned north into *Tejas*.

'Ten minutes,' the pilot said over the radio.

Hector checked his AK-47. They followed a narrow highway that cut through the lower portions of the Davis Mountains and passed through the little town of Marfa. They flew over cattle grazing and land that once belonged to *México*.

'Two minutes.'

His *soldados* got ready. Hector had brought a dozen men, even though he expected no resistance.

'In and out,' he said over the radio. 'No shooting except on my order. A Team makes entry, B Team secures the perimeter.'

Six men would go in; six men would stay out.

'Thirty seconds,' the pilot said.

A small town came into view. The streets remained vacant. They flew in low and fast searching for the red roof with the clock tower. Hector pointed.

'There!'

The courthouse. The sheriff's office, jail, and morgue occupied the basement of the two-story courthouse that sat on a grassy block surrounded by trees, apparently the only trees in town. The pilot pulled the nose up, and Hector and his men were out the doors—'*¡Vaya, vaya, vaya!*'—before the wheels touched State Street.

Fort Davis served as the county seat of Jeff Davis County. Both city and county were named in honor of Jefferson Davis, president of the Confederate States of America. But the Civil War was not on Deputy Sheriff Boone Huggins' mind at 5:45 that Tuesday morning. In fact, nothing was on his mind.

He was sleeping.

On duty. Sheriff Roscoe Lee worked the day shift; his deputy worked the night shift. The total population in the entire county was just over one thousand, so it wasn't as if they needed a SWAT team on stand-by. The biggest crime in the county was underage kids drinking beer at the fairgrounds on Saturday nights. So Boone made up a cell bed and caught six or seven hours of shut-eye every night.

What they call 'easy money.'

Consequently, Boone damn near shit his uniform pants when he opened his eyes to the business end of an AK-47 and six men dressed in black paramilitary uniforms.

'Jesús de la Garza,' the bald man pointing the gun said in a Mexican accent.

'No. I'm Boone Huggins.'

'Where is Jesús de la Garza's body?'

Boone pointed to the back.

'Show me.'

Boone led them to the morgue. Course, it wasn't really a morgue. It was just a walk-in freezer where the sheriff stored his deer during hunting season. But for the last month, it had stored three Mexican bodies wrapped in plastic, which creeped Boone out so he never went into the freezer. He unlocked the freezer door and stepped aside. The bald man went inside and checked the stiff bodies standing in the corner. He tapped one.

'This is Jesús.'

Two other men went inside and carried the body out. The bald man came out and said to Boone, 'Inside.'

354

Boone stepped into the freezer. The bald man shut the door. Boone was already cold.

Two hours later, Hector Garcia walked into Enrique de la Garza's office.

'I have brought your son home.'

'*Gracias*, Hector. Now, go to Austin and kill the governor.'

Lindsay Bonner knocked on the closed door to the Governor's Office then entered. Ranger Roy stood guard outside. She found her husband at his desk.

'Bode, East Austin Elementary, that's my school. That's Graciela Rodriguez's school. You can't close her school.'

'I'm not closing her school. Austin ISD is. Or they might.'

'Because you're cutting K through twelve funding.'

'Lindsay, the state is broke.'

She exhaled. It was time to tell him.

'I voted Democrat.'

'When?'

'Always.'

'I thought you switched to Republican when I did?'

'I didn't.'

'Don't mention that in public, okay?'

She gave him a look.

'Did you vote for me?'

'Yes.'

'Appreciate the vote of confidence.'

'You used to make me proud. Now I vote for you only because you're my husband.'

'Well, it's a vote.'

'It might not be this election.'

★ ★ ★

'Are you ready to go back to school?'

'I think so.'

Becca Bonner lied to her mother. She was not ready to go back to classes or volleyball practice. She might never be ready. But she knew her mother was ready to leave. She needed to leave. Her mother hated life in the Governor's Mansion. She hated being the governor's wife. Becca only hoped that her mother didn't hate the governor.

Jesse Rincón had gone into town to speak at a rotary luncheon. He arrived back at the clinic to find a network news truck with a satellite dish on top parked outside—no doubt another of Mayor Gutiérrez's Mexican Mafia—and inside Inez dressed as if she were auditioning for *American Idol*. Perhaps she was.

'They are going to tape the interview,' she said. 'It will run tonight on the evening news. Their "Difference Maker" segment. Do I look okay?'

Just before six, Lindsay sat alone in the master suite. She had a choice to make: the Governor's Mansion or *Colonia Ángeles*. The governor's wife or the doctor's nurse. Bode Bonner or . . .

She picked up the remote and clicked on the television. She switched channels without conscious thought but stopped when she saw a byline: 'From outside Laredo, Texas.' The video showed a *colonia*. Her *colonia*.

She increased the volume.

'There are over two thousand *colonias* along the border in Texas,' the reporter said over a byline that read NORA RAMOS. 'What makes this *colonia* so unusual is that it is situated between the border wall and the border, a no man's land

356

north of the Rio Grande but south of the wall that separates America from Mexico. Ninety-eight percent of the residents are Mexican nationals who . . .'

The segment continued with a voice-over video showing the wall and the river from the air above—she could almost smell the foul stench from the river—and the *colonia* situated between and then a ground-level view of the women and children living in conditions that seemed more desperate from afar, women and children Lindsay recognized. Little Lucia. And Teresa. And their *madre*, Sonia. The video ended with the reporter standing on the front steps of the clinic. She was young, she was Latina, and she was pretty. Jesse stood next to her.

'But while these people don't even have running water, sewer, or electricity, they do have one thing forty million Americans still dream of—a highly skilled doctor giving them medical care every day—for free. *Colonia Ángeles* means community of angels, but the angel in this community is named Jesse Rincón, a young doctor who was born in this very *colonia* and who returned home after Harvard Medical School to care for his people. He built clinics from Laredo to Brownsville, he trained midwives to staff each clinic, and he travels down the border when he is needed. But most days you will find him here, in the clinic in *Colonia Ángeles*.'

She turned to Jesse.

'Dr. Rincón, you care for six thousand patients in this one *colonia*? Alone, without a nurse?'

'I had a nurse, but she left.'

'Why?'

'A life on the border is a harsh life.'

'Will she return?'

Jesse stared into the camera a moment—almost as if he were staring at Lindsay—then shook his head slowly.

'I do not think so.'

Chapter 24

'Uh, Governor,' Ranger Roy said. 'I don't know how, but Mrs. Bonner, she, uh . . . she did it again.'

Ten days later, Bode Bonner sat at his desk staring out the window at the state capitol dome glowing yellow in the setting sun.

'I know.'

'I'm sorry, Governor. You want me to track her with GPS again?'

Bode shook his head.

'I know where to find her.'

It had been two weeks since she had left and taken all the color in the *colonia* with her. Her yellow and blue and green peasant dresses and scarves and those pink Crocs. And her red hair. The *colonia* was again gray. Gray lives, gray homes, gray dirt. Each day seemed grayer than the day before. Jesse had tried to focus on his work, but his thoughts always returned to her. To the governor's wife.

Where his thoughts now resided.

He cut the engine and got out of the truck at the post office in Laredo. He went inside and collected his mail. A few more checks. They arrived after each interview, then dwindled after a week or so. Perhaps the network interview the day before would generate more checks. The clinic needed an incubator.

He drove through downtown Laredo—it, too, seemed gray that day—and out of town. He turned south on the farm to market and onto his land. He parked next to the house and went inside.

He froze.

He sniffed. He followed the smell into the kitchen. She stood there at the stove. The governor's wife. In full. She turned and smiled.

'Hi, Jesse.'

Before he knew what he was doing, he walked to her and took her shoulders and kissed her.

'I love you,' he said.

'I know. I just don't know what to do about it.'

The next morning, the governor's wife was gone, and the governor woke next to Mandy Morgan in bed. Her bare backside was to him. He slid his hand down her side and over her hips and bottom and down between her legs. She stirred.

'Bode, I'm not feeling so good.'

'I hope it's not contagious.'

'Don't worry. It's not.'

He removed his hand. There would be no sex that morning. But it didn't matter. Even with the Viagra, his body wasn't working these days. Knowing that the most notorious drug lord in Mexico was gunning for you had a way of killing a man's sex drive.

Hank was dead. Darcy was dead. Becca could be dead. She was taking Darcy's death hard; she had moved out of her dorm and into the mansion. She refused to return to classes or volleyball practice. She was afraid. Bode was worried. The assassination attempt had pushed his political fortunes into uncharted territory. He now transcended politics. He was an icon. A legend. An American action-hero. This was just the sort of thing that could propel a man into the White House. Into the history books. One day his portrait might be on a White House wall with Washington and Lincoln and Roosevelt and Reagan. It was a heady thought. But his head was filled with other thoughts. With worries. Because he felt things . . . changing. Just like in a football game when something almost imperceptible occurred, just a feeling, when you knew the momentum had shifted to the other team.

When the game had turned against you.

THREE MONTHS
BEFORE

Chapter 25

Jesse Rincón ran the river at dawn on the third day of June. Pancho vaulted down to the riverbank to chase a jackrabbit, so he followed the dog down. He ran east along the hardened and cracked dirt bank toward the rising sun. He could not restrain a smile. She had come back. To the border. To the *colonia*.

To him.

He wanted desperately to go to her now, while she lay in bed, and to feel her body next to his, to wrap his arms around her and to be one with her. But now was not the time. She was still a married woman.

That day would come, but he would not dwell on it now. He would enjoy this day he would have with her as if it would be his last. And what a glorious day it would be. The sun now rose over the Rio Grande in the east where the sky was clear and held the promise of a—

He stopped.

He looked down. His shoes no longer tread on dry ground. Water lapped at his feet. He smelled a strange scent—the scent of rain. He turned back to face west. The distant sky was a dark black over the Chihuahuan Desert. There was rain in the desert. It seldom rained on the border, but when it did, a flood often ensued. Drought and flood, that was the weather cycle of the border. Rain in the desert ran fast and hard across the sunbaked dirt as if it were concrete, fast and hard to the *arroyos* that emptied into the river. He now studied the river. The water moved rapidly that morning.

And it was rising. Fast.

He climbed the bank and ran to the guesthouse. He banged on the door until the governor's wife answered in her night clothes.

'Hurry! The river is rising.'

'A storm comes from the desert.'

The rain fell gently at first. The wipers swept the water from the windshield without difficulty. Pancho rode up front with them.

'But we need rain,' Lindsay said. 'It hasn't rained since I've been here.'

'Yes, rain is good, but too much rain too fast is not good.'

The rain picked up strength. By the time they arrived at the *colonia*, the rain came down in sheets. The wipers could not keep up. She could barely see out the windshield. Jesse parked at the clinic.

'This will soon be mud,' he said. 'If the river comes over the bank, the entire *colonia* will flood. You will be safe here, in the clinic.' He pointed at the tall cinder blocks on which the small building sat. 'The water will not rise three feet here.'

'Where are you going?'

'To the river. Storms like this, they happen only once every few years. The children do not understand how dangerous the river can be. The rain collects in the desert then empties upstream. The river can rise fast, too fast to escape, if the children are playing in the river. Three years ago, we had such a storm. Two children drowned.' He braced himself for the rain. 'The children, they cannot swim.'

'I'll go with you.'

'No. It is too dangerous. You stay here.'

Jesse and Pancho got out on the driver's side and ran through the rain to the river. Lindsay hesitated then pushed her hat down on her head and followed. When they arrived at the river and Jesse turned and saw her behind him, he was not happy.

'Go back!'

She held her ground. Her mud. She pointed down at the river where a dozen children played in the rain and the river as if they were at a water park.

'¡*Salga del río!*' Jesse yelled to the children. Get out of the river.

They did not hear him, or they did not listen. They continued their play, as if the rain were a blessing from God. Jesse slid down the muddy bank to the river and went to them. Lindsay could not hear him over the rain, but he gestured to the low bluff where she stood. The children reluctantly obeyed. He herded them to higher ground then sent them home. He pointed down at the river and yelled over the rain.

'See how rapidly the river moves now, how fast it rises. It is up a foot since we arrived. They would have all drowned.'

They turned to walk back to the clinic, but Pancho barked. They turned back; the dog stood at the edge of the bluff and barked down at the river. A small boy was stuck in the river. The water was to his waist now.

'The mud!' Jesse yelled.

He slid down the muddy bank again. He waded into the river and to the boy; he reached down and yanked the boy's feet free of the mud. He picked the boy up and carried him to the bank. He held him high so he could get a handhold.

Lindsay knelt and reached down for the boy. She grasped his wet hand, but she could not lift him.

'I'll come up then pull him up!' Jesse said. 'Hold him.'

He climbed to the top of the bluff then knelt and reached down for the boy—

'Jesse!'

A wall of water swept around the bend of the river like a tidal wave. The water hit the boy and pulled him free of her grasp. He fell into the river. Jesse grabbed her, or she would have followed the boy into the river, then he jumped up and ran downriver, searching the water for the boy. She ran after him.

'There!'

She saw a bobbing head being swept away. Jesse ran fast to catch up then dove into the river. Pancho followed him. Lindsay ran downriver after them. She saw the boy thrashing wildly . . . then going under . . . and rising again . . . screaming with fear . . . Jesse swam after him, propelled forward by the river . . . Pancho followed his master . . . she ran and ran until . . . she did not see them again.

They were gone.

She collapsed to the mud. And cried. And on this border where there is no god, she prayed.

'Save them! Please, God! Save them!'

'Dive in!'

The Mexican consulate had located next of kin for all the children except Miguel, Alejandro, and Josefina. And they now stood next to Mandy on the limestone ledge of the Barton Springs pool just south of downtown wearing swim suits and expressions of doubt after dipping their bare toes into the frigid water. The spring-fed pool remained at a constant sixty-eight degrees year-round.

'Come on in!'

Two Texas Rangers book-ended the kids; two others manned the entrance and two more the far side of the pool. They had advised against an outing to a public pool as an unnecessary security risk—'Governor, if El Diablo can send two choppers into Fort Davis and take his son's body from the morgue, what can't he do?'—but the governor of Texas was completely unconcerned. Absolutely unafraid.

Because God was Bode Bonner's bodyguard now.

Bode Bonner had never been a religious man. He had gone to church as a boy to make his mother happy and as a man to make his wife happy, but he had never gone to make himself happy. Religion had never touched his life, like, say, football had. He had never really and truly *believed* in God, that God was a real and present force in his life. Sure, his reelection campaign theme was 'faith, family, and schools,' but that was just politics—until that day at Kerbey's. Father and daughter surviving an assassination attempt by Mexican hit men had been a religious experience.

And it had made Bode Bonner a religious man.

After the assassination attempt, Becca had moved back into the Governor's Mansion. She was too afraid to return to school. Or to leave the mansion. She lay in bed all day watching cable TV and texting. She had always been an outdoor person, but now she refused to leave the safety of indoors. Bode tried to talk to her, but he hadn't known what to say to make her feel better. To make himself feel better. Truth be known, the assassination attempt had rattled him. Scared the hell out of him. The idea that a drug lord in Nuevo Laredo could order three hit men to cross the border, purchase machine guns at a gun show in San Antonio, and travel north to Austin to assassinate the governor of Texas—and that they had come within a fraction of an inch of putting a bullet in his head and in his daughter's head—had unnerved him. He had not made a single public appearance since that day. Father and daughter had both lived in fear.

Until that day.

In the month since the assassination attempt, he had thought little about politics and a lot about life: The Meaning of Life. Death. Religion. God. Bode and Becca were alive; Hank and Darcy were dead. They had all occupied the same small space in front of the large plate glass window, but two had survived and two had died. How could that be? How could they have been alive and vibrant human beings one second and lifeless corpses the next second? How could life be so tenuous? Fragile? Fleeting? He felt guilty for being alive. 'Survivor's remorse,' they called it. Lying in bed each night, he had tried to come to terms with his survivor's remorse and make sense of the situation.

He couldn't.

And he had worried. The worries had become a part of him; he felt the worries with each breath he took. That he might soon die. That his daughter might also die if she were with him in public. He had been consumed with such worries for weeks. But then he woke at three that very morning, and the worries were gone. Because he woke with a sudden knowledge: It was a miracle.

God had saved Bode Bonner.

How else could his survival be explained? Two men wielding machine guns and firing at him from twenty feet away—*they had fired sixty bullets!*—yet not a single bullet had struck Bode or Becca. There was only one explanation: God had protected them, put up a spiritual shield that the bullets could not penetrate. God did not want them to die. He did not want Becca Bonner to die, and He did not want Bode Bonner to die. He would not *allow* Bode Bonner to die. Consequently, while that lunatic El Diablo had tried to kill him and might try again, he now lived without fear.

Bode Bonner had been bulletproofed by God.

But why? Why had God saved him? The answer came to him that morning as well: God wanted Bode Bonner to be the next president of the United States of America.

He had experienced a religious epiphany.

Of course, he had kept that epiphany to himself. He hadn't uttered a word of it aloud to anyone, not even Jim Bob. Especially not the Professor—he had always had an atheist bent about him, so he would simply scoff at such a notion. Truth was, Bode himself would have scoffed at the notion just two months earlier—before that day in the Davis Mountains. He had considered the meaning of his life leading up to that day in the mountains and all the days leading up to the assassination attempt, but he could not get his life's picture focused in his mind—until he had snapped to a sitting position in bed at three that morning and cried out, 'Yes!'

At that moment, the picture had come into focus.

It had been no mere coincidence that he had gone hunting for an African lion on John Ed's ranch, that he had been there that very day, on that ridge sighted in with a dangerous game rifle at the very moment that Josefina had attempted her escape from those cartel thugs—that his life and her life and their lives had intersected at that exact place and time.

God had put him there.

God had saved him from the assassination attempt at Kerbey's.

Because God had chosen His candidate.

God wanted Bode Bonner to lead America—to be the

leader of the free world. That's what He did when America was threatened. Of course, he could hear the nonbelievers saying, 'God has more important things to do than pick the next American president.'

Really?

The world is God's creation but America is God's country. God watches over America because America represents everything God had hoped His little experiment called mankind could achieve. America was God's hope for His world. God had handpicked George Washington to lead the new America, Abraham Lincoln to preserve America, Franklin Roosevelt to save America from the Nazis, Ronald Reagan to save America from Communism—now God had handpicked Bode Bonner to save America from the Democrats. In His divine and infinite wisdom, God had reached down and plucked him from obscurity as a state governor and put him on the path to the White House. God wanted Bode Bonner to be the next president of the United States of America.

So God would not allow harm to come to him.

Bode understood that now. He had nothing to fear. He could walk the streets of Austin, he could jog around the lake, he could make public appearances, and he could swim in Barton Springs pool without fear of assassination. He was again the old Bode. A better Bode. A bulletproof Bode.

'You guys gonna get in or not?'

Mandy dipped her toe into the water again.

'Not.' She turned to the kids. 'Who wants ice cream?'

Freeze your butt off in the frigid water or get down on some Rocky Road? That was not a tough choice for the kids. They skedaddled up the sloping bank to the concession stand. Mandy followed. She was wearing a black bikini, and Bode couldn't help but notice that she had put on a little weight.

Her tight abs seemed a little loose, her lean thighs a tad less lean, her round bottom a bit rounder. But then, what did she expect? You can't eat a triple chocolate ice cream cone with the kids every night and keep your girlish figure.

Lindsay did not know how long she had lain there, how long she had cried or how many prayers she had said, but the rain had stopped and the sun had appeared when she raised her head. She wiped her eyes clear of the rain and her tears and looked to the east. Downriver.

She saw a man, a boy, and a dog.

They walked on the bluff toward her. She pushed herself up and ran to them. She stumbled and fell twice, but she did not stop until she threw herself into Jesse Rincón's arms.

Chapter 26

Jesse stopped the truck at the gate in the border wall. Two Border Patrol agents stood guard. The one named Rusty walked over to Jesse's window. Lindsay averted her face.

'Mornin', Doc. They're waiting on you.'

'Who?'

'More TV folks. You're getting pretty famous these days.'

It had been a week since the storm. The river had

quickly returned to normal and the land to drought, as if the storm had never happened. They cleared the gate and drove down the dirt road and into the *colonia*. They found a TV truck parked outside the clinic with the satellite boom extended high into the sky—'More of Mayor Gutiérrez's Mexican Mafia,' Jesse said—and Inez waiting out front. She was wearing her faded blue dress and way too much make-up.

'She hopes to be discovered,' Lindsay said.

'In this *colonia*?'

Inez hurried over to the truck with a frantic expression on her face.

'Doctor, you must hurry! They have been waiting!'

'That morning show interview?'

'Yes! Live on national TV!'

'But, Inez, you do not have a television.'

'I can dream.'

They got out of the truck. Lindsay threw the satchel over her shoulder and walked down the dirt road. Jesse watched her, a moment too long for Inez's liking.

'Doctor! Hurry!'

She grabbed his arm and pulled him inside.

Jim Bob Burnet's office smelled like McDonald's. Eddie Jones had brought breakfast that morning. They now ate Egg McMuffins. Eddie had come to Austin to lay low after those incidents involving civilians in Iraq, which was fortunate for Jim Bob; he would soon collect on his insurance policy.

Spread across his desk were magazines and newspapers from around the country with Bode Bonner's image on the front cover and front page. And each story cited James Robert Burnet, Ph.D., as the genius behind the Republican

372

machine in Texas, the man with his finger on the pulse of politics in Texas. 'The next Karl Rove.'

Bode Bonner had transcended politics. He now occupied that rarefied airspace of an American icon. He had survived an assassination attempt by Mexican hit men in broad daylight, and he had shot and killed his three assailants. It was a scene straight out of a Hollywood action-thriller. Bode Bonner was a real-life American action-hero.

Which worried Jim Bob Burnet.

Because while the American people loved their heroes, the American press loved to bring their heroes down. Especially a conservative Republican hero. The liberal media would not allow a Republican hero to succeed in politics today. They would attack him—or her, in Sarah Palin's case—relentlessly. She's stupid, she's inexperienced, she's racist, she's danger-ous. The press knew that if they repeated a lie a hundred times every day for a hundred days, it became the truth. Then that flock of sheep known as the American people would believe it. Know it. Vote it.

It was a short journey from man of the people to scorned by the people.

They were a fickle crowd, the middle class. The rich and the poor shared the same motivation when it came to poli-tics: money. The poor voted to get more money from the government; the rich voted to keep more money from the government. It was that simple for them. But the middle class, their motivations were more complex, more fluid, more fickle. They didn't vote on money alone. Sometimes it seemed as if they voted on everything but money: abor-tion, gun control, gay marriage. Family values. Social values. Christian values. American values. The rich and the poor worked overtime to destroy any social values still standing in America, so the middle class voted to restore those values. Which had proved an exercise in utter futility, but that had not stopped the middle class from trying.

Every election.

Consequently, pollsters across America constantly tried to find the pulse of the middle-class voter, which usually proved impossible. Their views changed daily, hourly, apparently in response to the latest story on the evening news or *Entertainment Tonight*. But one response to the polls came through loud and clear: the middle class demanded a presidential candidate who portrayed family-social-Christian-American values, whatever they might be at the moment.

Not someone who betrayed those values.

So Jim Bob had examined Bode Bonner's middle-class values index and found it lacking in three distinct areas: (a) his daughter was a lesbian; (b) his wife had left him; and (c) he had a twenty-seven-year-old mistress. He could explain away (a) and (b), but Mandy Morgan was simply too gorgeous to explain away. Middle-class men might envy Bode Bonner, but their middle-class wives would hate him. And they would not vote for him. He would lose the election because of her. If Mandy Morgan were exposed as Bode Bonner's mistress.

Or should he say, *when*.

Jim Bob knew it was only a matter of time. He had no doubt—none at all—that at that very moment, somewhere out there, those sneaky liberal media bastards were readying an all-out attack on Bode Bonner, American hero. That's what they do.

And they would do it to him.

He knew the press had people poking into every nook and cranny of Bode Bonner's life. And everyone in his life. They would eventually happen upon Mandy Morgan. They would learn the truth. They always did. And when they did—when the images and stories were splashed across the televisions of America— the middle class would feel betrayed yet again. Bode Bonner, American hero, would be revealed as just another Republican hypocrite, preaching family values while screwing a girl young enough to be his daughter. And they would not vote for him. He wouldn't make it out of Iowa. So Jim Bob Burnet, chief political strategist for the leading Republican presidential candidate, had come to a tough decision.

Bode Bonner must end his affair with Mandy Morgan.

Jim Bob glanced over at the TV in the corner; it was on, but the volume muted. He wanted to catch the morning news headlines. But the screen showed a female reporter standing in a desolate scene of shanties and shacks with a river behind her. The byline read: 'Colonia on the Rio Grande outside Laredo, Texas.' Jim Bob pointed the remote at the TV and increased the volume. The reporter—a pretty Latina—spoke into a handheld microphone.

'They all fly into the Laredo International Airport, rent a car, and drive west on Mines Road to an unmarked dirt road that leads south to the eighteen-foot-tall border wall.'

A video played on the screen.

'They drive through the gates and another mile to *Colonia Ángeles*. It is as if they are believers journeying to a holy shrine. But they are television and print journalists coming to interview Jesse Rincón. He remains bewildered by the attention, but the *colonias* need the money the attention brings, so he grants the interviews. I too have come to meet Jesse Rincón this day.'

The screen switched to a live shot of the reporter and a Latino in a white lab coat.

'From the Mexican border in Texas, we're now joined by Dr. Rincón.'

'Good morning. Welcome to *Colonia Ángeles*.'

'Doctor, these *colonias*—these slums—they line both sides of the river, from here to Brownsville. Why?'

'NAFTA.'

'The trade agreement?'

The doctor pointed toward the river; the camera swung around to capture the Rio Grande and the slums on the far side.

'American companies relocated their factories across the river, for the cheap labor. Our cars, clothes, televisions, electronics, furniture . . . they are all made across the river. The factories are called *maquiladoras*. The word means "to submit to the machine." And submit the Mexican workers did. They are paid one dollar an hour for work Americans were paid twenty dollars an hour . . .'

Filthy brown kids gathered around the doctor, as if attracted by the cameras.

'Oh, look,' Jim Bob said, 'they put kids in the shot. He's politicking.'

'Maybe they live there,' Eddie said.

Back on the TV, the doctor was saying, 'Of course, they cannot live like human beings on a dollar an hour, so they live like animals in these *colonias* on both sides of the river, while the American managers live in fine houses in Laredo. But the jobs lured millions of Mexicans from the interior to the border. At the peak, the *maquiladoras* employed two million Mexicans. But the boom has gone bust.'

'What happened?'

'The American companies moved a million jobs to Asia. The poor Asians, they will work for twenty-five cents an hour. American companies troll the planet for the cheapest labor.'

'What happened to the Mexican workers?'

'Fired. The men went to work for the cartels, the women became prostitutes. NAFTA polluted the river and turned the borderlands into one big slum and an entire generation of Mexican women into prostitutes. Our leaders pass these laws but they do not foresee the consequences. Perhaps they do not even look, since they do not have to live with the consequences.'

The doctor waved a hand at the scene.

'This is the "international trade" you hear about on the evening news. *Maquiladoras* and *colonias*, sweatshops and slums, drugs and death, prostitution and pollution, that is what our desire for cheap goods does to the rest of the world.'

'The factories polluted the Rio Grande?'

'Yes. And the pollution makes the people sick.'

'Why doesn't the Mexican government stop it?'

'Calderón cannot worry about pollution when he cannot feed his people. If he cracks down on the *maquiladoras*, the Americans will take all the jobs to Asia.'

'Governor Bonner cut funding for the *colonias* during the last legislative session and is expected to veto all funding in the next budget.'

'So I have heard.'

'Perhaps Governor Rincón would not.'

'I am just a doctor.'

'Well, Doctor, prominent Latinos in Texas are promoting you as a possible Democratic candidate for governor, like Mayor Gutiérrez of San Antonio. I spoke with him yesterday in San Antonio. This is what he said.'

The screen switched to a video of the same reporter with Gutiérrez.

'Dr. Rincón could beat Bode Bonner. My people will vote for him.'

377

'The people of San Antonio?'

'All Latinos in Texas.'

'But Governor Bonner's polls show strong support among Latinos in national polls after he rescued those Mexican children and survived an assassination attempt.'

'Yes, that was a good thing the governor did. And I am thankful that he and his daughter survived the shooting. But Latinos in Texas have been waiting a long time for a Latino governor. That time has come.'

Jim Bob pointed sharply at the screen. 'That fucking Gutiérrez and his Mexican Mafia. This is his doing. He's still mad because we took Texas from Mexico. You'd think they'd fucking give it up—hell, we stole Texas fair and square a hundred seventy-five years ago. But they still bitch and complain and sue to get their land back. Mexicans actually sued to get back Padre Island, can you believe that?'

'What would happen to all the condos?' Eddie asked.

'Nothing. They're already owned by rich Mexicans.'

The screen went back live to the *colonia*. To the reporter and the doctor.

'Could Jesse Rincón be the first Latino governor in the history of Texas? Historically, Latinos have not come out to vote. But when they do, their numbers will decide who sits in the Governor's Mansion. That could be Jesse Rincón.'

The reporter put an arm through the doctor's and a devilish grin on her face.

'And ladies, he's thirty-eight and single. This is Carmen Cavazos, reporting live from outside Laredo, Texas.'

Jim Bob froze the frame on the handsome face of Jesse Rincón. He stared at his worst nightmare: a handsome, educated, articulate Latino. He felt like Apollo Creed's manager watching a young Rocky Balboa pulverizing a side of beef with his bare fists in that scene from *Rocky*. And he saw all his dreams dissolving into dust. Bode Bonner would not win the White House if he lost the Governor's Mansion. And James Robert Burnet, Ph.D., wouldn't be the next Karl Rove.

'I can't lose this election.'

'You?' Eddie said from the couch.

'You know what I mean.'

Eddie chuckled. 'I think I do.'

'Time to earn your pay, Eddie. Go down to the border, check him out, dig up some dirt.'

'He looks clean.'

'Everyone's got dirt, if you dig deep enough. And if you can't dig it up, you can always plant it.'

'You worried about that Mexican doctor?'

'I get paid to worry.'

'But the boss beats Obama—how can he lose in Texas?'

'Because he'd be running against a Latino in Texas.'

'Maybe he's gay?'

'The doctor?'

Eddie aimed a thumb at the TV. 'She said he's thirty-eight and not married.'

'We're not married.'

'We were.'

Jim Bob smiled. 'Latinos won't vote for a gay governor, would they? Even if he is one of them.'

Lindsay Bonner sipped her wine. She and Jesse sat on the back porch. The evening breeze was gentle and warm. The windows behind them were open, and the soft music drifted out.

'How did the interview go?'

'The reporter, she brought up my running for governor. Mayor Gutiérrez, he is at it again.'

'On national TV. Jesse, I know Jim Bob Burnet. He won't let this pass. He'll look for dirt . . . your dirt. If he can't find any, he'll make some.'

'But I don't want to be governor. I told the reporter.'

'She was pretty, the reporter?'

Like a teenage girl.

'Yes, very.'

Jesse stood and held a hand out to her. She put her wine down and took his hand. She stood, and they danced. Then he kissed her.

'Jesse, it would be a sin.'

'If love were a sin.'

'I'm still a married woman.'

'Your husband, he has forgotten that.'

'But I haven't. Jesse, I've lived my life a certain way. I can't change now, even if I—'

'Love me?'

'Yes. Even if I love you.'

And that was the question: Did she love him? It had been a long time since a man had found her desirable. Perhaps even sexy. A little. She enjoyed Jesse's attention. It felt good to be wanted, as a woman, not just as a photo op. But was she leading him on to fill a void inside her, an empty space her husband had once filled? And even if she loved Jesse, would she ever leave Bode? Of course, he was in Austin; she was in Laredo. Perhaps she already had. Dancing there in Jesse's arms, she felt a desire she had long forgotten. To lay with a man she loved.

Chapter 27

'Put it over the plate, Miguel. *Muy rápido.*'

Five of the last seven U.S. presidents had been left-handed. Bode Bonner would make it six out of eight.

Miguel's pitch was low.

Bode batted left-handed. Or he had when he played baseball in high school. He was a four-letter varsity man: football, basketball, baseball, and track. Football had been his ticket to UT, but baseball had been his first love. He hadn't picked up a bat in thirty years.

Miguel's pitch was wide.

The boys wanted to play *béisbol*, so Miguel was pitching and Alejandro was manning the outfield back by the tall wrought-iron fence and hedgerow surrounding the grounds of the Governor's Mansion. Bode was batting. Mandy and Josefina in her yellow dress sat on the bench. Bode glanced up and saw Becca watching from her second-floor window. She didn't want to come out, even though Ranger Carl, his replacement bodyguard, insured their safety within the confines of the mansion grounds.

Miguel's pitch was high.

Bode had been a power-hitting first baseman/center fielder for the Comfort High Bobcats. He had never hit for a high batting average, but he could put a fastball over the fence. And he had, often. Of course the fence around this lawn was considerably shorter than at his high school baseball field. So he was careful not to swing too hard.

Miguel's pitch was inside.

Bode had sent Ranger Carl to the sporting goods store to buy gloves, bats, balls, and bases. Bode was dressed in jeans and cowboy boots—he wasn't figuring on running the bases—and the boys were dressed in shorts and T-shirts. The scene reminded him of playing sandlot ball in Comfort, except this field wasn't right in the middle of town surrounded by houses. On more than one occasion, young Bode Bonner had put a baseball through a neighbor's window. The sound of glass shattering had sent the boys running to avoid paying for a replacement.

Miguel's pitch was right down the middle of the plate.

Without considering the consequences, Bode Bonner was that young boy in Comfort again. He stepped into the pitch and swung the bat hard at the white ball that seemed to hang in the air, begging to be belted, and felt the bat make solid contact.

Too solid.

As soon as he hit the ball, he knew it was gone. He watched the white ball sail far and high into the blue sky, still rising as it cleared the fence, and he felt that wonderful sensation wash over his body—*home run!* The boys whistled, Mandy and Josefina clapped, and Bode thought, *I've still got it*—until they heard the sound of glass shattering and a car alarm going off.

'Shit.' As soon as the word was out of his mouth, he knew it was wrong; a religious man shouldn't cuss. 'I mean, darn.'

The boys turned back to Bode with their eyes wide and expressions frozen, waiting for Bode's lead. Bode dropped the bat and ran for the mansion. The boys tossed their gloves and followed. Mandy and Josefina brought up the rear.

'You didn't see that, Carl!' Bode yelled to his Texas Ranger.

★ ★ ★

382

Jim Bob watched the scene on the lawn below. He shook his head. The governor's playing baseball with Mexican kids while Rome's burning. He sat behind his desk, again covered with newspaper and magazine articles and videos; but not of Bode Bonner. The last week, Jim Bob had read every article that mentioned Jesse Rincón and watched every video of every interview with Jesse Rincón. He now knew more about the doctor than the doctor knew about himself.

And none of it was good for Bode Bonner.

The guy was straight out of a Hollywood story: born in Texas of a Mexican mother who died in childbirth; raised by an uncle in Nuevo Laredo, attended Jesuit in Houston, and college at Harvard; graduated top of his class, which earned him a seat in the medical school; prestigious internship and residency; specialty in cardiac surgery; lucrative offers from hospitals across the nation; but he returned home to care for residents of the *colonias*.

It made Jim Bob sick.

His was exactly the kind of life story the liberal media loved, the kind of life story they would praise and promote— a Latino who made good and now did good. God, it was disgusting. And dangerous to Bode Bonner's presidential dreams. He could not lose the Governor's Mansion and win the White House. He had to win reelection in Texas. But liberals from New York to California would send wads of money to Texas to defeat Bode Bonner. The national Democratic Party would get behind Jesse Rincón and flood the state with campaign funds. Bode Bonner's reelection campaign had $75 million in the bank; the Democrats would soon have $100 million. Or $200 million. Or $300 million. Whatever it took to defeat Bode Bonner in Texas. To keep another Republican from Texas out of the White House.

But Jim Bob Burnet wasn't about to go down without a fight.

He would not let his chance slip away. He would do whatever was necessary to win. He had to prove to his ex-wife—and to himself—that he was not a loser.

So he had to win.

But he would not discuss any of this with the governor. Instead, he would wait for Eddie Jones to return from the border with dirt. Something he could use to eliminate this unpleasant threat named Jesse Rincón.

The Border Patrol agent named Rusty came over to the truck and handed Jesse a note through his open window. Lindsay ducked her head.

'Fella came out this morning, asking for you, like I'm a secretary or something. Course, I guess it's the least I can do, you being the next governor and all. Anywho, I told him how to find your clinic in the *colonia*, but he got kind of pale in the face, asked if the cartels killed people in there.' Rusty chuckled. 'Said to give you that note, said he'd be in Laredo.'

'Thanks, Rusty.'

'Sure thing, Doc.'

Jesse read the note then drove through the gates. He handed the note to Lindsay.

'This man wants to meet me at the La Posada. Who is he?'

Lindsay read the note. 'Clint Marshall. He's the chairman of the state Democratic Party. He hates Bode. It's mutual.'

Jesse drove into town at noon. Lindsay remained at the clinic. He parked on the plaza outside the La Posada Hotel and walked through the lobby and out to the courtyard pool where he found an Anglo sitting at a table under an umbrella with a cell phone to his ear and a big plate of enchiladas in front of him. He noticed Jesse and quickly ended his call. He stuck a hand out to Jesse.

'Dr. Rincón, I'm Clint Marshall.'

He was an overweight, middle-aged Anglo on his way to heart disease if he did not lay off the enchiladas.

'Mr. Marshall.'

'Clint. Please, have a seat.'

Jesse sat and declined Clint's offer of lunch.

'Doctor, I know you're a busy man, so I'll get right to the point. We want you to run for governor. We want you to be the face of the Democratic Party in Texas. The future of the party. With the growth of the Latino population here, the opportunity for a Latino to win the Governor's Mansion has never been better. You can make history.'

'Governor Bonner is unbeatable.'

'Have you seen the latest polls?'

'What polls?'

'Texas polls. You're gaining fast on the governor.'

'But I am not a candidate.'

'Doesn't matter. Your name is out there. Mayor Gutiérrez, he's a one-man campaign machine—and a formidable one. His Mexican Mafia, all the press you've gotten lately, you're a hot ticket. How many followers do you have?'

Jesse glanced around.

'No one is following me.'

'No. On Twitter.'

'Twitter?'

'You don't have a Twitter account?'

'Uh, no, I do not have that.'

'Well, you need one if you're going to be governor.'

'I do?'

385

'Yes.'

'Why?'

'People want to know what you're doing.'

'I am working. Treating patients.'

'No, no. That's too boring. You've got to make it sound exciting, like a pickup truck commercial.'

'A pickup truck commercial?'

'You want to be governor, social media's the ticket.'

'But I do not want that.'

'A Twitter account?'

'To be governor.'

'Why the hell not?'

'Because I am a doctor.'

'Who can be governor. The national Democratic Party has pledged as much money as it takes to beat Bode Bonner in Texas.'

'Why? Why would they care what happens in Texas?'

'Because Texas is the future of the Democratic Party in America. Once Latinos become the majority here and take Texas back for the Democrats, the other red states will fall like dominoes. Latinos are moving north, turning red states brown.'

'Why do the Democrats want so desperately to win this election in Texas?'

'Simple: If you keep Bode Bonner out of the Governor's Mansion, we keep him out of the White House.'

The governor of Texas sat behind his desk and gazed across at the Professor.

'You ready to come out of exile?' Jim Bob said.

'Yep.'

'You've been moping around the mansion for a month.'

Bode wasn't about to disclose his religious epiphany to Jim Bob.

'I'll schedule a press conference and get a "Bode Bonner for President" organization set up in the early primary states, start hiring staff—'

'This early?'

'You mean, this late? Romney and the others, they've already got staff up and running in Iowa, New Hampshire . . . Time to shift this thing into gear, Bode. If you want to be president.'

'I do.'

'Good.'

Jim Bob placed a stack of papers on the desk. Bode grabbed his signing pen.

'First item, pardon of DeSean Washington.'

'I hate pardons. I let someone out of prison, I'm soft on crime.'

'This guy served twenty years for a crime he didn't commit. Exonerated by DNA.'

'Another Dallas case?'

'Yep.'

'How many is this?'

'Fifty statewide, twenty-five from Dallas.'

'What were they doing in Dallas back then, putting every black man in the city in prison?'

'Apparently.'

Bode signed the pardon.

'Item two, you're appointing Hoot Pickens as chairman of the Texas Commission on Environmental Quality.'

'Hoot's an oil man.'

'Refinery.'

'Won't the press complain?'

'So? Now, item three . . .'

Jim Bob did not push paper across the desk. Bode had his signing pen at the ready, but he had nothing to sign.

'What's item three?'

'Mandy.'

'What about her?'

'It's over.'

'She's quitting?'

'You're quitting her.'

'You want me to fire her?'

'No. Just stop screwing her.'

'Why?'

'You want to be president?'

'Yeah.'

'That's why.'

'It's never been a problem before.'

'You never wanted to be president before. Look, you can have an affair with a goat and I can still get you reelected governor of Texas. But you get caught having an affair with a girl who looks like Mandy, even I won't be able to get you elected president. It's a different set of voters. You've got to clean up your act.'

'Quit sex?'

'At least until you're elected.'

'That'll be, what, almost two years? Damn, Jim Bob . . . I mean, darn, I haven't gone that long without sex since I was fifteen.'

'You had sex when you were fifteen?'

Bode nodded. 'The varsity cheerleaders.'

'But they were seniors.'

'Yep.'

'Which one?'

388

'All of them.'

'All of them?'

Jim Bob pondered on that for a moment then looked back up at Bode.

'They're gonna come after you.'

'They're all married by now.'

'Not the cheerleaders—the liberal media. They're playing Indiana Jones, digging all over Texas trying to find some dirt on you. They find out you're screwing a twenty-seven-year-old gal, they'll crucify you. All this—'

He gestured at the stack of magazines and newspapers with Bode's image on the covers and front pages now piled high on the corner of his desk.

'—ends. You won't *be* the wave—the wave'll be drowning you. You went from nobody to somebody in twenty-four hours. You can go back to nobody just as fast.'

'No more sex. That'll really disappoint Mandy.'

'Don't give yourself too much credit, cowboy.'

'The entire varsity cheerleading squad, Jim Bob. When I was fifteen.'

The thought of those sexual encounters made him feel guilty. Sinful. He was a religious man now. A man who could rise above desires of the flesh. Perhaps being celibate for a few years would be a good thing. Allow him to focus his mind on spiritual matters. Put his energy to work for God.

Still, he hated to see his year's supply of Viagra go to waste.

She had been seventeen and a virgin when she had first had sex with Bode Bonner. It had been a sweaty affair on a summer night in the front seat of his pickup truck. She prayed for forgiveness the next morning at mass, but she did not stop having sex with Bode, not for twenty-five years,

389

until he vetoed the CHIPS funding two years ago. The Children's Health Insurance Program. He knew how much that program meant to her, but he chose Jim Bob's opinion over hers, his political advice over her pleading for the children. Because of her husband, hundreds of thousands of poor children in Texas were thrown off the health insurance rolls.

How could she share a bed with a man who could do that to children?

She began sleeping on the day bed. She wished she hadn't. Once she had left their bed, she didn't know how to go back; once he had taken up with Mandy, she couldn't go back. Without their bedtime conversations when she had unimpeded access to his conscience, his transformation from a good man to a successful politician accelerated. She no longer recognized her husband. He had become a stranger to her. She couldn't have sex with a stranger, even if she were married to him.

But she missed sex.

She had never had sex with another man. On a few occasions, she had wondered what it would be like, if it would be better or worse or just different, but Lindsay Bonner had never been tempted to stray.

Until now.

TWO MONTHS BEFORE

Chapter 28

'He's not gay. The Mexican doctor.'

Jim Bob raised his eyes to Eddie Jones standing in the doorway holding a large envelope.

'How do you know?'

'He's got a woman. A married woman. Nice-looking broad.'

'How do you know she's married?'

'Wedding ring.'

Jim Bob gestured at the envelope.

'You got photos?'

Eddie stepped forward and dropped the envelope on the desk. Jim Bob opened the clasp and removed a stack of photos. He stared at the images a long moment. He blinked hard then stared again. They were photos of the doctor and a redheaded woman; they were drinking wine, holding hands, and dancing in each other's arms. A man and a woman who looked very much in love.

'Shit.'

'What's wrong?'

'She's working for Jesse Rincón.'

'Who?'

'You don't recognize this woman?'

'No.'

'That's the governor's wife.'

'You're kidding?'

'Do I look like I'm kidding?'

'You look like you're passing a kidney stone.'

'I might be.'

'The boss's wife, she ain't been around much since I hired on.'

'She's been down on the border.'

'Those unforeseen, unexpected, unpleasant things are starting to pile up, Professor. Figure I'm gonna start earning my pay pretty soon. Where's the boss?'

'At the capitol, for his press conference.'

On the fifth day of July, the governor of Texas stood alone in his office on the first floor of the state capitol. He never actually worked there; it was just a convenient place to meet legislators and lobbyists and give interviews to the press. The national press. They had all journeyed to Austin, Texas, to meet Bode Bonner, American hero. The man who would be president.

One big play.

A game changer.

And it had changed his game. Three months before, he couldn't pay the press to attend his weekly press conferences. Now his office had to issue credentials, so many media outlets wanted in on the action. No less than one hundred reporters and two dozen cameras awaited him in the press room. He was the most popular, most admired, most handsome, and most followed man in America. His favorable rating exceeded ninety percent and his negative was less than five percent. The world was waiting for him to announce his run for the presidency. He was waiting for the best moment to announce. But announce he would. His Super PAC now held pledges totaling $750 million. The Professor was hiring a campaign staff.

President William Bode Bonner.

Three months before, he wore Armani suits and French-cuffed shirts. Today, he wore what had become his trade-mark attire: buttoned-down, long-sleeved, starched shirts—white, blue, yellow, green, ecru, and even pink on Breast Cancer Awareness Day—jeans, always creased to perfection, a black silver-tipped cowboy belt, and black hand-made cowboy boots.

No hair spray.

Two months before, three Mexican *sicarios* had attempted to assassinate him. No second attempt had come. El Diablo had apparently given up on killing the governor of Texas. Of course, he now traveled with a half dozen Texas Ranger bodyguards. Mandy still served as his aide, but not as his mistress. He had expected tears when he broke the news that Jim Bob had ended their affair, but she had only said, 'We can wait.' He wanted to ask, 'For what?', but she had already exited his office. Becca still slept in the mansion, but she had returned to volleyball practice at UT. And the governor's wife had returned to the border. She had been gone forty-six days.

'Governor, we're ready.'

A young man stood where Mandy should be standing.

'Where's Mandy?'

The man shrugged. 'I don't know, sir.'

'Jim Bob here?'

'Yes, sir. He just arrived.'

Bode strode across the foyer with the same jaunty cocki-ness he had exhibited twenty-five years before when running onto a football field. Of course, it was easy to be cocky when God was your teammate. But Bode Bonner was about to learn that politics in America, like football, is a contact sport.

The Border Patrol agent named Rusty tackled the skinny Mexican boy.

The boy had raced past the front door of the clinic, where Jesse and Lindsay stood, as if he were running a race. He wasn't. He was being chased. By a green-and-white SUV driven by another Border Patrol agent. The boy glanced back, only to be slammed to the ground by Rusty, who had cut around the back of the clinic. Rusty now punched the boy in the face numerous times.

'Rusty, he's just a boy!' Jesse said.

'He just shot a Border Patrol agent in Laredo!'

Rusty removed a gun from the boy's baggy pants and tossed it aside. Next came a switchblade. Then a baggie of a black substance.

'Mexican black tar heroin,' Rusty said.

He turned the boy over and cuffed his hands behind his back then yanked him up. The other agent loaded the boy into the SUV then returned to Rusty. He slapped him on the back.

'Just another day in paradise.'

Two hundred thirty-five miles north, Governor Bode Bonner stepped to the podium and smiled at the sea of reporters. Network. Cable. Wire services. Newspapers. They had all come to him.

'Good to see y'all today. Questions?'

Hands shot into the air. Bode searched the sea of reporters and spotted a cute gal from cable waving as if desperate

396

to be plucked from obscurity by Bode Bonner and put on a national stage. Why not help her get ahead in the world? He pointed at her, and she stood. If he weren't a religious man, he'd say she had a nice body.

'Governor, are you worried about another assassination attempt?'

'No.'

'But they killed your bodyguard and your daughter's best friend. It was a miracle that you and your daughter survived.'

'Yes, it was.'

He thought it best not to elaborate.

'You really are an American hero.'

He smiled. No need to over-talk the obvious. He'd just hero his way through this nationally televised press conference. The little gal looked like a star-struck teenager. She had another question. He nodded at her.

'Governor, how are you going to reduce the federal deficit as president when Texas is facing a twenty-seven-billion-dollar deficit with you as governor? When you're going to fire tens of thousands of state workers and perhaps a hundred thousand teachers? How are you going to save a broke nation when you're governor of a broke state?'

'*What?*'

Right before his eyes, the cute reporter had transformed into Katie Couric, like that guy in the werewolf movie.

'Well, uh, the, uh, thing is . . .'

He glanced at Jim Bob by the door, who shielded his face from the reporters and mouthed, 'No deficit.'

'There is no deficit.'

'But—'

He turned away from the Katie Couric clone and searched for friendly faces. He found none, so he pointed at a familiar face, Carl Crawford, the reporter from the alternative Austin newspaper.

'But, Governor, I've obtained confidential documents written by your political advisor, Jim Bob Burnet, that prove the state of Texas is in fact facing a massive budget deficit and that you knew this when you said there is no deficit, as you just repeated.'

'There are no such documents, Carl, because there is no such deficit.'

Carl held up a stack of papers.

'Yes, Governor, there is a deficit and there are documents that prove it. One of your former employees, Jolene Curtis, gave these to me. You lied.'

Damn. The frisky gal betrayed him.

'Governor, she also gave us documents that prove you replaced the entire Board of Pardons and Paroles after they opened an investigation into the execution of Billy Joe Dickson to determine if the state executed an innocent person in order to derail their investigation.'

'She did?'

'She did. That's a cover-up.'

'A cover-up? That had nothing to do with any investigation, Carl. I just didn't want them to think it's a career.'

'Some people think Jesse Rincón might end your career as governor of Texas.'

'Who?'

'Jesse Rincón—he might be your Democratic opponent.'

'Jesse Rincón? Never heard of him.'

'I think you'll hear about him soon enough.'

Carl was grinning, as if he had finally found a scandal. Lying about the deficit, executing an innocent man, those are the best scandals he can come up with against an American hero? Please. Bode nodded at the reporter from the Houston paper.

'Governor, have you heard of Hoot Pickens?'

'Sure.'

'You appointed him to the Texas Commission on Environmental Quality even though he's in the refinery business?'

'Shouldn't the industry being regulated have a voice?'

'They shouldn't write their own regulations.'

'Lawyers do that.'

'Their lawyers.'

'Do you have a question or are you campaigning? You sound like my Democratic opponent.'

'Yes, Governor, I have a question: Can you explain how you made a half-million-dollar profit on a land deal with Mr. Pickens?'

'What land deal?'

'You bought a lot on Lake Austin from him two years ago, and you recently sold that lot to his son, and you pocketed five hundred thousand dollars.'

'I did? Look, I put all my assets in a blind trust when I was first elected governor, so I don't know anything about that.'

'But you know Mr. Pickens is active in Texas politics?'

'My auto mechanic's active in Texas politics.'

He smiled and moved on to the next reporter—but he was getting a bad feeling. This wasn't the hero's welcome he had expected. He pointed at a San Antonio reporter.

'Governor, did you appoint Joe Jack Munger to the UT Board of Regents in exchange for a million-dollar donation to your campaign?'

'No, absolutely not. I think it was only two hundred thousand.'

He chuckled, but no one else did. His bad feeling increased.

A little help here, God. He acknowledged the reporter from Fort Worth.

'Governor, we've learned from Democratic state legislators that you're personally rounding up votes for a special bill that would grant your biggest campaign donor—John Ed Johnson, a billionaire—the power to condemn rural land for his water pipelines. Is that true?'

'You're getting your information from Democrats? Those guys will say anything to discredit me because they know we're going to bury them in November.'

'But is it true? Are you supporting Mr. Johnson's attempt to condemn ranchers' and farmers' land for his pipeline?'

'No, of course that's not true.'

'So you'll veto the bill if the legislature passes it?'

'I can't answer a hypothetical question.'

'Sounds like you're dodging the question.'

God, feel free to step in anytime and smite these reporters down.

He gave up on Texas reporters and gestured to a network reporter.

'Governor, is it true that you employ illegal Mexican immigrants at the Governor's Mansion?'

'No, that's not true.'

'What about Guadalupe Sendejo?'

'Lupe? She's family. She's been with my family since I was a boy.'

'But she's undocumented. As are the Mexicans you employ at your ranch.'

'They're family, too.'

'But they're residing in the U.S. illegally. You're employing illegal immigrants while demanding that the president secure the border to keep illegal immigrants out—isn't that hypocritical?'

Please, God. A little help here.

A good-looking broad bounced up and down with her hand in the air. Surely she wanted to ask him about the shooting. He pointed to her. She jumped up.

'Governor, did your wife leave you?'

'*What?* Of course not.'

'Well, where is she? She hasn't been seen at her regular charitable duties in weeks now—the food bank, the homeless shelter, the AIDS clinic. Everyone is wondering where she is.'

He hoped he wasn't sweating through the armpits of his powder-blue shirt for all the world to see. He felt a single bead of sweat pop from a pore on his forehead. He couldn't reach up and wipe it off—the cameras would catch him sweating, just the kind of photo op he didn't need. So he ignored the sweat bead as it started its slow descent down his broad forehead. He tried to frown it off, but it hung tight to his skin. He finally reached up as if to brush his hair off his forehead and swiped the sweat bead with his palm. But his sweat pores erupted like Mount St. Helens with the next question.

'Governor, does your wife's absence have anything to do with the rumors that are running rampant around Austin that you're having an affair with your aide, Mandy Morgan. Is that true?'

'*Mandy Morgan?* She's barely older than my daughter—who's probably watching this press conference on TV. You should be ashamed of yourself for asking that question.'

'Which you haven't answered.'

He glared at her, which usually worked, but she held her ground. *Oh, God, your good buddy Bode is in deep doo-doo here!*

'Obviously, my political opponents have fed y'all with a lot of rumors so you'll air this on your shows and print it in your newspapers. Getting me to deny an affair with an aide is almost as good for ratings as me admitting it, right? This is exactly what is wrong with the liberal media in America today. You live for scandal because scandal drives ratings. So even if there's no scandal, you create scandal. And nothing drives ratings higher than a sex scandal involving a political hero, right? But the people of America will see this for what it is, a left-wing media attack. This is exactly what the liberal press does when the people embrace conservative heroes, when the liberal media's power to influence the people is challenged: you launch personal attacks. Tea partiers are racist, Sarah Palin is dangerous, I'm an adulterer . . . It's disgusting, and the people hate you for it. But worse than that, it's a cancer on democracy, a cancer that's destroying this country. I'm a tough guy, I played football, I took big hits, I'm used to cheap shots. But only football games were at stake. Our country, our way of life, is at stake now. And the press—so important an institution that it is protected by the First Amendment—goes down into the gutter to report filthy rumors like this. You can't hurt me. But you're hurting my wife and my daughter, and you should be ashamed of yourselves.'

But the reporter didn't seem the least bit ashamed.

'So it's all a lie? Your wife hasn't left you, and you're not having an affair?'

Bode jabbed a big finger at the reporter. 'It's a goddamn lie.'

Sorry, God, I'm winging it here. Alone.

He walked away from the podium and out the door. Jim Bob caught up with him a few steps down the corridor. Two Texas Rangers shadowed them as they marched down the capitol corridor and out the east doors and climbed into the waiting Suburban. Bode exhaled.

'What the hell was that all about?'

'That,' Jim Bob said, 'was the national press. See, Bode, you've played politics only in the friendly waters of Texas, where the press is compliant and we've only got two liberal media outlets in the whole state. Now you're playing politics in the big waters, where all the media are liberal and vicious.'

'And who's this Democrat, Jesse Rincón?'

'Your wife's doctor.'

'Her gynecologist is a Democrat?'

'No . . . well, I don't know, he might be . . . but this isn't about him. Jesse Rincón is her Mexican doctor.'

'She goes to a Mexican gynecologist?'

'Not her goddamned gynecologist! The doctor she works with, down on the border. He's a Latino named Jesse Rincón. He's getting a lot of good press for passing up a big-city practice to take care of those poor people in the *colonias*—'

'Oh, the liberal media love that, don't they?'

'—and Latino leaders around the state are pushing him for governor, they see him as the savior. Like the San Antonio mayor.'

'Gutiérrez? I gave him state environmental funds to clean up the riverwalk.'

'*New York Times* did a front-page profile on him. Rincón.'

'No one in Texas reads the *New York Times*, and no one in New York can vote in Texas. As long as he's not on *Fox*, we're okay. You think he's gonna run?'

Jim Bob shrugged. 'He hasn't said yes, but he hasn't said no.'

'Maybe he doesn't want to be a politician?'

'Everyone wants to be a politician.'

'I wanted to be a pro football player.'

'I mean, after they grow up.'

'Maybe he won't run.'

'They put kids in a TV shot with him.'

'Damn, he's running. A Latino. You figure the Latino vote will come out for him?'

'Does the Democratic vote come out for a tax increase?'

'Shit.'

'He'll sweep the Latino vote.'

'Which means he'll win.'

'They'll vote for him. And there'll be a Latino in the Governor's Mansion doing more than cooking. On my watch.'

The Suburban exited the capitol grounds and turned right on Eleventh Street.

'How the hell did they find out about Mandy?'

'Jolene, probably.'

'Damn. I thought she wanted to screw me.'

'She just did.'

'Maybe they found out from Mandy. Maybe she told a friend. Or texted someone.' He stared out the window. 'Jesus, this day can't get any worse.'

The Suburban entered the gates to the mansion and stopped in the rear driveway. Bode bolted out and marched inside the mansion and down the corridor to Mandy's office. He barged in without knocking on the closed door. Because he was pissed. *Excuse me God, but I am pissed*. Because his mistress had been talking out of turn.

'Damnit, Mandy, did you—'

A loud gagging noise interrupted him. Mandy was bent over behind her desk. Another gagging sound, and she sat up. She was holding the trash basket. The smell of puke permeated the small room.

'You sick?'

She spit into the basket, put the basket down, wiped her mouth with a tissue, and shook her head.

'I'm pregnant.'

Chapter 29

One hundred eleven degrees, and it was only the fifth day of July.

Lindsay Bonner had lived in Texas for almost forty years, so she knew heat; but the heat on the border defined heat. The air felt as if it were on fire. She wiped sweat from her face and drank another bottled water. Three hours she had walked the *colonia* on her morning rounds. She arrived back at the clinic feeling a bit woozy. She opened the door and stepped inside. Inez greeted her, but her words sounded distant. The girl's pretty face seemed vague.

'Doctor!'

Lindsay opened her eyes to Jesse and Inez hovering over her. She was lying on the examining table. Jesse checked her pulse; Inez dabbed her forehead with a cold wet towel.

'What happened?'

'You fainted.'

'The heat.'

'You are sure you are not pregnant?'

His question made her laugh.

'Only if I'm the Virgin Mary.'

They had tried to have a baby for four years, he and Lindsay. But she couldn't get pregnant. Not his fault. His sperm production was stupendous, the doctor had said. Her plumbing was fine. Just relax, it'll happen. It did. Bode would never forget that hot summer day nineteen years before when he had ridden in from the herd and found Lindsay waiting for him by the barn. Crying. He had dismounted and gone to her. He took off his gloves and wiped the tears from her face, sure she was about to tell him she had breast cancer. Instead, she smiled and said, 'We're going to have a baby.'

That day he had said, 'Thanks, God.'

Today he said, 'Why, God?'

That was still the happiest day of his life. This was not the second happiest day of his life. Bode Bonner's love child. It wasn't fair. Movie stars can have a dozen kids out of wedlock, and no one cares. In fact, they *ooh* and *ahh* over their baby bumps at the Academy Awards, as if they're the first women in the whole fucking world to have a baby. But let the leading presidential candidate sire one child—*one!*—with a woman who wasn't his wife, and you'd think the whole fucking world was ending.

And not just his political career.

Bode Bonner would be laughed out of the presidential race just as John Edwards had been, another cheating politician with good hair. And like all men who had ascribed their sudden success to divine intervention, Bode Bonner's thoughts now focused on one disturbing question: Why would God let this happen to him? To His chosen candidate? He stepped into Jim Bob's office, shut the door, and said, 'She's pregnant.'

'Good. Maybe she'll come home now.'

'Not Lindsay. Mandy.'

The news knocked Jim Bob back in his chair as forcefully as a two-by-four across his pasty face—which seemed even pastier now. He didn't speak for a long moment. When he caught his breath and regained his voice, he said, 'For Christ's sake, Bode, you never heard of condoms?'

'It was just once.'

'You been screwing her for more than a year.'

'Once without a condom.'

That one time was a problem.

'Why wasn't she on the fucking pill?'

'She said she went off because she was gaining weight, didn't want me to think she was fat.'

'And pregnant is better?'

'What are we gonna do?'

He could see the Professor's mind working through the five stages of political grief: anger, acceptance, recovery, strategy, polls.

'Treat it like the deficit: deny, deny, deny.'

'That didn't work so well for Clinton, Schwarzenegger, Edwards, Sanford, Weiner . . .'

'It buys time.'

'For what?'

'A mass murder, a war in the Mideast, a plane crash, that Lohan gal to do something stupid . . . for something else to come along and dominate the news.'

'Then what?'

The Professor shrugged. 'Standard political sex scandal procedure: confess, cry, seek treatment, promise to be a better man, vote for a liberal spending program.'

'I'm not crying on national TV.'

'No choice. It's in the playbook.'

While Bode considered that spectacle, Jim Bob put his elbows on his desk and his face in his hands. He exhaled like a dying man taking his last breath of life.

'The governor and the governor's wife, both having affairs. That's not in the fucking playbook.'

'*Both?* What are you talking about?'

Jim Bob looked up, as if surprised that Bode had heard his words. But he couldn't maintain eye contact. His gaze dropped to a large envelope on his otherwise bare desk. He reached over as if the act pained him and picked up the envelope. He hesitated, then held it out to Bode. He still did not look Bode in the eye.

Bode now hesitated.

He took a deep breath and the envelope. He opened the flap and reached inside. He removed a stack of photos. Jim Bob's eyes remained down. Bode looked at the top photo then sat down hard in a chair. He thumbed through the photos and saw his wife . . . with another man . . . a Latino man . . . a young, handsome man . . . sitting on a porch drinking wine . . . smiling . . . laughing . . . now standing and . . . dancing. His wife in another man's arms.

'Jesse Rincón,' Jim Bob said. 'I sent Eddie down there, to check him out.'

'Thought he was a gopher.'

'He is. He gets what he goes for.'

Bode fought not to look at the photos again, but he lost the fight. He now stared long and hard at the images of his wife with another man, but his mind conjured up images of his wife *with* another man, and he felt a hurt so deep that the images threatened to do what no opposing football player,

408

political opponent, disappointing poll, nasty reporter, or scathing letter to the editor could do: make him cry. But Bode Bonner had become such a consummate politician that he never considered that his own affair might have hurt his wife just as deeply. And made her cry herself to sleep many lonely nights.

'So she's . . . ? He's . . . ? They're . . . ?'

Jim Bob turned his palms up. 'He didn't catch them in the act, but you can see for yourself, they've got more than a doctor–nurse relationship. She's living with him . . . in his guesthouse on his land outside Laredo.'

'Jesus. Another man screwing my wife.'

'She's a good-looking gal, someone ought to be.'

'Never figured my wife for that.'

'No man does.'

Bode again looked at his wife's image in the photos. His smiling wife. He hadn't seen that smile since early in his first term. It was a real smile, not the smile of a politician's spouse. She hadn't been happy as the governor's wife in Austin, but she had found happiness as a nurse in the *colonias* on the border. With Jesse Rincón. The man who had his wife and now wanted his job.

The Professor spoke in a solemn voice. 'So let me sum up the situation for you, Bode: You and Jesse Rincón are now rivals for both the Governor's Mansion and the governor's wife. You're the top Republican contender for the White House, you're being hunted by hit men working for a Mexican drug lord, and your wife is working in a *colonia* with the man who wants your job and just across the Rio Grande from the man who wants you dead. And if that's not enough, your fucking twenty-seven-year-old mistress is pregnant.'

Bode looked up from the photos of his wife to his ace political strategist.

'Jesus, Jim Bob—you can't make this shit up.'

'Bode's Babe' ... 'Bawdy Bode' ... 'Bonner's Blonde Bombshell.' All three network evening news shows led with the press conference—*what, you don't have real news to report?* And then the cable talk shows had a field day. They splashed photos of Mandy ... Mandy and Bode ... Mandy and the Mexican kids ... more Mandy. They reported rumors—*they had no proof!*—about sex in the Governor's Mansion when the governor's wife was out of town. About a possible love child. And where was the governor's wife? Had she left the governor? Is the happily-married-man image just an image? Is Bode Bonner just another two-timing politician not worthy of his wife's trust? Or the American people's trust? How could Bode Bonner be president, a man who had hidden a twenty-seven-year-old mistress from his wife and a twenty-seven-billion-dollar deficit from the voters? On and on they went for hours and hours, until Bode couldn't bear to watch anymore, like watching a train wreck or Romney at a tea party rally. He forced himself to change the channel, but it was even worse. Leno and Letterman both made him the butt of their monologue jokes. He was no longer an American hero. He was the biggest punch line in America.

And his wife was having an affair.

Chapter 30

Jesse Rincón put on the coffee then dressed in his running shorts and shoes. He and Pancho were almost outside for their morning run along the river when the phone rang. He debated whether to answer, then relented.

'Hello.'

'Jesse, this is Jorge Gutiérrez again, from San Antonio. I am sorry to call at this time of the morning, but I wanted to catch you before you left for the *colonia*.'

'Mayor, you have been busy with your Mexican Mafia.'

'Have you received more checks for the *colonias*?'

'Many more.'

'Excellent. Did you see the news last night? The governor is now embroiled in scandal and the worst kind—a sex scandal.'

'What does that mean to me?'

'That means he is vulnerable. He can be beaten. By you.'

'I am not a candidate.'

'Not yet. Jesse, you have gotten very favorable press—'

'Thanks to you.'

'I do what I can. And you are rising fast in the polls. Jesse, you are now a household name in Texas and in most of the nation. You have gotten for free what most politicians can only dream of: name recognition.'

'But I am not a politician. I am a doctor.'

'You will be the governor, if you will only run.'

'I do not want to be governor.'

'All the better. People hate ambitious politicians, I know

this for a fact. It is best to be begged, and we are begging you, Jesse.'

'Mayor, I—'

'Jesse, will you at least meet with us? Allow us to make our case?'

'Us who?'

'Me, the chairman of the national Democratic Party, donors, Democratic senators, the entire Hispanic caucus in Congress, many of my mafia, perhaps even the vice-president . . . Jesse, they care about our people.'

'They are all going to come down to Laredo just to meet me?'

'Uh . . . well, no. They are coming to San Antonio.'

'Why not Laredo?'

'I am too old and too tired to travel to the border—the sun, the heat . . . and the Anglos, they are too afraid of the drug violence. You know how they are.'

Jesse laughed. 'No, I do not. They are too afraid to come to the border? Here is where our people are, Jorge. Here is where help is needed. If they want to help our people, they need to come see our people. Where they live. How they live.'

'Jesse . . . I am seventy-six years old. I have lived in Texas my entire life. I have suffered as a Hispanic, and I have seen the suffering of other Hispanics. Texas once belonged to us, but it was stolen from us. We can reclaim Texas for ourselves. This is our chance to take back what is ours. We can win. You can win. You can bring respect to our people. To us.'

The Governor's Mansion felt like a morgue the next morning, and with good reason: the governor's political career had died. Bode Bonner was a dead politician walking. The

412

staff averted their eyes when he walked down the hall. Even Lupe could not make eye contact at breakfast. He was now slumped in his chair in his office.

' "Bode's Babe." It's not even a good photo of her. You'd think if they're gonna blame me for having an affair with a woman half my age, they'd at least use a photo that shows how gorgeous she is. I mean, it's not like I'm cheating with trailer trash.'

'That's what you're worried about? Whether you're getting enough credit for the quality of your mistress? You'd better worry about the fucking poll numbers.'

'How bad?'

'You're going down faster than a drunk college coed at a frat party. The overnight flash polls—your numbers took a dive, nationally and in Texas, and your Twitter followers are dumping you in droves. You're below Eminem.'

'The candy?'

'The rapper. And Rincón's numbers shot up.'

'Great—he wants my job *and* my wife.'

'Which one do you want?'

He didn't answer because he didn't have an answer. Now that his wife had someone else, he found himself wanting her more than ever. But . . . he was so close to the Oval Office. So close. Why did he have to choose between his wife and his adventure?

'It's not fair. One illegitimate baby, and I can't be president.'

'Fair is where you go to see farm animals. Politics is winning and losing. And there's only one way you're gonna win now.'

'Which is?'

'You gotta get her back. Lindsay.'

'She won't want me back.'

413

'Not back like that—back here. In the mansion. Being the governor's wife. Standing by her man. At least until the election. People love her. If she stands by you, they'll stand by you. Beg her if you have to, Bode, but get her back to Austin.'

At least his daughter loved him. Bode found Becca standing in her room staring out the window. He went over to her and put his hands on her shoulders.

'Hi, honey.'

She turned and slapped him across the face. Hard.

'That's for hurting Mom.'

'Becca—'

'Are you fucking around on her? With Mandy?'

'Becca—'

'You are, aren't you? Goddamnit, Daddy, you're just like all those other politicians—a fucking asshole. Like all men.'

Disappointing your wife is a tough thing for a man. But disappointing your child—that's a worse thing. The worst thing. To see that look of utter disgust in his daughter's eyes cut Bode Bonner to his core.

Jim Bob knocked on Mandy's closed office door in the mansion then entered. She was crying. He was carrying that morning's newspapers.

'You okay, kiddo?'

She nodded like a little girl. Jim Bob sat down as if weary then tossed the newspapers on the desk.

'You see all this?'

She glanced at the headlines—'Bode Bonner a Cheater' . . . 'Bonner a Goner?' . . . 'Another Married Republican with a Mistress' . . . 'John Edwards Redux' . . . 'Schwarzenegger Sequel'—and nodded.

'And TV last night?'

Another weak nod.

'What are you going to do?'

'About what?'

'The baby.'

She shrugged innocently.

'Have it.'

'You're not considering an abortion?'

'An abortion? Bode's pro-life.'

'He might make an exception for you.'

'He would be disappointed with me.'

'Maybe not.'

'I could never have an abortion.' She smiled as if she were looking at baby clothes. 'Do you know that right now he— or she—is five inches long and weighs five ounces and has little hands and fingers and toes. I even felt a little kick.'

Jim Bob sighed. She had it bad.

'Donations to the reelection committee dried up, like someone turned off the money faucet,' Jim Bob said. 'The donors are pulling their pledges to the Super PAC. And John Ed called, wants to know if this will derail his special legislation.'

'I can't worry about his condemnation bill right now. I got Mandy to worry about.'

'She wants to have the baby.'

'*Why?*'

'Because you're pro-life.'

'But this is *my* life.'

It took four bourbons for Bode to work up the courage to call his wife.

'Is she pregnant?'

He couldn't tell his wife the truth.

'No.'

'You're not lying to me, are you?'

'No.'

He was lying about lying.

'Are you drinking?'

'Are you talking in an Irish accent?'

'So you had to drink to find the courage to call me?'

'I'm drinking 'cause my life just went into the crapper.'

'What did you tell Becca?'

'She slapped me before I could say much of anything.'

'Good for her. Ask her to slap you once for me. Maybe twice.'

'I'll make a note.'

She was silent.

'Lindsay, please come home.'

'Are you going to cut the school budget?'

'If I don't, will you come home?'

'I'm not negotiating, Bode.'

'I am. I'll do anything you want. To get you back.'

'Except love me.'

'Lindsay, I've always loved you.'

'Do you love Mandy?'

'No.'

'You're having an affair with a twenty-seven-year-old girl, but you want me to come home and stand by your side? Be the good wife?'

'I ended it. With Mandy.'

'You did? Why?'

'The Professor said—'

'Oh. For politics. Not for me.'

'What about you? Are you having an affair? With your doctor?'

416

'No.'

'If the press finds out you're having an affair with my only political rival, I'll never be president.'

'That's why you care?'

'Lindsay, I can be president.'

'Why do you want to be president?'

'Because I can.'

'That's it?'

'It's an adventure.'

'It's a game. Just another game to win.'

'Lindsay, life's just a game to men. Sports, business, politics . . . winning football games, making money, winning elections . . . you do it to prove you can.'

'Prove to whom?'

'Yourself.'

He heard her sigh, and then she was silent for a moment. Bode asked the question he had to ask.

'Do you love him?'

'I don't know.'

'But you might?'

'I might.'

'Your doctor wants my job and my wife.'

'He doesn't want your job.'

'Just my wife.'

'And what do you want, Bode? Your job or your wife?'

He loved his wife, but did he love politics more? He didn't answer quickly enough for her liking.

'Your job.' She exhaled into the phone. 'The Governor's Mansion is not my home. It never was. And the White House never will be. I don't want that life, Bode. You'll have to live it alone.'

Chapter 31

The next morning, Jim Bob greeted Mandy Morgan as if she were a visiting princess. He opened his door for her, he escorted her to a chair in front of his desk, he offered her coffee—

'I'm not drinking coffee anymore, caffeine is bad for the baby.'

—and otherwise treated her royally. He tried not to stare at her belly. There was nothing to see yet, but disaster was growing inside that belly. That being in her belly threatened everything Jim Bob Burnet had dreamed about and worked for the last twenty-five years of his life. That life threatened his life. He wasn't going to let this ex-cheerleader and her bastard baby ruin his life. He got right to the point.

'I'm prepared to pay you one million dollars.'

Her expression turned suspicious.

'To do what?'

'Abort.'

'No.'

'Mandy—'

'I wouldn't take a million dollars from Mr. Johnson for sex, and I'm not taking a million dollars for my baby.'

'John Ed offered you a million dollars for sex?'

'Yes.'

'And you didn't take it?'

'No.'

'Why the hell not?'

'I'm not like that. I know you think I'm just Bode's

418

plaything, but I'm not. I'm a lot smarter than you think. I'm not having an abortion.' She pointed at Eddie sitting on the couch. 'And he's scaring me.'

Jim Bob turned to Eddie and nodded to the door. Eddie stood and walked out.

'Mandy, you been watching TV? What they're saying about Bode?'

She nodded. 'It's terrible.'

'Yes, it is. Don't you want him to be president?'

'Yes. And I want to be the first lady.'

Jim Bob stared at this girl and thought, *What fucking world is she living in?*

She was sixteen, and she made her living as a prostitute in Nuevo Laredo. She flinched when Jesse stuck the needle into her arm. Penicillin. She had worked in a *maquiladora*, but had been laid off when the factory closed and her job had been moved to Asia. She had no other skills. Now she had syphilis.

'I need to see you again in one week,' he said to her in Spanish.

She nodded, but recoiled when the door swung open and two armed men entered.

'No!' she cried.

Jesse stood in front of her and blocked the men.

'What do you want?'

'Her. She is *puta*.'

'She is my patient. Get out.'

The man pulled a gun and put the barrel to Jesse's head.

'No!' Lindsay screamed.

The other man now stepped close to the man holding the gun and said in a low voice, 'El Diablo, he put out the order.

No harm is to come to the doctor. If you kill him, you will face El Diablo's justice.'

The man with the gun exhaled. His hand dropped. He turned and walked out. The other man followed. Jesse's hands were shaking. Lindsay came to him and put her hand on his shoulder.

'Jesse, are you okay?'

'I know I will die one day on this border, but I am very happy that this was not that day.'

'I thought the boss's official policy was abstinence,' Eddie Jones said. 'I guess only for school kids.'

'Funny.'

'I don't figure the boss is gonna get into the White House with a bastard child.'

Mandy had left, and Eddie Jones had returned to the sofa in Jim Bob's office.

'No shit.'

Eddie thought something was funny.

'These unforeseen, unexpected, unpleasant things are coming fast now.'

'No goddamn cheerleader is gonna take the White House from me.'

'I can make that unpleasant problem go away.'

'She won't get an abortion.'

'If she goes away, the baby goes away. I can make that happen.'

Jim Bob stared at Eddie Jones. He knew Eddie had a questionable past—shit, he worked in Iraq as a mercenary—but kill Mandy? From Eddie's expression, Jim Bob knew Eddie could kill her, dispose of her body, and then eat Tex-Mex for lunch without the need for a Tums. The guy was that cold.

But was Jim Bob Burnet? How far would he go to save Bode Bonner's political career? And his?

'Let me talk to Bode, make another run at her.'

His insurance policy shook his head.

'Woman like that, only a bullet will change her mind.'

Maybe Eddie was right. In five months, 'William Bode Bonner' would be typed under FATHER on a birth certificate in an Austin hospital. Jim Bob Burnet could not allow that day to come.

'Rest assured, Eddie—Mandy Morgan is either gonna come to Jesus or meet Him.'

'Is Jesús in heaven?' little Carmelita asked her father.

In the white compound in Nuevo Laredo, Enrique de la Garza was reading the *inglés* to his ten-year-old daughter. She smelled of strawberry shampoo. Her mother used to read to her each night, but the task had fallen to her father.

'Yes.'

'I miss him.'

'I do as well.'

'Is the man who killed Jesús going to jail?'

'No, *mi hija*. He is going to hell.'

ONE MONTH BEFORE

Chapter 32

Enrique de la Garza entered the chapel on the ground floor of his compound and dipped his finger into the font of holy water, then genuflected and made the sign of the cross. Each morning at eight he came into his chapel to pray and contemplate his life, to ask God for guidance and forgiveness, to confess his sins and receive the sacrament of Communion. He now walked up the short aisle to the altar rail where Padre Rafael awaited him, as he did each morning. Enrique knelt before him.

'*El cuerpo de Cristo*,' the padre said. The body of Christ.

Enrique turned his face up, opened his mouth, and extended his tongue. Padre Rafael placed the Communion host on his tongue. Enrique de la Garza accepted the true body of Jesus Christ into his own. He was supposed to confess his sins, venial and mortal, prior to receiving Communion, as he did each day. But he could not that day.

For his mortal sin was yet to come that day.

A 'come to Jesus' meeting, the Professor called it. Just like those evangelical tent revivals in the South where the faithful came down front to give their lives over to Jesus, to be born again, it was time for Mandy Morgan to come to Jesus, he had said. Or at least to Bode Bonner. It was time for her to give her life over to him so he could be the next president of the United States of America. It was the seventh day of August when Mandy marched into the Governor's Office where Bode and Jim Bob awaited her arrival, stood in front of the governor's desk, planted her fists in her ever-expanding hips, and announced, 'I'm not aborting our baby.'

Bode jumped out of his chair and came around the desk to her. She stood there breathing a bit fast, never a good sign with a woman and particularly a pregnant woman.

'Whoa, now, honey—no one's talking about abortion.'

'You're not?'

'No, absolutely not. We just wanted to figure out how we're gonna handle this, uh, situation.'

'Situation? You mean our baby?'

'Uh, yeah . . . that.'

Bode got her settled into a chair then stroked her narrow shoulders like he was calming a skittish colt. Once her breathing had returned to normal, he returned to his chair on the other side of the desk. The morning sun shone through the east-facing floor-length windows and directly on him. If not for the fact that he had sired a child out of wedlock, it would be a nice summer day in Austin, Texas.

'Mandy,' the Professor said, 'you're a smart girl. And you've been in politics for several years now. So you understand the political ramifications for Bode if it were revealed that the leading Republican presidential candidate fathered a love child—'

'*A love child?* What does that mean?'

As if Jim Bob had accused her unborn child of not being as smart as the other unborn children.

'A child by a woman other than his wife, that's all.' He quickly added, 'A woman he loves.'

426

'Oh.'

She smiled at Bode. Jim Bob gave Bode a look, as if he were setting her up.

'So, well, uh . . . here's the thing, Mandy. I . . . we . . . think it prudent for everyone involved to, uh, confirm the, uh . . . situation.'

Mandy Morgan was in fact a smart girl. She stood and again drove her fists into her hips, which from that angle appeared even wider.

'Confirm the situation? You mean prove that Bode's the father? That this baby is our baby? That I didn't fuck around on him?'

Bode had never before heard Mandy say the f-word, not even when they had sex. That was another bad sign with a woman. In their twenty-two years of marriage, the only time Lindsay had ever said the f-word to him was when he vetoed that CHIPS program providing health care for children in Texas, a cause near and dear to her heart. 'Fuck you, Bode Bonner!' she had screamed. Then she had moved out of their bedroom. Mandy now turned to him. On him.

'Bode Bonner—I love you. I've always loved you and I always will love you. Only you. I have been one hundred percent faithful to you—not even a million dollars could make me cheat on you.'

'A million dollars?'

'John Ed offered her a million bucks for sex,' Jim Bob said.

'While we were out hunting?'

Mandy nodded.

'That old son of a bitch.' He looked back at Mandy. 'You didn't take it?'

'No! I would never cheat on you, Bode. You're my man. My only man.'

She placed her hands on her belly; the baby bump was starting to show.

'This is your child. Our child.'

He knew she had been faithful. He knew the child was his. But he also knew that that child stood between him and the White House.

'I know all that, Mandy. But you know that baby will destroy my chances to be president. Since that press conference, my poll numbers have plummeted. And my Twitter followers are down to . . . what, Jim Bob?'

Jim Bob fiddled with his phone.

'Below Paris Hilton.'

Bode turned his palms up at Mandy.

'Below Paris Hilton.'

She threw her hands up.

'Why? If boys can marry boys and adopt babies and girls can marry girls and get pregnant with sperm from a donor and they can all be celebrated as wonderful families on *Good Morning America*, why can't we have this baby without being married? Why is their lifestyle okay but not ours?'

'Politics,' the Professor said. 'Gays and lesbians are liberal Democrats, so the liberal media celebrate their lifestyle. Not so much a conservative Republican married to one woman and fathering a child with another one—especially one who looks like you.'

'Mandy,' Bode said, 'you're absolutely right. It's not fair, the media shouldn't have a double standard for liberals and conservatives, it shouldn't matter. But politics isn't about right and wrong, fair or unfair. It's about winning and losing. Politics is played in the real world, and in the real world it matters. It matters to those voters who vote on family values because it's not their family values. Mandy, the reality is, they'll vote for another Republican. I won't make it out of Iowa.'

Mandy's expression softened a bit, so Bode pushed on. It was time to have the talk with his mistress.

'Mandy, you're young, and I'm old.'

'I know.'

'I'm not that old!' He sighed. 'But you're young enough to be my daughter.'

'I know.'

'You want children, I have a child. You're looking forward to your life, I'm looking back on mine. You need a young man, not an old guy. When that child goes to college, I'll be on social security, if it's still around.'

'The child?'

'Social security.'

'Oh.'

'Your best years are ahead of you. Mine are in the past. You're young and beautiful, and I'm old and . . .'

He waited. Nothing from Mandy, except a few tears, the first good sign that morning.

'. . . not as handsome as I used to be. Mandy, this isn't the start of my life. This is my last great adventure.'

'Having our baby?'

'Running for president. But if you have that baby, I won't be president. I won't be able to change the world, I won't be able to make the world a better place for Republicans— for their children. I won't be able to save America from the Democrats like God wants me to—'

Whoops. Bode knew he had made a mistake, but before he could repair the damage, the Professor pounced.

'*Like God wants you to?* What the hell does that mean?'

Jim Bob wanted a 'come to Jesus' meeting, Bode thought,

so let's give him one. It was time for Bode Bonner to share his religious epiphany with the world—or at least with the Professor.

'It means that God wants me to be president. It means that He put me on John Ed's ranch that day—'

'God and a Gulfstream.'

Bode ignored his sarcasm. Nonbeliever.

'—and on that ridge with that rifle at that very moment when Josefina made her escape attempt and—'

The nonbeliever rolled his eyes.

'Oh, for Christ's sake.'

'Exactly. And God gave me the ability to shoot those men and save her life. Because He wants me in the White House.'

'Well, He damn near got you killed at Kerbey's, you think about that?'

'No, He didn't. He saved me that day. Sixty bullets they fired, but not one hit me or Becca. It was a miracle, Jim Bob, a miracle. See, I figure God put up a shield, like some kind of force field—'

'*Force field?*'

'Yeah, you know, that the bullets couldn't penetrate. How else can you explain me and Becca surviving that attack?'

'Luck. She dropped her spoon.'

Bode pointed at Jim Bob like an eyewitness picking out the guilty criminal.

'Nonbeliever.'

'*Nonbeliever?*'

The Professor stood and gestured at Mandy.

'She thinks she's gonna have your bastard baby and still be the first lady of America, and you think God's picking Republican presidential candidates—I'm in a fucking insane asylum!'

430

Tears now streamed down Mandy's face. Her voice was childlike.

'My dad died when I was only seven. I missed him so much, growing up. My therapist says that's why I've always been attracted to older men, that I'm subconsciously searching for a father-figure, a man to replace my dad.'

She wiped her face and looked at Bode.

'Okay. I'll do it. For you.'

She put on a brave smile and started around the wide desk. The pregnancy had put a glow on her face that only made her more beautiful, if that was possible.

'Because I love you.'

She extended her arms to him, and he reached out to her. Just as she rounded the corner of his desk and stepped between Bode and the window and blocked the sunlight from his face, her beautiful face exploded and her brains and blood splattered all over Bode, and she tumbled into his arms.

'Jesus!'

The next thing Bode knew, they were sprawled on the wood floor . . . blood was everywhere . . . Jim Bob screamed, 'Help!' . . . the door flew open and Texas Rangers with guns drawn rushed in and shouted, 'Get away from the window!' . . . someone called 911 . . . 'We need ambulances at the Governor's Mansion! The governor's been shot! The bullets came through the east window. We need Austin PD's SWAT on the scene now! Cordon off the one hundred block of Congress Avenue, the sniper had to be positioned there!' . . . and Bode felt Mandy's warm blood flow from her body and soak his shirt and wet his skin until he lay drenched in her blood . . . and he felt life leave her.

★ ★ ★

431

Jim Bob Burnet stumbled out of the Governor's Office and down the hall and into his office. Eddie Jones followed him in and shut the door. He had rushed into the Governor's Office when he heard Jim Bob's call for help. He now holstered his gun.

'You okay?'

Jim Bob fell onto the couch. His heart was pounding out of his chest. He heard sirens coming closer. The last image in his mind was of Bode Bonner lying on the floor clutching Mandy Morgan's bloody head—what was left of it—in his arms.

'Jesus, her face . . . it was just gone.'

'High-caliber bullet,' Eddie said. 'Small entry wound, big exit wound.'

Jim Bob shook his head. 'Shit, if she hadn't stepped in the way, that bullet would have killed Bode.'

'The next one might.'

'The next one?'

'Sending a sniper to Austin—that drug lord ain't quitting until the boss is dead.'

'Can you kill him first? You were in Iraq, doing all that mercenary shit. You could get a few mercs, cross the river at night and kill him, get the hell out.'

Eddie snorted. 'You been watching too many action movies. Cartels got private armies, ex-special forces guys, and they're kicking the shit out of the regular Mexican Army. Sure, I could kill him. But getting out alive, that's the trick.'

'I had a million dollars set aside for Mandy. That money's available now.'

'One man with the right skill set . . . it's possible.'

'What if that were Bode instead of . . . ?'

Jim Bob couldn't clear the image of Mandy's face from his mind.

'You were right,' Eddie said.

'About what?'

'That she was either gonna come to Jesus or meet Him.'

Jim Bob lay his head back.

'I didn't want this. I just wanted her to get an abortion.'

'She just did.'

'Saving those kids, surviving an assassination attempt, now this—maybe God really does want Bode Bonner in the White House.'

'Well, if He does, He'd better find a way to stop that autopsy.'

'What autopsy?'

'On the girl. Homicide, they always do an autopsy. Problem is, they do an autopsy on Mandy—'

Jim Bob snapped to a sitting position.

'They find the baby.'

The Border Patrol agent named Rusty stepped through the front door of the clinic. Inez took one look at his olive-green uniform and his badge and gun and jumped up from her chair as if she were guilty.

'Doctor!'

Jesse looked up from his desk. The Border Patrol agents seldom came into the *colonias*, and then only to chase drug bandits, and only if they had shot an agent. Lindsay turned away. Jesse walked over to the agent and stuck his hand out.

'Rusty, how are you this day?'

The agent's expression was grim.

'Sorry to bother you, Doc, but I know you don't have

433

a TV or nothing out here. Seeing how you might run for governor, thought you should know.'

'Know what?'

'The governor's dead. Sniper killed him in the Governor's Mansion.'

The governor's wife screamed.

Governor Bode Bonner stepped out the front doors of the Governor's Mansion and onto the veranda. Cameras clicked and recorded the moment. He stepped to the microphones clumped together on a stand. He was still wearing the clothes stained with Mandy's blood.

'An hour ago, a bullet intended for me struck Mandy Morgan instead, killing her instantly. She was a wonderful, beautiful, smart young woman, and a tireless aide to me. She was my employee and my friend, but she was not my lover.'

He was lying, but Jim Bob said he had no choice.

'Governor, from what location did the shooter fire?'

'Apparently from the roof of an office building across Congress. The police and Rangers are investigating, but so far they've found no sign of the shooter.'

'El Diablo hasn't given up on killing you?'

'Apparently not.'

'What are you going to do now, Governor?'

'I'm going to bury Mandy Morgan.'

'Her mother wants to cremate her body,' Jim Bob said.

Two hours after Mandy had been murdered, Jim Bob Burnet had gathered himself. He had also convinced Mandy's mother that she did not want her daughter to be remembered as she was now but as she was before. Mandy Morgan's disfigured body now lay on a stainless steel table in the first-floor

434

morgue at the Travis County Medical Examiner's Office eight blocks away. Jim Bob had called to arrange a speedy transfer of the body to the funeral home, but the chief ME was having none of it.

'Only after we conduct an autopsy,' Dr. Paul Janofsky said.

'Why?'

'To determine the cause of death.'

'Cause of death? How about a bullet through her fucking head! I was in the room, Paul. I saw the bullet hit her. I saw her die. So did the governor.'

'Jim Bob, I'm standing next to the body. I've seen hundreds of gunshot deaths, I know what killed her, but—'

'Paul, an autopsy —the report, the photos—it'll all be public record. It'll be on the national news.'

It'll reveal that Mandy was pregnant.

'Jim Bob, look—'

'No, Paul, you look—at her. At her face. What do you see?'

'Her brain.'

'Exactly. You want her autopsy photos splashed all over the Internet? Her mother sure as hell doesn't. She wants the world to remember her daughter as the beautiful young woman she was, not with her fucking face blown off. Paul, she wants to cremate her daughter. Let her mother have her peace.'

He heard the ME breathing into the phone. Jim Bob gave him time to think it through. The ME finally spoke.

'As chief medical examiner for Travis County, I am responsible for investigating and certifying cause of death and manner of death in all cases of violent death. My investigation and certification as to cause and manner of death may, but is not legally required to, include an autopsy . . .'

He sounded as if he were rehearsing his response to the inevitable questions from the media as to why he did not conduct an autopsy.

'. . . and cause of death was clear and obvious, the death was witnessed by two credible witnesses, one of whom is the governor of Texas, and both of whom swore under oath as to the circumstances of Ms. Morgan's death. Thus, it was my . . .'

He *was* rehearsing. Paul Janofsky had been the Travis County ME for over thirty years. He had handled numerous high-profile murders. He had experience with the media circus. He was the only Republican holding elected office in the county.

'. . . professional opinion that, in light of the horrific trauma to her body and the family's wishes that an autopsy not be conducted and photos not be taken in order to preserve their daughter's privacy and dignity, an autopsy was not necessary or appropriate in this matter to determine cause of death. My official ruling is that Mandy Morgan died of a gunshot wound to the head. Manner of death was homicide.'

He paused.

'Sounds good to me, Paul.'

'Okay, Jim Bob. No autopsy. No photos. I'll need those sworn statements from you and the governor, then I'll sign the death certificate and issue a certificate for cremation. We'll release the body upon receipt of the next-of-kin's signed release form. Time of death was nine-thirty this morning, so she can't be cremated until nine-thirty Monday morning—there's a forty-eight-hour waiting period. You're on the clock, Jim Bob. Won't be as much press coverage this weekend, but come Monday morning, all hell's gonna break loose. You'd better get this wrapped up and the body in the furnace by then, because if the district attorney gets involved—and he will—and he requests an autopsy, I'm required by law to do it. And the DA's a Democrat.'

'The governor won't forget this, Paul.'

Jesse drove her into Laredo where there was cell phone service. She cried all the way. He was unfaithful, he was ambitious, he was a politician—but he was still her husband. She breathed with relief when she heard his voice.

'Bode—thank God you're okay. The Border Patrol agent said they killed you.'

'They killed Mandy.'

'Oh, no.'

He exhaled into the phone. 'Lindsay, you've got to come home. This guy ain't quitting. If he ever finds out you're right across the river from him—'

'He won't. How's Becca?'

'Daddy, I thought we were safe here. But if they can kill Mandy right here in the Mansion, they can kill us, too.'

Becca sat in her bed, where she sat or lay most hours of every day now, cuddling the oversized teddy bear Bode had given her for her twelfth birthday.

'Honey, you're safe with me.'

'She wasn't. Hank, Darcy, now Mandy . . . They're not going to stop until they kill all of us.'

Tears ran down her face.

'Daddy, who are those people?'

'You killed his girlfriend.'

Four hours later, Hector Garcia had just arrived back in Nuevo Laredo and the compound. He was weary from the long drive.

'*What?*'

'It is on the news.' Enrique turned the TV on with the remote. 'See? You did not kill him. You killed her.'

Hector had the governor's head in his cross hairs when he pulled the trigger. He knew the local police would lock down the area, so he had left Austin immediately and driven south to the border without stopping.

'Hector, go now and do not return without the governor's head.'

Darcy was dead. Hank was dead. Mandy was dead. Becca could be dead. He could be dead. But for Mandy, he would be dead.

El Diablo would not stop until he had his vengeance. As a father, Bode could understand that. If those hit men had killed Becca that day, he would hunt El Diablo down and kill him. If it took the rest of his life—if it took his own life—Bode Bonner would have his vengeance. Just as El Diablo wanted his.

Any moment, anytime, anywhere—a bullet could slam into his head. Bode turned his eyes up to the animal heads on the wall—now he knew how they felt. The only difference was, he knew he was being hunted. He knew they were coming after him.

Bode Bonner had hunted all his life. Now he was the hunted.

Chapter 33

Mandy Morgan's body, encased in a cardboard box, was slid into the natural-gas-fired furnace at the crematorium at nine-thirty the following Monday morning, exactly forty-eight hours to the minute after the time of her death shown on the death certificate signed by the Travis County chief medical examiner. Ninety minutes later, the sixteen-hundred-degree fire had vaporized her body tissues and organs and reduced the physical being that was Mandy Morgan (and her unborn child) to skeletal remains. Which remains were collected and pulverized by the cremulator until they were ashes. She had weighed one hundred ten pounds in life; in death, her ashes weighed only three and a half pounds and were placed in a silver urn at her mother's request. Madeline Morgan, James Robert Burnet, and Governor Bode Bonner witnessed the cremation. Madeline cried; Bode sat stunned; Jim Bob paid the $500 cremation fee from the campaign petty cash fund. The Travis County district attorney filed a written request for an autopsy with the Medical Examiner's Office at precisely 11:07 that morning.

Jim Bob drove Mrs. Morgan to the airport for her flight back to Odessa with the urn containing her daughter's ashes cradled in her arms like an infant. Bode returned to the mansion and found the kids playing soccer on the south lawn. With no adult supervision. He walked over to Josefina. She again wore the yellow dress, as if it were her only item of clothing.

'Where's Becca? *¿Dónde está Becca?*'

'*Duerme.*'

'*¿Duerme?*'

'*¿Qué?*'

'*Está durmiendo.*'

Bode turned his palms up.

'*¿Qué?*'

'Becca . . . she . . .'

Josefina put her hands together and lay her face on her hands and closed her eyes. As if sleeping.

'She's sleeping?'

'*Sí. Duerme.*'

Bode checked his watch.

'It's almost noon.'

He went inside and upstairs to Becca's room. He knocked but she didn't answer. He opened the door and peeked in. She was still sleeping. He went over to the bed and sat next to his daughter bundled under a blanket even though it wasn't cold. Becca Bonner never used to sleep till noon. Back on the ranch, she'd be up at dawn to ride her horse or brand cows or practice volleyball before school. She had been an active, athletic, fearless girl. Now she was a frightened, fearful, depressed child hiding from the world in bed. It was his fault. His actions had put her in this state. He put his hand on his daughter over the blanket and gave her a little shake.

'Becca, wake up. It's almost noon.'

No response.

'Come on, honey, you can't stay in bed all day. It's not healthy.'

Still no response.

'Becca.'

He stood and yanked the blanket off her. Saliva hung from

440

her mouth. Her face was pale. He shook her hard this time and slapped her face. No response.

She was unresponsive.

'Becca!'

'Don't tell Mom, okay?'

Two hours later, Texas Rangers stood guard outside the emergency room at Austin General Hospital downtown. Inside, Bode Bonner sat in a chair next to his daughter's bed. They had pumped her stomach. Alcohol and sleeping pills.

'I wasn't trying to kill myself. I was just trying to sleep. I'm afraid to shut my eyes.'

This was his fault, too.

'Daddy, I want to go home.'

'To the mansion?'

'To the ranch.'

Chapter 34

The Double B Ranch comprised five thousand acres of Hill Country land outside Comfort, Texas, population 2,358. The ranch had been in the Bonner family since 1868, when Samuel Bode Bonner, fresh off fighting in the Civil War, returned to Texas and bought the land for $800 cash. No one knew how he had come into such a fortune.

Samuel married Rebecca. They had five children. Two died before age ten; two more died without having married. Thus, the ranch went to the last surviving child, Benjamin Bode Bonner.

Ben married Jean. They had one child who survived birth, Henry Bode Bonner.

Henry married Elizabeth. They had two children. Emma Elizabeth, the daughter, died in a car wreck on Interstate 10 when she was sixteen. William Bode, the son, became governor of Texas.

Bode Bonner turned the Suburban through the gates under the Double B brand. Becca sat next to him in the passenger seat; Lupe, Miguel, and Alejandro sat in the middle seat, and Josefina sat in the third seat.

'¿La hacienda?'

'Yep. This is our ranch.'

Jim Bob had remained in Austin to write the keynote speech that Bode would give at the governors' conference in two weeks in Dallas. Bode had convinced his Texas Ranger bodyguards that if they stayed in Austin and made daily trips about town in the caravan of black Suburbans and Jim Bob issued daily press releases and tweets from the Governor's Office, everyone would think the governor was still in Austin; that he was safer alone than with large Rangers attracting attention. And besides, no one could find the Double B Ranch without a guide.

At least he didn't think so.

The long caliche road led to a modest house high on a hill that overlooked wide valleys east and west where the cattle grazed under the hot August sun. Bode parked the Suburban under the shade of an oak tree. The kids bailed out and stretched after the two-hour drive. A white-haired Mexican man rode up on a white stallion trailed by a big German shepherd. The man dismounted and embraced Lupe, his sister. The dog ran to Bode.

'Shep!'

Bode greeted the dog then stood to greet the man.

'*Señor* Bode, it has been a while.'

Ramón Sendejo's hands were strong from a life of hard work, the last sixty years on the Double B Ranch. He had come with his own father when he was only eight; he had never left the ranch. He turned to Becca and held his arms out to her.

'*Señorita* Becca, you have finally come home to Ramón.'

She threw herself into his arms and hugged him tightly. Ramón's eyes cut to Bode, his expression asking if she was all right. Bode nodded. When Ramón released Becca, he turned to the children.

'And who are these *niños*?'

'Miguel and Alejandro, and this little gal is Josefina.'

'And would you *niños* like to ride the horses? *¿Montar caballo?*'

The boys broke into big smiles—'*¡Sí!*'—but Josefina shook her head.

'I will make them *vaqueros*, *Señor* Bode, just as I made you. Come, Chelo has lunch for the travelers.'

Becca and the kids led the way to the house. Ramón lowered his voice to Bode.

'These are the children from that day in West Texas?'

'The ones I still have.'

'What you did that day, *Señor* Bode, that was a good thing.'

They went into the house where they found Ramón's wife

and the aroma of Mexican food in the kitchen. Consuelo—known as 'Chelo'—came to Bode and embraced him.

'*Señor* Bode. I am very happy that you are not dead.' She looked past him. 'And where is the *señora*?'

When Bode had called Ramón to tell him they were coming, he only said that Lindsay would not be with them. He had not explained why.

'She's out of town.'

Chelo looked into his eyes, then dropped hers. As if she understood.

'I have lunch.' She turned to the children. 'Come, *niños*, wash your hands.'

Everyone washed up in the kitchen sink and then sat at the table. Enchiladas, dark rice, and refried beans. Bode Bonner had grown up on Chelo's food.

His grandfather had built the hacienda-style house; his father had added on; Bode had put in the swimming pool for Becca and her friends. There were four bedrooms and four bathrooms, a great room with the kitchen at one end and the stone fireplace at the other, an office, laundry, and mud room. Bode had lived every day of his life in this house, except the four years he had lived in the UT football dormitory and the eight years in the Governor's Mansion. Ramón and Chelo lived down in the creek house. Lupe had lived with them until Bode had taken her to the Governor's Mansion. The four *vaqueros* lived in the bunkhouse. They ran five thousand head of cattle on the ranch. Some years they made a little money, some years they lost a little money. You didn't ranch cattle to get rich. You ranched because it was your life. What you knew.

★ ★ ★

444

After lunch, Becca took the kids swimming. Bode rode out with Ramón and Shep the dog. Bode's horse was named King. The big bay had been sired on the ranch and would die on the ranch, just as Bode's father and mother had died on the ranch. His sister, Emma, had died on the interstate, but she too was buried on the ranch. Bode and Becca were the last of the Bonner breed. When he died, the ranch would be hers. Given her sexual preference, Bode didn't figure on grandkids.

Who would take care of the ranch when Becca was gone?

They rode to the Bonner family cemetery where eleven white headstones stood. They dismounted and went inside the white picket fence under the shade of a tall oak tree. Bode's great-grandparents, grandparents, aunts and uncles, mother and father, and big sister. Emma had been special. Blonde and beautiful, tough and smart—she had been the queen of the rodeo and the rodeo star. She was the Bonner who would make the family proud. Then she was gone. Then they were all gone. His sister when he was thirteen, his parents when he was sixteen. Ramón and Chelo had taken him the rest of the way to manhood. They had cheered him in the stands as if he were their own son. Ramón was a wise old man who had helped Bode the boy through the dark days. He had something to say.

'When *Señorita* Emma died, I knew more death would follow. After your *madre* died, and then your *padre* so soon after, you were lost . . . until the *señora* came into your life. Your path is with her. It has always been so.'

Ramón mounted up and rode off to check on the herd in the west pasture. Bode rode on to the far hills, the highest point on the ranch. From there he could see the entire ranch—and the entirety of his life on the ranch. It had been a simple life, a good life, the country life. He had been happy living this life. He had been a boy here, until his father taught him how to be a man here. He had buried his mother here and then his father. He had married and become a father here. He had lived his life here. And the life he had lived here had been a real life.

Why had he left this life?

He had told himself back then that he was leaving to do good, and perhaps that was true at first. But there was no lying to himself now. His parents had put him on a straight path here on this ranch, but he had veered off course onto another path, one that took him to the state capitol and then the Governor's Mansion and might even take him to the White House. Was that Bode Bonner's path in life?

He sat on his horse and pondered Ramón's words.

And he wondered if Bode Bonner had made the family proud.

He rode back to the house and joined the kids in the pool. He put on a good face for them, but the image of Mandy's face being blown off kept him constant company now. He still couldn't believe she was gone. Because of him.

He got out and sat in a lounge chair under an umbrella next to Becca. It was good to have kids playing in the pool again. They had wanted more children, but the pregnancy was difficult; the doctor said the next one could be danger-ous. So Becca was an only child.

'I wish Mom was here,' she said.

'Me, too.'

'Do you really?'

He nodded. 'We need her.'

'You hurt her.'

446

'I know.'

'What are you going to do about that?'

'I don't know.'

'Are you going to try to get her back?'

'I'm not sure she wants me back.'

'You're part of her.'

Josefina played in the pool. The therapist had helped her. Each day Bode saw the little girl emerge from the frightened soul they had rescued that day in West Texas.

'We need to buy her a new dress,' Becca said. 'Her yellow one is getting ratty, she wears it every day.'

'Find her a new one in town.'

'I don't want to leave the ranch.'

Bode patted his daughter's hand. Josefina now climbed out of the pool and came over. Bode tossed her a towel. She wrapped the big towel around her little body then stepped to him and gave him a hug.

'What's that for?'

Becca had learned Spanish from Ramón and Chelo and the *vaqueros*. She translated. Bode had never bothered to learn their language. So he spoke Spanglish, the Tex-Mex butchered version, like a Texan cooking Mexican food. It was about time he learned the language.

'*¿Por qué tan cariñosa?*' Becca said.

'*Quiero ser tuya,*' Josefina said.

'She said she wants to be yours.'

Bode frowned. 'No, no, honey, it doesn't work that way in America. What those men did to you, that was wrong, okay? Men in America, we don't have little girls for our—'

'Daddy,' Becca said. 'She didn't mean it that way. She wants to be your daughter.' She turned to Josefina: '*¿Hija?*'

She nodded. '*Sí. Hija.*'

Becca grinned at Bode.

'I always wanted a little sister.'

'Lindsay, if El Diablo learns that you are the governor's wife, he will kill you before the sun again rises over the Rio Grande. You must go home.'

'I am home.'

Jesse and Lindsay got out of the pickup truck and walked into the house followed by Pancho. They placed the grocery bags on the kitchen counter next to the phone. The red message light was bright. Jesse hit the PLAY button and listened to messages from Mayor Gutiérrez and Latino legislators and business people from around the state—all pleading with him to be the Latino who takes Texas back from the Anglos. The latest polls showed Jesse in a dead heat with the governor.

'Of course,' the mayor said on the recording, 'we might not have to beat the governor-for-life because he might not be alive much longer.'

Jesse stopped the message and turned to Lindsay.

'Sorry. Gutiérrez and these other old Latinos, they are of another generation. They are still angry over past injustices. They want to fight the Mexican–American War again. But fighting past battles again does not help the people today, here on the border.'

'No,' Lindsay said. 'It doesn't help them at all.'

'And the leaders from the state and national Democratic Party, they think if I beat your husband here in Texas, he could not win the presidency.'

'Losing governors don't win the White House.'

'But they are just using me to further their agendas.'

'That's what they do.'

'The Democrats do not care about the people here on the border any more than the Republicans. I am just useful to them. They just want me to take the governor's job so to save the president's job. As if the president needs me.'

The phone rang. Jesse picked up the receiver and put it to his ear.

'Hello.'

'Dr. Rincón?'

'Yes.'

'Please hold for the president.'

Chapter 35

German immigrants settled most of the Texas Hill Country in the mid-1800s. The liberal Germans settled in Comfort. They called themselves 'free thinkers.' They opposed slavery and the Confederacy during the Civil War. Twenty-eight of those Germans paid for their beliefs with their lives; they were ambushed and massacred by the Confederates in 1862.

Located forty-five miles north of San Antonio on Interstate 10, downtown Comfort—which is to say, the three blocks of High Street—consists of antique shops, a bed-and-breakfast, a small library, a restaurant called the Texas Bistro, and a deli/wine bar called High's on High Street. It was eight in the next morning, and Bode Bonner stood at the corner of Seventh and High across from the old bank that was now a museum.

He did not look like the governor of Texas that day. No Armani suits and French-cuffed shirts or even jeans and starched shirts. He wore a knit shirt, khaki shorts, and sneakers. His blond hair stuck out wildly from beneath a burnt-orange Longhorns cap pulled down low. He wore sunglasses. He hadn't shaved. He had woken at dawn, as he had always done on the ranch, but not because there was work to be done; because he had woken in a cold sweat from reliving Mandy's murder. He could not erase the image of her face exploding from his mind.

Chelo had already been up at the house, but Becca and the kids were still asleep, so she was holding off breakfast. He grabbed a cup of coffee then drove into the town where he had grown up. He was searching for something.

The man he used to be.

A loud noise startled Bode, but it was only an old pickup backfiring. He was as jumpy as Jim Bob these days. The town had not yet come alive; of course, you could stand in the middle of High Street during rush hour and not risk getting hit. To say life was slow in Comfort was like saying it was hot in Texas in August. Bode needed breakfast and more coffee, so he walked down to High's. He entered, removed his sunglasses, and made eye contact with the proprietor behind the counter; he recognized Bode, but only nodded then turned back to an old-timer ordering.

'And a scone.'

The old man had white hair, a slumped posture, and a wood cane.

'Grady, you want two scones?'

'Why would I want two scones?'

'Because you already ordered one.'

'I did?'

'Yep.'

'I'll be damned.'

The old-timer named Grady turned from the counter, leaned hard on his cane, and eyed Bode a long moment.

'You look mighty familiar,' he said. 'Like someone I seen on TV.'

'The governor,' the proprietor said.

'No,' Grady said, 'not the governor. Someone else.'

Bode glanced over at the proprietor; they shared a smile.

'It'll come to me in a minute,' Grady said. 'You know he grew up here?'

'Who?'

'The governor. Helluva ath-a-lete.'

'That so?'

'Yep. One game he scored six touchdowns.'

'Seven.'

'Or was it seven? Can't recall. Anyways, he don't come back much no more, wants to be president they say. Damn shame.'

'That he wants to be president?'

'That he shot himself in the foot like that other boy wanted to be president, cheating on his wife.'

Bode again glanced over at the proprietor, who averted his eyes this time.

'Saw it on *Fox News*.'

'You figure that makes him a bad man?'

'Who?'

'The governor.'

'What'd he do?'

'Cheat on his wife.'

Grady shook his head.

'Nope. Makes him a selfish man. Man that don't think of no one but himself.'

'What am I supposed to do when the president calls and says he needs my help? That he needs me to beat the governor so the governor does not beat him?'

Jesse and Lindsay drove to the *colonia*.

'What are you going to do?'

'What do you want me to do?'

'I don't want you to run for governor.'

'Because of your husband?'

'Because of you.'

'What do you mean?'

'It'll change you. Politics. It changes everyone it touches. For the worse. You're a good man, Jesse, too good for politics.'

'How do you know this?'

'I've worked with you for four months now—'

'No. That politics will change me.'

'Because my husband was a good man before he became a politician.'

Bode Bonner had learned that he was special when he was twelve years old, when his superior athletic ability first became evident. Everyone—students, teachers, even grown-ups in town—assured him he was special. Often. Each year, the attention grew with his on-the-field exploits. By the time he was eighteen, that Bode Bonner was special was an accepted fact in town.

And in his mind.

That knowledge changes a boy. To walk into the feed store crowded with grown men and be greeted as if he were a god because he could play football, that changes a boy. Signing autographs when you're sixteen, folks wanting their photos with you when you're seventeen, college recruiters from around the country beating a path to your front door when you're eighteen: That becomes a part of you, like the blue of your eyes. It changes who you are, how you see yourself, how you view the world. Other people. Life. You start to believe that other people exist to serve you. That the world belongs to you.

It makes you selfish.

Ninety miles east in Austin, Jim Bob Burnet sat at his desk drinking coffee. Christ, Mandy's brains blown out and then Becca overdoses on sleeping pills. Now Bode, Becca, and the Mexican children had fled to the Comfort ranch. Jim Bob had elected to stay behind in Austin. He couldn't wait to leave Comfort when he was a kid, and he had never returned as an adult. And he never would. So he sat in his office.

With the blinds shut.

Bode Bonner had made a full recovery: the polls, the followers, the pledges to the Super PAC. They were all back. The scandal had been cremated with Mandy Morgan. The latest assassination attempt on the governor of Texas remained the number-one story in America. Reporters broadcast live from just outside the fence surrounding the mansion grounds, almost as if hoping to catch the governor's expected assassination live, like a reality show. Jim Bob stood and stepped over to the window; he stayed to the side and peeked through the blinds. Satellite dishes rose high above a dozen TV trucks lining Colorado and Tenth Streets. The camera lights shone brightly. He returned to his chair and increased the volume on the television. The reporter outside was saying, 'The governor of Texas remains secluded in the Governor's Mansion . . .'

He muted the volume. He would maintain the pretense that the governor was still in town with a steady stream of press releases and tweets. He picked up his iPhone.

At my desk. Won't let the devil himself keep me from working hard for the people of Texas.

'Cute.'

Enrique de la Garza read the governor's tweet on his iPhone. He was one of the governor's twelve million followers, not because Enrique cared what the governor was doing at any particular moment, but because he needed to know where the governor was in order for Hector Garcia to put a bullet in his brain. He started to put the encrypted cell phone to his ear and assure Hector that the governor was still in Austin, but—

A thought struck him.

The governor was not in Austin. He had left town. They were pulling the trick on Enrique de la Garza. He put the phone to his ear.

'Hector, the governor is no longer there in Austin.'

'But, *jefe*, we have had twenty-four/seven surveillance on the mansion. He is here. Yesterday, his caravan journeyed around town.'

'No. It is a decoy. He is gone. Find him!'

All his dreams had been born on that field.

Bode sat in the stands at the Comfort High School football stadium. On that field he had discovered two things: his football ability and his ambition. His ability fueled his ambition. His ambition expanded his world beyond Comfort and the ranch. He began to believe that there was more waiting out there for him. That his life would be played out on a bigger stage. That he belonged on such a stage. All he had to do was surrender to his ambition.

And he had.

'That you, Bode Bonner?'

Bode turned to an old black man standing there. It took him a moment to recognize the school janitor from thirty years before. He had been old back then, but he was ancient now.

'Mr. Jefferson. How are you?'

'Older. You still the governor?'

'Yep.'

'Thought they killed you?'

'They tried.'

Hector Garcia and one of his *soldados* followed the Texas Ranger into the restroom at the small taco bar near the University of Texas campus. They had trailed the Ranger in the SUV from the Governor's Mansion to the restaurant: lunch break. It would be this Ranger's last lunch. When they entered the restroom, the Ranger was zipping up. His *soldado* blocked the door. Hector pulled his switchblade and released the blade. The Ranger turned from the urinal, and Hector pushed him hard against the wall and swiped the blade across the Ranger's face, bringing the blood.

'Where is the governor?'

'Fuck you!'

Hector drove his knee into the Ranger's testicles; the Ranger went down. Hector felt the heat of hatred consume his body. He pushed the Ranger's head into the urinal and put the blade inside his nostril and slit it like butter. The Ranger started to scream like a child, but Hector clamped off his throat and all sound.

'Where is the governor?'

'Fuck you!'

Hector cut out the Ranger's eye. Before he died, he told Hector what he needed to know. Then they set fire to the taco bar to delay a warning to the governor.

They would only need that one night.

Bode Bonner had been a senior when Lindsay Byrne had moved to town, to this modest frame house. She had been the love of his life from the first time he saw her at school, looking lost in the main corridor. He walked up to her and said, 'Hi, I'm Bode Bonner.' He waited for the sense of awe to cross her face, but it didn't. It never had. Lindsay had never bought into his specialness. To her, he was not a god. He was just a man. She had brought him back down to earth that day. She had kept him grounded.

She had not idolized him as so many others had, but he had still been her hero. She had told him so one day on the ranch during spring roundup. They had worked side-by-side in the pens—he branded, she vaccinated. She had stumbled back over a calf; he had reached down and scooped her into his arms and off the ground before a cow could kick her. Her face was red from the sun and the work, and she was beautiful. He kissed her, and she kissed him back. Then she gazed into his eyes in that way she did, and she said, 'You're my hero, Bode Bonner.'

He had laughed and said, 'Hell, I just plucked you out of cow shit—I didn't rescue you from Indians on the warpath.'

456

'You're a good man,' she said. 'I'm proud to be your wife.'
She wasn't proud anymore.

Now, all these years later, for some reason that he could not put into a complete thought, Bode Bonner wanted desperately to make her proud again. To be her hero again. He needed that. It was the part of him that was missing.

They had married after she graduated from UT with a nursing degree. She joined him on the ranch. And there they would still be had Ronald Reagan not won the presidency in 1980. Democrats had controlled the state capitol since Reconstruction, but Reagan carried Texas and gave Republicans in Texas hope. That hope came to Comfort in the nineties. Republicans were plotting a takeover of state politics, and they needed young attractive candidates to run against old incumbent Democrats. Bode Bonner was thirty-one years old when ambition came into his life again. He had grown bored on the ranch. He again looked beyond the fences. Out there somewhere was excitement. Challenges. An adventure for Bode Bonner.

Perhaps in politics.

He had already run for the state legislature as a Democrat and lost to the incumbent in the primary. He then became a Republican and ran against the same incumbent in the general election. He won. The state legislature was a part-time job, only one hundred forty days every two years, so they had still lived at the ranch. Four sessions later, he ran for the Governor's Mansion and won. That was a full-time job, so they had moved to Austin. Four years after that, he had won again. His political career had soared—and his wife could no longer keep him grounded.

Between Comfort and Austin, he had lost his way.

He was governor-for-life, but it wasn't enough. It was

never enough. Ambition and testosterone drive a man to greatness—and then to self-destruction. No man can stop when he's ahead. Not when there's more to be had. More money. More power. Higher office. Younger women. Ambition drives him forward and testosterone makes him want more, always more—until he destroys himself. And those around him.

It is man's nature.

Was it God's desire? Did God really want Bode Bonner in the White House?

He stared up at the crucifix above the altar in the Catholic church he had attended as a boy with his family. Where he had received Communion and professed his faith in God. But he had lied. He didn't believe in God. He believed in Bode Bonner. Until that day at Kerbey's—until he had survived an assassination attempt—he had never thought much about God. He had thought about himself.

He had given in to his demon: ambition.

He wasn't God's chosen one. That was pure delusion fueled by ambition not faith. It was not real. What was real was that he loved his wife and daughter, but he had squandered their love. So his wife had left him and his daughter hated him. He had betrayed them both and now paid the price. Just as Hank and Darcy and Mandy had paid the price of living in the shadow of an ambitious man. It's a dark place. A dangerous place. They were dead, innocent bystanders caught in the crossfire of Bode Bonner's ambition. They would never laugh or love again; they would never have children or be someone's child again; they would never live again. Their lives were over—because of him. His ambition had killed them as surely as if he had pulled the trigger. Their deaths were on his tab. He turned his eyes up to the crucifix above the altar. They had died for nothing.

Unless.

At two the next morning, Hector Garcia and his two *soldados* parked the SUV under a stand of trees just down from the entrance to the governor's ranch north of San Antonio. They donned night-vision goggles and slung silenced weapons over their shoulders. Not that anyone would hear the gunfire—the ranch was in the middle of nowhere—or the governor's death cries.

They hiked up the caliche road to the house on the hill. A dog barked out front of the house. Hector put the beast down with one silent shot. When they arrived at the house, they tried the front door. It was unlocked. He shook his head; the *gringos* lived such sheltered lives. They entered the house.

Five minutes later, everyone sleeping in the house lay dead.

Hector removed his goggles and turned on the lights.

'The saw, for I must take the governor's head to *el jefe*.'

The *soldado* handed him the small serrated blade. They returned to the large bedroom and stepped over to the bed. Hector turned the bloody head over and—he recoiled.

'Who is that?'

'The governor?'

'No. That is not the governor. That is an old man.'

'Perhaps it is his father.'

They checked the other dead Anglos. None was the governor of Texas.

'Who are these people?' Hector said.

The *soldado* shrugged. They returned to the main room where they found the other *soldado* eating in the kitchen. He held up a chicken leg.

'Barbecue. It is good.'

Hector searched the room and found the mail. He read the name on the envelopes, blinked hard to clear his eyes of the gunpowder, and read again. He held up an envelope to his *soldado*.

'This is the Double V Ranch. I said Double *B*, as in boy. Not *V*, as in Victor.'

Hector threw his hands up.

'Ay-yi-yi.'

Chapter 36

Governor Bode Bonner stood naked—he had no tele-prompter, just his handwritten notes—before the other forty-nine governors finishing off their chicken entrées and pecan pie desserts and the cameras carrying his speech live on cable television. He was the keynote speaker at that year's gover-nors' conference in Dallas. He spoke in the voice of a man irrevocably changed by death.

'In the last two months, I killed six members of a Mexican drug cartel and survived two assassination attempts—but three people close to me did not. I went from obscure governor to American hero to leading presidential candidate to object of scorn and back to hero. After the last assassination attempt, I realized that I needed to reconsider my life. So I went back to where my life began, to the ranch that was my father's ranch and my grandfather's ranch before him, the land where Bonner men had lived good and decent and honorable lives for over a hundred years. I spent the last two weeks reevaluating my life—who I used to be and who I want to be. I decided I want to be the man I used to be.'

He glanced over at the Professor standing in the corner. His hands were spread and grasping his speech—the speech Bode was not giving that night. His expression was that of Dr. Frankenstein watching his creation think for himself. For the first time in his political career, Bode Bonner was his own boss.

'I used to be a cattle rancher. I wore old boots and old jeans and an old cowboy hat. I rode a horse. I drank beer. I never heard of Twitter.

'But once in the Governor's Mansion, I started wearing Armani suits and French-cuffed shirts and the finest hand-made cowboy boots. I drank bourbon. I sprayed my hair. I became more concerned with polls than people, more worried about how many followers I had on Twitter than how many teachers I had to fire.

'That's what ambition does to a man.

'I stand before you a man seduced by ambition and corrupted by politics.

'Politics changed me. I was once a Democrat and then I became a Republican and then a tea party favorite. I was once a good man and then I became a politician. I once had character but then I became a character.

'But looking death in the eye changes a man.

'I stand before you a changed man.

'I lost my way. That happens to men in politics. We're

driven by testosterone to make our mark on the world, but too often it's not a mark our children can be proud of. We play politics as if it's just a game, but it isn't a game to the people. Politicians have let the people of America down. I've let the people of Texas down.

'I'm going to try to do something about that.'

Bode Bonner walked off the stage to silence.

Chapter 37

The next morning, Bode walked into the Governor's Office to find Jim Bob waiting with the lieutenant governor and the speaker of the House. Bode sat behind his desk.

'Governor, what's this all about?' Mack Murdoch said. 'Calling us in on a Sunday morning.'

'Mack, Dicky, we're gonna revise the budget.'

'How?'

'We're not firing teachers, and we're not closing schools. We're not cutting education funding. We're increasing it. A lot.'

'Bode—'

He cut Jim Bob off with a raised hand.

'Where's the money coming from?' the speaker said.

'Your ideas, Dicky. Reform the property tax and expand

the business tax to services. All the revenues will be dedicated to pre-K through twelve education. Every penny.'

'We're gonna catch hell from the business community.'

'And we're gonna tap the rainy day fund. All of it.'

'We're gonna catch hell from the tea party.'

'Gentlemen, Texas is dying. The only way to save our state is to educate our kids. If we don't educate them, we're going to incarcerate them. I don't want kids sentenced to prison on my watch. We'll cut everything except education.'

'Why are you doing this, Governor?'

'Because we're those kids' only hope . . . and I don't want to make my wife a liar.'

Bode stood.

'That's the legislative agenda for the next session. Get to work, boys.'

'What about John Ed Johnson's special bill?'

'Forget about it.'

Jim Bob stood. 'Bode, he pledged fifty million to the Super PAC.'

There was a knock on the door, and Helen stuck her head in.

'Mr. Burnet, there's an emergency call for you.'

Jim Bob followed her out the door. Bode looked back at the speaker, who was eyeing him.

'What are you looking at, Dicky?'

'A real goddamn governor.'

'You cussed.'

'Special occasion.'

'Governor, I don't want to take the heat for raising taxes,' the lieutenant governor said.

'I'll take it.'

'I'll be by your side,' the speaker said.

463

'Aw, hell, now you boys are making me feel bad,' the lieutenant governor said. 'Guess we came this far together, might as well see how this story ends. I'm in. Let's kick some ass at the capitol.'

The door opened, and Jim Bob entered. His face seemed pastier than normal. He walked to his chair and sat down hard. He stared at his hands. Bode glanced at the speaker and the lieutenant governor. Both shrugged. After a long moment, Jim Bob blew out a breath and spoke.

'John Ed Johnson is dead.'

'*What? How?*'

'They killed him. That cartel. They killed them all. John Ed, Pedro, Rosita . . . all the animals, too. Except the lion.'

Manuel Moreno sat before a campfire on the Johnson ranch in the Davis Mountains. He was cooking breakfast. He had lived on the land for almost five months now, since the governor shot Jesús and the others that day. The *gringos* assumed he would make a run for the border, but he did not. He hid out on the ranch, and here he had been ever since.

Waiting.

He was promised much money for assisting the cartel with the marijuana farm. But the girl had attempted an escape the same day the governor had come out to hunt for the African lion; their fates had aligned that day. First harvest was only weeks away; Manuel's money was within his grasp, only to go up in smoke. The *gringos* burned the plants. And his future. He had watched the fire from the distance.

And felt the anger rise within him.

He had planned to take the money and go farther north, to buy land in Montana, perhaps, and to live the American Dream. But his American dream had been stolen from him by the *gringos*. Each day the anger grew. He watched as the Anglos came to the ranch and paid much money to kill *Señor* John Ed's game animals. He watched as *Señor* John Ed drove around the ranch in the Hummer as if he were a king. He watched through binoculars as *Señor* John Ed climbed on top of Rosita each night.

And the anger grew stronger.

Two days ago, the anger won out. Manuel had taken the AK-47 that Jesús had given him and gone to the lodge. He had walked inside at dinner time, when he knew *Señor* John Ed would be in the dining room and Rosita would be serving him food and Pedro would be pouring his bourbon. He killed them all. Then he killed every animal he found. He had never before eaten antelope, but it was quite good, especially when mixed with beans and wrapped in a tortilla, as he was now preparing. Manuel felt a presence and turned his head just in time to see the lion's jaws spread wide as the beast lunged at him. He felt the lion's mouth take his head and then the sharp teeth puncturing his face and skull. He dropped the tortilla.

Congressman Delgado rolled the flour tortilla filled with *migas* and *salsa* and took a big bite. Jesse sipped coffee. They were at Luis Escalera's café for Sunday breakfast. Jesse had heard that the congressman was in town that weekend; he had called his office and asked to meet with him.

'Are you troubled, Jesse?'

'Yes.'

'Is it about the governor's wife?'

Lindsay had told Jesse that Congressman Delgado had recognized her at the *Cinco de Mayo* festival.

'She is not my trouble.'

465

'Perhaps not yet. So what is now your trouble and how may I help you?'

'Mayor Gutiérrez and his Mexican Mafia want me to run for governor.'

The congressman leaned back in his chair. 'I have heard this. Jorge called me and asked me to intervene with you. I said I would not.'

'Why?'

'Because the decision to run for public office, to become a politician, is not made by committee or coercion. It is made in one's heart. A man must have the drive and the ambition and the heart to make a life of politics. You must make your own decision.'

'What is your advice? Should I run?'

'No.'

'Why do you say that?'

'Because your heart is here, on the border, with these poor people. You save lives every day in your clinic. Forty-five years, I have yet to save anyone in Congress.'

'But you do much good.'

'No. I do little good. Politics is no longer about good or bad, right or wrong . . . it is only about red and blue, winning and losing, profits and losses. Money. Some men are wired for politics and money, most are not. You are not. You are wired for love and hope. You love this land, and you hope for the people. Your heart is here, Jesse Rincón. Not in the Governor's Mansion.'

Just a mile south of where the congressman sat, Enrique de la Garza spoke on the phone with Hector Garcia in Austin.

'The wrong ranch?'

'Yes.'

'How many did you kill?'

'Five.'

Enrique sighed.

'I will pray for their souls. But why did you not shoot the governor during his speech? On national TV?'

'I was there, *jefe*, but I could not get into the building. Security was very tight. I was almost detained. Six Texas Rangers now guard the governor.'

'Come home, Hector. We will be patient. But the governor will die.'

'I will not be governor.'

'Good.'

'But you must leave. It is too dangerous here. If El Diablo ever learns—'

'He won't. And I won't leave you.'

They sat on the back porch. Jesse leaned to Lindsay and kissed her. This time, she kissed him back.

THE DAY BEFORE

Chapter 38

'That love child would've been the end of the boss,' Eddie Jones said. 'But Mandy takes the bullet instead, and his problems are gone. He's one lucky son of a bitch.'

Jim Bob's office again smelled like a fast-food joint. Eddie sat on the couch eating his Egg McMuffin.

'I'd rather be lucky than good,' Jim Bob said.

A month after the fact, Mandy Morgan was a distant memory, forgotten as fast as her body was cremated. She wouldn't even be a footnote to Bode Bonner's life story. John Ed Johnson's death had eliminated another scandal along with fifty million from the Super PAC. But Jim Bob had replaced that sum twice over with two phone calls. Bode's speech at the governors' conference had been hailed as groundbreaking in American politics. His polls climbed even higher. He now sat on top of the political world.

Bode Bonner *was* the wave.

'Course, you still got two problems to worry about,' Eddie said. 'One, that drug lord might get lucky and kill the boss; and two, that Mexican doctor might get lucky and win the election for governor. You figure the boss can still be president if he loses the election for governor?'

Jim Bob dropped five sugar cubes into his coffee cup.

'You up for another trip down to the border?'

'What for?'

'Because, Eddie, it's time to use your skill set to solve that particularly unpleasant problem for me.'

'Which one—the drug lord or the doctor?'

Dr. Jesse Rincón touched his nurse's sanitized hand.

'I am afraid for you. Lindsay, you should go home until this passes.'

'You mean, until El Diablo kills Bode?'

'I do not want that to happen.'

'I know.'

'But El Diablo, he will not stop.'

'I know that, too.'

'Lindsay, you must go home.'

'This is my home.'

'It is no longer safe for you here.'

'I'm safer than I would be in Austin. I'm hiding in plain sight.'

'Plain sight?'

'Yes. In Austin, everyone knows me. Here, no one knows me. No one knows I'm the governor's wife. Not even Inez.'

Inez Quintanilla strolled the sidewalks of the San Agustín Plaza in downtown Laredo that Sunday morning in early September as freely as an American citizen. Of course, she was not. She was a Mexican national residing illegally in the U.S., just like every other resident of the *colonias*. So she seldom ventured beyond the wall. She never came into town. But she was desperate to get out, to live beyond the wall, to have a life in Laredo. So she had ventured beyond the wall that day.

Not for a better life, but to pick up her kid brother. He had gotten into trouble the night before; Inez did not ask for the details. She did not want to know. He ran with a bad group of boys who fancied themselves gangsters. They desired the fast cars and faster girls that the drug money bought. But it also brought trouble. He had called that morning and asked her to come into Laredo and pick him up in the plaza at noon. So she had borrowed the neighbor's beat-up pickup truck and driven through the gate in the wall—the Border Patrol did not patrol on Sundays, so the doctor gave her the key code—and carefully into town. She had arrived early and decided to walk the plaza. Laredo seemed like heaven compared to the *colonia*. She dreamed of one day living this life, going to restaurants and nightclubs, buying nice clothes from the stores, becoming a wife and a mother, perhaps even obtaining a green card and working in a Wal-Mart and having a good life like—

She stopped.

Something had caught her eye.

A photo in a newspaper displayed on the newsstand.

A color photo of the governor of Texas. And the governor's wife. At a funeral. She wore a black dress and a black veil over her face. Her face was concealed but not her left hand when she had reached up to adjust the veil. And on one finger she wore an unusual ring. Two bands, one silver, one gold, twisted together at the end to form a lovers' knot. A wedding ring.

A wedding ring Inez Quintanilla had seen before.

'So, to summarize, we have killed two Texas Rangers, a college coed, the governor's mistress, and five innocents on the Double V Ranch—but we cannot seem to kill the governor. Why is that, Hector?'

The summer sun stood high in the sky and baked the earth brown. But the border was always brown. The land and the people. Enrique and Hector stood on the balcony overlooking the Río Bravo. Julio's piano notes drifted through the open courtyard windows. Chopin. Hector had returned to Nuevo Laredo because security around the governor in Austin had been increased to presidential levels and the Border Patrol had locked down the border. Apparently their attempts to assassinate the governor had proved an embarrassment to the *gringos*. So Hector needed to lay low for a while and allow things to die down, so to speak. Fortunately, Enrique de la Garza was a patient man. But justice and *venganza* would soon be his.

'The governor,' Hector said, 'he is a very lucky man.'

'His good luck will soon turn bad.'

'*Sí, jefe.*'

'Hector, did we also kill those people on the ranch where the governor murdered Jesús?'

'No. Manuel Moreno did.'

'The ranch foreman?'

'*Sí.*'

Enrique held up the Laredo newspaper.

'But they blame me.'

He sighed.

'So it was an employment matter?'

'*Sí.*'

'Good. That was unnecessary.'

'But I am afraid we also have an employment matter.'

'Another termination?'

'I am afraid so.'

Enrique walked inside and removed the machete from the wall rack.

★ ★ ★

474

That night, Bode Bonner sat on the couch in the family living quarters of the Governor's Mansion watching *Shrek* with the kids. They were laughing because Becca had changed the language to Spanish. Bode couldn't understand the movie, but it didn't matter. He was thinking about his life. About the people left in his life. Each day, there seemed to be fewer. For the last eight years, he had thought politics and power defined his life, but he now understood that his life was defined by the people in his life. These kids. His daughter. His wife. He wanted her back. Becca leaned into him.

'Daddy, call her. Get her to come back. Beg her if you have to. If you won't beg her for yourself, beg her for me.'

He kissed her on the forehead then pushed himself up. He went down the hall to his bedroom and called his wife.

'Hello.'

'It's Bode.'

'I have caller ID.'

'And you still answered.'

'How's Becca?'

'She's good. We're watching *Shrek* with the kids.'

'You're watching movies with the Mexican kids?'

'Movie night.'

'How are they?'

'Better.'

'How are you?'

'Better.'

'I liked your speech at the governors' conference.'

'You watched?'

'Of course.'

'I did a lot of thinking out at the ranch. About the old times. The way we were. The way I want us to be again.

475

Come home, Lindsay. You don't have to come home to me. Come home to Becca. Just come home.'

'Bode, these people here, they need me.'

'We need you, too. And you're not safe on the border.'

'No one here knows I'm the governor's wife.'

'Your doctor knows. And if your true identity ever gets out . . .'

'It won't.'

'Just so you know, we're going to fully fund the K through twelve budget.'

'For me?'

'For the kids.'

'Do you still love him?'

'I'll always love him.'

'And me? Will you ever love me?'

'I already do.'

They were on the back porch. The night air was warm, but the breeze off the desert made Jesse's arm around her shoulders feel good.

'One woman in love with two men,' he said. 'That usually does not have a happy ending.'

THAT DAY

Chapter 39

Lindsay slung the satchel over her shoulder. She had stocked it with medicine, supplies, and hard candy for the children. She would make her morning rounds before the summer heat set in. It would top 115 degrees that day outside and even hotter inside if Jesse was unable to repair the generator. Early September, but it was still summer on the border. Inez had not yet arrived, so Jesse came to her and kissed her, like a husband kissing his wife goodbye for the day. She felt like a married woman and she was; she was just married to another man.

'You look beautiful,' Jesse said.

She wore a white lab coat over a bright yellow peasant dress and pink Crocs. She draped a stethoscope around her neck. She tucked her red hair under a green scarf then pushed the wide-brimmed straw hat down on her head, to conceal her identity and her light complexion from the sun's rays.

'I will be out back working on the generator,' Jesse said. 'Inez should be here soon.'

Inez Quintanilla woke at seven. She had dreamed vividly of life beyond the wall. It was a colorful and wonderful life with pretty things and nice people. She had so enjoyed the dream that she closed her eyes and lay there a few minutes longer trying to recapture the moment. But she could not. The moment was gone. So she climbed out of bed. It was a work day.

She and her brother lived in a converted travel trailer. The wheels had been removed, so the trailer sat flat on the ground. Well, almost flat. Anything dropped on the floor would roll to one corner, but at least she knew where to find things. She had the small bedroom to herself; Roberto slept on the couch since he always came home late. She washed her face in the bathroom with the bottled water and applied her make-up carefully in case the television cameras came that day for the doctor. Two work outfits hung in the closet. She decided on the one she had not worn the day before. Once dressed, she would have Cheerios without milk for breakfast and then walk to the clinic.

She opened the thin metal door quietly so as not to wake her brother. She stepped out and froze. Her brother was not sound asleep on the couch as he usually was at that time. He was sitting and staring up at three men standing over him. Two held big guns. The man in the middle held a machete. The door behind them was open to the outside. The morning breeze blew hot and dusty.

'What is happening here?'

'Ah,' the man in the middle with the machete said. 'You must be Inez, the sister?'

Inez nodded.

'Well, Inez, your brother violated the code. I am here to dispense justice.'

'Who are you?'

'I am Enrique de la Garza.'

'I do not know you.'

480

'Ah. Perhaps you know me as the world knows me—El Diablo.'

Inez recoiled and sucked in air. She turned to her brother. He was crying.

'You work for him? You are a *narcotraficante*?'

'Yes, Inez,' El Diablo said. 'He works for me. Or he did. I have come to terminate his employment.'

'You have come to kill my brother? Personally?'

'Yes. I always terminate employees personally. It is company policy.'

'Why? What crime did Roberto commit?'

El Diablo turned to her brother. 'Tell her, Roberto. Tell your sister how you disgraced God and your family.'

'I did nothing!'

'But you did.' To Inez: 'Your brother gave heroin to a woman, a *Mexicana*.'

'So?'

'So our code does not allow that. We do not push the filthy drug habit on our own people.'

'That is a deed punishable by death?'

'She is a married woman. He gave her the heroin, and while she was under the influence, he raped her.'

'No!'

'Yes.'

'Roberto, is that true? Did you rape a woman?'

'No! She wanted sex with me.'

'Her husband demands justice,' El Diablo said. 'So Roberto must give him justice.' He turned to her brother. 'Roberto Quintanilla, you have not lived a life with honor. Will you now die with honor?'

'No!'

The two men grabbed Roberto and held his arms back and

pushed his head down. El Diablo raised the machete above her brother's head. Without conscious thought, Inez jumped between the blade and her brother.

'No! Please! He is my only brother!'

El Diablo paused in midair.

'I am sorry, Inez. But I must dispense justice. It is my duty. Please, stand aside.'

Inez Quintanilla's mind raced, trying to find hope for her brother. Where she found her only hope—*and it was her only hope*—made her sad. But she had no choice.

'I can give you what you want most in life.'

El Diablo lowered the blade, and Inez breathed a momentary sigh of relief. He looked her up and down and smiled as her father had once smiled at her when she was just a small child. When her parents were still alive.

'I can have pretty girls like you anytime I want. I can have you if I want. But I do not want you. And you should not offer yourself to a man, Inez, before marriage, in the church.'

'I do not mean me.'

'Then what do you propose to give to me?'

'What you want more than anything in this world.'

'What I want most in this world.' He thought a moment, and his eyes seemed to grow dark with his thoughts. 'Well, Inez, can you give me the governor of Texas?'

Everyone in the *colonias* knew that the governor of Texas had killed El Diablo's son and that El Diablo had attempted several times to kill the governor. Such news did not come from the newspapers or the television, but from word of mouth.

'No.'

'Then you have nothing I want. Stand aside. Please.'

He again raised the machete, and her heart grabbed at her chest.

'But I can give you something almost as good.'

He stopped.

'And what is that?'

'*La esposa del gobernador*. I can give you the governor's wife.'

He again lowered the blade, and she felt the relief again.

'Can you now?'

'Yes. I can.'

'How? How can you, little Inez Quintanilla living in this broken-down trailer in this *colonia* on the banks of the Río Bravo give to me the wife of the governor of Texas? Tell me, please, how can you do that?'

'I can tell you where to find her.'

El Diablo laughed in a way that made her afraid, as if she had taken something away from him. His voice became louder.

'Hector here can tell me where to find her. I do not want her. I want the governor.'

'But if you have her, he will come for her. He will come to you.'

El Diablo nodded. 'That is true, Inez. But it would be difficult to kidnap her in Austin and smuggle her across the river. Guns and cash we smuggle south every day, quite easily, but the governor's wife, that would be very difficult. The border is locked down.'

'She is not in Austin.'

'Then where is she?'

'She is here.'

'Where?'

'I will tell you where, if you will spare my brother's life.'

El Diablo's jaws clenched. His patience was running out.

'Inez, my child, it is not wise to toy with me, not about the governor of Texas. He murdered my son, and I intend to kill him. Between me and the governor is a dangerous place to stand. Now tell me what you know.'

'No. Not so you can then cut off my brother's head.'

For a moment, she thought El Diablo might slap her. Inez trembled like a leaf in the wind. But he blew out a breath and calmed.

'All right, Inez. I will not cut off your brother's head if you will tell me where the governor's wife is.'

'You promise?'

'Yes. I promise.'

Inez knew she had pushed him as far as she dared.

'She is here . . . in the *colonia*.'

'*Here?* In *Colonia Ángeles*?'

'*Sí.*'

'But that is not possible. I would have known. There is only one Anglo in this *colonia*, the—'

His eyes got wide with the knowledge.

'The Anglo nurse. Of course. I knew that she seemed familiar. She has the red hair, like the governor's wife.'

'She *is* the governor's wife.'

'But they said she was Irish.'

'She pretends. Sometimes she forgets, and her voice is different.'

'Thank you, Inez. You have made me a very happy man.' He turned to the man named Hector and said, 'Shoot him.'

'Wait! You promised not to kill him!'

'No. I promised not to cut his head off.'

The man named Hector raised a gun and shot her brother in his head. The bullet blew blood and brains out the back of his head. Hector shot him again in his heart. Her ears burned with the noise and her nostrils with the stench of the gunpowder, and her brother lay on the couch, his eyes

484

staring blankly at the ceiling, the teardrops still resting on his brown cheeks. Her only brother was dead. Inez Quintanilla was now alone in this harsh world.

'Now, where is the governor's wife? At the clinic?'

Inez stared at her brother's bloody face a moment longer, then she bolted out the open door and ran down the dirt road toward the clinic. She must warn the *señora*. She must save the *señora*'s life as she had failed to save her brother's. She heard the men yelling behind her and the loud engines of their trucks come to life. Coming after her. She cut between houses and under clothes hanging on lines and around morning cook fires until she finally arrived at the clinic. She burst through the door only to find the clinic vacant. The doctor's truck sat outside, but neither he nor the *señora* was there. She must be on rounds. Her body teemed with adrenaline. She had never before felt so alive, perhaps because she was certain she would soon be dead. She ran down the dirt road and screamed, '*¡Señora! ¡Señora!*'

But there was no answer.

Of every woman and child she encountered, she asked, 'Have you seen the nurse?'

One woman pointed down the road. Inez ran faster, calling out, '*¡Señora! ¡Señora!*'

Finally she heard the *señora*'s voice.

'In here.'

Inez pulled the blanket door aside and stepped into the home. The *señora* was kneeling on the dirt floor tending to a child.

'*Señora*, you must run away! You must hide!'

Inez tried to catch her breath. She felt the panic on her face.

'Why?'

'They come for you!'

'Who?'

'El Diablo! And his *hombres*.'

Chapter 40

Lindsay Bonner fought not to panic—because what she did in the next few moments would determine whether she lived or died.

Think, Lindsay, think.

A few minutes later, she had hidden her cell phone, and she stood alone, waiting for them to come for her and take her across the river and into Nuevo Laredo—and praying her husband would. She had not gone to him when he had needed her. Would he come now that she needed him?

Yes.

Bode Bonner would come for her. They no longer shared their lives, but he would give his life for hers. She knew that. And at that moment, she realized how much that meant— to know that he would always come for her. She heard the trucks stop outside and the sound of heavy boots on the ground. The blanket door was thrown aside, and a man now stood there. He held a black machete. He was tall and lean with jet-black hair and a goatee. He was the same man she had seen in the clinic that day.

El Diablo.

She knelt before him, her body trembling, and recited the Lord's Prayer.

'I am also Catholic,' he said. 'I am not going to kill you.'

She stopped praying and looked up.

'Then what do you want with me? I am just a nurse.'

He reached out and gently pulled her hat and scarf off, releasing her red hair.

'You are the governor's wife. He will come for you. And when he does, I will cut off his head with this machete. I will avenge my son's death. I will have justice.'

He held a hand out to her. She stood without taking his hand.

'Remove your clothes.'

'Is that what you want?'

'I want your husband's head on my desk. But I must ensure that you have no gun or knife or phone, and I prefer not to pat you down. Now, your clothes. Please.'

She removed her lab coat then unbuttoned her yellow dress and let it fall to the dirt floor around her pink Crocs. He waited. She unhooked her bra and let it drop. Then she pushed her panties to her ankles. She stood naked before him. His eyes took her in. He inhaled as if smelling a flower. Then he nodded.

'Yes, he will come for you.'

'How do you know?'

'Because I would come for you.'

He lifted her dress from the ground with the machete.

'Please. Get dressed.'

Chapter 41

The governor of Texas sat in his office in the Governor's Mansion staring blankly out the windows at the state capitol. He sipped his coffee. He had awakened early that morning; it was still before nine when the phone rang. He grabbed the receiver but realized that no lights on the console were lit. The phone rang again. It was his cell phone.

'Hello.'

'He took her.'

A man's voice.

'Who is this?'

'Jesse Rincón. Governor, he took your wife.'

'Who?'

'El Diablo.'

'When?'

'Not an hour ago.'

'Where?'

'Nuevo Laredo.'

The Mexican drug lord who wanted him dead now held his wife. It took Bode a moment to get his mind around that reality. He tried to think out his options.

'Governor, if you go public, he will kill her. If you call in the Border Patrol or ICE or the Mexican military, he will kill her. If you do nothing, he will kill her. We must go into Nuevo Laredo and take her back—before he kills her.'

Bode sat still for five minutes after he disconnected the phone call. He considered his next steps. Perhaps his last steps in his life. He would change clothes. He would pack his weapons and ammunition. He would fly to Laredo in the Gulfstream. He would cross the border into Nuevo Laredo. He would find El Diablo. He would kill him and save his wife.

He would not come back.

Two hundred thirty-five miles south, El Diablo said to the governor's wife, 'Does your husband really believe that he will be elected president? Another Texas governor?'

'Apparently.'

He grunted. They had just driven through tall gates leading into a white compound. Lindsay sat in the back seat of the Hummer with El Diablo. His driver and a bald man named Hector sat up front. She did not like the way Hector had looked at her. Her body still had not stopped trembling. El Diablo must have noticed. He reached over and patted her hand.

'You have nothing to fear from me, *Señora* Bonner.'

'Why not?'

'You saved my son's life. I told you I would not forget.'

'But you want to kill my husband?'

'*Sí*. He has much to fear. Because he murdered my son.'

The vehicle stopped, and the man named Hector opened their door. She got out, and El Diablo escorted her past armed guards and into the house. She glanced back at the guards.

'Do not fret, *Señora* Bonner, the guards do not come into the house where my children live.'

The exterior of the house resembled a prison; the walls were thick and seemed impenetrable. But once through the double entrance doors, she stepped into a magnificent open-air hacienda filled with color and art, soft Latin music and Spanish voices, plants and sunlight and servants dressed in black-and-white uniforms scurrying about. The entry opened onto a stunning courtyard and pool with palm trees and lush landscaping and a grand piano. El Diablo led her into a commercial-grade kitchen where they found a chef, a slender teenage boy, and a young girl dressed in a plaid school uniform fingering a cell phone.

'Are you texting that boy again?' he asked the girl.

She quickly ended her message and smiled.

'No, *padre*.'

He turned to Lindsay and turned up his palms.

'Children.' He sighed. '*Señora* Bonner, you met Jesús. I would like you to meet my other children, Julio and Carmelita. Children, this is *Señora* Bonner. She will be our guest for a few days.'

The children greeted her with good manners. The tightness in her chest lessened.

'Julio is a talented pianist, and Carmelita sings like the birds in the morning. Perhaps they will perform for you while you are here. Would you like something to eat, *Señora*?'

'No, thanks.'

'Perhaps you would like to freshen up, wash the smell of the *colonias* off. Come, I will show you to your room.'

When they exited the kitchen, Lindsay said, 'A few days?'

'I think it will take that long for your husband to arrive.'

'Mister El—'

'Please. Call me Enrique.'

'Enrique, this won't end well.'

'Not for your husband, I am afraid.'

'You don't know him. He can be a very hard man.'

'And what? I am a pushover?'

'I didn't mean—'

He laughed. 'I am just joking. Let us not talk about

490

unpleasant matters that are in the future. Let us enjoy the moment.'

They walked down a gallery fronting the courtyard— 'That is my chapel'—and past alcoves holding statues of Jesus Christ and the Virgin Mary, religious shrines, and a massive 'Ten Commandments' carved in marble. They arrived at an elevator and rode up to the third floor. They proceeded down another gallery overlooking the courtyard and into a spacious suite.

'I hope this will be acceptable.'

As if he were the concierge at a luxurious hotel. And the suite was luxurious. He opened the drapes to reveal a sliding glass door leading to a balcony that looked out upon Laredo across the river. They walked outside. He gestured at the river below.

'The Río Bravo del Norte.'

A Mexican woman dressed in a maid's outfit stepped out onto the balcony.

'Ah, Blanca. This is *Señora* Bonner. She is your only concern while she is our guest. Please bring her anything she desires.' He turned to Lindsay. 'Food, water?'

'Water.'

'Blanca, three bottles of Evian. And the lunch menu.'

Blanca departed, and they went back inside.

'Flat-screen television, all the cable channels. I love *Fox News*.'

He gestured at a painting on the wall.

'That is an original Picasso. I have an extensive art collection, perhaps you would like to see, after dinner.'

He showed her the bathroom, which was much larger than the master bathroom in the Governor's Mansion.

'Jacuzzi tub, shower . . . all the comforts of home.

Everything you need is here. If not, simply ask Blanca, and she will obtain whatever you desire. Anything at all.'

'Thank you.'

She was thanking the man who wanted to kill her husband.

'I will leave you now,' he said. 'Until dinner.'

He walked to the door but turned back.

'Oh, please do not leave the room.'

He shut the door behind him. She went over and locked the door. But there was soon a knock.

'Who is it?'

'*Soy yo, Blanca.*'

She unlocked and opened the door. The maid entered with three bottles of water and a menu. She then left, and Lindsay locked the door behind her. She sat on the edge of the bed and drank half a bottle of water then glanced at the lunch menu. Grilled salmon, char-broiled Gulf shrimp, chicken salad on a croissant, tortilla soup . . . She was abducted by a drug lord only to be fed like a hotel guest. The border was an entirely different world. She lay back on the bed and closed her eyes.

Bode knocked on Becca's door and entered her room. It was after ten, and she was still asleep. He sat on the bed next to her and stroked her hair. She stirred and woke. She rubbed her eyes and then reached over and turned the lamp on.

'Daddy . . . Where are you going?'

'To the border.'

'To get Mom?'

'Yes. Becca, the man who wants me dead, he took your mother.'

She sprung up in bed.

'Took her?'

492

'Kidnapped. He's holding her in Nuevo Laredo. I'm going down to get her.'

'Get the Rangers to go!'

'Becca, our military and police can't cross the border without permission from the Mexican government—and that won't happen. And if I sent the Rangers into Mexico, he'd kill her.'

'Go on TV!'

'He'd kill her.'

'What about our consulate down there?'

'Useless.'

'But, Daddy—'

'It's the only way to get her back.'

He saw in her eyes the realization that she might be seeing her father for the last time—and that she might never see her mother again. He cupped her face.

'I love you, Becca. I couldn't have asked for a better daughter.'

'I'm a lesbian.'

'You're my daughter.'

She stared into his eyes.

'You're not coming back, are you?'

'No. But your mother is.'

She threw her arms around him and hugged him tight. When she released him, she wiped tears from her face.

'Daddy . . . kill him.'

'Oh, you can count on that.'

Jesse Rincón entered the San Agustín Cathedral on the plaza in downtown Laredo for the first time in over three years. The church sat vacant. He walked up the center aisle and knelt at the altar rail. He gazed up at the crucifix on the wall above the altar. He spoke to God.

'I will make a deal with you. If you will spare her life, I will give you mine. I will do your work here, and I will never complain or question your will. Take her from me if you wish, but please do not take her life. That is all I ask.'

Just across the river from the cathedral, Lindsay Bonner woke to a man on top of her. Not El Diablo, but a foul man who smelled of whiskey and cigars. The bald man named Hector. She screamed, but he slapped a big hand over her mouth.

'*¡Cállete, perra!*'

He ran his hands over her breasts and down her hips.

'I tried to kill the governor. The next time I will succeed. But first I will have the governor's wife.'

'You'll fuck a dead woman!'

She had been born in Boston but toughened in Texas. She feared this man, but she was not afraid to fight him. She slapped at him and punched him, but he only laughed. He put his weight on her and his hand between her legs and tried to push his finger inside her. He froze.

'What is this?'

He raised up with her cell phone in his hand. Which gave her the opening she needed. She drove her knee into his groin. He wasn't laughing now. He groaned and doubled over. She kicked him in the face.

'*¡Puta!*'

He stumbled to the door but turned back.

'If you tell *el jefe*, I will come back and kill you before he kills me.'

'I won't tell him. But I'll make sure my husband kills you first.'

He cursed and left. She locked the door behind him then

494

wedged a chair under the knob. Then she ran into the bathroom and threw up.

'He'll kill her,' Jim Bob said. 'He probably already has.'

Jim Bob stood at the door to the master suite. Bode was packing weapons and ammunition in a duffel bag.

'No, he wants me. He won't kill her until he has me.'

'You thought this through?'

'Becca needs her mother.'

'You want me to go with you?'

'Thanks, but this is what *I* do.'

'You sure this is the only way? You go down there and kill Mexicans in Mexico—even a drug lord—it'll be an international incident. I don't know how many crimes you'll be committing. Bode, your White House dream ends tonight.'

'Jim Bob, I had a dream when I was eighteen. Her name was Lindsay. Last twenty-nine years, I forgot that. I remember now. I'm chasing my dream, Jim Bob, and it's not in Washington. It's in Nuevo Laredo.'

Bode Bonner zipped up the bag and stood tall.

'He took my wife. I want her back.'

Lindsay wanted the man's smell off her. She went into the bathroom and started a hot bath. When the tub was full, she undressed and stepped in. She sat then slid down until the water was up to her neck. She closed her eyes.

El Diablo wanted Bode to come for her. He would lay in wait and kill her husband. Or Bode would kill him. She didn't like Bode's odds against a drug lord on his turf. Bode always said that if you want to beat someone on their home turf, you'd better have a good game plan.

She needed a game plan.

She bathed with body wash and shampoo from Paris. When she got out, she put on a thick terrycloth robe. She heard a knock on the door.

'Who is it?'

'Blanca.'

She removed the chair and opened the door. The maid pushed a room service cart into the room, then went back out and returned with a rolling cart of hanging clothes and high-heeled shoes below. Evening dresses still in the plastic bags and new undergarments still in plastic wrap.

'What are these for?' she asked Blanca in Spanish.

'Dinner, with the *señor*. I will come for you at seven.'

Blanca left Lindsay alone. She turned on the television and switched channels, searching for news of her abduction. But there was no news. No one in Austin knew she was on the border. And no one on the border knew she was the governor's wife.

Except El Diablo.

She checked the room service cart: cheese and crackers and champagne. Hot tea. Coffee and cream. Butter cookies. As if it were tea time in Nuevo Laredo. She ate several crackers with cheese . . . and a few cookies . . . and drank the coffee. She hadn't eaten since early that morning. With Jesse. She wondered if he knew yet that she had been taken. Surely Inez would have told him. And he would have called Bode. And Bode would come for her. Soon. Not several days from now as El Diablo had said. But now. He was already on his way to her. She knew that. She also knew that when he came for her, El Diablo would kill him.

Or he would kill El Diablo.

★ ★ ★

The small jet taxied over to the private terminal in a secluded area of the airport. The door opened and a stairway dropped down. Only one man got off the plane.

The governor of Texas.

He spotted Jesse's truck and walked over with a duffel bag slung over his shoulder. He appeared much larger in person than on television. When he opened the passenger door and got into Jesse's pickup, he did not seem like the man who would be president.

Or who wanted to be.

The governor sat silent for a long moment—as if he were contemplating the final journey of his life. Jesse knew this because he had contemplated the same journey as he sat and waited for the governor's jet to arrive in Laredo. Perhaps they would take that final journey together, the governor and the man who loved the governor's wife. The governor finally stuck out a hand to Jesse.

'Bode Bonner.'

'Jesse Rincón.'

Jesse started the engine and exited the airport and drove east.

'We must wait until after midnight to cross the river.'

He took the governor to his homestead. They got out and went inside Jesse's house. The governor glanced around.

'This is where she's been living?'

'No. She lives in the guesthouse.'

Jesse led the governor to the guesthouse and unlocked the door for him.

Blanca knocked on the door at seven.

Lindsay had fallen asleep from fear and exhaustion. She had dreamed of Bode and Becca, Ramón and Chelo, Lupe and the *vaqueros* . . . and Jesse. She had woken with the vague outline of a plan. She dressed and now followed Blanca to the elevator and then to the second floor. They walked down a hallway and into an elegant dining room against a wall of windows facing the lights of Laredo. Enrique de la Garza stood by the windows, wearing a black suit and tie and checking his hair in the reflection, as if looking for gray streaks. He noticed her and turned.

'*Buenas noches, Señora* Bonner. My, you look beautiful.'

She wore a black dress and black heels.

'Blanca, champagne for the *señora.*'

He seemed oddly happy. So she decided not to upset his mood with Hector's attempted rape. She wanted him to remain happy and relaxed, to feel at ease with her. To enjoy her company. She wanted to appeal to his manhood.

Blanca returned and handed a flute filled with champagne to Lindsay.

'*Gracias.*' She turned to Enrique. 'Were these your wife's clothes?'

'Yes.'

'She liked short dresses.'

'Yes, she had beautiful legs. As you do.'

His eyes went to her legs.

'Congressman Delgado said we killed her.'

Enrique nodded. 'It was a mistake.'

'I'm sorry. There's been too much killing on the border.'

'Yes. Too much.'

He stepped closer and raised his flute as if to toast the moment, but she instinctively backed away.

'*Señora* Bonner, I said you have nothing to fear from me. But still you fear me?'

'Yes. I do.'

'Why?'

'Because you're El Diablo. The devil. A drug lord. You've killed thousands of people.'

'Who said that?'

Like a kid on a playground whose veracity had been questioned.

'Everyone . . . the newspapers, the government.'

'The American government?'

'Yes.'

'And, of course, the American government would never lie.' He sighed. '*Señora* Bonner, we live by a code of honor, Los Muertos. We do not kill women, children, or innocents.'

'You sell drugs.'

'Americans sell weapons to the world, but I am a bad guy because I sell marijuana to Americans?'

He shook his head.

'Your government, they are telling the American story, so Americans must be told that they are the good guys. They cannot be the bad guys. That is not allowed in the American story. God bless America. Americans must believe that God looks with special favor upon America. But if America is God's protagonist, who is the antagonist? Who is the bad guy? Every story must have a bad guy, is that not true? So your government creates bad guys for Americans to hate so they will not hate their own government. Yesterday it was Osama and the Taliban, Saddam and Gadhafi. Tomorrow it will be North Korea and Iran, although I must agree that those two guys, they do not seem right in the head. But, today it is me. Enrique de la Garza. I am the bad guy in the American story of this border. El Diablo. The devil. Your government gave that nickname to me, you see, so that I would sound like a very bad guy indeed—El Diablo, he must be a very bad *hombre*. And that is my role in the American tragedy. Because America must demonize its adversaries, anyone who will not submit to American rule. It is so much easier to demonize than it is to understand and acknowledge grievances against America, is it not? So, please, *Señora* Bonner, save the American self-righteousness for someone else. We Mexicans have heard it for one hundred and sixty-five years. Oh, here is Charles. Let us eat.'

He held a chair out for her. She sat, and the chef named Charles served soup.

'Tortilla soup,' Charles said. 'The entrée tonight is grilled sea bass flown in fresh from California served with a Greek salad and snow peas. For dessert we have cheesecake with a strawberry sauce or chocolate soufflé. Ma'am, would you like a glass of wine?'

'I have an extensive wine cellar,' Enrique said. 'Do you have a favorite?'

She shrugged.

'Surprise us, Charles.'

'Yes, sir.'

Charles left, and Lindsay tasted the soup.

'It's delicious.'

'Yes, Charles is an excellent chef.'

'He's not afraid to work for you?'

'Oh, no. You see, *Señora* Bonner, I am beloved by my people. I can walk the streets of Nuevo Laredo without fear. I employ the people and pay them well. I do not sell drugs to my people. I fund churches and schools. I love my country and my people. And they love me.'

'Congressman Delgado said you give away a billion dollars a year.'

'Yes, that is true. I tithe twenty percent. Of course, it is not as if I'm paying taxes.'

He had amused himself.

'Are your children joining us?'

'No. Charles prepared hamburgers for them. They enjoy the American food.'

'They seem like nice kids.'

'I like them.'

'Do they know what you do for a living?'

'Julio does, not Carmelita. She is a bit young, I think.'

'Do you think she'd be proud of you?'

'I hope so. I have tried to be a good father to my children, *Señora* Bonner. It has been difficult since my wife's death. And now my son . . . I apologize for my men endangering your daughter that day. That should not have happened. So, how long have you worked in the *colonia*?'

'Five months.'

He smiled. 'I have admired you since you came to Laredo in March, the census count, I believe, with Congressman Delgado. I saw you on television. And in the *colonia* that day after you saved my son, but I did not know it was you. Five months you have been just across the river from me. And I never knew.'

He stared at her from across the table, almost as if . . .

Bode Bonner smelled his wife's scent. It was there, in the small guesthouse, where she had lived the last five months. Where she had gone to escape her life with him. Because of him. She was another casualty of his ambition.

He would trade his life for hers, even up.

* * *

501

After dinner, they had wine on the balcony.

'The lights of Laredo are beautiful,' Lindsay said. 'I've grown to love the border.'

'Yes, the borderlands, it becomes a part of you. I was born here, and I will die here. This is my home. My country. *México*. Once, such a magnificent country. I often stand here and try to imagine what it must have been like when *México* extended from the Gulf of Mexico to the Pacific Ocean. Think what *México* would be today. What America would be today.'

'I would love to see Nuevo Laredo. I've heard it's a beautiful city.'

'It is indeed. I would love to show you my city. Perhaps that will happen one day.'

After you kill my husband, she thought but did not say.

Instead, she said, 'Perhaps.'

She wanted to give him hope. She dropped her eyes, then looked up at him, as if she couldn't resist. Men loved that little look. Why?

'You're not what I expected.'

He looked deep into her eyes, then broke away and gestured at the lights of Laredo.

'On that side of the river, you see life one way, looking south. On this side of the river, we see an entirely different life, looking north. We see the same land, the same river, the same sky, the same history—but we see it very differently. That is the borderlands.'

Jesse found the governor sitting on his wife's bed.

'Governor—it is time.'

He did not stand.

'Was she happy here?'

502

'I think so.'

He did not respond.

'Governor, may I ask you a question?'

He nodded.

'Why did you let her go? Why did you not come to the border and beg her to come back to you?'

'*Beg her?*'

'Yes. Beg.'

'I'm not that kind of man.'

'Not that kind of man? What, have you had so many women love you that you no longer respect love? To have such a woman as your wife love you, you should respect that. You should have fought for her love.'

'I'm here now.'

'You hurt her, with the young woman.'

'I know.'

'Okay. I just thought you should know.'

The governor exhaled heavily.

'Doc, when this is over and we get her back—and we will get her back—if she wants to stay here with you, I won't stand in the way. Hell, I don't deserve her, anyway.'

'Then why did you come for her?'

Now he stood.

'Because she doesn't deserve this.'

Lindsay had viewed Enrique's art collection and was back in her room by midnight. She checked the news, but there was nothing of her abduction. She lay back on the bed in the black dress. Enrique had said they would spend the day together tomorrow. Get to know each other. Breakfast, perhaps even a helicopter tour of Nuevo Laredo and the border. As if this were a vacation for the governor's wife. As if Enrique de la

Garza and Lindsay Bonner might have a relationship once the minor matter of killing her husband the governor was behind him.

But that would not happen. Not in this life.

Because her husband was not far from where she now lay. She could feel him. And she knew that by the time the sun rose over the Rio Grande, either Bode Bonner or Enrique de la Garza would be dead.

Chapter 42

The water was warm.

It was after midnight, and they were naked. They were not the only naked men crossing the river that night—the moonlight illuminated the river and the human beings holding their possessions aloft as they waded across—but they were the only naked men heading south into Mexico.

'Governor,' Jesse said, 'I am willing to die to save her. Are you?'

'She's my wife.'

'I did not ask if she were your wife. I asked if you are willing to die for her.'

'Yes. I'm willing to die to save her.'

'Good.'

'Why's that good?'

'Because we are going to.'

'Save her or die trying?'

'Both.'

'I can live with that.'

The doctor chuckled. 'I like you, Governor.'

'Oh, that's swell. Now I can die a happy man.'

'Happy or sad, it is of no consequence. You will die, and I will die with you. But she will live.'

'You love her that much?'

'I do.'

'Does she love you?'

'I hope.'

'I should probably be mad about that.'

'Be mad later, after we save her.'

'You just said we're gonna die.'

'Oh. Yes, that is true.'

They had waited until midnight and then driven to town and to the river. Directly across the water, only one hundred fifty feet away, a large white structure rose tall above the river.

'That is El Diablo's headquarters and home,' the doctor said.

'So everyone knows where to find him?'

'Oh, sure.'

'Why doesn't the Mexican government take him down?'

'Because he is beloved in Nuevo Laredo, as you are in Texas.'

'I'm just a politician.'

'You give the people what they want, as he does.'

They crossed downriver of the white compound. They arrived at the other side of the river, and Bode tossed the duffel onto the bank. They climbed out of the Rio Grande and stepped onto Mexican soil. They dried off then got dressed. Bode opened the 'tan in a can' and smeared the cream on his face.

'A large Anglo might attract attention on this side of the river,' the doctor had said.

Bode pulled a knit cap over his blond hair then put on a hunting coat with big pockets. He loaded the spare ammo in his pockets, stuck one six-shooter in his waistband and handed the other to the doctor, and secured the Derringer to his right wrist with a rubber band. He slung the dangerous game rifle over his shoulder.

'Probably won't get a second glance in Nuevo Laredo.'

The doctor held the gun as if it were a contagious disease.

'And do you know how to use these weapons, Governor?'

'I do.'

The doctor stared at the pistol in his hands. 'I have treated many gunshot victims, but I have never before shot a gun.'

'Well, Doc, you're fixin' to make some victims tonight.'

They sat quietly for a moment. Bode knew that his forty-seven-year career called life had come down to this one big play: saving his wife.

'Harvard Med School did not prepare me for this,' the doctor said.

'Nothing prepares a man to die.'

They stood and climbed the embankment, fighting their way through thick juniper and brush. They broke through to a four-lane east–west roadway, then quickly ducked back into the brush as cars sped past.

'Bulevar Luis Donaldo Colosio,' the doctor said. 'It leads directly to El Diablo's compound.'

'Let's go.'

'No. There is too much traffic on this road. *Federales* and cartel patrols. We must take the side streets.'

He looked both ways.

'Now!'

Governor Bode Bonner and Dr. Jesse Rincón jumped from the brush and ran across the four lanes and into Ciudad de Nuevo Laredo, determined to save the woman they both loved. Or to die trying.

And one of them would.

Chapter 43

'Calle Nicolás Bravo,' the doctor said. 'This street runs parallel to the boulevard. It will take us to El Diablo's compound. Maybe a dozen blocks west of where we stand. And the traffic is one-way toward us, so we will see cars approaching. But we must be careful. When it is dark, Nuevo Laredo is a very dangerous place. Here, you are either predator or prey.'

'I'm armed and dangerous, Doc.'

'*Mi amigo*, this is Nuevo Laredo.'

They walked down the cramped street past ramshackle residences so close to the street you could spit through the windows. Corrugated tin sheets and wood pallets fashioned fences that corralled chickens and goats. Old American cars were parked halfway onto the narrow sidewalk.

'I always wondered what happened to all the Oldsmobiles,' Bode said.

'Governor, what if she is not in the compound? What if we cannot find her?'

'She'll be there. He wants me to find her.'

Bode stopped and retrieved the handheld GPS unit from his coat pocket.

'And I can track her on this.'

Bode activated the GPS and got a signal. Good girl.

'How?'

'Her cell phone. I can track it.'

'But he would have taken her phone.'

'She hid it where he wouldn't find it.'

'Where?'

'You're a doctor, figure it out.'

'Oh. How do you know she would do that?'

'Because I've been married to her for twenty-two years. She's smart, and she's tough.'

He turned the GPS off and put it back in his pocket.

'Let's go get her, Doc.'

They continued west on Calle Nicolás Bravo and crossed 20 Noviembre San Antonio. Bode glanced down the side street and saw several groups of tough-looking men gathered outside cheap *cantinas*.

'Do not look at them,' the doctor said.

They walked fast down the south side of the street and crossed another intersection. Bode looked up at the road sign: José de Escandón. When he looked back down, a man jumped from the shadows and tackled the doctor like a linebacker flattening a quarterback. He apparently hadn't seen

508

Bode behind the doctor. Bode pulled his six-shooter and put the big barrel in the man's face. His eyes were suddenly wide. Bode spoke through clenched teeth.

'Get off my friend!'

He got off.

'Now git!'

He got.

The doctor stood and said, 'So I am your friend?'

'Depends.'

'On what?'

'If we get her out alive.'

They hurried on. The streets were lit with neon signs for *Corona* and *Tecate* and *Pesos-Dolares* and all-night *Farmacias*. Late-night partiers stumbled down the sidewalks until they fell over or were beaten and robbed. Hookers plied their trade for a few pesos. Austin's Sixth Street could be a bit wild at times, but the biggest danger was getting puked on.

Nuevo Laredo was the goddamn Wild West.

Headlights appeared in front of them, and the doctor abruptly grabbed Bode's coat and yanked him off the sidewalk.

'Governor, this way!' he said in a hushed voice.

He pulled Bode down behind a small adobe wall with a sign for 'Misíon Pentecostal.' They remained hidden until a military-style truck with armed soldiers in the back drove past.

'*Federales*,' the doctor said.

They stood and headed west again, faster now. They crossed Pedro J. Méndez and Santos Degollado streets. Each intersection seemed busier than the previous one.

'We are getting closer to the city center,' the doctor said.

The structures were low, and the tall white compound loomed over the buildings like a castle on a hilltop, so they had no trouble maintaining their bearing. They went through the Jesús Carranza and Leandro Valle intersections and past small auto repair shops with cars jacked up on blocks in the side yards and more *cantinas* and more . . . headlights coming toward them. They ducked behind a small *Tacos y Taquitos* stand and waited for the vehicle to pass. It was another truck with armed men in the back.

'*Federales?*' Bode asked.

'Cartel *soldados*,' the doctor said. 'Looking for a fight with the *federales*.'

The Wild West.

They jogged down the street. They had entered a bar district: El Paso del Norte, La Cascada, Aguilar Ladies Bar, and other such establishments lined both sides of the street.

'We are close now,' the doctor said.

They came to the intersection at Avenida Melchor Ocampo.

'We go north here. The next intersection is Vincente Guerrero, a very busy street. This street is not so busy.'

They hurried up the west sidewalk, which was shielded by cars parked along the street and shade trees. They were in a better part of town. Bode felt a sense of relief come over him—until he was slammed up against a building and a knife was jammed against his throat. A large Mexican man with whiskey breath put his weight into Bode.

'*¡Tu dinero o tu vida!*'

'Our money or our lives,' the doctor said.

'I'm the governor. I don't carry cash.'

The doctor dug in his pocket and produced a handful of coins. The man took the money then threw the coins on the sidewalk.

'*¡Más dinero!*'

The doctor shook his head.

'*No más dinero.*'

The man pulled the knife back as if to stab Bode, but his body suddenly clenched and his eyes bulged and he groaned. A hand—a white hand—emerged from the darkness behind the man and clamped over his mouth. The man dropped his knife and slowly crumpled to the ground. A shaggy figure leaned over the man a moment then stood and faced Bode.

'What the hell are you doing here, Governor?'

'*Eddie?*'

He stared at Eddie Jones' face in disbelief.

'What the hell are you doing here?'

'Saving your life.'

'Thanks, but why are you in Nuevo Laredo?'

''Cause you're paying me a million bucks to kill El Diablo.'

'I am?'

'Jim Bob is. Campaign expense.'

'Can you do it? Kill him?'

'Yeah, I can kill him. That's not the problem. Getting back across the river alive, that's the problem. So, Governor, what brings you to Nuevo Laredo?'

'He took my wife.'

'From the *colonia*,' the doctor said. 'This morning.'

Eddie nodded. 'Using her as bait. It's working. So what, you and the doc here figure on walking into that compound, killing the baddest drug lord in all of Mexico, rescuing the little lady, and then hightailing it back across the river before daybreak?'

Bode shrugged. 'As a matter of fact, that is the plan.'

'Well, Governor, as plans go, it sucks.' He glanced around. 'Come on, let's find a place to make a new plan.'

Bode pointed at the man lying on the ground.

'Is he dead?'

Eddie kicked the body.

'Oh, yeah, he's dead.'

'Maybe we should move him. A dead body on the sidewalk might attract attention.'

'In Nuevo Laredo?'

Enrique de la Garza did not sleep well alone. So he often worked late at night, after he put Carmelita to bed and read her a story in the *inglés* so she too could attend Harvard. He was in his office now, nowhere close to sleep, not with the governor's wife just one floor below in bed.

'You bring any weapons?' Eddie asked.

They had found a secluded alley around the corner between *farmacias* where the doctor said Americans cross the river to buy cheaper prescriptions. Bode now pulled his dangerous game rifle off his shoulder and showed it to Eddie.

'Jesus, Governor, you'll wake up all of Nuevo Laredo with this thing.'

'One of those three-seventy-five-caliber slugs, guaranteed to ruin El Diablo's day.'

'True, but we need to be a little stealthy.'

'I'm a good shot.'

'No doubt, Governor, but this ain't the turkey shoot back in Comfort. What else you bring?'

Bode pulled the six-shooter from his waistband.

'Colt Walker forty-four-caliber six-shooter. It'll blow a hole the size of a bowling ball through a full-grown man.'

Eddie blinked.

'A six-shooter?'

The doctor held his six-shooter out.

'I have one, too.'

512

'Anything else?'

Bode pulled his right sleeve up to reveal the small pistol rubber-banded to his wrist.

'A Derringer?'

'Forty-one-caliber double-barreled.'

Eddie shook his head. 'How 'bout you, Doc, you bring anything?'

'This.'

The doctor reached into his pocket and came out holding a scalpel.

'A scalpel? What else you got in there, a catheter?'

Bode was getting a little annoyed.

'So what'd you bring?'

'Just these.'

Eddie pulled a gun.

'Nine-millimeter Glock. Fifteen-round clip.' He screwed a long tube onto the barrel. 'With a silencer.'

Eddie opened his ratty jacket to reveal a sawed-off shotgun slung under one arm and a small weapon under the other.

'Uzi,' he said.

He lifted his pants leg to reveal a long knife with a serrated blade in a leg sheath. Taped to his other leg was an ice pick.

'You bring a can of Mace, too.'

Eddie chuckled.

'You came prepared.'

'This is what I do, Governor.'

'I thought you were a gopher?'

'I am. I get what I go for.'

Could the governor's wife love him if he killed the governor? Some women might be offended by such an act. But she had been working in the *colonias* for five months, perhaps she

513

had left the governor, as the rumors on cable suggested. And he had cheated on her; she could not feel that strongly about him. If Enrique had cheated on Liliana, she would have killed him herself. With the governor out of the picture, certainly Enrique would be the front-runner for her affection. Who else would be in the race? There were no eligible men for her in the *colonias* . . . except Dr. Rincón. Yes, he was also educated and quite handsome. But he was quite poor. A woman such as the governor's wife was accustomed to certain things in life, things that only a man such as Enrique de la Garza could provide. Perhaps it was the wine he had with dinner or the brandy he had after dinner—or perhaps it was his lack of sleep—but he actually entertained the thought that one day the governor's wife might be his wife.

The *federales* and cartels had set up competing roadblocks throughout the city manned by heavily armed men.

'And they wonder why tourists don't come no more,' Eddie said.

They evaded the roadblocks by backtracking and taking a longer route around, cutting through alleys, and even maneuvering through a side street of small motels manned by women dressed in lingerie. Shortly before 3:00 A.M., they arrived at the street on which the white compound was located. They ducked into a dark alley between two buildings. Bode accidentally kicked a beer can; it sounded like a siren as it careened down the concrete. Eddie put a finger to his lips.

'Shh.'

At each end of the street stood a man with a rifle slung over his shoulder.

'*Halcones*,' Eddie said. 'Lookouts. The far one is *policía*, on El Diablo's payroll.' He pulled out the Glock with the silencer. 'Wait here.'

He disappeared into the darkness. Bode and the doctor stood there, only their breathing breaking the silence.

'I miss him already,' the doctor said.

They peeked around the edge of the building and observed the *halcones*. First one, then the other, dropped to the ground. Eddie pulled the bodies out of sight.

'He is very good,' the doctor said.

'*¡No mueva!*'

They didn't move. They turned slowly to the voice behind them. A *policía* held a gun on them. Bode hoped Eddie returned soon. He didn't. But a large brick suddenly slammed against the cop's head; he collapsed to the ground.

'Hidi, Governor.'

Ranger Roy, sounding like a kid come to play.

'Roy—what the hell are you doing here?'

He wasn't wearing his Ranger uniform, but still, a six-foot-six Anglo in a T-shirt, jeans, and sneakers without a tan in the can stood out like a capitalist in Cuba.

'Mr. Burnet told me where you'd gone, so I drove down right after you left.'

'Why?'

'Because I'm responsible for her. Mrs. Bonner, she's like my mother.'

The boy's voice cracked.

'How'd you find us?'

He pulled a GPS unit out of his back pocket.

'Tracking your cell phone.'

'Roy?'

Eddie had returned.

'Hi, Eddie.'

Eddie turned his palms up.

'Anyone else coming?'

'Uh, no, I think this is it.'

Eddie shook his head.

'Let's get closer.'

They stayed in the shadows until they found another dark recess located directly across the narrow street from the front entrance to the compound. Standing outside tall iron gates were four massive *hombres*.

'I cased the place in daylight,' Eddie said. 'They've got sensors strung all the way around on top of the wall, so even if we could get over, we'd be dead before we hit the ground on the other side.'

'So how are we going to get in?'

'The front door.'

'The front door?'

'Who would be stupid enough to try that?'

'Good point.'

Eddie pulled out the Glock with the silencer again.

'Once we get in, we'll have to split up to find your wife.'

'No, we won't.'

Bode retrieved the GPS unit and activated it again. The signal came on.

'I'm tracking her cell phone.'

'No way he let her keep her phone.'

'She hid it.'

'Where could she . . . ?' Eddie smiled. 'Your wife's a tough broad, Governor.'

They looked at each other for a long solemn moment.

'Well, let's go get her,' Bode said.

Eddie pulled his knit cap down low and the collar to his ratty jacket up high. He dug into his pack and pulled out a small sealed foil container of cottage cheese that smelled sour. He poured the stuff into his mouth, but he didn't swallow. He kept his right hand free under the jacket to hold the weapon. He stepped out onto the sidewalk and began walking as if he were drunk. He stumbled back and forth then into the road, mumbling incoherently. As he approached the entrance gates, the guards started laughing. Eddie then dropped to his knees and puked the cottage cheese into the street. The guards laughed and stepped closer; Eddie rose up, leveled his gun at them, and shot all four men. They fell to the pavement. Not a dog barked.

'He's got skills,' Ranger Roy said.

They ran over and helped Eddie pull the bodies out of sight.

'I don't figure we got much time till we have company. Where's she at?'

Bode checked the GPS.

'East side.'

They slipped through the open gates and headed east along the perimeter wall. The base of the structure looked like a bunker half-built into the ground. Three floors extended above ground level. The entire structure was constructed of steel and concrete.

'Place looks like a fuckin' fort,' Eddie whispered.

The grounds were lush with palm trees and bushes that provided cover. At the east doors, Eddie took out two more men with the silenced gun. They entered the residence but encountered no more guards. They continued down a long corridor until they came to an intersecting corridor. Bode checked the GPS.

'Down here.'

'Governor, you boys go for your wife,' Eddie said. 'I'm going for El Diablo.'

517

'Why?'

'Because this is what I do . . . and I do it better alone.'

Bode, Doc, and Roy watched Eddie Jones disappear around the corner. Bode could hear their breathing in the silence of the corridor.

'I miss him again,' the doctor said.

'Let's find Mrs. Bonner,' Roy said. 'And get her out of here.'

Lindsay woke to Enrique's gentle touch on her shoulder. She jumped.

'Enrique—no!'

'Come. The governor, he has already arrived.'

They followed the GPS directions around more corners and down more corridors. They darted across a courtyard with a pool and continued along a dim hallway until they arrived at a steel door. They stopped. The signal came from inside that room. Bode put the GPS unit in his pocket. He drew the big Colt six-shooter with his left hand. Roy wielded a nine-millimeter pistol. Doc removed his six-shooter from his waistband. Bode slowly turned the door handle with his right hand. It was unlocked. He pushed the door slightly open. The room appeared dimly lit. He saw no one. He swung the door fully open and saw that the room had no windows and was empty—except for the cell phone sitting on the floor under a bright spot light.

'She is very clever, your wife.'

Bode felt a gun barrel on the back of his head and heard a man's voice behind them. The knit cap was yanked from his head.

'Please, step inside.'

The three Americans stepped inside.

'Put your guns on the floor.'

They put their guns on the floor.

'And the rifle.'

Bode dropped the rifle to the floor.

'My, that is a big rifle. You must be a very bad *hombre*.'

It wasn't a compliment.

'Now kick them away.'

He did.

'Turn around.'

They did. Standing before them was a bald Mexican man dressed in a black military outfit.

'I found the phone myself,' the man said. 'Your wife, she is very beautiful. And feisty. She told me I would have to fuck a dead woman, then she kicked me in my *cojones*. But before I kill her, I will have her. What do you think about that, Governor?'

'I think I'm gonna kill you.'

The man smiled.

'Against the wall.'

The three men backed up to the wall. The man pointed the gun at them.

'So, we have the governor of Texas . . . Dr. Rincón from *Colonia Ángeles*—I came with *el jefe* the day we brought the medicine and supplies—and . . .' He looked Ranger Roy up and down. 'My, you are a big *hombre*. And who are you?'

Roy stood tall. 'I'm a Texas Ranger.'

'Are you now?'

The man shot Roy in his heart. He fell to the floor, dead.

'Goddamnit!' Bode shouted. 'Why'd you kill him?'

'I hate Rangers.' He grinned. 'So, to finish the introductions, I am Hector Garcia. I had your head in my cross hairs,

Governor, but your girlfriend stepped in the way. You are a very lucky man. Not so much her.'

Bode wanted to kill this man standing before him.

'Where's my wife?'

'Why?'

'I came to get her.'

'But, Governor, how do you propose to get out of this room?'

'Did you not just hear me? I told you I'm gonna kill you. So after I kill you, where do I find my wife?'

'She is upstairs, with Enrique.'

Hector now had an amused expression on his face.

'Your wife, she said you would kill me first.'

'I've disappointed her many times—but not tonight.'

Bode swung his right arm up, and just as he did, the doctor dove for their guns on the floor. Hector turned toward the doctor and fired his gun. With his left hand, Bode grabbed the Derringer riding on his right wrist and ripped it free of the rubber band. He pointed the Derringer at Hector, whose gun hand was swinging back toward Bode. But Bode shot first. The .41-caliber bullet from the Derringer struck Hector in his forehead. He fell backwards. But the doctor now lay on the floor. Bleeding.

'Doc!'

Bode dropped next to him. He found the wound in his upper leg.

'Why'd you do that?'

'A diversion.'

'Damnit!'

'Save her.'

The doctor passed out. Bode needed to find his wife and save her, fast, so she could save the doctor. He searched the

520

doctor's pockets and found a handkerchief—and something else that might be useful. He stuffed the handkerchief into the open wound to slow the bleeding then took the doctor's belt and made a tourniquet. He put the Derringer in his pocket and grabbed a six-shooter and stuck it in his waistband then lifted the doctor and slung him over his shoulder. He had to find Lindsay and kill El Diablo.

Unless Eddie already had.

Eddie Jones had not confronted any more guards inside the residence. El Diablo apparently kept his *soldados* outside. Eddie now put his back to the wall and climbed the stairs to the fourth floor. Slowly. Listening for any sound. Any movement. He arrived at the fourth-floor landing. To the side that was visible from the stairs he could see an open door with a light on inside. But what was to his blind side? He stuck his head out beyond the wall and saw a flash of black.

'Damn.'

Bode had his gun drawn. He had carried the doctor down the corridor and up three flights of stairs. He had arrived at the fourth-floor landing and spotted Eddie.

His head.

His body lay on the other side of the landing; blood had oozed out onto the colorful Mexican tile floor. Neither Ranger Roy nor Eddie Jones would make it back across the river. Bode Bonner might not. But it didn't matter. What mattered—all that mattered now—was getting his wife and the doctor back across the river. Their lives were worth saving. Their lives had meaning. His did not. He was just a politician.

'*Bienvenido*, Governor! Welcome to Nuevo Laredo! Please, come in!'

The voice came from inside a room just off the landing. Bode carried the doctor over to the door and into a spacious office with a plate glass wall facing the lights of Laredo.

'Ah, the man who would be president.'

At the far end, a handsome Mexican man with a goatee stood against a desk holding an AK-47 pointed at Bode. A bloody machete stood against the desk. The governor's wife stood next to him. Wearing a short black dress.

'Oh, my God—is that Jesse?' she cried. 'Is he alive?'

'He's unconscious. Some *hombre* named Hector shot him in the leg. You El Diablo?'

'*Gringos* call me that. I am Enrique de la Garza. And where is Hector now?'

'Dead.' Bode turned to his wife. 'So is Roy.'

'*My* Ranger Roy?' Lindsay said. 'He came for me?'

'It seems that many men came for you,' El Diablo said. 'I did not expect you so soon, Governor. I took your wife, what, not twenty-four hours ago? You came quickly, and you have already killed Hector Garcia. I am impressed.'

'In a few minutes, you'll be dead.'

'Hmm. Well, perhaps you should drop your gun.'

Bode dropped the gun.

'Please kick it to me.'

He kicked the gun away then laid the doctor on the couch. He faced his wife.

'Why are you wearing a party dress?'

'Why do you have a tan?'

'Don't you think that dress is a little short for a woman your age?'

'A woman my age? Enrique thinks I have beautiful legs. Don't you?'

El Diablo seemed confused. Lindsay put her hands on her hips.

'You said I had beautiful legs. Do I or don't I?'

She pulled the dress up enough to expose her black panties. El Diablo couldn't help but look, and when he did the barrel of the AK-47 dropped slightly, which gave Bode the opening he needed. He pulled the Derringer from his pocket, pointed it at El Diablo, and squeezed the trigger.

Click.

El Diablo smiled.

'That must be disappointing, Governor.'

'A bit.'

He must have shot both barrels at Hector. He dropped the Derringer on the floor.

'But that was a clever try. Your wife does have beautiful legs.'

'I need to help Jesse,' Lindsay said.

'Yes. Of course.'

She went to the doctor and dropped to her knees next to him.

'I need to cut his pants leg.'

El Diablo tossed scissors from his desk to her. She cut the doctor's trouser leg.

'Will he live?' Bode said.

'He's in shock. I need blankets.'

'In the closet outside.'

Lindsay stood and went outside. She gagged at the sight of a decapitated man. But she went closer and picked up a gun with a long tube on the barrel lying nearby. She opened the closet and removed several blankets. She placed the blankets over the gun. She went back inside and covered Jesse with a blanket.

But she held the gun.

'I did not want that,' Enrique said to her husband. 'This is not about the doctor. This is about you.'

'You wanted me here. I'm here. Let them go. Let her save the doctor. Shoot me if you want, but let them go.'

'Yes, okay.'

Enrique raised the AK-47 and shot Bode.

'Bode!'

The force knocked him to the floor. Lindsay released the gun under the blanket and went to her husband. She knelt over him and checked his wound. The bullet had struck him in his right shoulder.

A hot, sharp pain burned through Bode's shoulder. He didn't think it was a fatal wound, but his right arm was useless. He reached into his coat pocket with his left hand.

'I love you, Lindsay. I'm sorry I hurt you. I'm sorry I didn't come here and beg you to come back to me. But I'm gonna get you and the doc back across the border. After I kill this son of a bitch.'

El Diablo snorted. 'You Texans, always with the cowboy talk.'

He again pointed the AK-47 at Bode, but then seemed to think otherwise. He placed the gun on the desk then picked up the machete.

'You killed my son, Governor, now I must kill you. But I will not kill you like a coward, as you killed my son. I will kill you as a man . . . *mano a mano*.'

He stepped closer with the machete. Bode pushed Lindsay away.

'I killed your son because he was gonna kill a young girl.'

'No! Jesús would never have hurt a child! He would never violate the code!'

524

'He beat her, and he raped her! A twelve-year-old girl!'

'No! I do not believe you!'

'You don't want to believe it, but you know it's the truth. The girl said he did. The other kids witnessed it. Your son was a sick fucking bastard just like his daddy!'

El Diablo glared at the governor of Texas.

'I will kill you now.'

'Bring it, you crazy-ass bastard! I'm not afraid to die!'

'Good—because you are about to.'

He raised his machete, but Lindsay threw her body over Bode.

'*Señora* Bonner, move away. I do not want you hurt. But the governor, he must die. Now.'

El Diablo reached down and took her shoulder to pull her away from Bode, and when he did his face came within reach of Bode's long left arm—which Bode swung up and across El Diablo's face. He stumbled backwards and grabbed his face. Blood oozed from between his fingers.

'*What* . . . what is that?'

Bode pushed himself up off the floor and held out the scalpel he had found in Jesse's coat. El Diablo seemed stunned.

'A *scalpel*? You brought a scalpel?'

'Doc did.'

El Diablo's face now showed his renewed determination to kill the governor of Texas. Bode searched for weapons. On a shelf were signed baseballs on small stands. He grabbed one.

'Do not touch my *béisbols*!'

Bode threw the ball at El Diablo. He ducked. Bode threw another. He ducked again. Bode threw baseballs until he ran out. Of baseballs, not balls. Because his only goal in life—his last goal in life—was to get his wife and the doctor back across the border. So he now fought with an energy that came from fear of failure, not of death. El Diablo stepped forward and swung the machete with both hands, again and again, blood dripping from the cut on his face. Bode jumped and ducked, but he felt the sharp blade slice through the skin on his left arm and bring blood. He knew the odds were against him, so on the next swing, Bode rushed El Diablo and tackled him with a ferocity he hadn't felt in twenty-five years. He wanted to drive this son of a bitch into the tile floor more than he had ever wanted to drive an opponent into the turf of a football field. They went down to the floor hard, and he felt the air come out of El Diablo as Bode's full weight landed on top of him, and he heard the machete's metal blade slide across the floor. Bode's right arm hung limp, but he punched El Diablo with his left fist as they rolled across the hard tile. He was determined to beat El Diablo to death, and might have, but a sudden sharp pain consumed his body. El Diablo kneed him in his balls. He released his grip, and when he looked up, El Diablo stood over him with the machete raised.

'I now avenge my son's murder. I now have justice.'

'Stop!'

El Diablo froze. Lindsay pointed Eddie's silenced Glock at him.

'Shoot him!' Bode said.

Enrique de la Garza smiled down at the governor of Texas.

'Oh, Governor, your wife and I have plans. She will not shoot me.'

She shot him. Twice.

Enrique fell backwards against the desk, the pain in his chest fierce and hot. He had been shot three times before, but

526

he knew instantly that this would be the final time. His eyes turned down to the holes in his chest. He put his free hand over the wounds, and it was soon bloody. His breath came harder now, and he spit blood. Enrique de la Garza would die that night in Nuevo Laredo. He turned his bloody palm up, then he turned to the governor's wife.

'But we had plans.'

'That was my plan,' the governor's wife said.

Enrique de la Garza would never again read the *inglés* to Carmelita or listen to Julio's Bach. He would never again experience romance or feel the love of a woman. He would die alone. He would die now. He dropped the machete and stumbled outside onto the balcony. He leaned against the railing and gazed down at his beloved Río Bravo.

Bode pushed himself up and wiped blood from his face, his blood or El Diablo's, he didn't know. He stepped out onto the balcony. El Diablo leaned against the railing, breathing hard and bleeding profusely.

'Please, Governor, do not let my children see me like this.'

'What do you want?'

'Help me over, so that I may die in the Río Bravo.'

'Why should I?'

'Because we are not so different, you and I.'

'How?'

'We both long for the love of a woman ... the same woman. Yet neither of us shall have her love.'

'You didn't kill me. I killed you.'

'No. She killed me.'

El Diablo turned and tried to hoist himself up and over the railing, but he was too weak. Bode shook his head then stepped closer and grabbed El Diablo to help him over the rail, but he suddenly felt a sharp pain. He groaned then backed away and looked down. El Diablo had stuck a switchblade deep in his gut.

'And now I have killed you, Governor. You will now die for murdering my son. That is justice. And I will now die with honor.'

El Diablo threw himself over the railing. Bode heard a scream and turned to see Lindsay staring at the knife in his gut.

'Oh, God—Bode!'

He leaned over and looked down to the river. In the moonlight, he could see El Diablo's body sprawled on the riverbank a hundred feet below. Bode yanked the knife out and dropped it over the railing. Lindsay examined his wound.

'It's bad, Bode.'

It was fatal. He knew it. He put his hand over the wound to stanch the bleeding. They went back inside and came face to face with a slender teenager with the face of an altar boy wearing black pants and a white shirt and pointing the AK-47 at Bode. The boy's hands trembled. Tears flowed down his face. He couldn't do it. He couldn't pull the trigger and kill a man. Bode walked to the boy and put his open palm on the boy's white shirt. He dragged his hand down and wiped his blood on the boy. He took the gun. Lindsay found a cloth and tried to stop the bleeding.

'Can you make it?'

'I'll get you both back across the river. If it's the last thing I do.'

And he knew now it would be.

Jesse Rincón opened his eyes on a bloody scene. The governor's clothes were soaked with blood. Lindsay's hands were bloody. His own leg was bloody. And a boy stood there as if in shock, his shirt red with blood.

'Where is he?' Jesse said. 'El Diablo?'

'Dead.'

The boy walked out onto the balcony and peered over the rail. The governor leaned over Jesse.

'I can walk.'

Jesse pushed himself up but fell into the governor's arms.

'The hell you can.'

The governor dropped the AK–47 then hefted Jesse onto his shoulder.

Bode Bonner was the governor of Texas, and he sure as hell wasn't going to die in Mexico. He would die like a Texan. In Texas.

'Hand me my pistol.'

His wife picked the gun up and held it out to him. He slid the Colt into his waistband. He then carried the doctor down three flights of stairs and to the front door. He stopped and drew the pistol.

'Open the door.'

His wife pulled the door open on two armed guards. Bode shot them both with the Colt .44. He saw no more guards so they hurried to the four black Mercedes-Benz sedans parked in the circle driveway. Lindsay ran ahead and stuck her head into the nearest car.

'Keys,' she said.

'Get in,' Bode said. 'I'll drive.'

'I will navigate,' the doctor said. 'I know the way out.'

Bode helped the doctor into the passenger's seat. Lindsay climbed into the back seat. Bode went around to the driver's side and saw two armed men running toward them. He put them both down with the Colt. He got in and started the engine.

'Go, go, go!' the doctor said.

Bode punched the accelerator, and the big Mercedes lurched forward and through the gates as shots rang out behind them.

'They're coming after us!' Lindsay said.

'We've got to get to the bridge!'

'No!' the doctor said. 'The *federales* will soon know we have killed El Diablo. They will not allow us to cross the bridge. We must go west, to the river. To the *colonia*. Turn right here. César de López Lara.'

Bode veered onto the road and drove past a string of *cantinas* and cheap motels.

'They're behind us,' Lindsay said.

'Left—there. Avenida Álvaro Obregon.'

Bode hit the brakes hard and made a fast turn, clipping a parked car. They were now driving down a dark road through what appeared to be a tenement of dilapidated houses and old cars parked right outside the doors. Groups of two and three men and women loitered on corners. Bode felt a fever washing over him.

'Did we lose them?'

'Yes,' Lindsay said.

Bode slowed so as not to kill a pedestrian on the narrow street, until he heard his wife's voice.

'No.'

He sped up—until he saw headlights coming directly at him.

'Shit—this is a one-way road, Doc! And we're going the wrong way!'

'Turn right—Calle Miguel Hidalgo.'

Bode swung the big sedan right onto another narrow street then sped up. His face felt hot and wet with sweat, and blood ran down his right arm and out of his gut.

'I grew up in this neighborhood,' the doctor said. 'A major road is just ahead. We can try to outrun them.'

Bode came to an *Alto* sign but he didn't *alto*. He veered to avoid cars parked along both sides through a little business district for five blocks then the road dead-ended into a four-lane roadway. The light was red, but—

'They're still behind us,' Lindsay said.

'Left!' the doctor said.

Bode gunned the sedan through the light and turned south. Now they heard sirens.

'*Policía*,' Lindsay said.

They had joined the chase from a side road and were now on their side.

'They're shooting at us!' Lindsay screamed.

Bullets hit the driver's side window, but did not penetrate the glass.

'I'll be damned. An armored car.'

He glanced at the *policía*. They too were stunned. Bode stuck his middle finger up at them. He floored the accelerator and soon had the sedan running eighty. Two lanes ran south, so Bode had room to maneuver. He swerved around slower-moving traffic and put some distance between them and the *policía* and El Diablo's men. He blew through another red light.

'Aw, shit.'

Traffic had stopped ahead. Cars were waiting to turn into a walled compound.

'Boys' Town,' the doctor said.

'Great.'

Bode blinked hard to maintain focus. He swerved around the line of cars. But just past Boys' Town the police had set up a roadblock.

'Hold on!'

Bode headed straight at the police cars then abruptly jumped the low median and drove around them in the northbound lanes then jumped the median back to the southbound lanes.

'They're coming after us.'

The doctor grabbed the dashboard.

'Turn around!'

'Why?'

He pointed. 'That is the Villareal, the motel where the *federales* stationed here reside.'

But they weren't just residing there; they were waiting for them in military trucks parked across all four lanes. Bode slammed on the brakes and swung the Mercedes around into the northbound lane. He stomped on the accelerator and sped past the *policía* and *soldados* heading southbound.

'Go left on Abraham Lincoln,' the doctor said.

Bode turned left and accelerated.

'Now right on Constitución.'

He swung right.

'Faster! No *alto*!'

'Don't worry, Doc. I ain't stopping.'

They flew through the stop sign at Venezuela.

'Left on Peru.'

Bode hit the brakes and turned the wheel hard. The sedan fishtailed and sideswiped a *Tacos y Barbacoa* vendor truck. He straightened out and headed west.

'Now go very fast,' the doctor said.

Bode went very fast. The traffic was one-way, and they

were going the right way for a change. They sped past *cantinas* with drunks loitering outside and small restaurants. In the rearview, Bode could see flashing lights. But they had a lead on them. His breathing came faster now.

'Bode, are you okay?' Lindsay asked.

'I'll get you home.'

'There!' the doctor said. 'Calzada De Los Héroes. The highway west.'

Bode steered onto the highway. Four lanes headed west, so Bode pushed the sedan. They soon cleared the dense part of the city.

'We are outside the city now. Perhaps they will not follow.'

'They're following,' Lindsay said.

'Faster!'

Bode pushed the sedan to ninety. The pain in his gut had gotten worse. Much worse. He clenched back a groan.

'What's that?'

Up ahead, he saw red taillights, as if cars were being stopped.

'*Bandidos*.'

'You gotta fucking be kidding me.'

'Do not stop, Governor.'

He didn't. He swerved into the oncoming lanes and around an eighteen-wheeler then back into the westbound lanes.

'You drive fast very well, Governor.'

'I been driving in Texas all my life.'

'We will turn soon, toward the river.'

'Bode,' Lindsay said, 'they're getting closer.'

'There!' the doctor said. 'The white cross . . . Turn!'

Bode slammed on the brakes and veered off the highway.

'There's no road.'

'A dirt road leads to the river.'

Bode steered down a path cut through the desert. The car bottomed out, so he couldn't go fast. His face felt hot; he fought not to pass out.

'They turned in behind us,' Lindsay said.

'The river is just ahead,' the doctor said.

'They're closer!'

'Just beyond that bluff is the river.'

'How do we get down to it?'

'We drive over the bluff.'

'Over the bluff?'

'It is a low bluff. We will drive right into the river. It is not deep, because of the drought. The *colonia* is just on the other side.'

'Lower the windows.'

'Punch it, Governor.'

Bode punched it.

'Hang on!'

The big Mercedes-Benz sedan flew off the low bluff and belly-flopped into the Rio Grande. The air bags deployed and cushioned the blow. The car settled into the river. They climbed out the open windows and into the river. The water was only a few feet deep. Lindsay and Bode pulled the doctor out of the river and to dry ground against a ten-foot-high bank.

'We must get to the riverbank above,' the doctor said. 'We will be easy targets down here.'

'I'll get you up, Doc.'

Bode hefted the doctor onto his shoulder again, and the pain told him that this would be his last living act. Lindsay scrambled up the dirt side as if she were that tomboy back in ninth grade. Bode grabbed a cane shoot with his left hand and pushed with his legs, the doctor hanging on and Bode's body bleeding out, and his right knee with the four scars burned hot with pain and his mind pulled up memories of lying on a football field with ligaments torn apart, of taking the pain and fighting through the pain, and sucking in air as he was now, and just as then, Bode Bonner refused to give in to the pain. Lindsay reached down to him and he reached up to her but he saw his sister Emma now and he wanted to make the Bonner family proud, so he grunted out one last massive effort . . . and he stood in Texas again. He dropped to his knees, and the doctor tumbled off his shoulder.

'Thank you, *mi amigo*,' the doctor said from the ground. 'You have saved our lives.'

Flashing lights appeared across the river.

'They're here!' Lindsay said. 'We've got to get into the *colonia*.'

She helped the doctor to his feet. He put an arm around the governor's wife. Bode pushed himself to his feet, but his time had come. He was born in Texas, and he would die in Texas. But he had gotten his wife home. He had come for her, as she knew he would. His last great adventure wasn't winning the White House—it was saving his wife. He now looked east and saw the sun rising over the Rio Grande. Over Texas. Perhaps it was the adrenaline or perhaps the delirium that now consumed his mind, but William Bode Bonner stood to his full six-foot-four-inch height and raised his good arm to God and shouted to Texas.

'That was a hell of an adventure!'

Just as he lost consciousness and his body collapsed to the ground, shots rang out from the other side of the river.

Chapter 44

Dying is a way of life on the border.

Lindsay Bonner knew that now. She was a nurse, but she could not deny death. She was a married woman, but she loved two men. Four men had come for her, but only one man would go home. She reached across the hospital bed and touched his face.

Bode Bonner opened his eyes. He blinked hard to focus. He was lying in a bed. In a hospital room. His wife sat next to him. He remembered.

'Doc?'

His wife clenched her jaws and shook her head. He felt tears come into his eyes.

'How long?'

'Four days. Since surgery.'

'Where am I?'

'Laredo hospital.'

'How?'

'Border Patrol. They brought us all here. The *federales* shot at us, from across the river. They hit you and Jesse. He died in the *colonia*. We buried him next to his mother.'

She cried now.

'I'm sorry, Lindsay. For Jesse . . . and for hurting you.'

She stared off a moment then turned back to him.

'You need to know something, Bode. I loved Jesse, but I didn't have an affair with him. Not a physical one.'

'Can you ever forgive me?'

'I already have.'
'Why?'
'Because you came for me.'

Chapter 45

Cameras and reporters from the networks and cable crowded into the press room and staked out positions in the corridor outside. Across the foyer, on the other side of the white marble statues of Sam Houston and Stephen F. Austin, the governor of Texas stood at the window of his capitol office staring out at the satellite trucks that lined the driveway circling the building. Since they had returned from Laredo, he had thought a lot about what it meant to be a good man, and while he hadn't worked out all the details, he had figured out the important points.

Honor.

Love.

Family.

Bode Bonner would be a good man again. He would live a life with honor, with love, and with his family. Jim Bob Burnet slapped him on the shoulder and out of his thoughts.

'It's been a great ride, Bode. Thanks for taking me along.'

'I know you wanted the White House as much as I did. I'm sorry.'

'Don't be. You got something better than the White House—a second chance with your family. Don't fuck it up.'

They shook hands. Left hands. Bode's right arm was still in a sling.

'Besides, I just might get to the White House without you.'

'How?'

'Palin called, wants me to come see her in Alaska.'

Now Bode slapped him on the shoulder.

'I'll be rootin' for you, Professor.'

Bode walked over and put his arm around the governor's wife.

Lindsay Bonner felt her husband's arm around her. Where it belonged. Where she belonged. She loved Jesse Rincón, but she had loved Bode Bonner longer. He had been a part of her since she was fifteen; he would always be a part of her. There was no denying it and no fighting it. She had loved him from the moment she had first seen him, and she would love him until the moment she died. They had shared twenty-nine years of life together, they had joined together to create the most wonderful child, and they had survived Nuevo Laredo. He had come for her. She had come back with him. He wasn't the same man she had married in Comfort twenty-two years before, and she wasn't the same woman who had left Austin five months before.

But he was her hero again.

And she would never again leave their bed. Not over politics.

Becca turned the volume up on the television. The

broadcast was from the press room just across the foyer. A reporter addressed the camera.

'Breaking news from Nuevo Laredo that Enrique de la Garza, also known as El Diablo, head of the notorious Los Muertos cartel that made two assassination attempts on the governor of Texas, is now dead, killed by Governor Bode Bonner himself. That's all we have now, but I'm sure we'll learn the rest of the story when the governor addresses us. Speculation is rife that Governor Bonner will use this opportunity to announce his candidacy for the presidency of the United States.'

Bode walked into the press room with Lindsay, Becca, Miguel, Alejandro, and Josefina in a new green dress. And Pancho. Bode stepped to the podium.

'Good morning. I have several announcements to make. First, I am resigning as governor of Texas effective immediately.'

The reporters jumped out of the chairs and began shouting questions. Bode held up his hand.

'My actions have resulted in good people dying. Hank Williams and Roy Rogers, two brave Texas Rangers. Darcy Daniels, my daughter's partner. Mandy Morgan, my aide. Eddie Jones, a campaign staffer. And Dr. Jesse Rincón.'

Seventy-five miles south, San Antonio Mayor Jorge Gutiérrez watched the governor on the television in his office in City Hall. Jorge knew he would die without respect.

'I've liquidated my blind trust,' the governor said. 'The money will be used to provide utilities to *Colonia Ángeles*, in honor of Dr. Rincón.'

★ ★ ★

One hundred sixty miles further south, the Border Patrol agent named Rusty stood at his post by the gates in the border wall one mile north of the Rio Grande. For the first time in his career, he wondered why.

In *Colonia Ángeles*, Inez Quintanilla sat at her desk in the clinic, as if awaiting the doctor's arrival that day. Tears streamed down her pretty face. She could not believe that the doctor was dead, but she knew he was because she had stood at his grave in the small *colonia* cemetery when his body was lowered into the ground. She knew she would never see him again. She knew life in the *colonia* would never be the same again, without her brother or the doctor. She knew there would be no laughter and no joy, no movie nights and no one who cared for them. She knew her life had been irrevocably altered. But she did not yet know that the doctor had executed a last will and testament that left his homestead on the other side of Laredo to 'my devoted assistant, Inez Quintanilla, who shall live beyond the wall.'

In his café in Laredo, Luis Escalera got drunk on whiskey.

Two hundred miles downriver in the clinic in *Colonia Nueva Vida*, the governor of Texas spoke of the doctor on the small television, and Sister Sylvia wept.

In his office in the U.S. House of Representatives, Congressman Ernesto Delgado watched the governor on television as he spoke of Jesse Rincón, and at that moment, he decided to retire. He did not want to die in Washington. He wanted to die in Laredo. On the border. Where he belonged.

★ ★ ★

'I will not be a candidate for the presidency.'

The reporters erupted as one, shouting questions at him. Bode held a hand up until they calmed down.

'I lost my way here in Austin. Ambition can do that to a man, blind him to what's important in life. I found my way again in Nuevo Laredo. I remember what's important now.'

He put his good arm around his wife.

'I'm going back to where I belong with my wife and my children, Becca, Alejandro, Miguel, and Josefina. And our dog, Pancho.'

The room had fallen silent. A reporter spoke softly.

'Governor, after killing El Diablo, you'll be unbeatable. You can be the next president of the United States of America. You're a living legend. There's even talk of erecting a statue of you here in the state capitol—next to Sam Houston.'

'A legend, huh? Well, I don't deserve a statue. You want to erect a statue, make it of Jesse Rincón. He made a difference in people's lives. I just wanted their votes.'

'Governor, you're really going to walk away from the White House? It's really over?'

Bode Bonner nodded.

'It's over.'

Epilogue

Two hundred thirty-five miles to the south, in the white compound in Nuevo Laredo overlooking the Río Bravo del Norte, the teenager with the altar-boy face watched the Texas governor's press conference on the flat-screen television on the wall of the office that was once his father's. He pointed the remote at the screen and froze the image. He was now *El Capitán*, head of the Los Muertos cartel. In the week since he had witnessed his father's death at the hands of the governor in this very office—*in his own home!*—he had finally become the man his father had always hoped he would become. And he had sworn to God that he would avenge his family's honor. That he would dispense justice. Julio de la Garza now raised his father's machete to touch the image of the *gringo* who had murdered his brother and father. He would seek *venganza*.

'No, Governor—it is not over. It has just begun.'

Acknowledgments

My sincere thanks to everyone at the Little, Brown Book Group in London, including David Shelley for his belief in my books and Iain Hunt for his brilliant editing. Thanks also to Wylie Jones Jordan in Acapulco for the Spanish translations and to Joel Tarver at T Squared Design in Houston for my website and emails blasts to my readers. And thanks to all of you who have emailed me with your thoughts and comments. I look forward to hearing from you again.

About the Author

Born and educated in Texas, Mark Gimenez attended law school at Notre Dame, Indiana, and practiced with a large Dallas law firm. He is married with two sons.